C000046288

Down, Out *and* Dead

by

Anne E. Randell

Grosvenor House
Publishing Limited

The right of Anne Elizabeth Randell to be identified as the author of this
work has been asserted in accordance with Section 78
of the Copyright, Designs and Patents Act 1988

The book cover picture is copyright to Inmagine Corp LLC

This book is published by
Grosvenor House Publishing Ltd
Link House
140 The Broadway, Tolworth, Surrey, KT6 7HT.
www.grosvenorhousepublishing.co.uk

This book is a work of fiction. Any resemblance to
people or events, past or present, is purely coincidental.

A CIP record for this book
is available from the British Library

ISBN 978-1-78623-134-5

About the Author

Anne Randell is a retired teacher. She grew up in Manchester and still lives in the North West of England. Having enjoyed writing Literacy texts and plays for her students, she wanted to continue writing once she left the classroom and completed several writing courses. Anne goes into her old school on a voluntary basis, taking writing and reading groups. Having travelled extensively, she has had travel articles published.

Down, Out and Dead is her third novel.

Previous novels: Next Time It Will Be Perfect
                          Look Right, Look Left, Look Dead.

Dedication

To Mary Edwards, a wonderful friend. 1935-2017

Acknowledgements

Once again many thanks to Peter for his patience and invaluable help when proof reading. Any mistakes remain mine. Thanks also to Sarah, Chris and friends for their continued interest and encouragement.

Prologue

Was it right to do the things I did? No.

Would I do it all again? Yes. Most definitely, yes.

So long ago. Such an ordinary day. No warning that lives were about to be torn apart. No premonition that the family was to be broken, the parts never to be reassembled: a jigsaw with a vital piece missing. The item in the local paper was so insignificant that only those who scoured every page would have noticed it. The report, hidden at the bottom of page eight, stated that Harry Whistler (aged 45) had disappeared from his home. He had been gone for almost two weeks and anyone sighting him was asked to contact the local police station.

Eve

Dad performed his vanishing act some twenty years ago in May 1995. When he materialised, I had been married (my eldest brother having walked me down the aisle) and divorced. An unfortunate, but necessary end to a union that was doomed from the start. We were both far too young and immature.

It was a Tuesday evening after work when Mum arrived at my flat, flustered and almost incoherent, to let me know he had been spotted in the park. She hadn't seen Dad, but a neighbour had enjoyed informing her that he was living in Elizabeth Park, one of the town's many homeless who called the park their home. The lost years have always been a black hole: where, and how, he had lived remains a mystery.

Since his return, weeks can go by without even a glimpse of him, but today makes three sightings in a fortnight. Recently, each time I've seen him, I've been shocked by his appearance: by how he has aged. He looks far more than mid-sixties. Hardly surprising when one considers his adopted lifestyle.

It's always tempting to pretend I haven't seen him, and we haven't spoken for six months. On that occasion, it was a very one-sided, uncomfortable conversation. It's so pathetic not to be able to converse with one's own father. Every encounter becomes more difficult and I've become an actress with acute stage fright: one who invariably fluffs her lines.

My brothers were annoyed when I suggested this journal, but it has begun. Asking them to contribute did not meet with much approval (somewhat of an understatement). I said that if we write it online it will be accessible immediately and can be added to by any of us at any time. None of them are keen, and being the middle child – a mathematical impossibility as there were four of us – has never given me much credence. It doesn't help that I am the only girl and my siblings invented the word misogyny.

The twins, Jacob and David, are three years my senior and Andrew is five years younger. Given time I hope that each of them will, somewhat reluctantly, write something, however mundane. Surely, they will feel compelled to add their version of events, the before and after of Dad. I know they will be tempted to write something – if only to belie my entries. One thing is certain, they won't allow me to have the final word. Andrew was livid when I said I wanted to amalgamate our thoughts on the events pre- and post that May. I know he's tried to obliterate it all from his mind. He yelled at me to leave slumbering dogs undisturbed (he loves altering adages, assumes that playing with words makes him sound superior). Of the four of us I think he has been the most affected by our family's somewhat unusual history.

Two years on I am reading this, the first entry. How naive I was – but how could I possibly have foreseen the events that were about to make our family front-page news?

We were never a television advert, the kind of family you envy as they sit laughing around a table in a state-of-the-art kitchen. But we were – for many years – reasonably happy. David, and especially Jacob, will almost certainly disagree with that statement and will remind me that I have somewhat sanitised my memories. They will argue that far from being happy, we were always a highly dysfunctional group, disjointed long before the schism created by Dad.

Yes, I wrote schism. What a word to choose. Rupture, the irreparable kind, like a post-operative lesion that refuses to heal, might be more appropriate. Easy to make alterations with hindsight. I will just read on.

What account will each of us give of that momentous day? It's so long ago; hard to recall events with any accuracy. What details will the boys provide of the before and after? I was the keeper of Dad's secret. I was the one he chose to burden with his confession, told late at night, both of us giving way to tears. They remain unaware of his sin, his alleged "crime". Would the Crown Prosecution Service be interested? Would he retain my services as his solicitor?

Questions, questions, questions. I never thought they would become reality. Be activated.

My poor father suffered, and continues to suffer, a self-inflicted torment, his religion telling him that sinners must be punished. Some would agree that he had broken one of God's laws, those essential rules that are fundamental to all religions and play a part in most moral codes. However, a jury would surely understand his reasoning, and I believe that few would convict him. The only one to give a guilty verdict is himself. (*Two years on I wept as I read that last paragraph.*)

I remember a late spring evening, the end of a glorious day. The weathermen keen to inform the nation that a record had been broken: the highest May temperature since records began noted at Manchester airport. We all sat at the end of the garden, under the old beech tree, going indoors not an option.

There was no warning. No indication that our lives were to be thrown out of sync, changed irrevocably. Yes, we had all known something was troubling Dad, but none of us had any inclination of the events that were to be put into motion that night. I had no idea what he was going to do. If, indeed, did he. I remain convinced that his actions were unpremeditated. The father I knew would not have inflicted such anguish on his family. Had any of us known, could we have stopped him? Probably not. By that stage even Mum was a bit player, with few lines and little influence on the drama.

It was a perfect evening in May.

Perfect. Apart from a man abandoning his family.

Chapter 1

Fordway Gazette

Body of Vagrant Found in Elizabeth Park

A body found in Elizabeth Park on Sunday morning remains unidentified. The man is believed to have been one of the rough sleepers who frequent the area. He is thought to be in his late sixties or early seventies. Anyone with any information about the gentleman is asked to contact the police and ask to speak to DCI Tarquin at Fordway police station.

Harvey Tarquin had been flattered when he was asked to take temporary charge in Fordway, the present incumbent off on long-term sick leave with heart problems. Following several years stationed in Preston, he had gained his longed-for promotion and become a Detective Inspector. Now, three years later, he had been seconded to the ever-developing market town, the carrot being a further promotion to Detective Chief Inspector. Harvey's recent "clear-up" record had been exemplary, and he was pleased that his immediate boss, Superintendent Grealy, had asked him to head the murder inquiry. 'You're an excellent copper with the necessary skills, and you're willing to put in the extra graft when it's required. Do well and this case won't do your career any harm. I'm here to give advice if you think it would help.'

Always reticent with his superiors, Harvey had mumbled his thanks. He sometimes experienced the same difficulty when communicating with his team. He enjoyed interviewing suspects, an aspect of the job where he was particularly skilful. Words came easily in the interview room; improvement required when dealing with other officers.

September 14th: three minutes past eight, the early morning air cool, a reminder that autumn was lurking, the surreal scene adding an extra chill. The SOCO team had arrived and erected a tent. The body deserved privacy when it was removed from the undergrowth. DCI Tarquin and DI Serena Peil donned the necessary protective clothing and stepped inside.

Manoeuvring himself into the space where the body lay, he yelled, 'Where the hell is the doctor? We can't do anything until death has been verified.' Harvey loathed the first moments of any investigation. He never failed to be moved by witnessing a body, seeing a life cut short. 'Has he or she been contacted?'

The answer to his question appeared at the tent door. 'Sorry if I've kept you waiting, the rush hour started early. I have to come all the way through town and the traffic lights are down on North Road.' Rosie Culkin, a local and very experienced GP, had recently volunteered to work with the police and this was her first call-out. After crawling into the bushes and examining the body, she murmured what everyone already knew: that the man hidden in the undergrowth was indeed dead.

'Any thoughts on the time of death?' Harvey asked, knowing that doctors were reluctant to commit themselves.

'Not in the past twenty-four hours. Rigor mortis has been and gone and some decomposition is obvious. That usually begins after forty-eight hours, so I think he's been here at least two days.'

'Cause of death?' When Harvey felt under pressure, he employed the fewest words possible, a characteristic his team often thought verged on rudeness.

'Hard to say. He's wrapped in so many layers of clothing I can't see enough to determine the cause with any accuracy. The post-mortem will furnish you with all the grim details. Sorry that I can't be more helpful, but you don't want me disturbing the crime scene.'

Thanking the doctor for her time, Harvey asked the SOCO team to begin their work. Numerous photographs were taken of the body and the surrounding objects: his worldly goods – such as they were – had been positioned almost reverentially around him. He lay, hands across his chest, as though an undertaker had already prepared the body for its coffin.

'Everything needs to go back to the lab. Let the forensic experts loose on that lot. You can move him into the open now. We've got all we need in here. Just one query: how was he discovered?'

'An anonymous telephone call, from a pay-as-you-go mobile we found discarded at the edge of the bushes.' Serena had arrived at work early, keen to catch up on the stack of paperwork that was beginning to resemble Jenga, the game she had played with her niece at the weekend, almost invariably managing to move the wrong block and cause the entire edifice to tumble down. She had taken the call and alerted the relevant people. Leaving the tent, she mumbled that she needed some fresh air, the stink inside making her nauseous. It was her first murder as a CID inspector and she knew she would have to toughen up if she was to do the job properly.

As her boss joined her she asked if there was likely to be any identification. 'There must be someone, somewhere who needs to know that their loved one is dead.'

'I doubt if he was carrying his passport or driving licence.' Harvey realised he had snapped and apologised. 'Identifying the body is, of course, a priority. First thing we need to organise is the PM then at least we'll know how the poor soul met his end.'

'Sir, we might be able to eliminate one of the homeless. I go to yoga with a girl called Eve Whistler. Her dad is one of the vagrants who frequent the park. We could ask her to look at the body. Terrible for her if it is him, but at least we'd know.'

'Too easy. In my experience, unidentified bodies remain just that: unidentified.'

Eve

No, it's not Dad. Not Harry Whistler, though I doubt whether he has much cause to use his name these days. Any form of individuality vanished a long time ago. I was asked to go and identify the body (everyone knows about my father. I live in a small town) and was so relieved that it wasn't him. I half-recognised the face and believe I've seen the man. If it's the one I'm thinking of, he liked to sit on the bench looking at the fountain in the middle of the park, and I spoke to him on several occasions. Dad almost certainly knew him: probably one of his drinking buddies. Someone must have called him Tommy as that's how I think of him and was the name I gave to the police. It's so sad that people in such dire circumstances become almost anonymous. The death has shaken me and made me determined to make more of an effort with Dad.

The PC, who looked too young and pretty to be doing such a gruesome job, led me into the viewing room and said that the death was being treated as murder. She didn't give any details but suggested that it might have been the result of a falling out amongst the homeless – apparently, a common occurrence – or a random attack by a stranger, the latter increasingly routine.

'Last year, on twelve separate occasions, people were hauled before the Magistrates for assaults or harassment issues involving the rough sleepers. People can be so heartless.' She had obviously forgotten I was related to one of the park's less welcome occupants.

Every November, hopefully before the winter makes itself known, I seek out my father and present him with his early Christmas presents: a fleece-lined anorak, warm trousers, jumpers, boots, thermal vests, ski socks and perhaps the most important of all, an Arctic-style sleeping bag. Last year's bag was an exorbitant price, but claimed to keep its occupant warm at minus twenty-nine degrees Celsius. Thankfully, even in the North West of England, the temperature doesn't usually go into such freefall. I've seen the one I want this time in the window of *The North Wall of the Eiger,* a huge venture catering for every conceivable type of outdoor pursuit. It opened recently and appears to be extremely popular; quite why in a small town with only an indoor climbing wall remains a mystery. This year's model claims to work at the same low temperature and to have the added advantage of being super light-weight. When all the air is squashed out it compresses into a tiny bag. Dad carries his life with him, so such details are important. I like the "super-efficient" draw string which surrounds the "mummy hood", words of great importance that I learnt a long time ago.

I'm not sure how he will react to the gloves I discovered on the internet. I hope he will see the funny side and wear them. When I was very young we all (yes, we were once a normal family) went to Chester zoo and I fell in love with the tigers. My obsession with them became a family joke and for years I received presents and cards with a tiger theme. Even my duvet sported one the huge cats sprawling its entire length. The thermal-lined gloves are striped, with tiger faces by the wrists. At the very least they will keep his hands warm and provide some amusement.

The speech, which I deliver annually, will beg him to overwinter at my house (like the birds which materialise and live for months at the Heron Hold Bird Sanctuary near here). I will remind him that he could retain his independence as my second bedroom is converted into a large en suite room – created with just such a scenario in mind.

'That's no longer the way I can allow myself to live. I did wrong and must pay.' Those or similar words are his yearly reply. Sinners must be punished. What a cruel religion that reprimands a man for so long. To him the deed was, and remains, beyond redemption. He will continue his self-inflicted punishment for the rest of his life and is, almost certainly, expecting the fully-extended version in the next one.

My parents were both members of the local church: St Bartholomew's in the middle of Fordway. It's a monstrosity of a building – the worst kind of early Victorian self-aggrandisement, sporting a ridiculously tall tower and hideous windows which can't decide whether, or not, they could be classed as stained glass. Dad was a lay reader and Mum taught the younger members of the Sunday School and arranged the flowers by the altar. As children, we were dragged out of bed every Sabbath to attend the eight o'clock service, though the complicated readings and litany meant nothing to us. Later in the morning Sunday School was compulsory. No excuses allowed: illness, homework crisis, or the coveted (and rejected) invitations from friends.

'Do you think God gives us time off purgatory for every hour we suffer in church?' Jacob asked after one particularly excruciating service. That was the only time I remember any of us being chastised physically. No doubt to my parents' ears he was blaspheming, breaking one of the Ten Commandments that had pride of place in our small entrance hall.

Jacob

Eve claims we were once a *normal family*: dream on dear sister. When I read the local rag, I knew the vagrant wasn't Dad. We couldn't be that lucky! Rough sleeper: what a ridiculous euphemism. Why not say down-and-out, homeless, itinerant, tramp, poor-soul-on-the-streets, destitute – or the more accurate, man who deserted his family and chose to make everyone's life wretched.

Eve's reminiscences will indeed be highly *sanitised* (her flattering word for inaccurate) and I feel duty-bound to write some sections for her ridiculous journal, or whatever she's calling it. David suggested naming it after the Narnia series which we all loved as children and call it "The Chronicles of the Whistlers". That suggestion didn't go down too well. Our dear sister is the only one who wants to produce a record of our family's travails. The rest of us find it too painful.

Andrew

Eve rang me. The man in Elizabeth Park was one of the other rough sleepers. I think I upset her when I suggested that it might be Dad next time. He would be no loss to the world. Absolutely none. This journal is a stupid idea. I shall make few contributions. Least said, the happier people tend to be.

David

I am, to say the least, on the hectic side of busy (three restaurants to oversee, a wife, two children, a menagerie of assorted pets plus an extremely time-consuming garden). Strange then that I appear to be the only one keen to write pieces for Eve. Her idea of a family history is an excellent one, hopefully helping each of us to understand, and perhaps even come to terms with, events which have lain hidden for far too long.

I was relieved that the gentleman reported in the paper wasn't our father. I use the word *gentleman* deliberately as the homeless I speak to in the park are unfailingly polite and keen to engage in erudite conversations. Andrew is wrong. Dad would be a great loss. I make sure I keep in touch with him. Several years ago, I gave him a mobile, so he could contact me in an emergency.

He remains a good man, if one who is extremely troubled. For him to have walked out on the family he loved meant that something had gone wrong, very wrong. I have a feeling that, of all of us, Eve is the one who knows the reason behind dad's desertion and the appalling lifestyle he endures. She has never said anything but perhaps writing will encourage her to tell us what caused such a tragic volte-face.

Chapter 2

Having set up the murder room, desks and computers arranged around the walls and officers assigned their duties, Harvey drove to the hospital. Attending post-mortems was something he hated, feeling the person was being assaulted a second time. Unfortunately, the pathologist Harvey preferred was on holiday. William Corke was proficient, but lacked the insights Alfie Morrison brought to any investigation.

The gruesome spectacle began, Dr Corke speaking into the microphone, his words recorded for future reference.

'The deceased is dressed in what look like unwashed clothes. He is wearing several layers and has a scarf around his neck. The body appears to have been attacked by animals, rats or foxes most likely, the damage to the face and hands obvious.' As the scarf was removed he said, in a voice devoid of emotion, 'There's your answer. The man was strangled.'

Duty-bound to stay for the rest of the unpalatable spectacle, Harvey stood and thought about the killer. What kind of man, or indeed woman, could strangle someone and leave the body in the undergrowth their worldly goods placed carefully around them? Harvey believed that if they had the answer to that conundrum they would be close to finding the killer.

'I'd say the man has been dead between three to five days. The weather has been warm, but as he was left outside the evident signs of decomposition make estimating the time of death harder. Almost impossible to be completely accurate.'

'Any distinguishing features?' Harvey wished for some scraps of evidence, broken bones, operations, tattoos, to aid in the body's identification.

'No, nothing worth mentioning. A large mole on his left shoulder, probably not too helpful. A mouthful of teeth that haven't been seen by a dentist for a very long time, so I don't think dental records will be of much use.' Pausing to look closely at the internal organs he was removing, he sighed. 'This man was not in a particularly healthy state: evidence of damage to heart and liver, the kind of harm inflicted after excessive alcohol consumption, almost certainly over a number of years. Lungs also display signs of long-term smoking.'

'Can you give an estimate of his age?'

'Well, nothing like living rough to age a person. Both externally and internally he is almost certainly presenting as far older than his chronological age. He gives the appearance of a man in his late seventies, or even early eighties, but with the abuse he inflicted on his body he might well have been considerably younger.' Examining the contents of the stomach he added, 'I'll send samples to the lab, but I rather doubt anything will move your investigation forward.'

Harvey was about to thank the doctor for his examination when the man exclaimed, 'Oh my goodness! I missed that the first time. There's a small gold cross at the back of his mouth. Small enough to be inserted and pushed towards the throat. It didn't get very far, but I can't imagine he wanted to swallow it. We have to think it was done post-mortem, or I sincerely hope that was the case.'

'If he had been alive would he have swallowed it?'

'Not necessarily, but it's not easy to insert something in someone's mouth if they don't want it there, and if he was asleep such an act would probably have woken him. One more thing…the deceased was a large man and his body must have been moved post-mortem. Strangling him in the bushes would have been almost impossible, insufficient room to exert the necessary pressure – strangling someone, even someone not in the best of health, takes a lot of strength – so I'm certain the attack took place elsewhere and he was then relocated. Moving him, and I'm not trying to be funny when I say he was a dead weight, must have taken a lot of muscle power, not to say determination. The murderer didn't want him to be found too soon. Wanted him to remain hidden.'

Harvey stood, deep in thought. 'The hiding place must have been known to his assailant. From the outside the bushes look impenetrable. However, once inside there is a large space, big enough for a small child to stand up. It's the kind of area one of the rough sleepers might crawl into on a cold night.'

'Interesting, though a lot of effort must have gone into concealing him there.'

'Are we looking for a male?'

'Or a very strong woman.'

Keen to update his team Harvey called a meeting as soon as he returned to the station. The gold cross inserted in the deceased's mouth caused Clare Jennings, the youngest member of the team, to say aloud what others were thinking. 'Sounds like some kind of religious nutter. Hands across his chest, worldly goods arranged like a sacrament around his body, and now a cross in his throat.' Few things annoyed DCI Tarquin more than unhelpful comments and the young officer received a warning to stick to more appropriate observations.

'We need to identify the man. That's our number one priority. Every one of the people who call the parks and streets of Fordway home must be questioned. One of them must be aware that a member of their group has gone missing. We also need a photo of our victim in the press: local and national. I've already contacted *Crimewatch*, and they will include our case this week. Until then I want all of you out talking to each, and everyone, of the homeless you can find.'

Serena stayed behind to speak to her boss. 'What's your thinking, sir? A fellow vagrant or a member of the public who had a grudge against their lifestyle?'

'I'm not ruling anything in...or out. The religious aspect is, to say the least, interesting and the gold cross makes me think it was a planned attack. Not much help in narrowing the field. I think this may take some time, and a lot of patient and thorough policework.'

Fordway Gazette

Rough Sleeper Named

The body found in Elizabeth Park has been identified as Thomas Granger (70) who went by the name of Tommy. His brother recognised him after seeing his picture on the television.

Tommy was originally from Manchester but went missing fifteen years ago, the family losing contact with him soon after he was made redundant. Jim Barrow, the manager of the car-hire firm where Mr Granger worked, remembered a hard-working, well-spoken man who was the victim of cut-backs during the recession. 'He was one of several employees we had to let go and I am very sorry to hear about the downward spiral he endured.'

DCI Tarquin, in charge of the investigation, refused to comment on how the case was progressing, but added that he was glad the victim had been identified.

This tragedy highlights the appalling number of rough sleepers in the town and a future edition will deal, in depth, with this sad situation.

As a child, Harvey Tarquin had been gregarious, with many friends (at times too many – he was often in trouble for socialising during lessons, one teacher chastising him for playing the part of the class clown, 'More like class idiot,' had been a whispered aside, his friend also then in trouble). Until he was eighteen he found it easy to make people laugh and became an excellent mimic.

He loved his first term at Manchester University where he had a place to read Law. A girl-a-week and heavy drinking did little to aid his studies and lectures were attended spasmodically. He was there to live the student life to the full. A few weeks into the second term his mother died. No warning. A massive stroke that felled her as she was unlocking the car prior to a shopping trip with a friend. The paramedics worked on her for forty minutes. 'We've got a pulse, let A and E know we're coming.'

An hour later Bill Tarquin was told that his wife had died. 'How am I going to cope son?' This and similar phrases became the chorus to any conversation. 'You'll stay and help with your brothers, won't you?' Harvey knew the question was rhetorical. Sam and Jeremy were two and four years his junior and he felt duty-bound to put his degree on hold.

One month morphed into two, then eighteen, and Harvey was forced to grow up. 'Thank you, son. I don't know what we'd have done without you,' became his even more pathetic new reprise. He had never realised how weak his father was. It was his mother who had been the reliable one, the parent who had encouraged her boys to achieve their full potential.

On many occasions, Harvey regretted agreeing to the new arrangement. Cooking, cleaning, shopping and washing all became his domain and the activities were not always undertaken with a good grace. 'Some help would be appreciated,' was apt to receive angry responses. Both brothers were miserable. Neither had Harvey's intellect and hated their academic studies. Dealing with the pain of bereavement made them volatile, and led to frequent arguments.

'We just wish some of the teachers would stop comparing us with you. They refer to you as "Tarquin senior" and say we need to be more like you. Fat chance.'

Feeling like a slave driver Harvey wrote individual homework timetables for them, prominently displayed on the kitchen noticeboard, and monitored their other activities. It was what his mother had done for him and therefore seemed appropriate.

'You're not our bloody mother,' was Sam's response one particularly unpleasant evening when he had been told he couldn't go out. 'She'd have known we need downtime.'

'You spent the entire weekend socialising, so I think that counts as downtime. And if you break your curfew again there will be consequences.'

'Curfew? Consequences? You may have started a Law degree, but you're not a High Court judge just yet. You'll soon be wanting to don the black cap.'

Walking into the room, Jeremy joined the argument. 'Bloody hell, Tarquin, you used to be fun. We remember how you lived it up. You've turned into a middle-aged, sanctimonious, bloody bore.' Asking his brother not to swear resulted in a tirade of abuse.

Returning to university was a mixed experience. He knew he wanted to gain a degree, but found the other students' immature and the social life, that he had once adored, puerile. 'That's how I behaved when I was here before,' he said to his tutor, 'how could I have been so callow?'

'Don't be so hard on yourself. You were a lot younger, maybe not in years but in experience. With your work ethos and the standard of your essays, I forecast an excellent degree for you. I'm just sorry you've had to go through so much to get to this point.'

Of average height, slim build and with unassuming looks (thinning fair hair and a nose broken in a drunken brawl) few would regard him as the archetypal policeman. During his final year at Manchester he was told about fast-tracking for graduates. Until reading about the possibilities for graduates with good degrees in the "New and Exciting Police Force" he had assumed he would become a lawyer, a career that had never really appealed. The promise of accelerated promotion was the key, with the likelihood of becoming an inspector after two years, and in time a superintendent.

Promotion was his aim. Unmarried and with no regular girlfriend (where did others find the time or indeed the inclination?) police work was his life. Having gained a First in Law he had stayed in the city, moving to Preston several years later. He loved the North West of England, so different to the levels of Oxfordshire where he had grown up.

His mentor in Preston, Lee Ritchie, had been a man nearing retirement, an old-school copper who had remained in the lower ranks, doing the job he went into: on the street, catching the criminals. He'd overseen many a young man through their initial year of promotion and always gave the same advice: 'You're doing well, but every policeman needs a hobby. The job can get you down and you'll need an escape route.'

Harvey's one form of relaxation was walking, preferably in the glorious surroundings of the Lake District. He had been asked to join the Preston Ramblers after a neighbour, Jim James, saw him setting off one morning dressed in boots, anorak and walking trousers.

'The PR is great fun Harvey, you choose the level of walk that suits you: easy, extended, or energetic! We organise rambles every weekend and, when the nights are lighter, one evening each week. You'd be more than welcome to come along and see how it suits you. We're a friendly bunch and love it when new members join us.'

Explaining that his work schedule was, to say the least, erratic, Harvey said that he would bear it in mind for the future. In truth, he far preferred walking on his own. His working life was overflowing with people and he loved the tranquillity that a solitary walk afforded. He was surprised at how stressful his work could be and loved the days when there were no time constraints and the walk could be long or short: almost invariably the former.

As always, the police station was frenetically busy. For a small town, Fordway enjoyed its share of criminal activity. The weekend had seen the cells fill up: the drunk and disorderly, the perpetrator of a particularly unpleasant domestic violence incident – the wife hospitalised – and a middle-aged man caught in the act of robbing a house, the owners returning earlier than expected.

After most of the morning had been spent assigning the "overnighters" and other weekend miscreants to his subordinates, he dedicated the rest of the day to the case that he was pleased to be heading: the murder of Tommy Granger. Although two weeks had passed with frustratingly little progress, it was good finally to dignify the corpse with a name and gain some background information on the man. Statements had been taken from several of the people who shared Tommy's way of living. All had spoken of a gentle man. One who spoke quietly. One who, in the direst of circumstances, had maintained his dignity.

Reading through his notes Harvey found little to raise his spirits, or help solve the case. The observations supplied by his fellow vagrants ranged from, 'He was never in trouble, liked a drink but wasn't the kind to start a fight,' to 'Old Tommy, a great character, would do anything for anybody and always shared his tuck.' The man had had no obvious enemies and had never come to the attention of the police, unlike some of his companions who were regular attenders at Preston Magistrates' Court for D and D, breach of the peace, fighting or theft. Harvey knew the gentlemen of the road, as he liked to think of them, stuck together (who else did they have?) and would often turn up in court mob-handed, frequently interrupting proceedings to make some loud comment. He did not remember seeing Thomas Granger there.

Harvey read his transcript of the telephone call to Thomas's brother, his only remaining relative. Ben Granger had said that Thomas had been a hard-working man who had been devastated when the firm, where he had worked for almost thirty years, had made him redundant. At fifty-five he had known it would be hard to find other employment.

'He tried to remain optimistic, but he couldn't seem to get another job, though goodness knows he tried. Application after application led to unsuccessful interviews or received no response. I could see he was losing heart and one day he told me he was going to the Preston area to look for work. He seemed quite positive when he left, but that was the last I heard from him. What a tragedy, what a terrible way to end up. But, the thing is, I can't imagine anyone wanting to kill him. He was always a caring sort, sometimes too much for his own good. Put up with his wife's affairs for years before he finally had enough and asked her to move out. No doubt she won't be too bothered.'

Today's task was to speak to Sylvia Granger. Finding the ex-wife had proved easy as she had retained her married name and had remained in Greater Manchester.

Chorlton-cum-Hardy, four miles south west of Manchester city centre, boasted many Victorian and Edwardian houses, now popular with commuters. Sylvia Granger lived in a detached property, the type of house favoured by the newly emerging middle class of the late eighteenth and nineteenth centuries. At that time, the village had retained its rural character. Being to the south west of the city it had the added advantage of avoiding the wind-blown smoke and smells from the factories. The factories where the well-to-do occupants were making their fortunes.

In her early seventies, the former Mrs Granger had not worn well, though she had obviously remained financially secure. Her brother-in-law's view was that Thomas had been "extremely generous, considering what the bitch put him through". Over-permed hair did little to enhance a face lined by years of heavy smoking. DCI Tarquin had been determined to interview her himself, thinking she may have some insight that might help to find the killer.

'Not seen him for years, he threw me out and kept his promise to have nothing further to do with me. Must be twenty-five years since we had any contact, but I never thought he'd end up on the streets. He was so house-proud, especially when we were first married. Did all the decorating and our garden could have been in a magazine: full of colour in all seasons. Oh, the time we spent in garden centres; paid out a small fortune. Mind you, he had a temper, could really lose it if someone crossed him. A bloke looked at me in the pub one time and Tommy threw a full glass of beer over him and threatened to break his arm if he did it again.'

'I know it's a long time ago, but did your husband have any enemies?'

'You mean apart from the man in the pub? No, generally he got on with people and I know he was popular at work. I was sorry when his brother told me that Tommy had lost his job. I know I've said he had a temper, but it wasn't bad enough for someone to want to kill him.'

Driving back to the station Harvey knew that the smallest altercation could lead to murder. Tommy's former employer, Jim Barrow, had made a statement which added little to the words that had appeared in the Gazette. Harvey thought it might be an idea to phone him again to ask about the possibility that Tommy Granger found it hard to control his temper.

'Good afternoon, Mr Barrow. DCI Tarquin here from Fordway police. We spoke last week when you were most helpful. I've just got one more question: did Mr Granger ever lose his temper?'

If Jim Barrow was surprised by the query he didn't show it and replied immediately. 'No, not that I was aware of. I don't recall him ever getting into an argument, though he did find some of our clients frustrating, the ones who returned cars late or in a filthy state. But, and it's a big but, he never let the customers see how he felt, always the professional, he just let rip after they'd gone.'

Thanking the man for his time, Harvey rang off and sat, not sure how helpful the day had been. There was so little evidence, but he reviewed what they knew. A body positioned almost sensitively in the bushes, the man laid out on his back, arms crossed over his chest and covered with a blanket. All his worldly goods – packed in plastic bags – positioned symmetrically around his body, an ancient rucksack parallel to his feet. He had been strangled, his neck covered by a scarf. From the dirty state of it almost certainly his. Perhaps most telling of all, a small cross had been placed in his mouth, fortunately post-mortem.

Someone had killed him and laid his remains out ceremoniously. Someone had cared enough to make his end look dignified. However, someone had wanted him dead.

Chapter 3

Eve

I am so afraid that the poor man was attacked just because he was one of society's outcasts. It made me determined to speak to Dad. Having delayed the encounter for most of the day, the light was beginning to fade by the time I found him. He was sitting by the smaller of the two lakes in Elizabeth Park, the one frequented by ducks rather than rowing boats. Always a sorry sight, today he looked worse than ever: a man unable to cope.

It is an unpalatable truth that he now regards the place as home. When we were children he used to tell us about the park. Queen Elizabeth the First is supposed to have spent a night in Fordway on one of her journeys north. She stayed, or so the story goes, with Lord Timperton in Fordway Hall, and what is now a public park was once part of his estate. When it became a park in the 1850s it was named in her honour. Dad, a staunch supporter of the Royal family, loved to think he took us to play where a queen had once walked.

Another of his retreats is the newly developed Ash Tree Park on the far side of town. It's a lot bigger and very busy, whatever the season. It's great for the children: swings, climbing frames, a paddling pool and a set of trampolines which the youngsters adore. The park is handy for the two large housing estates which were built recently, almost doubling the population of what used to be little more than a small market town.

I know Dad isn't too keen on this new park and doesn't go often. In one of our rare conversations he told me that he objects to the fact that the old allotments, there for generations, had to give way to "a glorified kids' playground". The open space that surrounded the allotments was also consumed, like a giant's snack: all in the name of progress.

I found him. The rain, that had threatened all day, had arrived. Dad sat, seemingly unaware of how wet he was getting.

'I'm not in the mood to talk,' was his opening gambit, 'leave me alone.' Over the years, he has made it obvious that he wants nothing to do with me, but today he was more vehement than ever.

I smiled and issued my usual invitation. His reply was slow and sounded rather confused. 'No doubt you mean well… middle class duty and all that… I'll stick with my routine…none of us want do-gooders interfering with us.'

I assured him that I wasn't trying to change the life he had chosen. However, following recent events I was worried.

After an age, both of us getting wetter by the second, he spoke so quietly I had to strain to listen. 'We're all so sorry about Tommy. He was one of the good guys, a real gentleman. I don't feel frightened, and in any case, some of us are needed to look out for a new girl who's joined us. She's very young and it's her first time living rough, so she likes to have as much company as possible. She's called Charlotte but prefers Charlie. She's a real tomboy. Reminds me of you when you were little, trying to keep up with your older brothers.'

It was strange to hear Dad talk so much. It was probably the longest conversation we had enjoyed for years. Unfortunately, that was the end of it as two of his friends arrived, turning up like the cavalry: rescuing him, armed not with guns but bottles of cider. Dad never used to be a drinker, indeed alcohol was banned from the house, deemed to be an evil influence which led to the all sorts of "sin", a physical phenomenon that my parents saw everywhere and were determined to avoid. What an interesting exchange of views his younger self would have with the alcoholic he has become.

When he walked out that May evening uttering the unforgettable phrase, 'I'm just popping out for a minute,' did he intend to return? What was on his mind? He took nothing with him: suitcase, wallet, passport or other forms of identity. The six o'clock news was on the radio and we were all finishing our tea (it was always tea, never dinner, maybe due to its early consumption). No reason was offered for the "popping out" and none of us questioned it. For a few months, he had been very down and had disappeared – on a regular basis – for solitary walks. But, until that evening, he had always returned.

By ten o'clock Mum was starting to worry. It was dark and none of us could imagine where he might be. The twins had been upstairs revising, the start of their A levels a few days away, and Andrew was fast asleep in bed. Sitting in the living room with Mum growing ever more nervous was something I shall never forget. In some ways, they were the worst moments of the entire experience, rather like the hours before an interview being so much worse than the actual thing.

Jacob came downstairs and took charge. When he was young he was the joker in the family pack, and that night he managed to relieve the tension by suggesting that Dad had joined the Foreign Legion or had been a Russian "sleeper" who had been activated. He was the one who rang friends to see if Dad was there.

'Don't be stupid, you're wasting your time phoning friends. He hasn't seen anyone for weeks. Not since Grandma died. He's been doing overtime at work, and then coming home and sitting incommunicado.' Mum's voice was shrill, the tension leaking out of her like a suppurating boil.

Three in the morning. The pressure unbearable. Jacob rang the police. The man he spoke to was sympathetic, but said that as Dad was an adult it was far too early for the police to become involved. 'Ring again if he still hasn't returned after twenty-four hours. In most cases people come home and have a perfectly good explanation for where they've been. Try not to worry. I suggest you all go to bed and get some sleep. I'll note down your call, but I fully expect him to be home soon.'

How wrong he was!

Jacob

Wrong? It's wasn't only the policeman who was wrong. The whole thing was wrong. Eve's memory is flawed. There were no funnies that night or, as far as I remember, for months afterwards. It was straight to panic mode, Mum's perennial reaction to anything unforeseen, a mood which, by morning, overwhelmed us all.

Sleep? What a relief that would have been. Five-thirty, a horrendous time of the morning, found the four of us back at the kitchen table drinking tea, the great British panacea. 'Where can he be? Why hasn't he come home?' Mum's wail the only interruption to the uncomfortable silence. She repeated these and other phrases until I'm sure I was not alone in wanting to escape. That was an impossibility.

Afterwards, when we discussed those first twenty-four hours, we realised we had all endured the same anxieties, staccato phrases that played on repeat in our minds. He was dead by the roadside, injured, lying unseen in a field. None of us thought he had deserted us, that truth was too painful. The man we knew (or thought we had known) wouldn't just have walked out. There must be some explanation. Our thoughts remained unspoken.

By morning it was David who took control and rang the local hospitals. I had contacted the police, so it was his turn to do something. By eight, friends had been contacted again. We were, and remain, a very small family, all relatives either dead or decamped to America or Australia, so there were few people to telephone.

Mum insisted that we all went to school, assuring us that our father would be home by the end of the day. During lessons my mind was occupied, the teachers reiterating their message that the exams we were about to undertake were vitally important. 'Revise, work, revise, work,' was their mantra, and whilst I now understand their desire for us to do our best, a few good grades were of little significance compared with Dad's disappearance. To give the teachers their due, a few weeks later each one was to write to the various Examination Boards to ask for extenuating circumstances to be taken into consideration.

How fortuitous that I had an after-school club: The Edible Garden. As I picked the spring asparagus I remembered Dad's vitriolic comment when I first mentioned my new hobby: "Gardening? Are you turning into a sissy?"

A strange comment when some of the world's great gardeners are men. I don't think it helped when I pointed out that Adam and Eve had started life in a rather famous one.

David

Extenuating circumstances, yes indeed we had those. The weeks of A Levels were hell. Should there be a celestial boss I am sure he has noted that we deserve a go-straight-to-heaven permit. How Jacob or I managed to pass them all (though in my case missing the high grades that had been forecast) remains one of life's mysteries.

Over those first days, then weeks, then months it dawned – gradually – that Dad wasn't coming back. Janine Fielding, the Family Liaison Officer assigned to us, said that it was surprisingly common for people to leave their homes. Hearing her say that he had, in all likelihood, come to no harm was of little comfort. She spoke of people who needed "time-out", of men suffering a mid-life crisis, or the very human desire for something totally new. 'You may never hear from him again, but it was his decision to walk away. Had he come to harm we would probably know by now.' The use of the word "we" was strangely comforting.

Andrew

Family memories of those first days? Not for me. I was excluded, dispatched with undue haste to live with Oscar's family. Oscar was, and remains, my only friend. End of that part of these ridiculous reminiscences. We all lived unhappily ever after.

Chapter 4

The phone call came in the middle of a walk. December can be glorious: clear blue skies, sunshine and fresh snow. The Saturday two weeks before Christmas was just such a day and Harvey Tarquin was enjoying a walk along Morecambe Promenade. He knew, from previous attempts, that trying to hike in the Lakes in such conditions would be inadvisable, the snow several inches thick and the paths not cleared. The local news had advised people not to go walking alone in the Cumbrian hills and one of his favourite alternatives was Morecambe Bay, a walk not undertaken for several months.

He had, on several occasions, completed the ten-mile hike from Hest Bank to Heysham and back, a splendid affair with stunning views across the Bay the whole way, but today he was undertaking a much shorter foray. Harvey always enjoyed the many bird sculptures that decorated the walk. The bird watchers in the area would no doubt be able to identify them all, but he was pleased to be able to recognise cormorants and the ubiquitous seagulls. He had read that all the birds on display were native to the Bay, though he wondered how often the eagle, perched imperiously on its balustrade, had been seen on the Lancashire coast.

The tide was venturing in, far more pedantically than the infamous "faster than a horse can gallop" which had caused many deaths. Harvey recalled the tragedy in February 2004 when twenty-one Chinese people collecting cockles drowned after being caught by the incoming water. Today the tide appeared to be breathing in and out as gently as a sleeping baby, though a mother would be concerned by the time-lapse between breaths.

Few people had ventured out, too early for most. Harvey passed two sets of dog walkers, out for their early morning constitutionals. 'Wonderful morning and there can't be a finer view in England,' the elderly man smiled, then added, 'southerners don't know what they're missing!' Looking across Morecambe Bay to Grange-Over-Sands and the hills beyond, with their icing sugar peaks, was indeed a sight to lift anyone's spirits.

Just as he was about to reply Harvey's phone rang. He hated allowing the ringtone (the *Adagio* from *Mozart's Clarinet Concerto in A major*, a calm prelude to calls that were invariably work related) to interrupt a walk, but in his elevated position it was essential that he remain in contact. Retrieving his phone, hidden at the bottom of his rucksack, took too long and by the time he pushed the answer button it had gone to voicemail. As he listened to the message asking him to contact Serena Peil he knew it was bad news. Serena had joined the Fordway CID team as an inspector and was proving to be extremely capable. She would not have interrupted his Saturday unless it was important.

Deciding to spend a further fifteen minutes enjoying the views he walked on towards Heysham, with its ancient church sitting so proudly on the promontory overlooking the southern shores of the Bay. The church had Saxon and Viking remains in its grounds, but the rumour that Saint Patrick had built it after arriving from Ireland was a myth: it was not erected until three hundred years after his death.

In the past, he had stopped to spend time inside the building and then have a drink in the adjacent café. He knew there would be no time for such indulgencies today. As he approached St Peter's he noticed a banner advertising an evening of music to raise funds for the grounds where it was hoped "An All-Seasons Garden" would be created. Remembering how beautiful the area surrounding the church had been on his last visit, daffodils creating a carpet of startling yellow, he punched Serena's number reluctantly into his mobile.

'Good morning, sir. Very sorry to bother you on your day off, but there's been another murder.'

Chapter 5

As Harvey drove down the M6 it was beginning to get busy. People were off to Manchester and the Trafford Centre – only thirteen shopping days left before Christmas. Harvey recalled the inspector's words. 'It's almost the same M.O. It's another of the rough sleepers in Elizabeth Park, but a female this time and very young. Early this morning a jogger went into the bushes to relieve himself and found her. Same as last time. She was hidden in the undergrowth and it looks as though she's been strangled. The Crime Scene bods are there, but we'll leave the body in situ until you arrive.'

It was her final comment that flitted, like a bird trapped in a room, round and round in his brain. The body would be left in situ. He imagined the scene: the woman strangled and abandoned in the bushes. Wondering how long she had lain there, he found himself repeating the same words: Why is someone targeting the poor souls who are homeless?

After weeks with little progress he had assumed that Tommy Granger's death had been a one-off, the result of an altercation. Perhaps there had been a dispute over sleeping arrangements, or someone's drink had been stolen, the kind of events that occurred with depressing regularity amongst the gentlemen of the park. However, he realised that such disputes seldom resulted in extreme violence – and never, in his experience, to murder. The religious features of the first murder occupied his thinking: the laying out of the body, the arrangement of the man's few worldly goods laid like offerings around him and, most intriguing of all, the positioning of a cross in the deceased's mouth. Was this the same?

Thomas Granger's case had gone cold, as cold as the sub-zero temperatures which had swept down from the north and affected the whole country. Harvey was very afraid that this new case would prove as hard to solve as the first one. He didn't know that the two cases were linked, but it was more than a coincidence that within the space of a few weeks two people, who spent their lives wandering the streets, sitting on park benches and sleeping rough, had been strangled, their bodies left hidden in the bushes.

Andrew

A woman this time. Young: in her late teens. Eve rang, distraught. She said she's more and more worried about Dad. Well, there's nothing we can do. She didn't like it when I suggested that he might be the killer. It's a thought! Who's he keeping close to him...friends or enemies?

Eve

There are times I can't believe Andrew is my brother. He has no regard for anyone else, not a compassionate bone in his body. He's always been the same – must have had an empathy bypass at birth. Jacob and David both rang last night when they saw the local news. We met for lunch today and they said they are frightened for Dad's welfare. At least they understand.

They were disgusted by Andrew's suggestion that Dad might be the killer, and Jacob said that was typical of him. 'He says the first thing that comes into his head and doesn't care how much it upsets anyone else. How Mum puts up with him living at home is anyone's guess.' Jacob went off on one of his rants, the kind he indulges in when stressed.

'The problem with our mother is that she needs someone to "molly-coddle" (his words). She doesn't want him to leave home, afraid she'd be lonely.' He may be right. She does everything for her *baby boy* as she refers to him and continues to do all his washing and ironing. She even changes his bed and has a hot meal ready for him at six o' clock every evening. Even I think it's all rather pathetic.

David, normally the calm one, got quite agitated when we were discussing Andrew. 'He's spoilt, utterly ruined. However, I've always thought that he's the one, out of all of us, who has been the most affected by Dad's shenanigans. He was only ten at the time of the "popping out", but his teenage years were blighted by it with those awful depressions and long periods of silence. Do you remember the days when he didn't speak? They were horrendous and in many ways, he's never outgrown them; even now he only enters a conversation when it suits him. Mum doesn't help as she is so delighted to keep him as her Peter Pan.'

We are going to see Dad together. Mob-handed! He won't like it, but with three of us there he might be persuaded to come home with me. Probably no point asking Andrew to accompany us, but David said we should try.

Jacob and David have excuses for not asking him to live with them. David's house is overflowing with people and animals: a wife, Elspeth (the less I say about her the better) two children, a large out-of-control dog and three cats. It's understandable that he wouldn't want Sasha and Caitlin to have too much to do with their grandfather.

Jacob was obviously embarrassed when he said that he couldn't offer to take Dad. He's got a holiday booked. Two weeks over the Christmas holiday in the Appalachian Mountains playing his banjo. No, none of us could believe it when he first mentioned it. He's always been the musical one and can play the guitar and ukulele as well as his beloved banjo.

'It was advertised as "The Ultimate Banjo Bonanza". It's a fortnight of lessons, group sessions, solo opportunities and then several gigs: my idea of heaven. The blurb also says there will be lots of time off to explore the glorious countryside.' I'm pleased for him. Being a peripatetic music teacher can't be easy. He finds it frustrating when his pupils aren't as passionate about the instruments as he is and don't practise from one lesson to the next.

We're going on our Dad-hunt on Sunday. Maybe if he knows how scared we are he'll agree to leave the parks.

Andrew

Crazy! A ridiculous venture. Dad invented the word stubborn. He won't budge. In the very unlikely event that he does agree to their plan, Eve will be throwing him out after a few days.

Has she forgotten what he was like to live with? Me, me, me. Nowadays even Mum acknowledges that he wasn't an easy man.

Did they tell me what they were planning and ask me to accompany them knowing I would decline the offer? They like to make me look bad. So, so superior, my elders if not betters.

Chapter 6

Fordway Gazette

Second Murder in Elizabeth Park

A second body has been discovered in Elizabeth Park. Three months ago, a rough sleeper, Tommy Granger (aged 70), was killed and his body left under some bushes in the middle of the park. Last Saturday a second body was discovered in similar circumstances.

The body has been identified as that of Charlotte Carraway, a young rough sleeper, aged 18. She had arrived in Fordway only recently having been on the Missing Persons' list since April.

Charlotte is believed to come from Bolton where she lived with her parents and younger sister.

The police refused to comment or to say whether they think the two cases are linked.

DCI Harvey Tarquin knew the cases were linked; the similarities impossible to ignore. With little progress made, the early morning briefing bristled with frustration. Harvey scrawled on the case management board. 'I know it's almost illegible, so I'll read each line aloud and hope someone has ideas about where we go from here.' The room was quiet. No gallows humour suggesting that games of hangman might help to decipher his scribble.

'To recap: two murders. One a man of seventy, the other a young woman. Two bodies strangled and left under the same bushes. Both victims covered with their own blankets, scarves around their necks, their arms crossed over their chests.'

'The Press has not been made aware of those details,' Serena interrupted, 'and we want it left that way.'

'The bodies were shown respect.' Harvey was keen that the team should adopt the same stance.

'Apart from being strangled.' Roger Symmons, a long-standing member of the Fordway team, was the only one to find his aside amusing.

'As I said the bodies were respected. Covered up, left in an almost ritualistic fashion, small crosses placed inside both mouths. The killer – if it's the same person – hid them from view. Now he, or of course she, might have done that to prevent them from being found too soon, or maybe they didn't want them viewed as entertainment.'

'Surely, we're not looking for a woman, sir.' P.C. Symmons stopped, realising he'd interrupted his superior. 'I was just thinking that the killer must have been strong to move the bodies into the bushes.'

The silence that ensued told him that his idea was not popular. 'We must keep an open mind about that,' Harvey murmured, then continued. 'Was the killer sorry for what he'd done? Both victims were rough sleepers, both were known to the others who live as vagrants. Were Tommy and Charlotte known to the killer? Both victims appeared to have been well liked. No one has had a bad word to say about either of them.'

Serena stood up to speak. 'Those are the similarities. Now the differences: one was a man, one a woman; one was 70, the other 18; one a long-term gentleman of the road, estranged from his family, the other a recent arrival, missing from home for almost eight months, her family desperate to find her.'

One of the most harrowing parts of any murder investigation is speaking to the relatives. Harvey hated it but never delegated the task. He knew he had the skill and necessary tact to elicit information from people at their most vulnerable: information that might prove vital. He thought back to the harrowing meeting with Charlotte's parents.

Mr and Mrs Carroway had travelled from their home in Bolton. They had entered the room with a dignity that appeared almost misplaced. Both had been dressed professionally, in black and navy suits respectively, and had obviously been keen to make a favourable impression. Ursula Carroway's hair looked as if she had just been to the hairdresser's and her make-up had been immaculate. Any tears had long since been shed and the two had stood to attention, like members of a regiment called in to speak to a senior officer.

Following the usual commiserations Harvey had asked the necessary questions. Edwin Carroway had done all the talking, his answers reminding the inspector that he was dealing with a professional, one who spent his life delivering lectures. He appeared unmoved as he explained that many months ago, Charlotte had walked out after a particularly unpleasant argument. She had informed her parents that she hated them and everything they stood for. To begin with they thought it was just a teenage tantrum; that she was punishing them for not giving her permission to go to a party. She had gone anyway.

'Can you give me any more details?' Harvey had asked, knowing that he was asking for information the parents might not want to divulge.

After a brief hesitation, Edwin Carroway had spoken. 'It was a Wednesday night and Charlotte had school the following day and exams coming up, so a late night was out of the question. When she didn't come home on the Thursday morning we rang all her friends. She'd gone to Angela's "Eighteenth Extravaganza" at a nightclub in the middle of town, but had left with her boyfriend in the early hours of the morning. He said she had walked off, telling the young man that we were picking her up. Until the event in the park no one had seen her since that night.'

Harvey thought Mr Carroway's description of Charlotte's murder was unusually callous and his use of the word *event* totally inadequate to describe his daughter's demise. Suspecting that the man was keeping some details back he had asked, 'Had she ever done anything like this before? Was it out of character?'

Edwin had looked at his wife who was sitting very upright in her chair, eyes focussed on the painting on the wall. She seemed almost amused to see a copy of Renoir's *Boating on the Seine*. Harvey had purchased it on a recent visit to the Musee d'Orsay in Paris and hoped it would help make people more relaxed. From his position, he could enjoy one of Van Gogh's self-portraits, a painting that suited its setting as it could be viewed as a personification of mankind's travails. The small office he was using to speak to Charlotte's parents was the one he'd been allocated whilst in Fordway, and he had wanted to personalise it. Others had family photos. He relied on the Impressionists.

Following a prolonged silence Edwin had continued, his voice now less authoritative. 'Charlotte was always an independent girl and in the months before she left home she had got in with a crowd of whom we disapproved. Most were older than her and had left school, with no intention of enjoying a further education. The young man she brought to our "Open House" last Christmas was most unsuitable. He looked as though he was on something. I recognised the look from some of my less salubrious students. When we talked to her about drugs she told us that everyone took them and that they were no big deal. "Only a few E's not the hard stuff," had been her somewhat naïve comment.'

Ursula had then interrupted. It was the first time she had spoken, and Harvey placed her accent a lot further south than Manchester. 'She had a place at Oxford…to read Classics. She was such a clever girl and, up to a year ago, worked hard and we were so pleased with her progress. Her younger sister, Emily, is even brighter and is going up to Oxford a year early.'

And thereby hangs the tale. Harvey still felt saddened by the woman's words. Poor daughter, hot-housed, grown for public approval. Charlotte wanted out of Mummy and Daddy's plans for her and the only way was to abscond, get as far as possible from the life they had scheduled. How sad that her choice of lifestyle had to result in such a tragic outcome.

Nothing Mr and Mrs Carroway had divulged had helped. There was still no obvious motive for the murder of an eighteen-year-old runaway. He doubted very much that either of the parents had been involved, though a greater display of sadness at her demise would have made him think more compassionately about them. Perhaps people in their elevated circles hid their emotions and did their grieving in private. He hoped so: Charlotte deserved it.

Serena Peil was horrified to realise that she was enjoying being part of a murder investigation. Only recently promoted, she felt that she was involved, finally, in "proper policing". But no one should gain satisfaction from the death of another. She would not have admitted her feelings to anyone. Did other officers feel the same? She was sure DCI Tarquin didn't. His reputation as a consummate professional was well-founded, and Serena knew how fortunate she was to be working on her first serious investigation with him in charge.

She had spent the morning in the two parks looking for the rough sleepers and trying to persuade them to come into the station to talk to the police. Knowing most of them would be phased by the word investigation, or the thought of being questioned, she had opted for the phrase less likely to intimidate them. Most had lost any sense of time, so arranging an appointment for a specific hour would have been pointless. Opting for this afternoon was as close as she could come to a timetable.

They had already "helped the police with their enquiries" but very informally, mostly sitting on a park bench, the one festooned with flowers, well-wishers keen to make the seat look like a florist's shop. The second murder meant that a more formal system of gaining information had become necessary. Both she and Harvey hoped that at least one of the men (no females now that Charlotte had been killed) would have some information, something that might appear insignificant, but that might help solve the cases.

And...there was always the possibility that one of them might be the killer.

Chapter 7

Eve

We found Dad eventually. It was early afternoon and he was drunk and almost incoherent. Slurred words did little to lighten his venom. He informed us that not only did he not want to leave the park, but that he didn't want anything to do with us. Any of us. When I suggested that he had punished himself enough he yelled that eternity wouldn't be enough time to atone for what he had done. Redemption unattainable. A strange conviction for one who had been such a firm believer in the Salvation offered by Christ.

Total failure. The day was not only a waste of time but left us all feeling dreadful. Standing beside him, we were rendered speechless by his swearing and the profanities he shot at us: bullets that hit their targets every time. We told ourselves that the obscenities were his way of dealing with the unbearable loss of two of his companions. The man is in the depths of despair, the murders having affected him more than he is willing – or able – to articulate in any other way.

David and Jacob asked me what Dad had meant about his needing to be punished. I replied that I didn't want to talk about it. I said I would, at some point, include it in the journal. Not yet. I promised my father that I would never tell anyone, and it feels too soon to break that vow.

Of the two I think Jacob is finding it the most difficult to admit that we can do nothing. David has his family and menagerie – another kitten added last week – to occupy his life. Thank goodness Jacob is off on his banjo break.

I will immerse myself in work and spend the next week attempting to keep my clients out of prison! It's my turn to be the overnight duty solicitor. Oh joy! Two a.m. meetings in the delightful ambience of the police cells with the reprobates of Preston. Living in Fordway means that I have several miles to travel to work. Thankfully, when I'm on overnight call, I stay with Philip, though he's getting far too serious and thinks the relationship is going somewhere: church. I keep telling him once was more than enough for me.

Andrew

So, siblings coping.

Eve losing herself in work.

David with his new kitten.

Jacob escaping, pretending to the world that he has talent… and of course growing his prize-winning vegetables on his allotment. Don't we all have to hear about that!

Each looks at life through their own selfish prism. What a pathetic excuse for a family we are. I am so pleased not to be a part of it. Ever since I was side-lined, sent to live with Oscar during those first weeks when Dad opted not to come home, I've felt like the missing ingredient that ruins a cake. I still wonder how it was possible that sixty days could feel like a lifetime. Oscar's mum was kind and tried to make me feel welcome, but I overheard his dad asking how long I'd be staying.

I was ten and understood what was happening at home. The fact I was being treated like an ignorant child didn't help. Being ostracised made the whole thing so much worse. Not knowing any details was agony, my mind imagining the vilest possible scenarios. I felt as though I'd lost the others, not just Dad. I needed to be included. It was harder, indescribably so, to be excluded. Have you got my point, Eve?

Mum says that she was thinking of me, that she wanted my life to be normal. Normal? How normal can it be to live two streets away from your own home knowing you weren't wanted – either at home or with a different family? There really wasn't room for any more in the Slade's small house and even Oscar grew tired of sharing his bedroom.

I found out later that Dad had made contact (the one and only letter), making it clear he wasn't going to return. They were all at least two weeks ahead of me in coming to terms with that gem.

Why did they wait to tell me? Why not when we all met up on the day I turned eleven? My birthday party was at the local cinema, followed by a meal at McDonalds, all arranged by Oscar's mum, my lot arriving at the eatery (hardly a restaurant) with presents and stupid cards. I was old enough to be told the truth.

Finally, almost two months later, I was allowed home. As I walked through my own front door Mum sat me down. It must be admitted that she did look rather shame-faced. 'Andrew love, I've got something to tell you,' this was my mother in all her stuttering glory, her modus operandi for anything contentious. 'Dad won't be coming home.' Five words with the capacity to destroy a life: mine has never returned to what most people would deem "normal". I know who I blame: Dad, the man who deserted me, left me with the quartet that comprises what is euphemistically called a family. What a joke! What an absolute joke!

My depression is returning. A marauding army is invading, raping and pillaging, annihilating all the positives and leaving my brain overwhelmed by black thoughts. It's like drowning in a sea of negativity. I can't sleep so feel permanently shattered, lose concentration at work and can hardly eat. That's the one that worries Mum as she does love to feed me: roasts, suet puddings, pasta and every rich pudding devised by Mary Berry. Thoughts of death consume me, both mine and others.

A miserable entry for your bloody journal. Hope you're all satisfied.

Chapter 8

Harry Whistler walked into the police station just after two o'clock. It was slightly too early in the day for him to be completely inebriated, though the stench of booze emanating from him made Serena Peil think that anything he had to say might be unreliable. Like all gentlemen of the road he carried his life with him. Harry had learnt early on to travel light – everything remaining in sight.

Carrier bags were overflowing with clothes, a sleeping bag, plastic matting and, somewhat surprisingly, what looked like a pair of brand-new trainers. A large rucksack bulged under the weight of its unseen contents.

Showing him into the interview room Serena introduced him to DCI Tarquin.

'Don't waste your breath, I've talked to him before.'

'Indeed. I came to the park soon after Thomas Granger was found dead and we spoke then.'

'And you think dragging me in here is a good idea? I've nothing to add to what I said before. If you think I know anything, you're very much mistaken.'

After thanking the man for coming, Serena offered him a cup of tea. Drinks and biscuits in front of them she was keen to begin, knowing that he hadn't come for small talk. The arrangement was that she would do the talking and her superior would listen and observe. 'It's often not what someone says as the way they say it.

I'm a great believer in the theory that body language can be louder than words.'

Informing the man, sitting so belligerently in front of them, that their talk (careful not to use the word interview) was being recorded, Serena began. 'Mr Whistler, how well did you know Thomas Granger?'

'If you mean Tommy then say so. No one ever called him anything else. Thomas Granger departed a long time ago. The man we knew was called Tommy and if you don't call him by the name he *chose* to be known by then I'm leaving.'

Realising that she had insulted the man she apologised, and after a few uncomfortable seconds tried again. 'How long had you known Tommy?'

'Another bloody stupid question. The world I occupy has no reason to observe days, weeks or even years. Don't ask me what day of the week it is or even the month. Summer is better than winter, dry is better than wet, and that's about it.'

Deciding to try another tack, she continued: 'Tommy's death is being treated as murder and we are keen, as I'm sure are you, to find the perpetrator. In the weeks leading up to his death were you aware of anyone who held a grudge against him? Anyone who might have wanted to harm him?'

Serena was about to rephrase her question, no answer forthcoming, when Harry spoke, his voice so quiet she had to strain to hear him. 'Everyone liked Tommy. Everyone knew they could trust him. Some of the others would rob you as soon as look at you but Tommy wasn't like that. I once left my cider with him and he didn't touch a drop. We weren't friends, but we respected each other. As far as I know everyone felt the same. So, no, I can't imagine why anyone would have wanted to hurt him.'

46

'Mr Whistler, I realise this is a difficult question, but have you heard any rumours or gossip amongst your fellow rough sleepers? Has anyone indicated that they know what happened?'

'Rough sleepers! What a bloody euphemism. But if you're asking whether anyone has confessed to the murder, then no, no one's done that, or at least not in my hearing. If they had it would make your job easy.'

Serena looked to the DCI for some help, her questions obviously antagonising the man who sat fidgeting and glowering at the floor. So far, his body language was of little help.

Harvey knew the next few minutes were vital, the man in front of them likely to walk out. 'We really appreciate your coming in to see us Mr Whistler...and anything... however minor or seemingly insignificant, might be of help. Shall we move on to the sad news about Charlotte?'

Taking her inspector's cue, Serena continued more cautiously. 'We believe that Charlotte had only been living on the streets for a short time. Did you have much cause to speak to her?'

The change in the man, who had so far appeared to be antagonistic, was chameleon-like. Slumping in his chair, he bowed his head and began to sob, the sound growing louder by the second.

Passing him a box of tissues Serena assured him he could take his time. Minutes passed as he sat crying and shaking and repeating over and over, 'Oh, not poor Charlie, not poor Charlie.'

The DCI took over. 'Mr Whistler we are very sorry to have upset you. You were obviously very fond of the girl and her death at such a young age is abhorrent.'

Looking up for the first time since he had entered the room, Harry Whistler began to speak. 'Charlie was a delight, a breath of fresh air. Everyone loved her from the moment she came to Fordway. I remember the first time I saw her. She was sitting on the bench outside the café in Elizabeth Park and she looked like a little stray, the kind you might take pity on and deliver to the vet's. She was cold and hungry and didn't know how to cope living rough.'

The effort of such a long speech had tired him and the officers allowed him time to recover.

'Bigman and I took care of her. We showed her where the best places were to sleep, and Bigman lent her his spare sleeping bag. She never went hungry when we were around. Within a few days she was good at begging – usually in the middle of town until your lot moved her on. After that she was the one who came back to the park with some food which she always shared.'

Knowing that Bigman was the nickname of a fellow gentleman of the road, Edward Trendell in a previous incarnation, the next question seemed obvious. 'Is there any chance that Bigman might have wanted to hurt Charlie?'

Leaping to his feet with an agility that surprised those watching, Harry Whistler yelled, the words loud enough to be heard along the corridor. 'Just because we don't live like the rest of you doesn't make us murderers. There is no way on this earth that Bigman – or any of the rest of us – would hurt a girl like Charlie. That's not how we behave. We look out for each other. Yes, we fall out, like all people do, but I repeat that being homeless doesn't make us killers. You are looking in the wrong place.'

After asking Harry to sit down Harvey apologised, saying he had not meant to infer anything. He was interrupted mid-sentence by Harry's final comment, one that neither listener had envisaged. Storming out of the room, Harry Whistler slammed the door and could be heard stomping down the corridor.

'I know it's the obvious thing to say but that went well!' Harvey's attempt at a joke failed miserably.

'I'm sorry, sir. I think that was my fault. I didn't handle him well.'

Assuring her that these occasions were never easy, they started to discuss the interview. Little appeared to have been gained, Harry's final remark, thrown almost carelessly as he left the room, causing the most debate. What exactly had he meant? Should they pursue it further or was it the ramblings of a man whose brain had been addled by drink?

Chapter 9

Eve

Dad has been interviewed by the police. I should have known. It was inevitable as the homeless must be the obvious suspects. Serena Peil and I go to the same yoga class, the one held at the primary school on the outskirts of town. Neither of us attend regularly, both having jobs with unsocial hours. However, the odd time we are both there we tend to do our contortions side-by-side. Afterwards we go for a drink in the pub around the corner and, as we are in the same line of work, can talk for hours – about our jobs and how hard we find certain yoga positions!

She probably shouldn't have told me about Dad, but I asked how the investigation was going and she said that all the homeless had been invited into the station. So, of course, Dad was mentioned, and I made a feeble joke about that interview being fun. She didn't want to say too much but, obviously rather embarrassed, told me about his final comment. I know my reaction must have startled her. If only I had been prepared I would have spoken differently. As it was she must have known that his final rejoinder came as no surprise. Does this mean she will feel duty-bound to take the matter further? Oh, my dear man, why did you have to say that?

Jacob

Back from a delightful two weeks in glorious scenery and with the most amazing music sessions. Back to reality. Wonderful to miss a family Christmas, though Eve assures me it went quite well. It was only the three of them, David insisting that he wanted to spend The Day with his entourage. Eve is so good at keeping the peace, and Mum would enjoy the extra company. Shame Philip felt duty-bound to go to his parents' as Mum really likes him.

It's never easy to resume everyday life after enjoying a break so much, but this time it's harder than ever. Does Eve's latest missive mean that Dad is a suspect? David assured me that the idea is ridiculous, that even though we don't really know him these days, he is positive that Dad is incapable of killing – not one, but two people. 'If they thought for one second that he might be the one they're after he'd have been dragged back to the police station and would have needed legal advice. Maybe even asked for Eve.'

Why did she write about his comment not being a surprise? She's the calm, assured lawyer and never panics. It sounds as though she did just that. Maybe we should meet up and ask her.

I do find the notion that Dad might be a killer rather delicious!

Andrew

Not another conspiracy theory. A few months after our dearly beloved Dad absconded, I overheard my dear sister having a conversation with Mum. My mother had no idea what Eve was talking about. I heard her get cross and say that Eve was wrong, that Dad hadn't gone because he'd done anything wrong, and he most certainly wasn't guilty of breaking any of God's laws. When I asked her about it she clammed up and said I was too young to get involved.

The "Mindless Murders of the Truly Vulnerable" as one newspaper had called them were fast becoming cold cases. Although it had taken several days, every member of the homeless community had been interviewed in the police station, their answers recorded and studied in minute detail. Only Terry Wendover, a vagrant who had been walking the streets of Fordway for decades, had said anything of real significance.

'Old Harry was far too fond of that new girl. We don't like having women around, they cause far too much trouble. I caught him with his arm around her, and he looked guilty when he saw me looking. Said he was just comforting her because she was upset, that she hadn't known it would be so hard on the streets. Load of rubbish if you ask me, anyone with half a brain knows being homeless is more than difficult. Bigman kept his distance once the girl had been around for a few days, but Harry was always there, asking if we'd seen her and then making a fuss of her when she turned up. Maybe she spurned his advances and he got rough with her.'

Harvey had suggested that he and Serena review all the interviews. 'Harry Whistler certainly broke down when we mentioned Charlie,' Serena said, adding, 'he was obviously very fond of her. Maybe he did think he'd try his luck, and when she said no it got nasty.'

'But that wouldn't explain the first murder and we're pretty sure the same person committed both. The M.O.'s are identical and a lot of the details of Thomas Granger's annihilation were not revealed to the public. Both bodies were hidden in the bushes, both were laid out, arms crossed, worldly goods arranged around them. Both had gold crosses inserted in their mouths. Both were strangled.' Harvey felt as though he was trying to convince himself. He knew that if cases weren't solved within the first few days then trails went cold. And this was one was fast becoming freezer-like.

Serena asked the questions that had been raised many times. 'Is there any chance that we are looking at the wrong people? Why do we think one of the homeless was responsible? Why have we ruled out the possibility that it could be someone who lives locally and has a *thing* about these down-and-outs?'

'We haven't ruled anyone out. But, let's be honest, where would we start? Joe Bloggs the postman or Josephine Bloggs who works at the corner shop? That would make our job impossible. Let's face it if we start thinking like that then it could be anyone. Thousands of people live in Fordway.' For the next few minutes they were both aware they had not done the obvious and widened the net of possible suspects. However, limited resources meant that it was not an option.

Trying to be positive, Harvey managed a smile. 'Back to our gentlemen friends. I read an article, based on some research that's just been undertaken in Boston, that interviewing people from minority groups is sometimes more successful when they are all together, gives them more confidence. We know some of the men we brought in thought we were being judgemental and that we were down on them because of the way they live. Maybe if we see them as a group they will be more forthcoming.'

'We are getting desperate if we're looking for help from across the pond. Some crack-pot ideas have come from there.'

'Agreed. But it might be worth a shot. We could include snacks and drinks – non-alcoholic of course. I'm sure our meagre budget would stretch to that. I'll pass it by the Super and get back to you.'

Chapter 10

Eve

Christmas passed. Mum, as always, had put a great deal of thought and effort into the day: a real tree with fairy lights; cards on display; a ridiculous number of presents (including stockings with satsumas, puzzle books and socks…she still treats us as children) and more food than we could manage. Andrew was just about bearable, though I think he may be entering one of his downward spirals. He didn't like it when I suggested that the doctor had said he should seek help the moment it starts.

Boxing Day became tense. David and family came in the afternoon and things seemed to deteriorate. I love my oldest brother, but he can be rather pompous and must always be right. As they were putting on their coats to leave, he made the mistake of talking to Andrew in front of everyone. We'd discussed Andrew: I assumed any conversations would remain private.

'Do you think you need a bit of help Andrew?'

'I don't interfere in your life, so please return the favour.'

'Sorry Andrew, I don't mean to intrude, just trying to help.'

'Help? Help? How is Eve digging up the past helping? Let bygones go by.' With Andrew, everything seems to go back to the journal. I'm not sure why he hates it so much.

No news on the murders. It's all gone quiet, even the press has lost interest. I haven't seen Serena for weeks, what with the Christmas break, and then missing the first three yoga sessions of the new term. Work has been all consuming and I haven't even managed to make time for the "ten minutes a day" Amy, the young and enthusiastic instructor, advocates as a way of maintaining our "yoga persona".

As a defence lawyer, a lot of my time is spent listening to my clients' colourful accounts of their misdemeanours (alleged!). Archie Brigand was before the Magistrates today charged with dealing drugs. He's well known to the various courts and I'm sure the trio on today's bench were tempted to weigh rather than read his list of convictions. However, despite my repeated warnings, he stuck to his "story". He had been on the building site a few miles out of Fordway to park, intending to walk back into town to meet his friends for a meal.

'If I walk there and back it means I can allow myself a pudding.' He's certainly enjoyed a lot of those and doesn't look as though he could put one foot in front of the other for more than a few metres. He claimed to have discovered the drugs on the waste ground, and merely picked them up intending to hand them in at the police station. He's been sent for trial at Preston Crown Court as *if* (not quite the right word) he's found guilty, the Magistrates' sentencing powers would have proved to be insufficient. It looks like another prolonged spell of board and lodging at the taxpayers' expense for Mr Brigand.

Many a citizen would agree with the Chairman's final comment. After ordering the collection and destruction of the drugs, he added that he was tempted to request the same for the defendant! Fortunately, the latter was said as a joke once Archie had left court – muttering about his human rights.

I haven't felt like adding much recently to the content of the journal. George Solomon, of Solomon, Jones and Whelan – and my immediate boss – keeps adding to my workload, and I can hardly complain that it's interfering with my writing.

David

Ah yes, Eve's writing. That was what got Andrew so irate. Before we went to Mum's on Boxing Day I texted the others, to say that for her sake we should maintain a united front. The last thing she needs is for her offspring to quarrel and make snide remarks. The afternoon started well. It's been a winter of heavy snow falls, but it was a day late at Christmas. When Mum opened the door on the 26th there were comments on how beautiful it made everything look. There was the usual spread and some half-decent wine (for Elspeth and me, the others remain tea-total. As I was driving and planning to visit my restaurants later I restricted myself to one small glass).

We played the usual games: Wink Murder, Charades and a long-winded game of Monopoly which Sasha and Caitlin still love. Andrew isn't into games, too frivolous for his tastes, but he was joining in until I suggested that he put hotels on Mayfair. Such a trivial aside to cause such a reaction. He stormed up to his room and only reappeared as we were leaving.

The end of the day was worse than Eve has acknowledged. With most of the family there (minus Jacob, lucky sod) it wasn't the best moment to ask him if he needed help, and I'm sorry I upset him. He's always been super-sensitive, seeing slights where they don't exist. When I mentioned Eve's journal he really lost it. 'If you can't see the danger, lurking like a spider watching its web, then I can't explain,' was his slightly esoteric remark.

My reply was perhaps not as measured as it might have been. 'You are being paranoid, but nothing new there!' The look on his face made me continue in a quieter fashion. 'Eve just wants to try to understand what happened to our family. She's hoping it will help us all to come to terms with events: past and present.' The audience didn't help, our mother shifting nervously from foot to foot, the girls desperate to leave and Eve attempting to intervene. I have tried to phone and have emailed and sent a few texts to apologise. So far, no reply.
Better write an entry for the journal:

My father tried to be a good man. Being the oldest (five minutes ahead of Jacob and so able to enjoy bragging rights) I always felt that I knew Dad better than anyone. Jacob was usually in his room, playing his music, when Dad and I spent time together. When Dad's day off (a different day each week as he was the main pharmacist in the local branch of Boot's) was a Saturday, hours were spent playing the board games we both loved: draughts, chess and our favourite, Scrabble. The latter really needs more participants and Eve and Mum would, when press-ganged, join us. Dad never worked on Sundays and no games were permitted on the day dedicated to worship, prayer and silent contemplation.

We were both interested in politics and discussed the relative assets of the candidates in the local and national elections. We loved election fever and sat up to watch the

General Election results as they came in, sometimes witnessing the dawn if the outcome looked uncertain. When he was young, Dad worked for the local branch of the Labour Party, but became disillusioned when they became, 'Nothing but watered-down Tories!'

I'm not sure if this is the kind of entry Eve wants but it puts a different perspective on the man.

Jacob

Bully for you, David. How lovely to have such fond memories of Dad. You always were his favourite son. There was a time he had high expectations and wanted us all to become successful, but only you and Eve have managed it. When I bumped into him last year (on the High Street, a busy Saturday morning and incredibly embarrassing) he had just walked past your third restaurant – the one with Whistler in enormous letters – and was full of your success. 'David has done so well.' As if I needed reminding. He then regaled me with the tale of your first restaurant when you were very young, and which was an overnight phenomenon. 'You should ask David for a job, I'm sure he'd find you something.'

'I have a job, Dad, and it's one I really enjoy.'

'Strumming a banjo. Call that a career?' The sneer in his voice made me want to hit him.

'Actually, I do. I am the peripatetic music teacher at three secondary schools and am starting some primary school work. That to me is more important than feeding overweight, self-indulgent people.'

'You were never going to amount to much. No desire for real achievement.' How ironic that the disaster of a human being in front of me was lecturing me on achievement. Walking off I thought one day...one day... My time will come.

Andrew

So, David wants to apologise, and Jacob is pleased he missed Christmas, though it's news to me that he has had any dealings with Dad.

It was obvious that he'd planned his fortnight of cacophonous banjo strumming so that he could miss the horrendous yearly ritual. Did he wear dungarees and a neckerchief and pretend to be part of the great American folk scene? Mum had asked me to "make an effort". She always wants me to talk to my siblings and remain pleasant. I was managing until David did what he does so well: patronise me. Then to speak like that in front of the others. Unforgiveable.

Chapter 11

By mid-January Harvey Tarquin needed to do something to revive the *Murders in the Park* investigation, its designation on the information board in the Major Incident Room. He had been given the express order to "clear up these bloody killings". Pictures of the two victims were displayed prominently, lest anyone forgot that they were investigating the demise of real people.

Serena was completing some over-due paperwork and looked up as Harvey approached. 'Good morning, sir. I'm just writing up the domestic abuse interviews then I thought I'd look again at the statements we have on the park murders.'

Pleased that at least one member of his team remained interested in the investigation which had hit a barrier, more impenetrable than the cell doors below stairs, he perched gingerly on the edge of the desk.

'Several weeks since we had any contact with our homeless friends. We could re-interview them individually or see them en masse. Remember I mentioned the research in America, the idea of seeing people together, well I got the go-ahead – with refreshments – so maybe it's time to try it. After all what else can we do? Maybe, just maybe, one of the men will inadvertently reveal one tiny snippet that will guide us in the right direction.'

Serena looked dubious, but was willing to support anything that might break the cases.

Knowing it would be hard to bring the town's homeless together under one roof, Harvey spent two days walking round issuing invitations which promised an afternoon indoors with food and drink provided. As the gentlemen of the road often had little concept of time, the arrangement was that police officers would find their "guests" by twelve noon on the day in question and drive each man to the meeting.

'Better be worth it, this is going to cost a lot in man-hours,' Harvey said, knowing his meagre budget was already extended to its limits. 'But the main problem is I don't think everyone will attend. Terry Wendover wasn't exactly enthusiastic. I couldn't possibly repeat what he said, but he feels he has helped us as much as he can, and even added that he's pointed us in the direction of the killer.'

'I remember he said we should be looking more closely at Harry Whistler. He doesn't strike me as being capable of murder, though his daughter's reaction when I told her about his final remark, you remember the one that surprised us the first time we spoke to him, was interesting.' As soon as she finished speaking Serena realised she had opened her mouth only to plant at least one foot firmly inside. 'Sorry sir, I know Eve from Yoga classes and I shouldn't have said anything, but she asked me about her father and whether he'd been interviewed. I know I said too much, and when I repeated his final rejoinder she did a triple-take. What I said really bothered her, but she clammed up and rushed off.'

'Interesting, but you should not discuss the cases with anyone outside the station. As you are aware that can be a disciplinary matter.'

Apologising again, Serena left to organise the refreshments for the following Friday. She was almost certain that nothing would be gained from such an occasion, but, like Harvey, knew the existing trail was like a path, deep in the forest, that peters out for no obvious reason.

Threatening clouds hung low, predicting further rain. The morning had begun with torrential downpours of Biblical proportion. The weather forecasters on the local radio station had appeared to enjoy conveying their warnings of wide-spread flooding and dangerous driving conditions. It was a day when those with little shelter would surely welcome the opportunity to be undercover.

'The men have gone out to round up our guests, sir. Some of them weren't best pleased, not in these conditions.' Serena was nervous, the enterprise new and untried. 'They'll speak to any of the homeless they find, and bring them back as soon as possible.'

It had been arranged that the food would be available from early afternoon. The hope was that most of the men they wished to see had arrived by then.

'Not the best day to be out hunting for the rough sleepers. No doubt George will have something to say about the smell in his car. Rain-sodden clothes are bad at the best of times without the addition of a certain aroma!'

George Eventide was the same age as Harvey, but was wedged a couple of ranks below. He had failed his OSPRE, Objective Structured Performance-Related Examination, to move from Sergeant to Inspector three times. He resented the fast track approach to policing, believing that it was hours on the beat that taught the job, not a fancy degree.

Sergeant Eventide was giving his partner the benefit of his thoughts. 'What the hell is he thinking? Bringing those itinerants in. They'll be no bloody use, rather like our hoity-toity inspector.' Clare Jennings was used to his rants and remained silent. The rain had returned, and it was all she could do to drive, the windscreen wipers turned on full, merely adding to the confusion, every arc producing a kaleidoscopic image.

Seven men were escorted into the interview suite, the one usually reserved for the more sensitive interviews of children or victims of domestic violence or rape. The room was set up with comfortable chairs and low tables on which were spread a variety of sandwiches, sausage rolls, biscuits and cakes. Tea, coffee and soft drinks were available on a side table.

Harvey Tarquin knew he must get something from the afternoon. The venture hadn't met with much enthusiasm from his superiors or indeed the rest of his team. Even Serena had voiced her doubts. 'I hope we get some new leads or we'll be the laughing stock, funnier than the new sitcom on TV last night.'

'Thank you for coming this afternoon, gentlemen. I hope you've enjoyed the refreshments and the escape from the next apocalypse.' Realising any attempt at humour was inappropriate he cleared his throat self-consciously before continuing. 'You all know why we have invited you this afternoon. We all want the same thing…to find the person who has murdered two of your friends.'

'You think it's one of us, one of us that's doing the killings, and that's the real reason we're here.' Bigman sounded resigned. He knew the world viewed the people he regarded as friends as a sub-class, capable of anything.

'If, and I'm not saying it is, but if it's one of us I know who it is.' Terry Wendover looked worse than the last time he had been invited into the station. His overcoat had recently been torn and his boots would not be serviceable for much longer. 'I told you last time…but you took no notice. I bet you didn't even write it in your book. How many deaths will it take before you lot do something?'

Mutters turned to shouts as several of the others agreed with him. Harvey's plan of a gentle chat was disappearing. At least the food was proving successful.

'Gentlemen, I will repeat that the reason we have invited you here today is to see if any of you has any information that might help us. We do want to find the person responsible for these atrocious and cowardly acts. Mr Wendover, we did listen to you last time and will discuss your suspicions with you privately.'

'No bloody fear. I told you once, and now I've told you again. The person you want is in this room, and I suggest you arrest him this afternoon.'

'Thank you, Mr…'

'Thank you nothing, I'm off.'

Harry Whistler watched him leave. 'He thinks it's me. He's shouted it at me enough times, and said he'd told the police.'

Coming to his friend's defence, Bigman was adamant that the killer was not one of them. 'We may be homeless, considered by many to be the dregs of society, but we know each other, our darkest secrets; the reasons we're on the streets. We are the only family we've got. I came here today to assure you, Detective Chief Inspector Tarquin and Detective Inspector Peil, that you will not find the killer in our midst. We'd do anything to protect each other.' His use of full titles added a certain gravitas to his statement.

It was the longest speech that Harvey had heard from him and he realised that he was dealing with a highly educated and erudite man. How he would like to know the man's darkest secret, and the reason he was homeless.

After another hour, when very little had emerged, the men were thanked for coming, and told that cars would take them where they wanted to go.

'The Ritz would be acceptable,' Eddie Bond's remark was his first that afternoon.

Alone in the room, the debris from the meal strewn on the tables, Harvey and Serena felt like students who had just been informed they had failed every exam.

'Nothing. We've learnt nothing.' Harvey sounded as despondent as he felt.

'Terry Wendover was interesting. Do you think there is any point in pursuing his allegations?'

'Maybe in the morning. I for one need a walk, a take-away and a hot bath. Definitely in that order.'

Chapter 12

Eve

Saturday: normally my day off, but this is my week (one in four) to be the duty solicitor, and the week goes into the weekend!

A horrible day: the kind one wants to forget.

It started just after three in the morning, an hour no sane person wants to know even exists. My strident ringtone (the only way to ensure I change from comatose to compos mentis in zero point one seconds) meant only one thing: a summons to the cells. Nothing wakes Philip, and I left him to his slumbers.

A light frost was forming, the moonlight creating glistening patterns on the road. Although the scene was quite stunning, I would still rather have been in my warm bed. Fortunately, the gritting vehicles had been alerted to the dangerous conditions and I had an incident-free drive into the middle of town. Few things are as scary as losing control on black ice. I speak from experience.

The car park adjoining the police station was full, the cars, dressed in their combat regalia, stood to attention, ready for the next offensive. Entering the station, I thought how like a mid-budget hotel the reception area looked. Recently refurbished, it was far more welcoming than its previous bleak incarnation. The sergeant on duty, a young man I had not seen before, checked my credentials and buzzed me through.

The interview room I was designated was in the far reaches of the building. It is blessed with one meagre window which has a cobweb encrusted mesh covering. During daylight hours, the room is small and inhospitable, but at night feels claustrophobic. Many an innocent man must have signed a bogus confession just to escape those four walls.

'Good morning Miss Whistler, always a pleasure to see you. Welcome to the asylum.' Sergeant Witherspoon never failed to greet me like his best friend. His cheerfulness was ever-present, whatever the time of day – or night. He once told me that he enjoyed working at night so that he could spend time with his grandchildren during the day. What a life: miscreants kicking off at night, and the under-fives during daylight hours.

'We've got a real corker for you. You really will be so pleased to be the duty solicitor.' Assuring him that such an enticing-sounding scenario was extremely unlikely, I asked him why I had been summoned.

'We have a Mr Hughes – Mike Hughes – here. He's drunk out of his skull, and was arrested after shouting the odds in Market Square. Apparently, he's the murderer we've all been looking for. He reckons he killed the vagrants in Elizabeth Park. He claims to visit Fordway regularly, and says he always spends time in the park. As soon as he arrived he demanded to see a solicitor, and insisted he wasn't going to say another word until you arrived. So here we all are.'

'But not as happy as can be,' I added trying not to let my true feelings show.

Mike Hughes was new to me. Most defence solicitors will tell you that they become very well acquainted with many of their clients – and indeed their families. Three generations of the same tribe can all appear before the Adult and Youth Courts – sometimes on the same day! As far as I was aware Mr Hughes had not used our firm before.

He was extremely drunk. I suggested that any interview was rescheduled for later in the day.

'No way, no bloody way. I want to confess...I want to get it off my chest...tell you what I did. Listen... listen...' and with that he fell asleep, his head landing gently on the table.

Driving home, I was annoyed at the monumental waste of time. I seldom get back to sleep after a seeing the wee small hours; this morning proved to be no different.

Getting up after such interrupted slumber is never easy. Philip was his usual ebullient self, and had made me toast and a large mug of tea (my lifeline). These, and his cheery smile, were waiting for me as I stumbled bleary-eyed into the kitchen.

'It has just been reported that a third body has been found in Elizabeth Park.' The voice on the radio stopped all logical thought. I felt like Lot's unfortunate wife as I listened to the rest of the report. 'The person found is believed to be a member of the homeless community who are to be seen regularly in the town's central park. No further information is available.'

No further information. I must have repeated the final words as Philip took my hand, and asked if I was OK.

'They didn't say a name. No name. They shouldn't put it on the radio until they know who it is. They need to inform the relatives before they broadcast the tragedy. What a way to find out that a loved one has died.' By now I was shaking, the tea slopping out of the mug I didn't realise I was still clutching.

Philip sat beside me, and put my drink on the table. 'I know what you're thinking, but it's very unlikely to be your Dad. There are a lot of gentlemen who frequent that park. It is terribly sad, but it could be any of them. Try not to worry…as I said it's almost certainly not him.'

By the end of his speech I was ready to scream. As I yelled at him that he couldn't possibly know it wasn't Dad, I knew I sounded like one of the women who, in times past, would have had a Scold's Bridle inserted. 'There are only a handful of men who sleep in Elizabeth Park, and my father is one of them. It's just as likely to be him as anyone else. It might be him…it might be him. What if it is him? What if…'

Philip enfolded me in a bear-hug, something I hate. 'Let's find out if they have a name. I'll phone Fordway police, and ask to speak to the man in charge.'

Bursting into uncontrollable sobs, I managed to mutter that it was the thing to do. In court, I have often seen people, both defendants and witnesses, lose control. I had thought I had more self-control. Rushing to the bathroom I was sick, and slumped, shaking over the toilet bowl. I could hear Philip's voice and realised I was truly afraid: that I didn't want to know the outcome of the conversation.

'Thank you for your time. You'll let us know as soon as you have more information.' After giving his mobile number, I heard Philip put down the phone.

'Sorry love, but they don't have a name yet. It was definitely a man, but they haven't identified him.'

'Why not? WHY NOT?'

'I spoke to Detective Inspector Tarquin and he will let us know. The dead man was tall and heavily bearded, but he couldn't say any more.'

'That could be Dad. Oh God! That sounds like my father.'

'Yes, and no doubt like most of the others. Shall I ring your office and say you won't be in today?'

'What, and sit worrying here? No, I'll be better kept busy.'

Busy meant dealing with a full quota of the cells' overnighters. It started with a man I know well, and I was not surprised to see his name on my worksheet. Kyle Powers was recently given a suspended prison sentence following an assault in a pub. Last night it had been his wife's turn.

Although only in his early forties, Kyle looks a good two decades older. He has been an alcoholic for as long as I've known him, and the drink has wreaked its revenge. Frequent spells in hospital – with a liver beyond repair – has not persuaded him to alter his life-style. His wife, Shelley, is also well-known to the courts, appearing on a regular basis for a variety of offences: Drunk and Disorderly, possession of drugs and shoplifting: the last time for three pieces of rather expensive meat from Asda, which she had informed me she hoped to sell on.

This morning Mr Powers was a sorry sight, and his words were so slurred he was hard to understand. 'She kept going on and on…moaning about me never being in. I just lost it. She really knows which buttons to push.'

'Your wife is in hospital, Mr Powers. I don't think the magistrates are going to think your actions were commensurate with a few comments about your penchant for being out.' I realised that he might not understand every word, but he got the gist.

'Silly cow winds me up. I know I went too far. But I did call for an ambulance.'

'Well, that makes it OK!' My sarcasm was totally lost, so I suggested that his actions were too extreme to be ameliorated by a 999 call. Yes, I was using over-the-top language, but it was that or lose it, and that was not in my remit. I said I would defend him to the best of my ability, but I suggested he pleaded guilty, and warned him that he was very likely to be remanded in custody awaiting an appearance in the Crown Court.

'Bloody hell, it was only a slap, no more than she deserved. She's always on my case, drives me loopy.' After reminding him that his defence was rather weak, I left saying that he wasn't due before the bench for a couple of hours. That would give him some time to sober up. I knew that was one case I wasn't going to win.

My attention then turned to my night-time confessor. Before seeing him, I needed to ascertain when the latest body had been found in the park, and if anyone could give me a time of death. More than anything, I needed to know if they had a name for the poor unfortunate.

Smokers are a modern-day plague: despatched outside to face the elements. Unfortunately, my need for nicotine is in direct proportion to my stress level. Sleet was descending with metronomic regularity, and the temperature remained well below zero. Standing in the freezing conditions I was unaware of the weather, my constant shaking the result of overwhelming, mind-numbing fear.

I wondered if my legs would support me. I was like a toddler who hasn't quite mastered the art of standing. It was only as the cold from the rough brickwork soaked through my jacket that I realised it was the wall that was keeping me upright. My hands trembled so much that it took me three attempts to dial the inspector's number.

'Good morning Detective Inspector Tarquin. My name is Eve Whistler. My partner rang you earlier to ask about the body found in Elizabeth Park. You may recall we met briefly when I was asked to verify that the first body in the park was not my father, Harry Whistler.' I explained the reason for my call, barely managing to remain professional. I was longing to yell down the phone, demanding details about the latest victim. I wanted to know why the hell no one could assure me it wasn't Dad. Stuttering, almost incoherently, about the man in the cell, the one intent on confessing, I asked if a time of death had been established. For one horrendous moment, I understood what Kyle Powers had meant when he said he had "lost it".

After a few niceties (which I could have done without) the inspector said that he was still unable to tell me the news I wanted to hear. No identification had been made. How could they not know who the latest victim was? Realising my distress, he continued in a calm voice, giving me more information than he might other- wise have done. 'You asked about the time of death. The body was found very early this morning by a woman returning from her night shift at the hospital. It hadn't been hidden as the others were, and lay across her path. The pathologist thinks death occurred between two and four a.m.'

'That would appear to rule out the man we have in the cells. He was here from just after two, and so drunk I doubt he could have committed the murder and got himself to the middle of Preston so quickly.'

'Nevertheless, I had better come to see him later. I need to have a few words. It may be a different killer this time, so we'd better rule him out of the first two. Sorry I can't go into more details.'

Ending the call Eve felt deflated, a meringue that collapses the second it leaves the oven. Hardly able to walk, she staggered back inside. She knew she wasn't in the right frame of mind to interview the self-confessed killer, and was glad she didn't have to deal with Mr Hughes again, except to inform him that a senior officer would be arriving later.

Chapter 13

Elizabeth Park had been shut, the gates guarded by uniformed officers. A huge sign informed would-be visitors that the park was *Closed until further notice*. A crowd had gathered, bad news travelling faster than the express train that could be heard in the distance.

'Another one? When are you lot going to make Fordway safe again?' With his dirty-looking clothes and dishevelled appearance, the youth who shouted this question looked as though he might be one of the homeless community. The rest of the ever-growing throng added their comments about the lack of interest the police had taken in the murders, many voicing the opinion that more effort would have been made if the victims had come from the gated Elmwood estate on the outskirts of town.

Harvey Tarquin and Serena Peil were standing inside the tent that had been erected to protect the crime scene. A wider perimeter had been cordoned off with barricade tape. The inspector was determined that there must be no contamination of the evidence.

It was their second visit of the day: they had waited to return until the pathologist had been to give a possible time of death, and the SOCO team had completed their duties. Before anything could be touched, moved, or further investigated, numerous photographs had been taken. Evidence markers had been placed next to the body. Sketches of the entire scene had been drawn: an extra form of documentation; a detailed reminder of the horrific scene. Notes, now in Harvey's hands, had been recorded to gauge distances, and other information that might not be easily detected from the photographs.

Looking at a body is never easy, the police agreeing that it was one of their more unpleasant duties. In this case, it was worse than usual.

'Why in the world would anyone want to do that to another person? He may have been homeless, but he was still a human being. Why set fire to him? Does the killer not think it's enough to kill someone without desecrating the body?' Serena had witnessed several corpses, and had been present at post-mortems, but she had never seen one as horrendously disfigured as the one that lay in front of her. The remains hardly looked human.

'The things we see and deal with make any TV drama look like Children's Hour.' For a moment, Harvey was finding it hard to remain dispassionate. 'Though his initial visit was brief, the pathologist said he was almost certain that the injuries were inflicted sometime after the man died. It would be good to know he didn't suffer these atrocities, but of course the cause of death has yet to be established. That's one PM I'll attend without you.'

'Thank you, sir.' Serena's voice wobbled, and to her horror she thought she might faint if she stayed much longer. The smell in the small enclosure was overpowering, a barbecue left on too long.

Realising his colleague was becoming emotional, Harvey maintained his professional demeanor. 'We'll know the reason for these barbarities when we do our job and find the perpetrator. I'd like you to go back to the station and see how many people are available to contact the others in the homeless community. I think the only way we can identify this tragic soul is by eliminating the others. Ask for names to be recorded, and find out their whereabouts overnight. Not a good way to identify a body, but it's the best we can do.'

'No, it's not as if anybody is going to file a missing person report. Whoever he is, it's likely that the only people to grieve will be his fellow vagrants.' As she pulled the tarpaulin aside to leave the tent, she gave way to the tears that had threatened all morning.

Chapter 14

Eve

Three days and still no news. Despite numerous phone calls I have no further information. I left work early (sent home more like). Shirley, our ever-caring clerk, insisted that I go and rest: an impossibility. She said she'd call later to make sure I'm OK. How can I possibly be all right until I know? Phoning my brothers was a waste of time. They know no more than me, but seem resigned to the possibility that this time it may well be Dad. My brain is stuck on a repeat setting...*it is Dad, it's not Dad, it is Dad.* It's like a song one hears first thing in the morning then can't block out... however much one tries.

Jacob

As usual my sister has gone straight to panic mode. Why does the female of our species always, and I mean always, go straight to the worst possible scenario? I told her there are a great number of gentlemen who frequent the park. The rules of probability would indicate that there is only a one-in-however-many-men chance it is our father. I reminded her that it took some time to identify the first bloke, Tommy, or whatever his name was, so she shouldn't read anything into the fact that they can't say who this latest man is.

David

Yes, Eve rang and said Jacob hadn't been much help, so I told her we've got to be patient. We will be informed as soon as the police have an identity: there must be some reason they are unsure. Last night I overheard a couple in the restaurant saying they had heard stories that the body had been mutilated in some way. That didn't happen to the first two.

Eve

I wish I hadn't phoned David. I've heard some of the rumours that are flying around. I feel as though they brush against me, rather like the daddy-long-legs that used to take up residence in my bedroom. To think that I found them scary and called for help. I didn't know what fear was!

Andrew

I refuse to join in with this speculation. We will be told if it is Dad. What I MUST comment on is David's latest venture: Whistler's Wild West. At least someone's life is continuing. His latest restaurant is in Rusholme, on Curry Mile, student land, on the outskirts of Manchester. I love his slogan: *You've tried the Indians: now try the cowboy!* I went the other night. It's all decked out like a wild-west saloon bar, even down to sawdust on the floor! The waitresses are dressed like cowgirls: checked shirts, Levi's, boots with jangling spurs (could get annoying) and the obligatory Stetsons which hang at a variety of ludicrous angles down their backs. The menu has a selection of enormous steaks, and the longest list of burgers I've ever seen, all accompanied by fries, and followed by milk shakes and ice cream. Nice one brother!

Mum, the twins and Eve went on the opening night, but I prefer restaurants when they are quieter...and I don't have to pretend to like my family.

Good for you, dear brother of mine. It must be wonderful when one's life travels along so smoothly: no leaves on the line or cancelled rolling stock for you.

Serena walked into Harvey's office. 'How did the interview go?' She knew her superior had been to Preston to question the would-be confessor. The man had been held for a couple of days: an extra thirty-six to ninety-six hours granted by the magistrates as it might prove to be a murder investigation.

'No use at all. A total nutter. One of the weirdos who wants his moment in the spotlight, though I stopped myself from using such torture tactics.'

Serena was pleased to hear Harvey in lighter mode. She knew he was having a hard time. The superintendent had been overheard yelling that he needed a result.

'Mr I-want-to-confess, claims to have committed the first two murders, but now says he didn't do the last one. We know he wasn't responsible for number three, as he was picked up, drunk, in the middle of Preston about the time of the Tuesday morning murder.'

'We have said there might be two people doing the killings. The last one was so different to the first two: no respect for the body; no laying out his possessions; no hiding him in the bushes. Is there any possibility he was responsible for Thomas Granger and Charlotte Carroway?'

'As I said, Mike Hughes is looking for attention. According to the sergeant on duty, the man has been a nuisance in the past. He's confessed to other crimes, including the theft of a lady's underwear from her clothesline! So far the CPS hasn't been interested.'

'Probably not our man. I'm sorry sir, but there's not much progress here. Three of the nine people we know frequent Elizabeth Park are still unaccounted for, including Harry Whistler and Terry Wendover. We know it's not unusual for the homeless to visit other locations, but irritating that two of the men we are keen to meet have gone missing.' Harvey was about to interrupt, but saw that Serena wanted to continue. 'Jimmy McDowell, another rough sleeper we said looked too well-groomed to be on the streets, informed us that he saw Harry and Terry arguing after they'd been to the afternoon get-together. He was sure it was the same day. He said it had been such a treat to have a social event, as he put it, that he claimed to recall every moment of the day.'

Drumming his fingers on the desk, a nervous habit of which he was unaware, Harvey replied. 'We need to find either Harry or Terry. I've a horrible feeling one of them might be the killer and the other the victim.' His right hand was accelerating in both the speed and sound: an irritating finale to their conversation.

Leaving Serena staring into space, Harvey dashed into the incident room, a cavernous space with its many desks set well apart. Most were occupied with officers completing their paperwork. Barking orders, something he seldom did, he addressed his team. 'I want Harry Whistler or Terry Wendover, and preferably both, found. ASAP.'

Chapter 15

Eve

Andrew says life at home was awful long before Dad left. There were good years, Andrew. Perhaps you were too young to appreciate Grandma Jo (never Josephine). You must remember calling her Grandma "Jam". David and Jacob thought they were comedians making that up from the initials of her full name: Josephine Alice Morrell. Jam came to live with us when her husband died. You were only three at the time, so may have forgotten the years of light she shed on our often-gloomy house. When her beloved Bill died she was still very fit: in mind and body. However, after six months of widowhood, she decided she didn't want to live alone, and so took over the large bedroom on the second floor, the twins ascending to the enormous space in the attic. You used to love going up to the top of the house, and were always made welcome. There was a time you were all friends.

Grandma Jam was Mum's mother, but how such an ebullient character had produced the quiet mouse we knew was beyond my comprehension. 'Your Mum was very different when she was a girl. Always singing and dancing, and she loved the latest fashions; spent her first wages on a ridiculous outfit she'd seen someone wearing on *Top of the Pops*! I know children find it hard to imagine their parents being young, but this view of our mother was unreal. Her youthful attributes had, most unfortunately, fallen into a black hole.

I must have been about twelve when she gave me this different version of Mum, too young to have my questions answered about what had caused the change. The twins remember many arguments between Grandma and Dad, and it is only now that I realise she blamed Dad for the change in her daughter.

One row I do recall was on a Wednesday night. Jacob wanted to play football for the local team. Never normally sporty, he had developed a sudden enthusiasm for the game, largely due to his friend's dad running the side. When he came home after the practice he was so excited. 'I've been picked! Mr Allison wants me to play in defence.'

'That's wonderful,' Mum said, sounding more animated than usual, 'when is the match?'

'Sunday at three, on Millington Field.' Poor Jacob, he was far too excited to notice the stony look on Dad's face.

'Sunday is the Sabbath: The Lord's Day. There will be no going out to play a game.'

As he fled the kitchen, Jacob could be heard yelling about the unfairness of life. I suspect we all agreed with him, but none of us spoke: we sat in an uncomfortable silence, slowly finishing the evening meal (Mum's rhubarb crumble ruined).

Grandma Jam slammed down her spoon, and used a tone of voice I had not heard her employ before. 'That child needs to play football this Sunday, Lord's Day or not. Does your god really not allow fun – and more important a feeling of fulfilment on *His* day?'

'This is my house, Mrs Morrell (his use of her title a common occurrence), and my family will keep the Lord's Day holy.'

'What in the world is holy about your child being miserable? Has your god not got a sense of human worth? Playing in a team will be far more beneficial than sitting listening to a sermon he probably doesn't understand.' At this point we were all sent to our rooms, but could hear raised voices continuing the argument. Jam had told me she was an atheist, a concept totally outside my experience. She never tried to influence us, but over the months following Jacob's disappointment (he never went back to the practices) I knew she hated her son-in-law's rules. Dad kept a firm control over his family. Jacob has always maintained that once we got over the shock of his leaving it was a kind of blessing – and not the sort we received in church.

Andrew, you must remember inadvertently upsetting Grandma when you pulled up the flowers in the garden and brought them into the kitchen. They were Sweet Williams: at least a dozen in full bloom. Mum was annoyed with you, and Grandma reacted even more vehemently by bursting into tears. Grandpa's name had been William, and she often called him her "Sweet William", and could never look at the flowers once he died. Realising you were upset, she sat you on her knee and fed you sherbet lemons, such confectionary not normally allowed on a weekday.

She lived with us for four years, and I'm sorry if you don't recall them. A heart attack, totally unexpected, ended her life one blustery morning as she walked into town. Mum was devastated, as was I. Someone said that the dead have never gone completely whilst there is a person left who can resurrect them in their minds. I often find myself remembering Grandma Jam. If I could speak to her one last time I would thank her for adding so much to my formative years.

Hers was my first experience of a funeral: a joyous occasion; a celebration of her life. It was totally unlike the more sombre affairs I attended afterwards, and is the one that had real meaning. She had left her requests, perhaps afraid that my parents would give her a religious send-off full of hymns whose sentiments she abhorred. The crematorium rocked to Queen and Duran Duran! She had brought something special to our home, and I had lost a great friend. A year later Dad's mother arrived, but that's another story, and the cause of that fateful May.

Andrew

No, dear sister, I have very few memories of that Grandma. Mine are of the second one. As you say, that is better not recorded.

How obvious can you get: Mum is, and always was, better off without Dad. Is this journal really descending into stating the bleeding obvious? (Yes, we all agreed not to use swear words...but that had to be included.) If she began life as a "singing, dancing girl" who took an interest in clothes, there was, at some stage, a cataclysmic change. And we all know who was responsible for that.

Eve

Still no news. No rumours (strange, as lawyers usually pick up most morsels of gossip). No invitation to view this latest body. No cessation to the worrying. No nothing: an appalling double negative which seems to encapsulate the situation.

I have had that three-in-the-morning feeling all day: the one where one wakes up afraid, often for no apparent reason, the dreams and dreads jitterbugging frantically around one's brain. One then lies trembling, unsure whether to wait for the dance to end or get up and fill the kettle!

Philip is good when I become depressed. This evening he made scrambled egg (he's no chef but can break eggs with the best of them) followed by Ben and Jerry's Chubby Hubby: comfort food par excellence.

It's bedtime, and I have convinced myself that the body is not Dad. He's a survivor, unlike the rest of us. We have all suffered to varying degrees. Only David seems immune to his upbringing. We could all benefit from some of the divine intervention we learned about as children. As that is unavailable we adopt different coping mechanisms:

Jacob: loses himself in his music
Andrew: remains a mummy's boy
Me: thank goodness for work…and cigarettes
David: success, success, success.

Chapter 16

Harvey was walking: circuits of Elizabeth Park occupying his day off. Bulbs were beginning to make their annual appearance, and for the first time in over a week the sun was shining. There were many routes round the park, the more popular busy with people exercising their dogs and parents their children. He loved the fact that no two perambulations were the same, the park having so many pathways. Looking south, the view over the gently undulating hills was glorious: the winter sun lighting the tops.

Avoiding the children's playground, recently updated at a cost that had made headlines in the local paper, Harvey continued up the steep slope to the Victorian tea shop. Many of the original nineteenth century features had been kept, including a huge glass-covered porch which ran the length of the building. Modern folding doors had been fitted, allowing the area to be used for extra seating during the summer. Three wrought-iron boot scrapers stood ready for action by the main entrance. They were still used occasionally. Inside, the Victorian theme was evident, with geometric red and brown floor tiles, a large fireplace and the main attraction – that was in all the guide books – a stained glass window showing the Barrington family: patriarch in Mayoral robes, wife and ten children. A plaque commemorating Mr Barrington opening the café was given full prominence above the counter. To the modern, more cynical-eye, it was obvious he enjoyed displaying his philanthropic duty by providing a location for his workers to enjoy their leisure.

'Lovely day for a change,' the lady behind the counter believed in talking to every customer. Her outfit complemented the room: a black dress, long white pinafore and mob-cap.

'First time in weeks I've walked around the park in the dry,' was Harvey's uninspired reply.

'It's so attractive in the sunshine, just such a pity it's been spoilt by the terrible goings-on. It's about time the police caught whoever is killing those poor souls.'

Harvey had been walking for over two hours and needed a rest. The last thing he wanted was to be reminded of the murders, or his team's lack of progress. Sitting inside, all the outside tables taken, with a strong coffee and slice of fruit cake – some type of cake essential on every walk – his body stopped, unlike his mind.

The post-mortem on the latest, still unidentified, body had been gruesome. Alfie Morrison, the pathologist once called "The Einstein of his trade", spoke as little as possible to the living, but became garrulous when dealing with the deceased. He regarded them as people who deserved dignity in death. A staunch Christian, he believed the soul had gone on to greater things, and it was his duty to respect the body.

'An autopsy is like a sacrament, a rite of passage for the earthly remains.' When Harvey had first heard Alfie say this, he had been impressed. Other pathologists used black humour whilst conducting the autopsy, something the policeman loathed.

Alfie's strong Scouse accent had bounced off the walls of the autopsy room. 'Good morning Rushy, or is it

Rushelle?' Any unidentified person was dignified with the name of one of his football heroes. A lifelong Liverpool supporter he had been known to give the deceased his raucous rendition of *You'll Never Walk Alone*. 'Yes, you're most definitely Rushy: a male, a narrow pelvis. You've been burnt, thankfully post-mortem judging by the blisters which are dry, hard and yellow.' The pathologist stopped to readjust his microphone which was recording his findings.

'How did you die? I bet you weren't a pugilist, but the fire has given you a boxer's posture: legs fixed at knees and hips, and arms flexed at elbow and wrists. Fingerprints destroyed, but we'll extract some DNA from your bones. Hope you don't mind, but someone wants to know that a man they once loved has died.'

Alfie Morrison turned to the living, warning them that any DNA might be highly degraded or contaminated. He added that he would produce a dental chart, and take an X-ray of the man's jaw, though he thought it doubtful whether either would prove helpful.

'How tall were you? What did you weigh old fella? What colour was your hair? If only you could tell us; the fire has changed all these things. Was your hair dark? If so, you'll be pleased to hear it hasn't changed. But if it was lighter the fire has blackened it.' In truth, very little had survived the flames.

Harvey hated the moment when the internal organs were removed.

'My goodness Rushy, you liked a drink. Didn't do your liver much good. And the old ticker was in poor shape. Something tells me you might not have been long for this world, but I am so sorry you had to leave it this way.'

Sitting in the café, aware that most patrons were enjoying normal, everyday conversations, Harvey recalled the moment when Alfie had spoken so softly he had asked him to repeat his comment. 'Oh, my dear friend. You were strangled. What an awful way to die. May you rest in peace, safe in the Good Lord's keeping.'

Strangled. Like the others. The question was why had the violence escalated to such an extent? The body burnt beyond recognition. No respect shown.

'Have you found a cross?' Harvey didn't know if he wanted an affirmative answer.

'No, not this time, which probably means there wasn't one as gold only melts at inordinately high temperatures, and there would, at the very least, be some fragment remaining. Gold melts at 1945 degrees Fahrenheit. This is average for a metal, being three times higher than the melting point of lead and a third of the melting point of tungsten. Sorry, I have a photographic memory for such details.'

'So, no cross. Did the killer not have time to insert it before setting the body alight, or are we looking for a different man?'

'Or woman, DCI Tarquin. We both know the female of the species…'

On leaving the café Harvey decided to clear his head with one last stroll around the park, this time taking the route that led past the ornate bandstand. In summer, the highly elaborate structure housed Sunday concerts which were always well attended. Almost all the musicians were local, the town's brass band and male voice choir featuring on a regular basis. As he approached the circular edifice, with its plaque proclaiming that it had been erected in 1854 to provide entertainment for the masses, he saw Bigman.

'Good afternoon.'

'And a very good afternoon to you Detective Chief Inspector Tarquin.'

'Please call me Harvey, I'm not on duty now, merely enjoying the park.'

'Harvey, it is. I've not used my name for years. Feels like another life. Nowadays everyone knows me as Bigman, but there are times I'd like to revert to the name my mother, God rest her soul, gave me.'

'If you want me to use it I'd be more than happy to oblige.' A long pause made Harvey wonder if he had overstepped the mark and upset the man.

'I was christened Edward Jonathan Trendell. I used to get Ed, Eddie and Ted but to my family I was always Edward. Formalities mattered. You probably find it hard to believe but I had a good upbringing and a loving family...in the past...all a long time ago.'

'Have you got time for a cup of tea? The café's still open.' Harvey was keen for the conversation to continue and a return to the café wouldn't be a hardship.

Large bowl of tomato soup, cheese sandwiches and two slices of cake added to the drinks, Edward spoke of his horror at recent events. He remained adamant that the murderer didn't come from the homeless.

'We're society's outcasts, all down on our luck, but I guarantee that we are not hiding your man. We think it's someone with a grudge against us, though why we should distress anyone enough for them to commit murder is beyond me. We keep ourselves to ourselves.'

'The police are keeping a very open mind. Our problem is we have so little evidence. We have not ruled anyone in or out, but anything any of your friends can tell us might help.'

Edward laughed and said that the "get-together" at the police station hadn't exactly been a roaring success.

'We all have our own stories, our tragedies that reduced us to this way of living. Perhaps a different approach, where you get to know the real us, might be advantageous. Few of us chose to live as down-and-outs, the words that I use to sum us up, but life's vagaries led each of us to this point.'

Harvey had suspected that the man he had known as Bigman had fallen further than some of the others. The man was erudite and obviously well educated. Asking if he'd like to tell his story Harvey assured him he was ready to listen.

'University, a job in the city, a wife, two children…all thrown away. I was a gambler. It started with a flutter on the horses and an occasional bet on the football. The first time I did that I won five hundred pounds as Arsenal beat Chelsea three nil and David O'Leary scored a hat-trick, so I got it all right and thought I had the magic touch. After that I just couldn't stop. The debts started, and my wife insisted I go the Gamblers' Anonymous. Unfortunately, by then it was too late. I re-mortgaged the house, sold the car and some of Celia's jewellery. She'd had enough and went back to her parents with the children.'

'They do say such an addiction is an illness.'

'A self-inflicted one. I still can't believe what it made me do: steal, lie and start drinking. I lost everything. Stupid thing is, even today if I ever get any money, I still want to go into the betting shop. Good job the one on the High Street has banned me!'

Chapter 17

The post-mortem report had arrived, Alfie Morrison delivering the gruesome reading personally. 'I knew you'd want to see this sooner rather than later. Nothing that you didn't hear at the time, but the good news is I managed to salvage some surprisingly decent DNA. Often impossible when the body is so badly burnt, but this fella's left humerus had escaped the worst of the fire and it was just possible to extract a smidgen of the stuff.'

'Is it enough to send to the data base?'

'Not sure, but Helga Reinhardt is the person to ask. She's the expert to contact at the UK Police National Database when the sample is tricky. Good luck. I'd be grateful if you would inform me when you know something. I'd love to know who this man was.'

Promising to keep the pathologist informed Harvey got straight on to the nation-wide database, set up in 1995 and now housing almost eight million DNA records. If, and it was a big if, the latest victim had a criminal record his information would be stored there.

Asking to speak to Miss Reinhardt, he realised his hand was shaking so much the phone was almost falling from his grasp. Could this be the breakthrough they needed? Was he about to learn the identity of the deceased? Was it Harry Whistler or Terry Wendover?

And, even more pertinently, if it was one of them did that mean the remaining man was the killer?

Helga Reinhardt had been born in Devon, her parents arriving in England a few weeks before her birth. Harvey had expected to speak to a woman with a German accent and reproved himself for such an assumption. 'How soon will we have a result?'

'These days the system is state-of-the-art and if we have the DNA on our system we will be able to find the match and let you know…hopefully sometime today. Is that soon enough for you?'

Realising the last comment was a rebuke for the impatience and lack of manners he had shown, Harvey apologised and said it was much quicker than he'd expected.

'Don't worry Chief Inspector, I know the police want immediate answers and the half a million spent recently has given us an amazing new device, rather like a state-of-the-art printer. I hate to admit it but it could be used by someone with almost no expertise, a fact I don't admit to just anyone. I'll phone you later this morning and I hope I'll be able to give you a name.'

Waiting had never come naturally to Harvey who wandered round his room, stopping to gaze at every picture and file. All he needed was an umbrella and he could have been a tour guide.

Serena was the last person he wanted to see. Before he knew the truth, he had no desire to discuss the latest developments. Working a different case, Serena merely wanted his advice. 'Maureen Tuart is here, sir. She's accusing her partner, Abbie Winsome of putting photos of her on the internet.'

'Well you know the drill. Get a statement and take it from there.'

'The name Abbie Winsome rang a bell and when I went on the HOLMES site I found her. She's on licence, only released from Style prison last year, having served five years of a ten-year sentence.'

Feeling he was being asked about trivia, and by an officer who should have known what to do, he started shouting, the words bouncing off the walls like a game of squash.

'Well it's bloody obvious. She needs to be locked up again. You know as well as I do if someone is out on licence and they are accused of committing another crime they go straight back inside. And she'll be there until the case comes before the magistrates and even longer if it goes to trial or to Crown Court.'

As Serena left the room, slamming the door behind her, the telephone rang. 'Good morning again, Chief Inspector... and I have to point out it is still today.' Speaking with a calm he didn't feel Harvey asked the inevitable question.

'Yes, our wonderful equipment can provide a name for you. Terrence Wendover. He's on the database as he has served time at Her Majesty's Pleasure. He was in Wandsworth for fraud. It's a long time ago but we keep the information forever.'

Thanking her, Harvey ended the call.

Eve

Inspector Tarquin called. It's not Dad. He said a name, but it meant nothing to me. The relief was overwhelming. I sat and cried, then sobbed down the phone to David. He said he'd tell the others. The police want us all to go into the station to see if we can help them locate Dad. Good news: it's not him. Bad news: he must now be a suspect.

Once the body had been identified the next step was to inform his relatives. The man had lived as a rough sleeper for years, but someone would want to know what had happened to him. Harvey was subjected to the shakes he invariably experienced when he knew there was a breakthrough in a case. On one occasion, he had been asked if he was developing Parkinson's Disease.

Without realising how vehemently he was speaking, he addressed Serena like a candidate seeking election. 'The Police National Computer: get on to it right away. If, as we now believe, Mr Wendover has a criminal record, everything we need will be there: arrests, sentences and more importantly his personal details. I want this within the hour and then we can begin our search for his killer. The person with three murders to his name.'

Serena was becoming accustomed to her boss's dramatic changes of mood. She also knew he was right, that Terrence Wendover's documentation would be on the PNC, all police records kept indefinitely, the only exception being when an individual could demonstrate special reasons for the removal of their details. She knew that current policy was to retain all records until the person reached a hundred and she was sure Mr Wendover hadn't had his birthday card from the Queen.

Half an hour later, Serena knocked on the Chief Inspector's door. 'It's all here, sir. DOB, former address, next of kin and a rather impressive list of misdemeanors. The magistrates knew him well, as did some of the Crown Court judges. Everything was tried, from fines to curfews to unpaid work, but the final thing on his record was five years' imprisonment.'

Wanting to get to the point, Harvey grabbed the information from her. 'Released from Wandsworth over a decade ago. Never arrived home. Reported missing five days later. It looks like his wife left it a few days, thinking he'd gone to celebrate his release in the usual fashion. She says in her statement that she wasn't unduly concerned initially when he didn't manage to find his way back.'

'He was released at the same time as a man he'd got friendly with in jail.'

'Yes, thank you inspector, I can read.'

'I'll leave you to it then, sir.' Serena had learnt that being on the "naughty step" was all part of working with her superior. Good job she admired the man.

Unaware of his rudeness, Harvey sat and made notes. Terrence Wendover was last seen leaving Wandsworth prison at eight o'clock on the morning of July 14th, 2003. Howard Mackay had left with him. The next step was obvious: contact his jailbird friend. Mr Mackay must also be in the system. Too wound up to begin the search, many a clock being damaged by such tension, he called Serena back in and ordered her to get coffee and sandwiches and several bars of chocolate from the canteen.

Chapter 18

Jacob

What a monumental waste of time. We were all hauled down to the nick to be interrogated about Dad. Detective Chief Inspector Tarquin doesn't inspire confidence. He'd make a good contestant on 'Mastermind' (specialist subject: asking-questions-to-which-there-are-no-answers). He seems to think (totally erroneously) that we know where Dad is living. The man is obsessed with the notion that we must have some idea where he went twenty years ago, before he resurfaced as one of the great unwashed of Fordway.

His sidekick, the extremely attractive Inspector Peil, looked rather embarrassed when her boss pursued his line of questioning which drifted ever more aimlessly, like a becalmed ship.

'DCI Tarquin, you have to believe us when we say that we wish we did know where our father is living. However, the fact is, we don't. He may have returned to the life he lived for the best part of a decade, before his return to this town. We had no knowledge of him for ten years and he has never spoken of it.' Having delivered his speech, David looked to the rest of us for confirmation.

Eve then surprised us by saying that she had spoken to Mum. These days we try not to involve her in anything to do with Dad. She becomes agitated when we speak of him and we're all aware of her heart problem.

'Mum thinks he might have spent time in Scotland. His godfather went to live in Craigton, to the southwest of Glasgow, when he was a boy. She remembered him talking about Bellahouston Park and rolling Easter eggs there with his cousins, as he called the children of the family. Mum is sure he stayed with them quite regularly when he was small and that he loved the visits.'

Andrew interrupted, 'Why in the world did she think he might have returned to Glasgow? We all lost contact with them yonks ago. I never remember any of us even meeting them. And let's be realistic, he never showed any interest in taking us north of the border.'

Eve found Andrew's negative input annoying. 'Well...Mum told me that on one of the few occasions they talked – after he came back following his decade's absence – he kept repeating that Craigton Cemetery was a wonderful place with its chapel that was in daily use. He claimed it was an easy place to seek shelter. She did add that he was extremely drunk at the time so maybe it doesn't mean anything.'

By this juncture wild geese weren't just being chased but had been caught, cooked and eaten. The afternoon was not only a waste of our time but an insult to our intelligence. Doesn't the man think we'd have said if we had any idea where Dad is living? None of us care enough to protect him. If indeed that's what he needs.

Andrew

Mum was terribly upset when I got home. She'd told Eve about the Glasgow connection in confidence and was appalled to think that the police might now think she knows more than she does. My sister should leave her out of it. Too many cooks in the kitchen produce an inedible meal.

Calling a team meeting, Harvey updated them on the recent developments. Spending time informing the group of the autopsy report and DNA sample, which had been successfully identified, he announced that they had a name for the latest victim. Terrence or Terry Wendover.

'So, does that mean we're looking for Harry Whistler? Is he now our main suspect?' Sergeant Roger Symmons was in belligerent mode, finding his superior's rather pedantic updating extremely frustrating.

Ignoring the interruption, Harvey continued with Mr Wendover's criminal record and release from prison. Informing them that the last person to see Terry before he disappeared, only to surface in Fordway some years later, was Howard Mackay, a fellow inmate, released at the same time. 'Inspector Peil, find out the whereabouts of Howard Mackay. Sergeant Symmons I want you to track down Mrs Wendover and the rest of you keep looking for Harry Whistler.'

The meeting had not gone well. A fact Harvey did not need to be told.

Chapter 19

Wedding invitation, the third friend in less than a year to hope that Serena and partner would attend a reception that would cost many thousands. Amy would undoubtedly attempt to outdo the first two. Another day of utter boredom loomed, sitting on her own, no partner available, next to people she didn't know and with whom she had nothing in common. There would be hours of dancing; everyone else with their significant other. She daren't tell her mum as it would lead, as inevitably as her grass grew faster than she could cut it, to more hints about time passing, especially if she wanted a family, the sub-text being that Serena was her only hope of grandchildren.

'Why you ever let Brian go is a mystery. Such a pleasant young man and a doctor. He was very fond of you and I know it was your decision to end it. Such a shame after three years together.'

Instead of spending her days doing the job she loved, catching criminals and gaining promotion, she should, according to the font of all wisdom, 'You don't get to my age without learning what's important in life,' be a hausfrau with a brood of mini Brian's. Her mother had settled for a life of service to her overbearing father, and years of anguish when Serena's younger brother died, very suddenly, the fault in his heart undetected for fifteen years.

'Thank goodness I've got you close, Serena, the pain of losing Ryan doesn't get easier, whatever they say. Your father doesn't understand, but I know you do.'

How wrong she was. In her job, Serena was forced to confront tragedy every day, listen to people whose lives were performing somersaults, not knowing which way was up. She had seen bravery and resilience and the desire to cope in the direst of circumstances. Her mother allowing herself to wallow, week after month after year was becoming tedious. Sympathy in short supply.

Although she was delighted to be independent, the beautifully designed invitation upset her. Not a good start to the day, she knew she should have left the cream envelope unopened. Hopefully, Harvey would be in a better mood today. She wasn't in the right frame of mind to cope with his brusqueness.

Walking into the incident room she was only too aware that she would have to and that she hadn't helped the situation.

Three murders in Elizabeth Park. Progress almost non-existent. Even snails had been known to move faster. Over three months had elapsed since the most recent murder. Harvey was concerned. As always when he became stressed he turned to food – the wrong kind. The words "comfort eating" might have been invented for him. If he carried on much longer new clothes would be needed, and he didn't have the time or inclination to go shopping.

Superintendent Grealy had sent a memo demanding a breakthrough. If only! When he had relayed this gem to Serena, she had made the situation worse by indicating that there were rumbles of discontent amongst the officers involved. 'Roger Symmons can't understand why we haven't had "all those bloody layabouts" in for formal questioning, and someone else (I don't want to say who) thinks we need a new DCI.'

The recent events in Fordway were so unusual, like a non-league team making good progress in the FA Cup, that none of his team had much experience of working on murders. He knew they were working hard and were feeling as frustrated as he was. He tried not to blame the individuals for their comments: long hours with little to show for them always created a negative atmosphere. How he longed for a unit like the Homicide and Serious Crime Team that operated in London. At the last count, London had thirty-one murder investigation teams, experts at their jobs: what he wouldn't give for just one.

Desperate to break the cases, he believed that the key was finding Harry Whistler. Were his family hiding anything? The brothers had been cross with Eve when she had referred to their father's connection to Glasgow. A trip up there would, almost certainly, be a frustrating waste of time, but if Harry had lived there before he just might have returned. The idea had been planted and needed nurturing.

Mid-morning, the rush hour traffic long gone, made the trip up the M6 almost pleasurable. Harvey was finding it hard to stay below the speed limit. A few others obviously felt the same as they rushed past.

Stopping at the Tebay services, Harvey admired the view. Open countryside stretched in all directions and he thought that the lakes and trees surrounding the services must make them the most beautiful in England. As he waited for his *Mega Mouthwatering All-Day Breakfast* with its proud boast there would be no need to eat again today, he read the leaflet informing him that Tebay was one of the few independent, family-owned motorway services in England. Harvey was pleased to see that the buildings had been constructed of timber and local stone, designed to blend in, unlike many of the recent utilitarian disasters in Fordway.

Since his mother's funeral, Harvey had always hated anything to do with death, a rather unfortunate detail in his job. At work, he managed to maintain a professional detachment when dealing with a murder victim or even the remains of some poor soul involved in an accident. Suicide was the one appalling phenomenon he left to others, incapable of dealing with the fact that someone had been unable to continue, their life deemed intolerable.

The wide, tree-lined avenues of Craigton Cemetery did little to lighten his mood. Tomb stones, many from the Victorian era, leant at gravity-defying angles. Stopping to read some Harvey felt the anguish of parents who had buried six, seven, or in one case, eleven children. He knew that each loss would have scarred the souls of those left to mourn.

'Good afternoon, doesn't make pleasant reading, does it?' The question, although almost certainly rhetorical, seemed to require a response.

'No, indeed not. I don't know why but I always find myself reading tomb stones. Somewhat macabre. They make me wonder about the people involved.'

'From your accent, I would hazard a guess that you're not a Glaswegian.'

'No, just visiting. My name's Harvey and it's my first time here.'

'Good to meet you Harvey. I'm Robert. I come here each week. My wife is buried over there, in the modern section. Dead these three years and I miss her as much as the day she died. They say it gets easier but that's not been my experience. Still you don't want to listen to the maudlin ramblings of an old man.'

'So very sorry about your wife. I know my father still misses Mum. He says he talks to her every day.' Pausing to consider how to continue the conversation, Harvey suggested that they walk on together. The graves situated on the next avenue were from the First and Second World Wars.

'We've got too many of these; young men dead before their time. There was a military hospital in Glasgow during The Great War and the records show we've a hundred and sixty-five buried here, plus eighty-four soldiers from the fracas with Hitler. My father and grandfather are by the west gate. Both were working on the Clydeside shipyard the first night it was targeted: 13th March 1941. Nine hours of bombing. The buggers, pardon my language, but what else do you call them? came back for another go the following night. Seven and a half hours that time. Five hundred and twenty-eight civilians killed and too many injured to count. Sorry about all the statistics. I was a maths teacher and have a photographic memory of numbers.' Standing to attention he added, 'Five years to my century, a number I find myself wanting to achieve. Doris would have loved the idea that I might get the official birthday greeting. Ironic, as in my youth I was a card-carrying member of the Communist Party. At a time when many people had a picture of the King on the living room wall, we had Karl Marx.

Genuinely amazed by the man's longevity, Harvey commented on how well he looked and the fact he obviously still had "all his marbles" a comment that made them both laugh.

Looking more serious, Robert continued, 'My grandma lost her husband and son and was one of the forty-eight thousand who lost their homes. A few months later she lost her mind.'

As the old man paused for breath, Harvey said that anyone one who hadn't lived through it couldn't really imagine it.

'It all broke Grandma's heart. She ended up in the Gartnavel Royal Hospital, sounds better than the Glasgow Lunatic Asylum! I used to visit her there with my mother.'

Rounding a wide corner, the Crematorium came into sight. Harvey had read that it was fifty years old and had been renovated the year before, making it *"A fitting venue to say a fond farewell."* Whitewashed walls were surrounded by shrubs and with its well-maintained Garden of Remembrance it belied its daily use. Had Harry Whistler once sought shelter here...and more pertinently...was this his latest refuge?

'Robert, there is a reason I'm here.' Pausing briefly, Harvey wondered how much to say. 'I'm a police inspector from Lancashire, and I'm trying to locate a man from my home town.'

'Sounds ominous. I like a good mystery. Tell me more.'

'Over twenty years ago, a man disappeared from his home in Fordway, that's a few miles north of Preston. He left without saying goodbye and wasn't seen again for over nine years. When he resurfaced, he was one of the town's homeless, living on the streets and in the local parks. His family regained some contact with him. However, he's gone AWOL again and we would very much like to speak to him.'

Realising he wasn't explaining the situation clearly, Harvey decided to be more honest. 'The man I'm looking for is called Harry Whistler. One of his children thinks he may have spent time in Glasgow the first time he absconded – not sure that's the right word as he may not have done anything wrong, but he is a *person of interest.*'

'My dear Inspector, Glasgow is a huge town. Why are you looking in this cemetery? The man would do better on Sauchiehall Street or Bellahouston Park.'

'Mr Whistler's wife remembers her husband talking about Craigton Cemetery…and indeed that park, whose name we pronounce somewhat differently! Apparently, he once said that it was possible to find shelter here at all times of the year.'

'Well, the gates are open from dawn to dusk and it will be warm in the crem.' Realising what he'd said he laughed and apologised for the last comment before continuing. 'We do get the occasional rough sleeper here. I've not seen anyone recently, but then I only come once a week and don't always walk round here. Too sad to see the mourners follow their loved ones inside.'

Thanking Robert for his time, Harvey gave him his card and asked him to phone if he saw a man matching Harry's description: 'Above average height, grey hair, unkempt beard, and was last seen wearing a black overcoat and brown bobble hat.'

'That would probably describe most of the rough sleepers we see here, but I'll be in touch if anyone like that materialises.' His curiosity becoming cat-like, Robert asked why the police wanted to find the missing man. 'He must have done something awful to bring you all this way.'

'He may not have done anything at all. We just want to ask him some questions. Sorry that's all I'd better say. Thank you for your time and the best of luck. Hope you receive the Birthday Card!'

Bellahouston Park wasn't too far away, so Harvey decided he'd call in before heading home. He hadn't realised the park was so big, far too many acres for one man to cover. Should Harry be here the chances of finding him were equivalent to his chance of winning at chess (a game his family loved but which he invariably lost, his brothers far more proficient). Turning for home, even tuning the car radio to Classic FM, did little to lift his mood.

Chapter 20

Eve

I was worried by Andrew's comment about Mum, so I went to see her after work. Andrew was there and is obviously not speaking to me. He's like one of my less cooperative clients who answer, "no comment," to every question. Why don't people realise they only make things more difficult for themselves. Whether he likes it or not we are all involved and should stay in contact. We need to maintain a united front, if only for Mum.

It's hard to see one's parents becoming frail. Today Mum looked like a twig about to snap in the wind. After apologising for upsetting her, I reassured her that the Glasgow link would be treated carefully, but added that the police had to find Dad. She didn't like it when I said that I'd heard the inspector had gone up to Glasgow to look for him.

'Why can't they leave the man alone? That's what he wants, all he's wanted for twenty years.' At that point, I could hardly tell her that Dad is a suspect, that he might have killed three people. Not what one wants to hear about your husband, though my brothers would say that word was no longer applicable.

There was a horrible silence: several elephants rampaged around the room. When she spoke again her voice had aged into an old lady's croak. 'I keep wondering where it all went wrong. If only we'd had more children. When we married, we both said we wanted a large family. Each one would have been a Child of God, sent by Him to increase His flock.'

Mum was off on her usual soliloquy. 'Would it have been different if Adam had lived? Three weeks and two days was all God allowed him before He recalled him to His Glory. Harry took it really hard.' This was a well-travelled path, one trodden on most visits. People say they have defining moments, ones that change their lives, that have the propensity to derail them, and this was Mum's. Her final comment only told half the story. It was she who took to her bed, unable to face her other children, or I suspect her husband. It was Mum the rest of us lost for weeks, then months and, to a lesser extent, years. Dad coped: Mum didn't. I was four, my brothers three years older; all too young to understand or help, though I remember David holding hankies to Mum's face and offering to make the tea. Andrew arrived a few years later and was the final addition. Is that why he has remained the baby? That's understandable. But so sad. So wrong.

Fordway Station was like the morgue: the morning briefing a discordant rendition of *Abide with Me*. Serena Peil had made what felt like an inordinate effort: new navy suit, cream blouse, hair controlled by *firm control* lacquer and full combat-style makeup set like concrete. Ready for her important announcement, she waited like a child about to open a birthday present. Harvey sounded dejected, like a sergeant major, unable to raise his troops, defeat deemed inevitable.

'Nothing to report from my trip to Glasgow. I gave my card to a man who visits the cemetery regularly (smirks from Clare Jennings, the youngest member of the team) and I spoke to the site supervisor and Reverend Astley. Both said they often get members of the homeless fraternity. Some merely wander aimlessly in the grounds, whilst others seek solace and shelter in the chapel. Unfortunately, neither could recall seeing anyone new recently. All in all, a wasted journey.'

Leaning awkwardly on his desk, fingers drumming incessantly, Harvey was irritating Serena. He wasn't the only one who had been busy. Deciding to take the initiate she launched in. 'As expected, Howard Mackay, the man released from Wandsworth at the same time as Mr Wendover, was in the system and easy to locate. He's still at the address he gave in 2003 and I contacted him on his landline. His wife answered and confirmed that he is the Howard Mackay we are seeking.'

'Can we get to the point Inspector Peil? So far you've given us nothing.'

'When I phoned the first time, Mr Mackay was at work. He's employed, full time, in a gym in Salford, used his time in prison wisely and gained the relevant certificates. His wife said he came out a different person. It was his "first and last time" inside.'

Harvey's fingers had accelerated, a sign he was about to bite someone's head off and Serena knew she had to get to the main point. 'I made an appointment with Mrs Mackay to speak to her husband in the evening. Always better to speak face to face, so I went to Pendlebury, north-west of Salford, last night. Howard remembered Terry Wendover, he said they'd become quite close when they shared a cell. He recalled that Terry wasn't interested in any of the educational opportunities at Wandsworth, and said that when he was released he was going to "do his own thing; be his own man." He was sure Terry had no intention of going home.'

'Has he any idea where Terry was thinking of going?'

'No sir. He knew they wouldn't keep in touch, and after they had a drink at the nearest pub they parted. He's never heard from him since. The one thing he did say was that Terry was Scottish and came from Glasgow.' Knowing she had everyone's attention she added, 'Maybe Terry Wendover and Harry Whistler go back further than we thought. Did they meet up in Scotland and travel down to Fordway together?'

Sergeant Symmons stood to speak. Never a charismatic individual, his demeanour this morning was almost antagonistic. 'As asked I tracked Mrs Wendover and gave her the news. She wasn't in the least bit bothered and told me he's been dead to her for years. No contact since he was released from prison. If he had gone back to his house, he wouldn't have been made welcome: she had a new fellow by then. She had no idea where he went after prison and didn't seem to be interested. The only time she showed any emotion was when I said he'd been sleeping rough, but Fordway meant nothing to her, a town she claimed not to have heard of.' Sitting down he gave his superior a look that spoke volumes: ask me to do a menial task and I'll give you a mundane feedback.

Was any of the day's information useful? Uncertain. The smallest snippet can crack a case, but the fact the two men might have associated for years brought them no nearer to finding Harry Whistler who, for the time being, was their chief suspect.

Eve

Strange how everyday life continues – even in the middle of a crisis. My day was spent in Courtroom Five defending an assortment of villains whose misdemeanours ranged from petty theft (two bottles of wine from Marks and Sparks, so not just any wine but...) to Eric Herd arrested for being Drunk and Disorderly. The man's an alcoholic and until he gets some help we will have the pleasure of his company on a fortnightly basis. At least he's consistent.

I came home exhausted having talked for almost eight hours. Words dominate my life. My profession is ruled by language (some say arguments) which I employ to defend my clients. Jacob asks how I can "champion" – his word – the guilty. I point out that everyone is entitled to a lawyer who will represent them in court. English law retains the concept of *innocent until proven guilty* and it is the prosecutors' responsibility to establish guilt (beyond reasonable doubt) and mine to speak for the defendants. Yes, there have been times when I have managed to convince the magistrates that defendants are innocent when I suspect they might be guilty. My job (and I have been told I do it well) is to present the facts my clients have given me. I can have no opinions. I am merely their mouthpiece.

How strange then that words abscond every time I attempt to have a conversation with family or friends, like soldiers deserting their regiment. The journal helps: no one is listening and there is little response. Strange to think that when I started it I could not have envisaged that its content would run parallel with a series of murders. It was meant to be a record of our family, each member adding their own comments.

Tomorrow will be difficult. Serena wants to meet me. She assured me it's just an informal chat, but every word I utter will be analysed and reported back. Maybe I should pretend I'm helping a client and prepare my arguments. It must be about Dad, but am I speaking for the innocent or the guilty?

DCI Tarquin feared that he would not be leading the Elizabeth Park murders indefinitely. Superintendent Grealy had indicated as much in a rather terse phone call where he'd been warned that more progress was essential. 'Bloody well get on with it.' If only he could *get-on-with-it*. Until Harry Whistler was found the investigation had stuttered to a halt, a car in need of a new battery.

Recently, his obsession with the case meant that every spare minute was taken up with endless perambulations of the park: no Lake District or Morecambe Bay walks to lift his spirits. Sitting by the duck pond, many of them devouring the bread thrown by a group of children, he was aware of someone sidling up to him.

'Good afternoon, Inspector Tarquin. Do you remember me? Eddie Bond. When you asked where we'd like to go after our afternoon tea party I asked for the Ritz. Think I was the only one who laughed!'

'Sorry that our budget didn't extend to such luxury. Good to see you again. How are you?'

'Very well, thank you. It's rather fortuitous–yes, I had a good education–seeing you. I believe you're looking for old Harry. The day after poor Terry was killed I met Harry in Ash Tree Park. He knew he'd be a suspect after their fracas the day before and told me he was going away.'

'Did he say where?'

'He mentioned Lancaster. Said he'd spent some time there, back in the day, and that there was a reasonable hostel for the homeless on the edge of the town. You might not recognise him, I hardly did. He's shaved his beard and given himself a crew cut. Got some new clothes as well, no idea where they came from.'

'Did he give any indication that he knew he'd be wanted for questioning?'

'Indeed. One hundred per cent. That's why he went. I did tell him he looked too good to be allowed to stay in a hostel, but he indicated that he knew the man who runs it. Rick something, sorry can't remember any more.'

'Thank you, Mr Bond.'

'Good grief, I haven't been that for a long time. It's Eddie now, or the eagle after that mad so-and-so in the ski jumping.'

'Well, Eddie, you've been very helpful.'

'It's not him. Harry's not the man you want. I've known him for years and he's no murderer. All the people who've been killed were his friends. It's just not him. He's been devastated by the deaths. I repeat, they were his friends. It's almost as if someone is trying to hurt him.'

Chapter 21

The Press were in full cry: police incompetence and the lack of progress had produced lurid headlines: "Do These Murders Not Matter? The Homeless of No Value. Are We a Country Still Ruled by Class Divisions?". When he got back to the incident room an ear-splitting silence descended. Several of the day's papers were lying on desk tops, the written words the only sounds screaming at him. For several moments, it felt like a scene from a poorly acted film, the characters all given non-speaking parts to save on the budget.

Calling Serena into his office, he growled at her. 'You're going to Lancaster. Harry Whistler might have gone there. Take someone with you, be good experience for Clare Jennings, let her lead the interview. I've contacted the local police. They're happy for you to be there, and said to let them know if they can be of assistance. Remember, Mr Whistler has a new look: clean shaven, neat haircut and smart clothes. Apparently, he used to frequent the homeless shelter on the outskirts of the town. I phoned the man in charge, a Rick Bolton, and he's expecting you.'

Arriving rather later than planned, the A6 blocked by an accident immediately after the motorway exit, the two officers went straight to the rather prosaically named *Home from Home Hostel*. The building looked dilapidated. It had originally served as a community centre, before reinventing itself as a shelter. A plaque by the front door announced that a *Help the Homeless* charity was responsible for its upkeep. More funding was obviously required. Several men were standing patiently in a straggly queue, waiting for the doors to open, females conspicuous by their absence.

'Good afternoon and welcome.' Rick Bolton was not what they had been expecting. Smart suit and bow tie looked totally out of place in an establishment for those who had fallen on such hard times.

He was obviously used to the looks the visitors failed to hide. 'I dress like this as appearances are important. The men are reminded that they remain of worth, that my staff and I respect them and value their time with us.'

'How long can anyone stay?' Clare liked to ask direct questions. Serena made a mental note to have a discussion with her about her interview technique.

'As a general rule for a maximum of three nights, but there are exceptions. We had one gentleman with us for two weeks. He was unwell and needed hospital treatment. It took that long to persuade him to go to Casualty. Most of our friends are aware that this is a last resort, not an escape from the streets. We have a vetting system and monitor them very carefully. No drinking, drugs, arguing, stealing or bad language allowed. That may sound heartless, but it's the only way to cope with the numbers. We can only sleep fifteen at any one time and feel it's best to shelter the most vulnerable. It's a sad fact that there are more and more people living rough and our small enterprise hasn't got the space, volunteers or money to help them all.'

Having nodded in the appropriate places, Clare asked about Harry Whistler.

'When your boss rang, I looked at our records. We do try to keep a list of our friends, though we are aware that some use false identities. I can't say I remember him, so many come through our doors, and only a few…usually those who cause trouble…stand out. It's a salutary thought that they tend to remember our names.'

The men hoping to stay the night had started to enter the building. 'Harry Whistler. That's a name I've not heard for a long time.' The two officers turned around to see a man grinning at them, his mouth almost devoid of teeth. 'Harry and I were mates, must be years ago. He was OK was old Harry.'

'This is Ted Derby, one of our regulars.' Rick sounded fond of the old man who stood leaning awkwardly against the wall.

Introducing herself, Serena took charge of the questioning. 'Mr Derby,' the use of his title resulted in another toothless grin, 'we are keen to talk to Harry Whistler. We believe he may have returned to Lancaster. Have you seen him here recently?'

Ted removed himself from the wall and lent towards the officers. 'I believe there is usually a reward for information.'

'Now, Ted, you know better than that. Money doesn't change hands inside these walls.' Rick was speaking to Serena as much as the vagrant.

After making a mouth zipped movement, Ted began to walk away.

'Wait Ted. How about an extra night in the hostel if you talk to the police officers?'

'Two and it's a deal.'

'Done. Now come to my office where you can talk more privately.'

Mugs of tea and a plate of biscuits in front of them, Ted started a monologue. 'When I said it's many years since I heard Harry's name, it didn't mean I hadn't seen him. Indeed, I was talking to him only yesterday! Talk about déjà vu: there he was in the very spot he used to call his own...down by the canal. He looked better than he used to but it was the same Harry. We spent ages catching up and he said he'd returned to his home town... Fordway. Funny to do that, most of us avoid anywhere to do with our previous lives, too many memories. When I asked him why he'd come back to Lancaster he went quiet, so I didn't press the matter and...'

Clare interrupted the flow. 'Can you tell us exactly where Harry's spot is?'

'I was coming to that. It's just after the Horses' Rest pub, the one they've done up. Proper posh it is now, but at least they kept its name, good to be reminded that the animals got a break after pulling those canal barges. There's a hump-back bridge just to the south of the pub with an old warehouse beside it. Long ago it was a place to store the goods the canal barges transported; still got the hoists they used. Harry and I used to doss down inside. It was in quite good nick, built to last. Few draughts, especially upstairs. You can't miss it these days as its covered in great notices – it's going to be redeveloped into town houses, whatever they are. No good to the likes of us now.'

'You said you saw him yesterday. Did he give any indication that he was planning to stay in the area?'

'You can never tell with Harry. Could be weeks, or he could be gone by now.'

Thanking the man for his time and adding that they hoped he enjoyed his nights in the hostel, Serena and Clare asked for directions to the canal.

Chapter 22

Jacob

I have just got home after one of the most unpleasant evenings of my life. Mum rang me and asked me to go home. She wanted me to help David sort through Dad's things…yes, she had kept a wardrobe full of his clothes.

Bags full of trousers, jumpers, coats and even a pair of blue-striped pyjamas are ready to go to a charity shop. She begged me to take one or two things he might want: a winter anorak, scarf and shoes which look new. She is keen for me to find him and hand them over.

When I asked why she had kept them for so long she gave the wonderful answer, 'I have always hoped he would come home. I now realise that isn't the case. If the recent awful events in the park haven't made him return, nothing will.'

Strange that she wanted me to help David sort through it all. No point asking Andrew, he's such a baby, he'd have balked at the notion and probably had to lie down in a dark room for at least a week. Mum didn't ask Eve, though she'd have made a good job of it. For some unfathomable notion, it was David and me, not that he was much help, just grabbed a couple of mementoes and vamoosed. Mum was in such a state that I didn't ask her why she wanted me to be involved.

David

Fancy Mum keeping his stuff this long. She never said. I left most of it to Jacob. Cowardly I know, but sorting through the remains of Dad's life was too upsetting. It must have been an horrendous task and well done for completing it, Jacob. I take it that the wardrobe is now empty. As you say, Andrew would have found it too hard, and I suspect she asked you as you were always the one to get to the nub of any problem: as Dad would have said "sort the wheat from the chaff" or "sheep from the goats"! You don't dilly-dally, and spend ages deciding the best course of action. If I'd stayed I would probably still be studying each item and trying to decide what to do with it: charity shop, pass it back to its original owner (!) or bin it.

Do you remember when Mum lost her cool with all four of us and ordered us upstairs to tidy our rooms? We had separate rooms by then, the one enormous room divided in half, and yours didn't need too much attention, so you came next door and did mine. Were Eve's and Andrew's also immaculate due to your administration?

If you want me to take the clothes you're supposed to give to Dad I don't mind. They sound like things he might need.

Mum is more worried than any of us about the murders in the park, scared that Dad will be next. She continues to care about him, though I can't think why. He deserted (Andrew's word is dumped) her as well as us all those years ago...more so in some ways. We've had the chance to grow up and get on with our lives whilst she continues to be more like a widow, without the comforting thought that her husband didn't want to leave her. I'm surprised she would even contemplate taking him back.

Why had he not gone to Lancaster himself? Why had he not accepted the help offered by the local police? They were the ones who knew the terrain. When Serena had told him that they had seen Harry, been within touching distance of him, and let him run off, he was so angry he couldn't speak. The man couldn't be fit enough to outrun two young women.

'Sorry, Harvey,' the use of his Christian name totally inappropriate, 'he looked up as we approached and legged it. He obviously knows the alleys and hiding places and by the time we were over the bridge he'd disappeared. At least we know where he is.'

'Shame you didn't know when you were there.'

'Sir,' back to formality, 'I know Harry Whistler is a person of interest and we want to interview him, but the papers think we should be making more progress and I wondered if it was too late to widen our search.' Trying this tack again was as successful as the first time she'd mentioned it, and the look she received told her she remained persona non grata. She didn't think she'd done anything wrong. Her boss obviously needed a scapegoat.

Chapter 23

At first glance, it looked as though Harvey was enjoying a day off. Some would disapprove and deem it inappropriate. Wasn't he supposed to be the one in charge of three murder investigations? He was, however, indulging in a "blue-sky thinking day", the terminology employed by a man he'd heard on the radio. He recalled the somewhat esoteric advice to "walk whilst allowing one's mind to operate beyond the confines of the office". He hoped that creative ideas might emerge, those not limited by staying indoors and being interrupted by members of his team. Such a strategy had worked in the past, long before it had been awarded such an intriguing label. The entire day was to be spent strolling in the fresh air whilst allowing his brain to wander freely.

Deciding to keep well away from the local parks, Harvey drove to Beacon Fell. Normally just over twenty minutes, the drive had taken almost double that, road works on the A6 and an irritatingly slow tractor extending the journey. There was a time the Fell had been a regular haunt, the extensive views from the trigonometry point on the hill top magnificent: weather permitting. The information plate informed visitors that Morecambe Bay, the Forest of Bowland hills, Preston and even Blackpool Tower could all be seen. Underneath, in bold letters were the words: **On a clear day, the Welsh hills,**

the Lake District and even the Isle of Man may be visible.
Unfortunately, the day was overcast and there was little
to observe.

Numerous paths crisscrossed their way around the
area, assault courses and playgrounds recently added.
Not interested in such activities, Harvey enjoyed his
own, more sedate, form of exercise and reckoned to
walk at least ten miles on each visit.

A party of school children was racing round, clip-
boards and pens in hand. Beacon Fell now advertised
itself as a mecca for those interested in orienteering
and was used by both amateurs and professionals.
On his last visit, there had been a Lancashire trial taking
place to select the most accomplished for the national
team.

A harassed looking teacher stopped him as he began
his descent. 'Have you seen three boys who look as
though they're lost?'

'Sorry, all the groups I've seen looked as though they
knew what they were doing.'

'My trio should have reported back twenty minutes
ago. They're supposed to come back every half hour to
get the new directions. I think they must still be looking
for the first markers.

'Good job it's boys. The people I work with would be
making all sorts of comments about the female of the
species having no sense of direction.'

'Oh, we've had that from the girls already. The boys
are in for some teasing when they do eventually turn up.'

Agreeing that he would direct them back to the coach
park they bade each other farewell.

Unable to let his mind roam as freely as the lost boys,
Harvey decided to start by putting the events of the past
few months in some sort of order.

First murder: September 14th Tommy or Thomas Granger. Aged seventy. Strangled and moved under the bushes, body treated with respect. Belongings, such as they were, laid reverentially around the body. A small cross placed inside his mouth. Long-time member of the homeless fraternity. One brother, one ex-wife, both ruled out of the inquiries with solid alibis.

Second murder: December 11th Charlotte Carroway. Aged eighteen. Strangled, and once again, left underneath bushes in the park. All her belongings beside her. Again, a cross inserted post-mortem. Missing from home for several months. Parents and sister had been involved in a nation-wide search. Not considered as suspects. Charlotte had only joined the people in the park shortly before she died.

Third murder: February 10th Terrence or Terry Wendover. Aged fifty. Strangled, body burnt post-mortem. Belongings scattered, and body left in full view. No cross present, though it might have been incinerated. Ex-prisoner. Ex-wife. Ex-life. No obvious suspects. Former wife out of the country on the day of the murder. Terry vamoosed when released from prison, no contact with his former life. Long-time vagrant in Fordway.

The only thing the three had in common was that they had all shared the unenviable experience of living as rough sleepers. Had they been selected? Why them and not some of the others? There were many to choose from, an increasing number living that way.

Arriving back at the reception area, Harvey was pleased to hear that the missing boys had returned. They were being chastised loudly enough for the whole of Lancashire to hear. They all looked suitably subdued, a situation exacerbated by the smirks on the faces of their classmates. How simple life was when all that mattered was that it was someone else suffering an ear-bashing from an irate teacher.

Tea and cake were needed. Perhaps those might invigorate some brain cells. As he sat, watching the children step onto their mini bus, he realised he was no nearer to following his own orienteering clues. He was at least as lost as the unfortunate boys had been. Think, you fool, think...all three strangled, the third then mutilated, burnt beyond recognition. Alfie Morrison, the one pathologist he could trust to do a thorough job, had asked, 'Who in the world would want to do this to a fellow human being? Unless of course he was a Man U supporter!' Harvey hadn't asked him if he meant the victim or the assailant: no doubt either would have done. At the time, he had been surprised, as black humour normally had no place when Alfie was performing a post-mortem.

Thinking about Dr Morrison he recalled being the officer asked to attend Charlotte Carroway's PM. The pathologist had been in tears. 'Sorry. I don't usually blub, but when it's someone so young, all her life ahead of her, it's just so incredibly sad. All so futile. Even worse when it's a baby or a young child. When that happens my faith is sorely tested, and I often ask Him why? Why wasn't He looking after them?'

Harvey had agreed, and had been moved himself when Alfie started to sing 'We love you Charlotte, we do,' to the time-honoured football tune.

Following his break, he was pleased to see that the sun was beginning to win its battle with the clouds which had lingered over the entire country for the best part of a week. The main path, which led to the west of the Fell, had a steep incline, the effort making his spirits lighten.

He knew there was a vital clue: someone had said something important. What was it?

Serena had once again suggested widening the net, looking beyond the homeless for their killer. If that was to be the case, the problem was where to start. They had interviewed each of the deceased's relatives. Foreign holidays, seventieth birthday parties, work commitments and hospital appointments had ruled them all out. He felt certain they needed to be in contact with Harry Whistler. Should they also speak to his family again? Harry was the only one with relatives in the immediate vicinity. They must know more than they were saying.

After another ninety minutes walking, managing not to retrace his steps, he was no nearer to a solution. So much for blue-sky thinking. More like foggy day's deliberation.

Eve

What a day. The kind every lawyer dreads. A totally uncooperative client, with at least one bottle inside him, who annoyed the legal adviser and the magistrates with his appalling attitude. He slouched into Court Two, muttering under his breath. Hands firmly in his pockets, he scowled at the three who had the dubious pleasure of sitting on today's Bench.

The legal adviser, a very experienced woman who has seen it all before, opened the case.

'What is your name?'

'None of your business.'

'You have to give the Court your name.'

'Get lost, I know my human rights.'

'Is your name Joel Rushworth?'

'Yeah.'

'Thank you. Now that wasn't so hard, was it?' Mrs Knowles continued, requesting his address.

'Ain't got one.'

I intervened and said he could be contacted via his sister. Anticipating the next question, I added that as far as I was aware he did not possess a mobile phone, at which point Mr Rushworth totally lost it and started effing and blinding, calling everyone in Court names I can't record! The Chairman asked, very politely in the circumstances, for my client to be taken down to the cells to cool off and speak to his lawyer, neither of which happened. I wasn't surprised when, on his all-too brief return to Court, he was remanded for twenty-four hours: we will go through the whole palaver again tomorrow. At least by then he should be sober. Rather appropriately, he's charged with being Drunk and Disorderly, and stealing two bottles of wine from Waitrose.

My next case stumbled like an inept hurdler falling at the first frame. Paul Kingsley's partner, and the only witness to the alleged domestic violence, failed to arrive. A common occurrence: always infuriating. Several phone calls, to ascertain her whereabouts and enquire if she was planning to come to Court, went unanswered. As there was no case to answer the CPS withdrew the case and Mr Kingsley was free to leave. The man is a pugilist and has several convictions for assaults on previous partners. As he swaggered out of court he gave a good impersonation of a boxer who has just won his fight. Unfortunately, the disturbing fact, and fact is the word, is that the absentee Sonia will continue to be his punch bag; that is until she leaves him, or he puts her in hospital ...or worse.

Most unusually I was home early. I haven't been to yoga for weeks, but tonight I went, having allowed my early tea to settle. Always an advantage before the contortions. As soon as I walked in to the school hall I came face to face with Serena who looked nonplussed to see me.

'Hi, I've not been for ages. Have you been coming?' was my rather weak opening. The woman was obviously in police mode and didn't know how to respond. 'We are a right pair. You'd think we hadn't heard of a work-life balance. It must be six weeks since we were both here.' Realising I was rambling I sat down on my exercise mat and started to take off my shoes.

'My first time for about a month.' With that brief rejoinder, she moved to the other side of the room. The evening had been ruined. It was obvious that she had no desire to talk to me. What had happened that she was afraid to discuss? As always, my thoughts flew in all directions: there'd been another murder and this time Dad was the victim; Dad had been arrested; I was a suspect and was about to be questioned under caution; or the more likely scenario that Dad was still missing, and she thought I knew more than I was saying. As a lawyer, I knew it was probably nothing more than her not being allowed to discuss an ongoing case with me, but my mind wasn't operating logically.

My goodness, were the yoga positions hard work! Even the Low Lunge and Cat Pose had me aching in places I'd forgotten I had. As for the Handstand and Plow Pose, not a chance. I did what the oh-so-intense instructor said we could do if we were finding a position too hard (the sub-text being that as one had paid good money to be there one should attempt each movement and not be lazy and opt-out) and lay on my mat and attempted one of the relaxation meditations. To say the least that was futile. I ended up even more tense than when I arrived. To top it all off, towards the end of the session, that normally glorious moment when we all lie down whilst she lulls us with soft music and even softer words, telling us to relax each part of our bodies, the man next to me fell asleep and snored gently, much to the amusement of the lady on his other side.

Serena had left by the time I arrived in the car park. I know when I'm being avoided. Just not sure why. Thank goodness, I am in my own house tonight. Not sure I could take Philip's attempts at reassurance. He means well, but has no idea how my thoughts become blacker by the day. Must ring Mum and see how she is.

Andrew

Yes, dear sister, you rang Mum. The poor woman hasn't been right since Dad vamoosed again. That man puts Houdini's escapades to shame. Eve was in one of her moods, reminding me that she's always been a drama queen. I once suggested she had chosen the wrong career and should be on the stage until David pointed out that lawyers are acting all the time, reciting the lines their clients have instructed them to say. Women crying down the phone do not impress me, and I knew she would upset Mum if she spoke to her. I told my beloved sibling that Mum had gone to bed; a lie, but in the circumstances excusable, and that I would tell her she had rung: another whopper!

Not a word about how I am – not that she cares – and she hardly mentioned Mum. How she copes as a solicitor I don't know, as for the next half hour she rambled, so randomly that she was extremely hard to follow. Tangents led to non-sequiturs and back to tangents: Dad, the murders, who would be next, and would the police want to talk to us again all gushed out, like the contents of a fizzy bottle that has been shaken before opening. As I half-listened, flicking through the pages of the latest B&Q brochure that was lying by the phone, the thought occurred to me that she is feeling guilty about something. She knows more than she lets on. Jacob didn't like it when I said that to him. It's true. Must try to see the boys. Without Eve.

Chapter 24

Monday morning. The start of a new week or the banal continuation of the old one? Sergeant Roger Symmons stood up. When he had information to impart he enjoyed his moment in the spotlight. 'I was in early this morning to catch up on some paper work when a call came through. The caller wanted to speak to someone dealing with the Terry Wendover murder. It was Terry's brother, a Martin Wendover. He's coming in later and thinks he may have some information for us.'

'What time is he arriving?' This was one interview Harvey wanted to conduct, though he knew his sergeant should be involved.

'He lives in Manchester. Said he would be here by mid-morning.'

'Did he give any indication of the nature of his information? Did it sound useful? We'd better be prepared before we meet him.' Harvey knew he was sounding pompous.

'Just that he saw his brother recently, in fact the night before he died, and that he had said something that might be of interest, something that might help us find the killer.' The room was still, everyone working out the possible importance behind the sergeant's convoluted sentence. All present hoped that this might be the breakthrough they needed.

Martin Wendover was nothing like his brother. Hard to believe they were siblings; the years had been much kinder to the one now in the interview room. Looking extremely nervous he fidgeted, eyes darting everywhere but at the two policemen. He had dressed for an interview: smart suit, white shirt and a blue and grey striped tie that looked brand new. Hair and shoes had been brushed to a shine. Stuttering slightly, he apologised, 'Sorry I'm late, the traffic was horrendous.'

Wanting to put the man at his ease a well-appointed room had been chosen, where discussions rather than interviews were held. Someone had taken care to make the space as welcoming and unthreatening as possible: neutral colours, soft furnishings and vases with real flowers. The aim was to put people at their ease. Those not used to involvement with the police found any interaction disconcerting. Others regarded it as such a regular occurrence that they might as well timetable it on their tablets.

Sitting on the settee, covered in a corded beige, Martin sat up straight ready to begin. Having practised his lines, he was keen to deliver them.

Harvey had decided that he would lead the discussion with his sergeant taking notes. No tape recording had been deemed necessary. 'Thank you so much for taking the time to come. I'm DCI Harvey Tarquin and this is the sergeant you spoke to this morning, Roger Symmons. Please accept our sincere condolences on the loss of your brother.'

'Sad to say I lost him a long time ago. There was a period we were the best of friends. When we were growing up we were inseparable. Then, when we got married, we went on lots of holidays together with our wives, and when the children came along we met up at each other's houses most weekends. We both worked for Bolton Builders. I was a brickie and he drove the lorries. It was all fine until he got in with a bad crowd and started with some petty crime which soon became more serious. He seemed to be in trouble on a weekly basis. It was inevitable that he would end up in jail, and after he got out we lost touch.'

A long pause made both policemen wonder where the discussion was leading. 'When you phoned this morning, you said you had some information that might be helpful.'

'Yes, sorry, I'll get to the point, just wanted to give you some background. Wanted you to know that for many years Terry was a hard-working, upstanding citizen. It's hard to believe how wrong things can go. Out of the blue. No warning the first time he was involved in anything criminal. But I never thought he'd end up on the streets. What a shock I got when I saw him recently. Sorry I haven't come sooner. I was so upset when I read about him and then his wife, well in fact his ex-wife – she got a divorce – said you'd been to see her and I thought I ought to come and talk to you.'

Assuring Martin that it was never too late, Harvey asked him to continue.

'The wife's cousin lives in Fordway. We'd come to see her. Took her grandchildren to the park. Elizabeth, I think it's called.' The man was getting nervous and had started to speak in staccato sentences.

Keen to calm their visitor, and realising they had been in such a hurry to begin their discussion that they hadn't offered any refreshments, Harvey asked if he'd like a drink.

'Sorry. I just get so upset when I think of the way he died. He'd done a lot of bad things, and gone a long way from the old straight and narrow, but he didn't deserve to be murdered. He was still my brother.'

Drinks in front of them, Harvey assured Martin that there was no hurry; that he could take his time telling them about the meeting with his brother.

'As I said we were in the park, by the kiddies' playground up near the café. What a shock I got when I realised the down-and-out standing in front of me was Terry. He must have seen the look of horror that I couldn't hide and laughed. "Well, well, well, if it isn't my big brother." He always called me that – I was eighteen months older than him.' Finding it hard to continue, Martin took a sip of his coffee.

Harvey spoke quietly. 'The years hadn't been kind to him. That way of life takes its toll. He must have looked very different to the last time you saw him.'

'I went to visit him in prison. He was family, though I didn't like what he'd done: armed robbery. Thank goodness, our parents didn't live to see how low he'd sunk. I never doubted he deserved his punishment. On my final visit, just days before he was due to be released, I told him that I'd help him when he got out. A mate of mine had got a huge contract to build hundreds of houses in Salford and had said he'd take Terry on. He knew his background, but said as he was my brother he'd trust him, and I promised to keep an eye on him. Terry seemed pleased. However, that was the last time I saw him. Until that afternoon.'

A long silence was broken only by cups being replaced on the table. Harvey knew he had little influence on the speed of the interview. Given time, their visitor would speak when he was ready.

'The wife and her cousin took the kiddies off to feed the ducks and I stayed to talk to Terry. He looked so awful. Truly horrendous. He was always fond of a drink, but that afternoon he stank of alcohol; it seemed to emanate from every pore. I managed to stutter some sort of greeting and said it was good to see him. It was. For years, I'd had no idea where he was living or what had happened. I even wondered if he had died. We had been so close I couldn't believe he wouldn't try to contact me. Keep in touch.'

Martin needed a few moments to regain his composure. 'Sorry. So, sorry, I still can't believe that having found him again I lost him that night. We promised to maintain contact: yes, probably minimal, but I planned to meet up with him on a regular basis and he seemed pleased with the idea. My offer for him to come to stay with Sandra and me, was rejected. Then, just as I thought he was going to make a bolt for it, he agreed to meet up with us in the park – nothing regular – just the occasional get-together. I suggested once a month. He laughed, said that such dates meant nothing any more. He called the park "his home" and said he was there most of the time, so I would be able to find him.'

Raised voices in the adjoining room interrupted the story, Harvey failing to show his displeasure. 'Please carry on Martin.'

'The rest of the family had gone home, but I sat outside the café with Terry to have a drink. It was chilly and still damp, but he said he wouldn't be welcome inside. It was then that he told me he'd spent the afternoon in the police station. When he saw my face, he was bullet-quick to assure me that he wasn't in trouble, just there with the other homeless to talk to the police about the two murders. I'd read about them, who hadn't? Never imagined my brother could be involved. I remember asking if he had been of any assistance, able to help in any way. "Me, help that lot…never. I've no time for them: they stitched me up too often. That spell in prison would have been halved if a certain Inspector Matthews had told the truth. I only agreed to go to today's little get-together to lay a false trail. Haven't had so much fun for ages."'

Stopping to consider how to proceed, Martin gazed out of the window, the one that had the uninspiring view of a brick wall. 'I asked him what he meant. Laughing raucously, he told me that he'd suggested that one of the other vagrants was the murderer. When I asked him if that wasn't dangerous he said that there was no way that the man would ever be charged, but it would be wonderful to watch the police going around in stupid circles trying to find sufficient evidence to take him to court. He said the man was called Harry Whistler and that they usually got on well, but just recently they'd had a falling out and this was his vengeance. "Get Harry and the old law enforcement. Two hits for one lie." Didn't sound like the man I used to know.'

'Your brother did indeed indicate that one of the gentlemen who frequent the park may well be the killer.' Realising he had sounded aloof, Harvey said that it was most useful to know that Terry had been trying to mislead them. 'We do however have an open mind as to who the killer might be, and indeed what strata of society he or she comes from.' Once again, Harvey hated his turn of phrase. He'd gone from unfriendly, to pompous.

Their visitor didn't appear to notice. 'It was what Terry said next. That's the real reason I'm here. He claimed to have seen the person who killed the second victim, a young girl.' A prolonged silence followed this statement.

Sounding calmer than he felt, Harvey spoke quietly. 'Yes, she was an eighteen-year old called Charlotte

Carroway. You said you read the papers. They were full of her murder.'

'Indeed, it was headline news. I repeat that it was so strange to realise that, at the time, I had no idea there was any link to Terry. Well anyway…Terry claimed to see a person backing out of the bushes, late on the afternoon when Charlotte was murdered. He thought nothing about it at the time, just assumed the person had been caught short or was looking for a dog.'

'You keep saying person. Did your brother say whether it was a man or a woman?'

'No. I asked him that and he said it was getting dark, night coming early in December, and he was too far away to tell. He remembered some details about them. They looked about medium height, so not much help, and they were dressed in the usual uniform: trainers, navy denims and a dark hoodie which was up. However, the main thing that made him suspicious was that they were wearing dark glasses. Definitely not needed.'

Allowing Martin to pause, Harvey assured him that this could be vital evidence. 'Terry's final comment was that the man or woman he saw was definitely *not* from the homeless community. Far too well dressed, and as he said, "I know them all and would have recognised them even in the twilight. I'm good with body shapes and this wasn't one of us." He was adamant about that. He also said that he got the impression that the person was quite young, or at least a lot younger than most of the people he knew in the park.'

'I wish your brother had told us this. He might still be alive.'

'It has crossed my mind that the killer knows he was seen and came back to murder Terry.'

'A possibility, but if so he waited a long time. Charlotte was killed in December and your brother in February. Although Christmas came in-between, seven weeks is a long time to defer the annihilation of a witness.'

Thanking the man for his help, and assuring him that any information was treated seriously, Harvey left him with Sergeant Symmons to write a statement.

Serena had been waiting to hear the outcome of the meeting. 'Any help, Sir?'

Almost apoplectic, Harvey yelled, loud enough for everyone to hear, 'Terry Wendover. The bloody man deliberately misled us. He had vital information that might have helped.' Relaying all the facts only helped to increase the inspector's blood pressure. 'The person he saw might have been totally innocent...or could have been the killer. Frustrating that so much time has elapsed before we got this description.'

'Doesn't sound of much use, sir.'

Not what her boss wanted to hear.

Chapter 25

Elizabeth Park had always benefitted from the very generous legacy left by George Barrington. It was more than a rumour that it still amounted to several millions. No contribution for its upkeep had ever been requested from the town's council. All wages paid, grounds maintenance – the Peace Garden winning a national prize last year – the upkeep of the café, lakes, fountains, paths and bandstand all came from the legacy. Much of the fortune had been carefully nurtured in stocks, shares and, more recently, off-shore accounts.

One of Mr Barrington's final innovations had been the erection of a theatre, a large, imposing building on the northern edge of the park. Both professional and amateur performances were well attended, and it was often said that their founder would be pleased that the people of the town were still able to enjoy the many and varied entertainments the theatre, bearing his name, staged. *The Pirates of Penzance* was due to be performed in a few weeks, the Fordway Players mounting twice-yearly shows.

The Board of Trustees met on the first Thursday of every month, many meetings a mere formality. Tonight, was different. An extraordinary meeting had been called, and on a Monday. The other members were intrigued.

Gerald Moreton, the Trustee's chairman, had drawn up a very short agenda: one item of great importance.

A confident man, he was sure he could get his motion passed, the police presence he had requested would add further weight. PC Clare Jennings was the first to arrive.

'Good evening, ladies and gentlemen. Thank you for attending this unusual meeting. As you can see from the extremely short agenda I wish to discuss the recent appalling events in our park. I realise it is some weeks since the last murder, and as I'm sure you are all aware the police do not seem to be making much, if any, headway. The time has come for us to be proactive.'

'Not sure what we can do to solve three murders if the police can't.' Ella Norris was the one negative member of the board. No one could recall the last time she had made a helpful comment.

Gerald continued, her interruption ignored, like background noise that goes unheard. 'We are not here to assist the police in their enquiries. My idea is to prevent any such future events. DCI Tarquin, leading the investigation, informed me that a constant police presence was unrealistic. Rather disappointing, though understandable. I would therefore like to suggest that we do something that, in the past, we have tried to avoid. CCTV cameras. Several of them at strategic points.'

'Oh, Mr Chairman,' Ella was at her most vehement, 'we all know why we have never accepted them. The people who come for a pleasant stroll in the park, or tea in the café, don't want to be filmed. There are few places where big-brother isn't watching, and our park has always been one of them.'

Looking none too pleased by her comment, he said that PC Clare Jennings was here to speak for the police.

As Clare stood up (she invariably stood to give her evidence in court, feeling more self-assured that way) she knew she was making a tomato look pale, her lifetime affliction not improving. She sounded more confident than she looked – or felt.

'The police find CCTV footage to be a great help in many of the cases they deal with, and the CPS often rely on it when they bring a case to court. If the cameras are unobtrusive, they usually cause no offence. Indeed, most people wouldn't even know they were there. However, Fordway has tried to keep cameras to a minimum, all in the centre of the town, where most crime occurs. But, in the circumstances, it would feel appropriate to place several cameras in the park and I have a list of possible locations. Both gates are the obvious starting point. Had they been in operation at the time of the murders we would at least have known who was in the park.'

Hilda Thaw, the longest serving member of the board, butted in. 'That's assuming the two gates are the only way into the park. Only last week I saw some youths pushing their way through the bushes by Elgin Road. They were in before I could stop them.'

Clare agreed that determined individuals could find different ways into the grounds, adding that other cameras would be needed to cover as much of the park as possible. 'The bandstand, theatre, fountain and café are some of the obvious locations. It's not possible to have eyes everywhere, but my boss asked me to say that he thinks the idea is a good one.'

Ten minutes later the motion was passed and an order for ten cameras sanctioned.

Jacob

Never again. I am not meeting for a conflab, Andrew's word which says it all, with my brothers ever again. When Andrew first suggested it, I said no. It was David who persuaded me, saying he was worried about Eve. She's a female, so ipso-facto neurotic: nothing we can do about that.

We have all suffered her fixated phone calls, the ones where she grieves, bewailing the loss of Dad. Andrew and I would be more than happy if he were to be lost permanently. She says she has nightmares where she awakes, screaming in terror, thinking that he has been killed or is due to be the next victim in the park. She hates it when we suggest that he might have gone walkabout to avoid being arrested for the trio of tragedies. That was my phrase which I rather liked, but which met with little response.

David suggested that we all talk to her. 'If we decide what to say beforehand, I'm sure we can allay her fears.'

Andrew got it right when he replied that she was traumatised because she knows far more than she is admitting. David's reply that if we are all together she may tell us what she knows made Andrew laugh and me yell, 'Well why in God's name hasn't she let us in on her little secret before now?'

Not a pleasant evening, though as we met at David's new restaurant at least the food was good. American size burgers, more chips than any of us could finish, followed by waffles, blueberries and a mountain of ice cream that looked like a poor man's Mont Blanc. Good job we weren't presented with the bill. If one was lacking in the readies there is no way one could afford to eat chez David. We left our dear brother to sort out a meeting. I will simply have to be there. I don't want to miss the excitement.

David

Eve, I know you will have read Jacob's latest entry and I'm sorry that he hasn't worded it more carefully. We are all concerned for you. You are obviously in a state about Dad. I feel certain that he will return, just as he has in the past. To put your mind at rest I do not, for one moment, think he is the killer. He may be many things however, I cannot imagine him murdering even one person, and definitely not three.

Apart from anything else, where is his motive? These people were his friends and he was fond of them, especially Tommy Granger and of course, more recently, the young girl, Charlotte. I met him a few days after her body was found and he was bereft. Weeping for her. Hardly the action of her killer and no, he isn't that skillful an actor. His grief was genuine.

Had the police suspected him he would have been arrested and charged. You, of all people, know the drill. I think the whole sorry mess got too much for him, and he has once again run away, like the coward I fear he has become.

When you feel up to meeting us let me know. In the meantime, we will keep in touch and share anything we hear.

Eve

Thanks David. Jacob's rant did upset me. He accuses me of knowing more than the rest of you. This is true, but until I discuss it with Dad I don't feel I can talk about it. I do think it would be a good idea to all meet. If only for mutual support.

I've been feeling very isolated. Serena, the young inspector I sometimes meet at yoga, was there the other night and she avoided me as if I had some deadly disease. I might as well have been walking along ringing a warning bell. Does she know something she thought she might divulge? Yes, I'm worried…but not neurotic Jacob.

Following the meeting with Terry Wendover's brother, Harvey was keen to update his team. Wanting to encourage his sergeant, he had asked Roger to relay the details from the discussion which had lasted well over an hour. The room was eerily silent as Roger Symmons read the statement made by Terry Wendover's brother.

'So, are we now thinking that the murderer isn't one of the homeless fraternity?' The question, though obvious, bothered Harvey, who glowered at Clare.

'I don't think we're quite ready to make that leap just yet. The person Terry saw that evening, and remember it was dusk, might not have had anything to do with the murder.' Harvey waited for some response. Several people spoke at once.

'And poor Terry's no longer here to corroborate any details.'

'He was also rather well-oiled when he came to our little get together.'

'It's not much help as he couldn't even identify the sex of the person he saw backing out of the bushes.'

'The man or woman might have been taking a leak.'

'It all depends how much credence we give to a tale from a down and out.' The last comment receiving scowls and loud tuts: most present wanted to give the appearance of political correctness, even if they agreed with the sentiment expressed.

Harvey watched the men and women sitting around the table. Empty cups and discarded food wrappers littered its surface and summed up the air of despondency that had fallen, like the persistent drizzle that had forgotten to stop, belying the weatherman's promise of sunshine. They were all frustrated by the lack of progress, and he could tell that the meeting hadn't done anything to encourage them. He had to admit that a possible sighting of an unidentifiable man or woman relayed by the brother of a deceased vagrant wasn't exactly what the CPS would call strong evidence. Thanking them all for attending he told them to go home, relax and come back refreshed in the morning.

'Sir, are we going to widen our list of suspects?' Serena asked as she walked out with her superior. It was at least the third time she'd mentioned the possibility in a short space of time and her superior knew she had a point.

'I have no idea. Absolutely no idea.'

Chapter 26

Time off. If past-experience was anything to go by, Harvey doubted whether he would be free to enjoy the whole weekend. The day had started badly when he realised that his fridge, freezer and cupboards were all bare. Shopping was not an activity he enjoyed. There were times he envied his married colleagues who went home to an organised house, then laughed when he thought how Serena would react to such sexist stereotyping. He stood disconsolately in the first aisle of his local supermarket clutching a very long list, mostly essentials. Reading down the piece of paper he had torn from the *At Your Age Don't Rely on Your Memory* notepad a young colleague had given him as a joke saying that the years were beginning to tell, he wished he had written it in a more logical fashion. Bread, fruit, washing powder and cereal were all located in far-flung parts of the store.

Mozart interrupted him. Maybe the time had come to change to a less beautiful melody on his mobile, the sublime clarinet playing inappropriate for the bad news it almost invariably announced. 'Jonathan Astley here, Reverend Astley from Glasgow. We met a few weeks ago, and you gave me your number, asking me to contact you should someone matching your missing homeless man come this way.'

'Yes, indeed I remember it well. How are you and what can I do for you?'

'I'm extremely well and it's hopefully what I can do for you. A gentleman of the road has visited our church twice in the past week. He's not one of our regulars. I didn't manage to speak to him initially as by the time I was free he had gone. He wandered in again, late yesterday afternoon, and I sat with him for about half an hour. The reason I'm ringing is that he fits your man's profile: he has an English accent, though I can't tell which part of the country he is from, and kept repeating that he needs to atone for his sins. He asked me for absolution. I explained I could help him, talk through his perceived sins, but that it is not within my remit to forgive them. It would need a Priest to do that.'

'Does he fit the description I gave?'

'Well, he's probably in his late sixties, though it's hard to tell as the poor souls who are homeless age so rapidly. He's well spoken, but it was his asking for redemption and the accent that made me think of your man. He's remarkably smart for a gentleman of the road. I think you said the man you are looking for has shaved and acquired new clothes.'

'Did he tell you his name?'

'Not really. He asked to be called Henry, but I'm almost certain that was an alias. Most of the men, and women, I talk to want to forget their past personas and invent a whole new incarnation. I suspect most adopt a different name.'

'Do you know where he's living?'

'Sorry. He declined my offer of a place at our homeless shelter, said he's OK now the better weather has come.'

'Did he give any indication where he's been recently? Anything about moving north of the border?'

'Once again, sorry. Most of our conversation was about his need to be forgiven. He said he has done terrible things and broken several of the Ten Commandments. I got the feeling that he has a church background. Quite suddenly he needed to go. I asked him to come back any time, and assured him that I would gladly discuss his misdemeanors with him. He may or may not take me up on the offer. Sometimes I see a person several weeks running, then they disappear and I'm left feeling frustrated, not knowing how they are. On the other hand, I've been counselling a young man every week for many months. I'm hopeful he'll return to his family and has asked me to contact them. Dear me, you don't need to know all that.'

'You've been very helpful Reverend Astley. Just one more question. Did the person you think might be my man give any indication when he might return?'

'No, the first time was a Sunday and then it was yesterday, Friday. I asked him to come to see me this evening. The last funeral is four o' clock and I said I'd be free from about five. I'm not sure if he'll take me up on my offer, but you're welcome to be here just in case.'

Thanking the man, *call me Jonathan,* for the information, Harvey paid for the items he had in the trolley and drove home. He knew he was too tired to drive to Glasgow and didn't want to involve any of his team on what was, almost certainly, a waste of time, so he took a taxi to the railway station.

Trains from Fordway to Preston were every twenty minutes on a Saturday, and from there the main line trains to Glasgow were every hour. Second class was busy, but Harvey refused to pay the extortionate first-class supplement. He started to regret his frugality when at the next stop, Lancaster, students poured into his carriage like lemmings hurtling en masse to their fate.

'It's reading week and we're all escaping for some mollycoddling at home. Some of us might even open a book!' Harvey smiled at the young man and remembered his first, carefree year at university: so very different to the ones after his mother died.

Jamie, plus large rucksack, iPad and laptop, had crammed into the last vacant seat next to Harvey. During the next couple of hours, the young man barely paused for breath. He was reading chemistry but might change course as he wasn't enjoying the subject; he was the youngest of five children and the only boy. 'I made sure I lived in a house of blokes when I arrived at uni. At home, even the cat was female! Lancaster's got some great nightlife and I'm really enjoying student life.' Wishing he could just admire the delightful scenery, Harvey's contributions to the conversation were some occasional grunts which he hoped he managed to time appropriately.

Glasgow. Saturday afternoon. The usual onslaught: shoppers defying the Chancellor's gloomy talk of austerity; teenagers already inebriated; the pubs busy since lunch time; hen and stag parties under way, the hens teetering on ridiculously high heels and dressed as fairies; raucous Celtic fans rejoicing in their midday victory in the Old Firm encounter with arch-rivals Rangers. The taxi weaved its way through the busy streets, the driver bemoaning the behaviour of people, especially the young. Finding the man's strong Glaswegian accent hard to fathom Harvey was once again in grunt mode.

The Day Thou Gavest Lord Is Ended could be heard clearly, every word distinct. As Harvey approached the chapel he was amused to think that the Scots obviously sang more enthusiastically at funerals than the English. There would be no hymns at his final service. Not wanting to become caught up with the mourners, he retreated to a nearby seat and watched as they exited the building. Jonathan Astley spoke to each member of the deceased's family, and Harvey thought again that his first impression of the minister had been correct: a very decent man doing an excellent job. Lacking any kind of faith himself, he still understood how vital it was to others, and for those mourning a source of great comfort.

As the last car drove away, Jonathan spotted Harvey and invited him in. 'Lovely to see you again, Harvey. I trust you had an easy journey and that I haven't wasted your valuable time. The man I spoke to might not be your man and this could be like trying to catch a snowflake.'

Assuring the minister that any lead needed to be pursued, the two men went into the chapel and sat in a pew near the door. 'The main reason I contacted you was the poor soul's evident desire for absolution. I know you indicated that your man...Harry Whistler? has the same demons. As we both know the appearance of our homeless friends can be deceptive, but this gentleman would seem to be the appropriate age and, as I said, would appear to fit your bloke's description.'

The two men sat and talked, each enjoying the other's company. Jonathan had only trained for the ministry a few years before, having been a merchant seaman for over thirty years. 'I saw the world, or at least many of its ports, most of them not particularly salubrious. The job was enjoyable. I didn't exactly have a Road to Damascus moment, just one stormy morning looking over the sea, which was chopping and churning, it felt as though my life was like that: tossed here and there, with little purpose and even less direction. It was like an awakening and I knew that I wanted, indeed needed, to follow a different path. Serendipity: we were carrying some civilian passengers back to England and one man was returning home after years working as a missionary. We spoke at length and I saw my future.'

'Did you never marry?'

'I was married for ten years to a lovely lady called Moira. At the beginning, she didn't seem to mind that I was away so much. I was devastated when she divorced me, saying that she felt like a single parent, and if we were apart she could be totally independent. I'm fortunate that I see my boys and the grandchildren. I've always regretted the separation, though being absent for months at a time – I worked in the Far East – didn't make for an easy relationship. I never knew whether she preferred me away for most of the year or at home, for weeks on end, interrupting her routine.'

As he completed his story the chapel door was thrown open. Staggering and swearing, laden down with bags and bottles, the man they were waiting for arrived. He wasn't Harry Whistler. Knowing he was in the way, the vagrant needing time with Jonathan, Harvey took his leave. The return journey felt interminable.

The remainder of the weekend was ruined. Relaxation impossible. Harvey was almost relieved when the alarm, on its highest, ear-shattering setting, announced the start of the working week.

'Bloody, stupid waste of time. Pardon my French.' Back in DCI mode, Harvey was in a foul mood. 'Traipsing up to Glasgow on my day off for nothing, absolutely deleted expletive nothing.' Serena was tempted to agree. Fortunately, she didn't give voice to her opinion. Had she been asked, she would have doubted it would be Harry, such good fortune seldom aiding an investigation. It was going to be a long week.

Morning briefing was tense, their leader's attitude affecting all present. Unwilling to confess his weekend's activity, Harvey bawled, like an irate teacher losing his temper with a class of children who had been inattentive. 'In case any of you have forgotten we still have three, yes three, that's as in one more than two, murders to solve, and we can't find our chief suspect. What in the world are you all doing? I want an update from each-and-every one of you on my desk by lunch time. Do not even think of eating until I have your report, and I sincerely hope you all have something to impart. If not, I will want to know why. Now get on with it.'

'Sorry, Serena, I know that's not the way to get the best out of the team, but surely a vagrant can be found. We don't exactly need Interpol's assistance.'

'You have to remember the man was AWOL for almost a decade the first time he made a break for it, and it was only when *he* decided to resurface that anyone knew his whereabouts. He's obviously good at living underneath the radar.' The look on her superior's face told her that she had not been helpful. 'Every officer wants him found. However, as you know only too well, they are all up to their eyes in other tasks. They're checking statements and alibis, and trying to gain further insights into the victims' backgrounds.'

'What? Are any of those as vital as ascertaining the whereabouts of a killer? Maybe if they had their priorities right we'd have Mr Whistler locked up in the cells by now.'

Serena had learnt that when her boss was in a belligerent mood he was best left alone, and she was ready to walk out, stopping by the door when he spoke again. 'The thing that's bugging me is that I know there's a gorilla in the room.'

'Don't you mean an elephant?'

'No nothing that can't be spoken about. The gorilla reference indicates something so obvious one misses it, rather like looking for wood amongst the trees.'

'New to me; explain please.'

'I first became aware of the phenomenon on a training course a couple of years back. The final speaker, one of the better ones on an excruciatingly boring two-day let's-all-pretend-this-is-making-us-better-officers meeting, was reminding us how unreliable eye-witnesses could be. He showed us a short video clip and asked us to concentrate on counting the passes made by one of the two basketball teams. I was pleased with myself. I was sure I'd counted the correct number. Twenty-two passes. When he asked if anyone has spotted anything unusual a few people laughed. He then re-ran the video telling us that this time we were not to watch the players. Half way through the game a man in a gorilla suit appeared at the front of the screen, jumping up and down and being generally silly. Most of us – all experienced officers – had missed the gorilla entirely. We'd have made very poor witnesses.'

'So, you think we are staring at a vital clue and can't see it.'

'Exactly. Though I have no idea quite what we do to make it jump out at us.'

Chapter 27

Harry Whistler had moved on to Manchester. The centre was crowded, thousands of AFC Ajax fans in their bright red replica shirts were enjoying themselves prior to the evening's football match against Manchester City. City fans hoped that the second leg of the Champion's League encounter would be as much of a walk-over as the first had been when the two had met the previous month. City were taking a four-nil lead into the game, as their fans were keen to remind the Dutch visitors.

Determined to stop any trouble before it started, the high alcohol intake likely to fuel trouble, there was a noticeable police presence in Piccadilly Gardens. A constable, who looked as though he should still be at school, was talking earnestly to one of the visiting fans. 'I had a wonderful holiday in Amsterdam last month and was so pleased to visit the newly refurbished Rijksmuseum. Rembrandt was so incredibly good.' The look he received indicated that his listener thought Rembrandt might be the new goalie needed to assist his team's sieve-like defence: twenty goals against them in recent weeks.

There was a time when Harry had been interested in football. His father had done the Pools every week, seldom winning more than a few pounds, but listening avidly as the scores were read out at five o'clock every Saturday. Woe-betide anyone who interrupted the announcer whose voice went up and down depending on the result; away wins causing a rise of several semitones.

It was Harry's first time in Manchester. The weather had so far made a mockery of the city's reputation for rain. Sunny days had given way to cold nights, the lack of cloud cover sending the temperature plummeting. Harry had never minded the cold: it was always possible to stay reasonably warm. Rain was another matter; shelter essential. Once wet it was impossible to sleep, sodden clothes making the wearer wretched.

Manchester felt right. It was possible to lose himself amongst the many homeless. After some initial misgivings, he had soon realised that he could move around incognito, something that felt imperative. This time there had been no planning. A decision of such suddenness had left him surprised. Terry's murder had been the catalyst. He had fled the park, walked to the motorway slip road, accepted a lift from an accommodating lorry driver, and been dropped-off on the outskirts of Manchester.

Sitting, listening to the so-far friendly badinage, passed the time: 'Thought Ajax was a cleaning product – we'll clean you out later'; 'You might as well have a row of tulips as your defenders'; 'Never mind, there are plenty of canals to throw yourselves into when you go home'; were some of the polite comments and Harry found himself smiling. His father had taken him to one match: Preston North End versus Middleborough, a Saturday 3 p.m. kick-off. The legendary Tom Finney had been playing and scored the winning goal three minutes from time. It hadn't made him into a fan, but he had enjoyed the afternoon.

The nights still felt as though they arrived too early, and once the sun disappeared Harry left the city centre and walked the three miles out of town to Platt Fields.

Since arriving in Manchester, several weeks ago, he had spent every night in the park, usually sleeping near the under-fives playground, the noticeboard announcing that the area was for toddlers only, and that any older children should use the playground designated for the "up to nine years" nearby. Judging by some of the vandalised swings this rule had not been followed. Both playgrounds were situated near the large lake where boating and the use of pedalos were advertised. Neither occupation was much in evidence. Harry imagined it must be a different scene in high summer.

On his first evening, he had met Billie, a garrulous gentleman of the road, who had delighted in telling Harry all about the park he had called home for twenty years. 'It's a place of great historical significance,' had been his opening gambit. 'I love history, and feel proud to live in a park that can trace its beginnings back to 1150. It was first known as the "lands of Platt" and was given to the Knights of St John by William, son of William – I guess they didn't have much imagination when choosing Christian names.' By this stage, Harry had found it increasingly difficult to maintain any interest. His new friend was not to be deterred. 'During the winter of 1908 to 1909, over 700 men re-laid the park and made Gore Brook into a lake with an island in the middle, only accessible by boat.' The history lesson had continued for several minutes, very little of it heard. At least Billie had shown no interest in Harry: where he had been or why he was there.

It had been necessary to leave Fordway. Going to Lancaster had been a bad idea, though how the police had known he was there remained a mystery. On his final night in Fordway, he had been sleeping in an outhouse that the park's gardeners sometimes forgot to lock.

The noise of the police cars with their pervasive herald of doom (good news rarely following their raucous racket) had shaken him awake. Fear, such as he rarely experienced, told him that the blues-and-twos arriving at such an early hour meant only one thing: a third body had been discovered. It was the morning after Terry Wendover had accused him of committing the first two murders and he was not going to wait in Elizabeth Park to be arrested.

Twenty years ago, the first time he left Fordway, there had been a great deal of secret planning. For several weeks, he had taken small amounts of money from his account and secreted it in a bag at the back of his wardrobe. Clothes had been placed in a locker at the railway station, along with toiletries and a small suitcase. He had found it surprising how little he wanted to take, or indeed think he would need in his new life. Had he been asked, he would have admitted that he had no idea what he was going to do or where he would be living. All he knew was that he had to leave the town where he had lived all his life. Escaping his family and the comforts of home were vital. He was all too aware that his sin would follow him and he sought only one thing: punishment. That was his aim. How to achieve it he left in God's hands.

Since that fateful evening in May, when he had informed his family that he was "popping out for a minute", he had accepted the chastisement that he knew he deserved. His deity had ordained that he should become homeless. Over the years, the penance had been harsh. That he deserved it was never in doubt. His faith had never wavered. He knew that this time God had meant him to come to Manchester and continue to live amongst societies' outcasts. Would the same God want him to return and confess? If so ordered, was he strong enough to obey such a command?

Had anyone been looking for Harry in Platt Fields they would not have recognised his clean-shaven, short-haired new incarnation. When "all hell had broken out", battalions of police invading Elizabeth Park, dogs straining at their leashes as they apprehended the vagrants, Harry had managed to escape through the woods situated near the south entrance. Over the years, David and Eve had kept him supplied with a small amount of money, some of which he had kept for the proverbial rainy day. Three bodies meant there was a deluge. Hurrying into town he had purchased scissors, shaving foam and razors and had transformed himself in the toilets by the market. People off to work had been too preoccupied to notice a tramp walk into the toilets and a gentleman, dressed for a day in the office, emerge several minutes later. The new coat and trousers his daughter had given him were worn for the first time. Harry Whistler was ready to begin the next act.

Eve

No news of Dad. *I grow more afraid that he is the murderer*: I have never written those nine words before – or not in that exact formation. I almost laughed when they reminded me of Eric Morecambe's famous comment about playing all the right notes, just not necessarily in the right order. Unfortunately, humour is misplaced. The words feel somehow momentous. Crucial. Dad was last seen at the afternoon meeting in the police station, just before the third murder. Why hasn't he been spotted since?

Gossip is flowing, like an uncovered sewer: Harry Whistler is wanted by the police for all three murders;

Harry committed the third one – of Terry Wendover – following the man's accusations at the end of the meeting; someone else killed Charlotte and Tommy; our family know more than they are admitting and will be questioned. Paul Tottering, a lawyer in my firm, and one I've always found it hard to like, suggested that it will be more like formal interviews under caution. He then had the audacity to offer himself in a legal capacity.

Work is, as always, a great panacea, if stressful. Quite often I have great sympathy with my clients though this doesn't excuse their behaviour. This morning I felt both sympathetic and unbelievably exasperated by an adult and how he had behaved. Alan Houghton had never been in trouble until Wednesday night. He assaulted a man in The Last Retreat's car park. At the time, he was so drunk, described as "reeling and rocking", that this morning when I interviewed him he had very little recollection of the event. It had taken over twenty-four hours for him to be sober enough for us to meet.

'I got wasted. Deliberately. Wanted to forget. Cheryl, my partner lost a baby last week and it felt like the final straw. It was the same week that my father was told that his MS had got worse and that he would soon need a full-time carer. It's been me and my sister so far, and with work – I'm away a lot – I can't do much more. Mum buggered off...pardon my language...a few years ago, and it's all down to us.'

I knew that the magistrates would be sympathetic to his situation. However, the fact remained that he had hurt someone badly enough for them to need medical attention.

'Cheryl and I were due to stay at the hotel that night, a sort of look-on-the-bright-side moment but I got a bit obstreperous...Cheryl's word...broke some beer glasses, and the manager said we couldn't stay. I've never done anything like this before. Please tell the judges that.' The fact that he misnamed the people about to hear his case helped me warm to him.

The CPS evidence was irrefutable. There was very clear CCTV footage, both inside at the hotel's reception area and then in the car park. In the first video, my client could be seen attempting to hit the manager, who only avoided the clenched fist by moving aside at the last moment. The car park footage was nasty and made me realise that mitigating circumstances would not be of much help. Sympathy would be for the victim, an elderly man called Brian Coulton. My client had punched the old man, who had asked him if he was fit to drive, to the ground, then kicked him several times once he was down. Both Cheryl and Brian Coulton's wife could be seen trying to reason with Alan and restrain him.

The magistrates took a long time discussing the case. As they returned to the bench Alan was asked to stand. Recording their summation my hands were shaking, a most unusual occurrence as I pride myself on my ability to remain detached. The Chairman was an extremely experienced lady who must be approaching seventy, the compulsory retirement age for JP's. From past dealings with her I knew that she was fair but not afraid to deliver the toughest sentences. She has an excellent speaking voice, one that she had employed for years in the classroom. Many a youth must have quailed in her presence.

'Mr Houghton, you have pleaded guilty to an assault occasioning actual bodily harm. Several facts are undisputed. You were drunk. You attempted to assault the manager of The Last Retreat Hotel. You then assaulted and injured Mr Coulton in the hotel's car park. We have listened carefully to the mitigating circumstances presented by your lawyer and feel sympathy for your family troubles. However, nothing excuses your behaviour in the early hours of that morning. Because of you an elderly and vulnerable member of the public required hospital treatment. You used both your fists, and your shoes which are classified as a weapon. The fact you were in drink, adds to the seriousness of this case. The offence therefore falls into Category Two in the guidelines. We could have put it into the higher category, but took your personal circumstances into consideration, leaving it in the middle section. Had it been placed in the top category you might well now be facing a custodial sentence.

To your credit, you have shown great remorse, and we have noted that this is your first appearance in court. We do not believe that your acts were, in any way, premeditated, but they did display a total lack of self-control. We are therefore ordering a report from the Probation Service with a view to a Community Order.'

Alan was told to remain in the building to see the probation officer who agreed that he was capable of undertaking hours of unpaid work. I think he was more than willing to pay the court costs, the rather impressive fine, and the generous compensation to Mr Coulton. I doubt if we will see Alan Houghton before the bench a second time.

If only my dilemma was as easily solved. Should I go to the police? Or wait for them to ask to see me? It will be one or the other.

Jacob

Once again, no Dad.
David and I have been discussing the events leading up to Dad's first vamoose. Our grandmother, Dad's mum

this time, had lived with us for two years. We no sooner got rid of one grandma than the next one appeared. We joked that they were a bit like buses. Our maternal nan had been a lovely lady. David stopped me saying much about grandma number two as she was ill most of the time she was with us.

Towards the end, the cancer affecting her mind as well as her body, she became extremely confused. Most worrying was her penchant for wandering. She would leave the house (how she unlocked the door remains a mystery: Fort Knox had nothing on Dad's somewhat idiosyncratic system of fortifications) and saunter off down the road, often being returned, like a lost umbrella, by one of the neighbours.

Several times she thought I was Dad. Of all of us I was the one who most resembled him. Not true these days, or I sincerely hope not. 'Ask the doctor for more morphine, Harry. I'd go quicker and that's what I want.' When I repeated this to my father he got very cross and said it was the ramblings of a poorly lady.

'She's a devout Christian and knows that the Good Lord will take her in His own time. No one can read the mind of the Almighty. "The Lord gives, and the Lord takes away." It will be His decision.'

I still think that when He eventually decided that Grandma's time to be taken had arrived it wasn't a second too soon. A spell in the local hospice, a few weeks before the end, helped. She came home with excellent pain relief, but unfortunately by that time her mind had deteriorated, and she could be heard ranting and raving through the night, and much of each day, crying for her husband and family members who had "gone to the glory".' How irritating that such unwelcome phrases have taken up permanent residence, cluttering my mind.

'Let me join you, I'm ready. Come for me, please come and take me home.'

The day she died Eve commented on the silence. We had become almost accustomed to her noise, which sounds callous, but we were young and, I must admit, self-centered. It never entered our heads that one day it might be us enduring such torment.

Following her demise Dad suffered terribly. He had been very close to the old lady and mourned her passing, though as he believed it was to a *better place*, none of us found such extreme anguish easy to understand. As the weeks passed, the funeral over, her body committed to the grave next to her husband's, Dad seemed to sink further and further, like an out of control submarine, to the depths of despair. He grew more and more despondent and started to spend untold hours at church. At home, he was mostly monosyllabic and almost totally unresponsive to any aspect of family life. I realise now that he was suffering from depression, that most horrific of afflictions. Mum tried to get him to see the doctor, but he tore up the appointment slip she handed him. 'I don't need pills. They won't cure this pain.'

When he wasn't weeping, he was slouching in front of the television: the programmes unseen, his eyes staring at the floor. In the week leading up to his exodus (I'm sure he'd approve of the Biblical reference) he seemed to regain some energy. He would leave the house, saying he was going for a walk, and return several hours later. We all assumed he was spending time hiking by the canal, a favourite pastime, or be on his knees in church, and didn't question him. Had we done so I rather think he would have lied to us.

Eve always asks if we should have made more of an effort. Would it have made a difference? The fact is we were young and didn't interfere. He was the adult: in our naivety, we all thought he should be able to help himself. Even David, the son closest to him, made little effort. Something he has regretted. I was always in awe of my father, and if truth be told, presumably what Eve wants, I never liked him. At times, he was not a very pleasant individual: autocratic, belligerent, callous. That's the ABC of him! I could complete the alphabet though that's not necessary. Three words suffice.

Recently my sister used the word lament. She said she has lamented for over twenty years. But how can one lament a loser? That would be my L!!

Andrew

Well, well, well! My dear siblings. Despite my unwillingness to have much input to this silly epistle, I must add my four-pennies' worth today, double the usual value I think you will agree. What news I have! Nothing to do with Jacob's recent ramblings, though I would love to see the A to Z in its entirety.

I know what you all think of me, a namby-pamby little boy who has never grown up. For your information, I started a new job recently. Yes, shows how much you know or care. I quit the library and got the first job I applied for! I am now Assistant Editor of the Out and About section of our local rag. Impressed? I've always known I could write and now I can prove it. An Open University writing course reignited my passion for the written word. None of you will recall that I won first prize in the top-class competition at primary. Mrs McBain said it was the best short story she had ever seen produced by a boy of my age. That was a few weeks before Dad messed with our minds and I lost all desire to commit words to paper. Hard enough to utter them.

Time to get to the point of this unexpected entry. Are you all ready?

Monday morning, bright and early. First assignment: to visit Manchester and report on the less obvious attractions of the city. It's not too far from here, ideal for a day out, especially in the school holidays. My task wasn't to cover the high-profile venues, so not the Arndale Centre or Trafford Park, the main museums and most especially not the tours of The Etihad or Old Trafford, for those brain-dead enough to follow football. No, my remit was to write about locations that are easily accessible and that visitors, new to the city, might not have on their agenda.

Naturally I had googled possibilities before I went, and managed to go to the Greater Manchester Police Museum, Chetham's Library and the Town Hall in the morning.

This is where it gets interesting...keep reading dear trio. After lunch, I caught the number 42 bus and travelled a few miles out of the city. My destination was Platt Fields. Still with me? My reason for going was to see if the Gallery of Costume was worth including in my list of suggestions.

Now it gets exciting! Alighting from the bus, one of many that travel up Oxford Road, I made my way into the delightful park – just practising my article – and...guess who I saw standing in the park's main entrance. Dad! Mr Harry Whistler. The loser himself. It's a cleaned-up version of our dear papa. Hair cut short, beard gone, and tramp trousers replaced with smart ones. I didn't just do a double take but a quadruple one. I don't know who was more shocked, him or me? A short conversation ensued. Not worth repeating, nothing new.

Chapter 28

David

Sorry Andrew, but you must go to the police. They are looking for him and you can't keep such vital information to yourself. You were the one to see him, so it's your responsibility. You claim to have grown up. Now prove it.

Eve

Shall we all go to see Dad and ask him to come back with us? He will need our support.

Jacob

Why? Let the police deal with him. He is not, and I mean NOT, our problem.

Following almost ten months in Fordway, Harvey Tarquin applied for his secondment to become permanent. The previous DCI had taken early retirement.A prolonged bout of ill health had shown no sign of improvement and his doctor had advised him it was time to leave. George Griffith had worked at Fordway for over twenty years and had been a popular boss. A phone call, the previous day, had confirmed Harvey's position as the new DCI.

Telling his team hadn't been easy. The announcement of George's premature retirement was hardly a surprise, but had been greeted with groans and mutterings. 'I know many of you will miss George. We all wish him a long retirement with better health. I sincerely hope that I will prove to be a successful, approachable leader, able to step into the great man's shoes.' He hated such phrases, but the words had escaped like a bird fleeing a cat's open mouth. The looks he received let him know his analogy was at best a paltry size six. He had never felt more inadequate.

During his months in charge at Fordway he hadn't made many friends. He knew he had the necessary attributes to be a successful DCI. He was hard working, with the skill to direct individuals to the tasks that suited their talents, and highly proficient in the interview room. There was one area he was only too aware he needed to develop: empathy for the more recalcitrant officers. He needed to improve his interpersonal skills, to build a rapport with every member of his team. He knew he needed to listen more, be willing to accept their ideas. Charismatic and approachable had been the words used of the previous DCI.

As he left the room, he overheard one of the young PC's mutter, 'Griffith and Tarquin are bloody poles apart. Reminds me of that experiment everyone does in school using a magnet. One end attracts the iron filings and the other end repels them. Need I say more?' The ensuing sniggering rang in his ears. Harvey knew he would have to engage with the men and women in his team, but knowing was one thing, doing it a different matter entirely.

There was one positive. The station was always busy, and he was delighted to be able to boast a high rate of successful outcomes. Whilst in charge of the murder investigations he had proved good at delegating, assigning the appropriate officers to the more mundane cases. If it had been a boxing match the villains of Fordway would have lost on points. The great disappointment was the lack of progress with the murders in the park.

Having delivered the obviously unwelcome news, he began the day's business. With no new developments, the park murders had been put on the we'll-keep-looking-and-hope-something-develops pile. His warning that he only had a short time left to solve the incidents had been rescinded, following an extended, and at times uncomfortable, interview with his boss. Having studied all the available material, the witness statements, interview records, forensic information, pathologists' reports, accounts of trips to Glasgow and Lancaster, Superintendent Grealy had been surprisingly understanding. But he was told only Inspector Peil and a couple of other officers could be spared to pursue the meagre clues that might solve the trio of killings. Every other member of the team was now allocated new work.

Serena interrupted his maudlin thoughts. 'Sir, there's been a phone call. A man of sixty-four has gone missing. He's only been gone a few hours, not normally long enough to raise alarm bells with an adult misper, but he is extremely vulnerable. His daughter is concerned as he has early-onset Alzheimer's. She recently organised a group of live-in carers. Apparently, Edwin York vanished whilst two of the carers were in the kitchen. 8 a.m. this morning and swap over time. Neither of them heard the front door open, or were aware that he had left the house until about 8.15 when Jason, the overnight carer, went through to say goodbye to Mr York. Edwin York has walked out before but has never left the garden.'

'Have we been given a photograph and description of what he was wearing?' PC Clare Jennings was keen to be involved, her great aunt in a local Home with the devastating illness.

'Mr York's daughter is coming in. I'd like you to interview her, Clare, and write a report ASAP.' Harvey knew Clare was one of the people on whom he could rely with such a sensitive case, and giving the extra responsibility seemed appropriate. Within half an hour of the meeting Clare's report had been circulated to the entire team. To make it feel more personal, it was handwritten.

Missing Person: Edwin York.
Vulnerable man, aged 64

Information from the meeting with Mr York's daughter, Sally Brown. 10.30 Tuesday 5th June

Mr York was last seen just before 08:00 in the living room of his house, 64, Ashworth Drive, Fordway, when his night-time carer, Jason Cole, took him his extra cup of tea. Breakfast had been eaten in the kitchen, and the routine had been established that Edwin had a second drink "watching" the news in the lounge.

Mr Cole then went to complete the hand-over sheet with the day-time carer, Shirley Knowles. It was about 08:15 when they realised Mr York had left the property. Edwin doesn't get dressed until he's had his second drink, so must have walked out still wearing his nightwear: pale blue pyjamas, navy dressing gown and brown slippers.

This is the first time that Edwin York has gone missing, though he has, on occasion, been found wandering in the garden (the gate is kept closed). His daughter said that it is a long time since he has been out on his own and she is adamant that he will have no idea where he is. The Alzheimer's has been developing for three years, getting gradually worse, reaching the point where he needs twenty-four-hour supervision.

Mr York has lived in Fordway all his life. The addresses of his two previous homes are recorded below and need to be visited.

- 61, The Orchards, Fordway: the house where he lived as a child
- 127, Broadoaks, Fordway: the large family home where he lived for thirty years before moving to his present address three years ago, following the death of his wife.

It is doubtful whether Edwin could find his way to either of these properties, but they need to be checked. I will go to his present address and make sure he's not anywhere in the house or in any outbuildings, though his daughter said everywhere has been searched. There is a garage which is kept locked, and a large garden shed.

Sergeant Symmons will attend the two former addresses. An item will be broadcast on the local news requesting the public to go to the assistance of Edwin, whose description will be aired.

I have issued the day's foot patrol with a recent photograph of Mr York. They have been asked to spend time in the town centre, both parks and the canal, though as these are a distance from his house his daughter is doubtful that he would be able to walk to any of them. He has some problems with mobility.

Edwin York's son has been informed and is coming from Preston to help with the search.

Satisfied that everything was being done, Harvey concentrated on reading the previous day's reports, not an aspect of management he enjoyed.

Eve

Andrew, have you been to the police? You can't prevaricate. If you don't go, I will. Let me know which you'd prefer. I went to Manchester yesterday. No sign of Dad. There was a man selling *The Big Issue* outside The Arndale Centre and he said there was a new bloke sleeping rough who looked too well dressed, not a typical down and out. However, he wasn't much help, didn't know a name and had never spoken to him. In the evening, I went out to Platt Fields and wandered around until closing time. No luck. None of the other homeless, and there were plenty, had any idea who I was talking about.

Andrew...go tomorrow, or let me know if you'd rather I did. Someone HAS got to let them know.

'Serena, could you come to my office, please.' Harvey didn't know whether the recent phone call would advance their investigation or drive them down another cul-de-sac, one that's hard to exit. Too many weeks had passed without any progress. Three bodies remained in the morgue and demanded justice. Keeping himself busy with the numerous other matters that came his way had done little to improve his mood. Most of his team continued to avoid him.

'Come in and shut the door. I've just had a message from Andrew Whistler. He says he has some important information and is coming to see us at ten.'

'Did he give any indication what this info is?'

'No, just said he needed...that was the word he used...*needed* to see us urgently. He sounded most uncomfortable.'

Andrew

Police visited. Message delivered. Are you all happy now?

David

Stop being so belligerent. At least tell us how they reacted to the information. Which officer did you see?

Andrew

The big chief: DCI Tarquin and his rather gorgeous side-kick – can never remember her name. She's far too attractive to be working for the police. I was rather surprised that there was very little reaction, though I suppose that's their training. They did say they were grateful for the details I furnished (a Deputy Editor's word!) especially about his new appearance. Clever me: I had a couple of photos on my phone which they were extremely keen to copy. *Harry Whistler Vanishes Part Two* might be a best seller. Freedom soon to be curtailed. Poor old Dad.

Jacob

Good on you, Andrew. I didn't think you'd do it. However, you won't like this. Are you all sitting down? Right, I've just looked at the Manchester Evening News online. I think the police may be too late.

Breaking News.

The body of a vagrant has been found in Platt Fields in Manchester. The man's body was seen floating at the edge of the large boating lake in the centre of the popular park. A fellow member of the city's large homeless community has identified him as Barry Lambert. Anyone with any information about the deceased, or anyone who may have witnessed anything unusual in the park last night, is asked to contact the local police station.

Jacob

Now there's a coincidence. Three homeless massacred in Fordway, Harry Whistler Esq. in the vicinity, then another in Manchester…ditto! And my dearest siblings, just in case you're not in *Cluedo* mode, shall I repeat the common factor? Oh, my word! It's our one and only Dad, with or without the dagger in the library. Now which one of us is going to ensure that the local police are aware of this latest episode?

Chapter 29

'Any sign of Edwin York? Two days since he went missing, that means two nights without shelter.' Harvey hated the thought that such a vulnerable man was alone and possibly frightened. He knew the old man would be unable to help himself.

'He may be in a garage or shed somewhere. The house owners could be away, or have had no need to go into their outhouses. We've asked everyone to check, but it would only take one to remain unopened.' Clare Jennings felt personally responsible and wondered whether more could be done. 'The local rag comes out today. There's a large spread on the front page with a recent photo and a plea from his children for people to watch out for him.'

Looking as though she was about to burst into tears, she addressed the team. 'We have to consider where he might be. People like him don't just vanish. He's apparently too confused to be able to plan anything. He must, at the very least, be cold and hungry. I've organised for the sniffer dogs to be used. PC Strong is at Edwin's house getting some clothes for the dogs to work with. I wish I'd done that as soon as he was reported missing.'

Harvey thought that Clare was the most self-critical officer he had ever worked with. A commendable trait until it made her doubt her actions.

Remembering to thank her, Harvey continued. 'Moving on...we've had what might be valuable information about Harry Whistler. His youngest son, Andrew, came to see Serena and me. He told us he'd seen his dad in Manchester. He's still living as a vagrant, but has retained his change of appearance: hair cut short, clean-shaven and well dressed. Andrew told me he spoke to him and that he seemed OK. Nothing was mentioned about Harry's reason for leaving Fordway, or any future-plans he may have. Nothing about a sojourn in Lancaster.'

'Manchester. We might know he's there but trying to find him will be like looking for a grain of sand on Blackpool's beach. Manchester's a heck of a big place and if he doesn't want to be found, and I'm assuming that's the case, then a lot of police time will be wasted.' George Eventide was in his usual negative mode, for him the glass was only ever ten percent full.

Serena glared at the sergeant, a look that could freeze hell, and snapped, 'Thank you for your positivity Sergeant Eventide. Andrew spoke to his father in Platt Fields, a few miles out of the city centre. I've already asked the local police to do a quick sweep of the area. Andrew was very helpful and gave us a copy of a photo he took on his mobile. Apparently, Harry didn't like that at all and fell as he tried to grab the offending article. Andrew said he delighted in leaving him sprawled on the ground.'

'Do some of us need to go to Manchester?' Roger Symmons asked, keen to make progress on the case that was so infuriating it was giving him sleepless nights.

'Indeed. Serena and I will go, and as you are all aware we've been allocated more personnel. I'd like four volunteers to accompany us. As Sergeant Eventide so helpfully reminded us, it is a large city and finding someone who does not want to be found will be difficult. However, we must make a concerted effort. I need not remind you that the man remains our chief suspect in three murders.'

Several hands were raised. Harvey selected the officers who would have the unenviable task of searching for the man they were so keen to interview. Thanking everyone for their continued hard work, Harvey brought the briefing to a close and asked to speak to the day's volunteers.

'Meet in the car park in fifteen minutes; two vehicles have been allocated. We each need a copy of the photo Andrew gave us.'

Serena's howl would have made a wolf proud. Leaping up from her desk she yelled, 'Sir, come and look at this. I've had an email from Jacob Whistler. Cryptic. He suggested I look at yesterday's *Manchester Evening News*.'

The article was open on her computer.

Manchester was continuing to enjoy a spell of good weather, the organisers of the concert in Platt Fields glad they wouldn't have to distribute the waterproofs that were sitting in their boxes behind the recently erected stage. This being the city infamous for its rain they knew they would be of use at some future event. Crowds were starting to gather, most prepared with camping seats, picnic bags and sun cream. Half an hour to the start of the day's music, an eclectic mix of rock, pop and classical. The poster at the gate read *Entertainment for all the Family. Something for everyone. Music to suit all tastes. Money back if you don't find at least one act that has you singing along or your feet tapping.*

Serena smiled, 'I like the irony... it's free entry!' The park was crowded, people there to enjoy an afternoon's entertainment.

'We've as much chance of finding Harry Whistler as I have of being in a good mood.'

'We knew it was a long shot, that he might not be in the park. He could be anywhere in the city...or even have moved on again.'

The local police had been informed that Harry Whistler was a "person of interest", and had been busy. Fordway's officers were dispatched to scour the park, then the streets of the city centre, with the help of some local bobbies. Knowing it was almost certainly a monumental waste of time did not lighten her boss's mood.

Two hours later Harvey and Serena realised they were covering the same paths, meandering aimlessly. Background music ebbed and flowed, a tide driven by a frenetic force, the sounds filling the park. They knew their target had altered his appearance and kept checking the recent photo Jacob had supplied.

Walk a Mile with God and He Will Listen, the base was pounding, the words raucous.

'God is certain to hear that along with the entire population of the North West of England.' Serena's half-hearted attempt at humour raised a brief smile. They stopped and walked towards the crowd, most of whom were on their feet, singing a discordant accompaniment to the gospel rock band. Hands were held aloft, swaying in time to the hectic rhythm.

Serena found herself singing along to the words she knew by heart, an ex-partner fanatical about gospel-rock. 'This is the kind of music Harry might like. If he's here he'll be listening to the religious songs.'

'You walk around clockwise, and I'll go the other way. The crowd is about forty-deep, but I would think he'd stay on the periphery.'

'This is pointless. He could be hiding in plain sight and we wouldn't find him. We'll go into the city then leave it to the local police. The man is a past master at avoiding detection. I don't know why we thought we'd track him down, but I felt we had to try.' Harvey sounded as despondent as he felt.

Chapter 30

Eve

The thought of the homeless man found dead in Manchester is making sleep as elusive as good art work in the recently opened gallery in town. Ten rooms full of pretentious, pointless pieces. I've always believed that if a picture needs an explanation the artist should keep it to himself. Boys, have you read the blurb on the one made up of red and green splodges? "Life as a futile exercise". Was he talking about the painting or the stupid people taking it seriously? Sorry, I digress.

Darcy Williams, the new legal adviser in Preston, asked if I was OK this morning. I know I look awful and feel haunted by Dad. He's like an ever-present phantom, there and not there at the same time. What he might have done is an ever-present nightmare.

My first client today didn't help! I hadn't had the pleasure of her company before, though it wasn't her first appearance in court. She has an impressive list of previous convictions and is well known to our firm. Named Olive Della Dalthwaite by parents who should have known better (her initials must have caused some mirth at school), she swaggered into court on perilously high heels and gave her name in a voice already husky from cigarettes. When asked for her address she looked blank.

'Please will you tell the Court your address.' As the request was repeated she looked at me.

'Where do you live?' I mouthed.

'Oh, 46 Bleasewood Flats,' the word address now understood.

The same happened with "plea". Guilty or not guilty the easier terminology. There are times I despair. An article in the weekend's paper warned that the gene pool is not improving as the better educated are having fewer children whilst the remainder…Ms Dalthwaite has already produced six offspring, at least two already known in the Youth Court, and still has years of possible procreation left. As with so many of my clients she looked a great deal older than her thirty-five years. I sometimes wonder if Darwin was misheard and didn't say "survival of the fittest" but "survival of the thickest".

I was on a loser (judicial terminology) as she was caught outside our local Tesco's with an array of items, no doubt intending to sell them on. The ever-helpful probation service said they were willing to assist and she was given a community penalty to work with them on her problem with alcohol. Call me a pessimist, but I think she'll be back in court within the month. Some people can't be helped. This was one of those occasions when the job is really depressing.

I'm on my own this week which doesn't help. Philip has gone for a week's rock climbing in Scotland. When I got home I looked on the internet, but there was no update on the body in Manchester. Despite a few shaky notes, playing the piano helped. Chopin Preludes: music to console. Mum said ages ago that I can have the Bechstein. It's a family heirloom and a magnificent instru-ment, far superior to my Welmar. Mum rarely plays, and Andrew was the only one who didn't learn, so it's a shame to leave it untouched. I'll suggest we swap. Be good to do something positive.

Andrew

Yes, thanks dear sister. Another of my failings: "the only one who didn't learn". By the time I was old enough Mr Sallenger was the only teacher in the area. I loathed him from the very first "relax your fingers, they look like pokers" lesson. A Venn diagram of our family would relegate me to the empty space outside the impenetrable circles. Andrew doesn't play an instrument; Andrew doesn't garden; Andrew can't play board games; Andrew is the odd one out!

Eve, you didn't look very carefully at the follow-up in today's *Manchester Evening News*. The man they found in Platt Fields died of natural causes. So, nothing to do with our dear father this time. Not murder numero quattro. Is everyone pleased about that?'

Fordway station felt like the K2 basecamp; people frustrated by a lack of progress. The news from the mountain had filled the weekend's headlines, dreadful storms delaying the ascents that were being covered and relayed across the globe. An unprecedented number of British climbers were hoping to set new records. There were so many individuals involved, the hoped-for speed to the summit was growing increasingly unrealistic. The room in the depths of the station lacked energy, and, like the mountaineers, required an input of oxygen.

Harvey had been dreading morning briefing. Recently, the relentless routine experienced every day had been demotivating, and he knew he had to regain momentum, to press the team's accelerator pedal. He was all too aware of the inevitability of the boring, the routine, the time-consuming tedium of so much that his team undertook. It was his job to inspire them, to make them believe again. The cases would break. They had to.

'I have been informed officially that the homeless man discovered last week in Manchester died from a heart attack, so nothing to do with Harry Whistler.' DCI Tarquin didn't know how he felt. It meant that the Manchester police were no longer interested in assisting in the hunt for the elusive vagrant.

'One less crime for us to solve. Can't be too many left before I leave, escape.' George Eventide was counting the weeks and gave anyone who would listen regular updates. 'Any news on the old boy who went walkabout?'

'Edwin York is still missing. Following the short item on *Crimewatch* there were the usual unhelpful calls. He was in Tesco's car park, the library and floating in the canal. That last sighting turned out to be a coat someone had thrown in.'

Clare Jennings almost interrupted her boss. 'His daughter is distraught. She's here every day and wants to know why we can't find an old man with dementia. She remains adamant that he must be in the vicinity. He had no money with him, and she says he hasn't known how to use public transport for about a year. There's no point widening the search, but we need to revisit every shed, garage, outhouse. Apparently, he likes to be inside and retreats to the potting shed in his garden whenever he's taken outside.'

'OK. I'll leave that with you, Clare. All foot patrols to be given an area to search...thoroughly. Give them the instruction to look everywhere a man might hide. My feeling is that he's got himself shut in somewhere and doesn't know how to get out, poor soul.'

'Sir, can we use the dogs again?'

'Expensive…especially as they were employed a few days ago, to no effect. Let's rely on the men on the beat. They know their routes. Please emphasise vigilance.'

Hiding her disappointment, Clare decided to join the constables on the streets. How she would love to be the one to find the missing man. Hopefully still alive.

Chapter 31

Ash Tree Park was deserted, the rain keeping all but the most determined dog walkers indoors. Harry Whistler was glad of the quiet. He had liked Manchester, but it was good to be back home. City life had proved an interesting interlude, a sub-plot in the story. He knew it was only a matter of time before the police apprehended him, and he reasoned that he was merely delaying the inevitable: coming back deemed the best option. If only he hadn't…

Arriving in Fordway in the early evening he had gone straight to the allotments on Aldwin Road, the many plots kept in mostly pristine condition. The one he was interested in was in a far corner, isolated from its neighbour by a fence, the gate in the middle newly painted, a rather garish red, to match the shed's door. Shed was a euphemism for what was a home from home. Net curtains were hung at the window, a table and chair placed underneath. A folding *Campingaz* stove sat beside an array of crockery and cutlery. This was the nearest Harry got to comfort and he used it sparingly.

Walking up to allotment number twenty-three, Harry retrieved the key to the shed from its rather prosaic hiding place: under the second plant pot to the left of the door. He knew that Jacob was a creature of habit, that the key would be secreted there forever. Placing the key in the lock, he was surprised to find he didn't need it. As he pushed the door open the smell hit him. When the shed hadn't been used for a few days it became musty, like the sets of old comics he had once discovered in a cardboard box in his basement, the previous owners forgetting they were there. This was different. A malodorous stink: decay and putrefaction assaulted his nose, the odour making him gag. As his eyes grew accustomed to the gloom he saw the cause of the stench. A body, or what had once been one, the skin bursting open revealing muscle and fat, was facing him.

It was the face that made Harry recoil, the bones visible through the flesh. Numerous questions cavorted like an out of control horse across his brain; neurotransmitters in overdrive. Had he seen the man before? Why was he sitting here, dead, in his son's shed? Why was he wearing night clothes? Who was responsible? How had he died? Did Jacob know? He hadn't visited the shed for some time and wondered why he had chosen to return. How long the man had been there?

Stumbling backwards he retreated outside, glad of some fresh air. Panic ruled, the key remained in the lock, the door stood open. His hands were trembling, and he knew he was about to be sick. Number twenty-three was the final allotment before the scrub land, recently awarded planning permission for over four dozen new builds. Leaning over the fence that separated the allotments and the soon to be *Houses for the Discerning: two, three and four-bedroom properties available in the autumn*, he ejected his egg sandwich and half litre of cider.

Jacob knew that his father slept in his chalet (he never called it a shed, far too plebeian), and was appalled. An infrequent event, he managed to deal with the empty bottles and use of the exterior as a toilet. It was nearly two decades since he had begun to grow fruit, vegetables, and his favourites, a wide variety of flowers in the space where he felt most at peace. The down-payment for the allotment had come from the money left to him by his maternal grandmother. At the time, his father had been scathing. 'You're throwing your inheritance away on what? Gardening! Flowers? My son the pansy!' He recalled his father's attempt at humour. The scorn had been nothing new.

'At least I don't spend my time on my knees talking to the ether, or rather moaning and wailing to some unseen and absent force.'

'Sir, he's been found. Edwin York. A woman went to work on her allotment early this morning, one of the ones on the outskirts of town, and went into the shed next door to borrow some shears. She has an agreement with the owner and they share equipment. The door was ajar, and when she looked inside she discovered the body. To say the least she is extremely upset. SOCO have been alerted and will meet us there.' Clare Jennings was finding it hard to hold back the tears. In charge of the case from the beginning, she had retained some hope of a happy ending. Her next job was to inform the daughter. Then attend the post-mortem.

The *Crime Scene: Do not enter* was already in place at the entrance to the allotments, with a constable standing guard. Signing the crime scene entry log, Harvey walked the quarter mile to the final plot. A large tent surrounded the shed, the appalling odour permeating the thin canvas. Stepping inside he smelt death's familiar perfume. Not one found in the shops.

Dr Rosie Culkin arrived five minutes later. 'Oh, my goodness. How awful, the poor, poor man. Is this the case they covered on the television, the elderly man who disappeared from his front room?'

Agreeing that they had indeed found the missing person, the DCI asked for the death to be confirmed, and for an estimation of when the final goodbye happened.

'Time of death 10:31. From the state of the body I'd say we're talking weeks not days. Nails and skin have loosened, and the insects are enjoying themselves.'

'So, soon after he walked out of his house. Why in the name of all that's holy wasn't he discovered before now?'

Her job done, the GP left Harvey with the horrific discovery.

A length of rope had been tied around the dead man's neck. Close by there was a large ball of the same material, popping out of packaging that read Kingfisher Heavy Duty Jute Twine.

'Whoever did this used the first thing that came to hand. Makes me wonder if this murder wasn't premeditated.' Harvey was thinking aloud and added, 'You could say the same about the ones in the park, all strangled with their own scarves. No need to carry a weapon when what you need is right there.'

Photographs taken, evidence removed, the body was placed gently, and with the usual respect, in the bag ready for its transportation to the mortuary. As he followed the attendants down the communal path, he noticed an allotment that had obviously been abandoned in a hurry, the gardener no doubt leaving as soon as he was asked. A spade stood to attention, a flat cap placed enigmatically on the handle. Harvey smiled, almost expecting the cap to be doffed.

Alfie Morrison was waiting at the entrance to the morgue. Most of the population would regard it as the grimmest of workplaces. For Alfie, it was his showground, the place where he became the ringmaster, in charge of the circus that followed any unexpected death. Already dressed in his protective clothing, he led Harvey and Clare Jennings into the dissecting room, a stench of chemicals making the newcomers gag. A tall man, the pathologist stooped to avoid the powerful lights, positioned to illuminate the proceedings.

Turning to the young constable, he grinned. 'Not your first post-mortem I hope.'

Murmuring that she had already attended two, Clare added that this one would be hard as she had been heavily involved in the case, and was bitterly disappointed that Edwin York had not been found in time.

'If it's any comfort, I would think that he was probably dead by the time you became involved.'

Turning his full attention to the man on the table he donned gloves, mask and goggles, giving him the appearance of an escapee from an X rated film: what he was about to do seldom shown on the big screen. Standing by the deceased he contemplated the body, then made the sign of the cross.

Speaking into the microphone that recorded his findings, Alfie began. 'Good morning Mr York. You remind me of Peter Beardsley, same shape of face. He was a wonderful striker and a gentleman, and I have a feeling you belonged in that category. I'm very pleased to meet you, though not here, and definitely not in these circumstances. So, sorry, my dear man. You were murdered. Now who would do that to a man like you?'

Moving forward to survey the body more closely, he continued, 'My assistants are just going to take some photos of you in your night clothes, and then once you're undressed they'll take a few more. Hope you don't mind, but we need to find out how you met your end and one small detail could be vital, so everything must be on record.' The pathologist's voice was a calm backdrop to the assault about to be undertaken.

Harvey was always impressed by Alfie's ability to connect with each corpse. Some pathologists he'd worked with treated a corpse as a puzzle to be solved, devoid of humanity. Alfie Morrison dealt with each one as they had been in life: an individual, worthy of respect.

'What did you like doing, my new friend? Walking? Fishing? Solving crossword puzzles? Or was there a time you were keen on football? I expect so with your resemblance to Mr Beardsley. Did you stand on the terrace with your dad and yell as your beloved team scored a goal, or berate the ref for an appalling decision? You should have been with me on the Kop last weekend: it was never a penalty! Though maybe you were a Spurs supporter and then you'd have sworn the official got it right,' adding as an aside, 'though even the most die-hard Liverpool fan would have said they deserved to lose as they only had a skeleton defence on Saturday!'

Having seldom heard the man employ black humour, Harvey was unsure how to respond and said nothing.

The twine around the deceased's neck was left in situ until his clothes had been removed. Once the man was undressed, Alfie began to undo the knots, the twine refusing to yield. Using tweezers, and much patience, the knots surrendered, their deathly task complete.

'I know it's obvious, but I'll say it for the record: death due to ligature strangulation. Mr York was killed after heavy-duty twine was tied tightly around his neck. Asphyxiation is another way of putting it.'

The PM continued, the pathologist thorough as always. He sounded almost up-beat, as he maintained a one-sided conversation with the deceased. Harvey was surprised when Alfie's tone changed. 'By all that's holy, what have we here? Have a look, Chief Inspector.'

Harvey stepped forward, something he usually tried to avoid. A small gold cross nestled at the back of Edwin York's mouth.

'It looks the same as the others. We've visited every shop within a twenty-five-mile radius that sells such items. Many man hours have been spent going as far south as Manchester and as far north as Kendal. There was a jeweller in one of the outlets in Bolton who was sure he'd once stocked something similar, but that was as close as we got. The internet looked hopeful, but the crosses they advertised were much bigger.

Chapter 32

Needing fresh air, they walked along the road discussing the case, Harvey doing most of the talking. 'Another killing; another strangulation.'

Clare was feeling ill, the smells and sights of the autopsy room lingering, her body requiring the attention of a power shower. 'You can't think this has anything to do with the homeless murders. Edwin York had gone missing, but no one could have mistaken him for one of the vagrants.'

'I don't see how we can avoid linking this to the events in Elizabeth Park. Despite the difference in choice of victim, it is one heck of a coincidence. Yet another person has had their life ended by strangulation and a cross inserted in their mouth. However, the first thing I want answered is why he wasn't found earlier. We need to know who owns that allotment and whether it was searched. Alfie Morrison said that death occurred at least three weeks ago, in other words, around the time Edwin York went AWOL. If the body was there that long someone must have known about it.'

Mozart's ringtone interrupted them. Expecting the call to be police business Harvey answered curtly and was surprised to hear, 'Harvey, so sorry to contact you at work, but it's your dad. He's had a fall and is in hospital.'

Recognising the voice, Harvey felt irritated. The woman was paid enough, the agency charging above the normal rate, an expense he and his brothers had felt was necessary as their father deteriorated: day and night visits now essential. Controlling his temper, he asked how seriously his father was hurt.

'A broken leg and bruised ribs. They think he'll be in for some time. The trouble is it's made him even more confused. He keeps asking for your mum and I don't think he knows where he is.'

Saying he needed to deal with the call, he informed the young constable that he would see her back at the station. A trip home seemed inevitable. He hadn't seen his dad for many months: too many. The last time had been in late February, an unseasonably bright winter's day. A day out had been planned. He had been surprised when the old man had been unable to open the car door or understand the workings of the seat belt. As they had turned out of their drive onto the main road his father had hit the dashboard, like a driving instructor indicating an emergency stop.

'Where are my keys? My keys, I can't find them. Stop the car. NOW.' The outing had not improved, the elderly mind unable to cope with choice: the selection of a drink and cake creating panic and more shouting. Harvey had been devastated that his father was all too aware of his brain's deterioration. 'What's happening to me? I can't join up the dots anymore. Nothing makes any sense.' The doctor assured Harvey that, though sad, most individuals became calmer and more accepting as the illness progressed.

'The moments of lucidity are fewer and the person becomes unaware of their shortcomings. Probably better for them, if not the family who have to watch the decline.'

Harvey wondered how much his father would know of this latest episode.

Train journeys can be pleasant: time to day-dream as the scenery floats past, or lose oneself in the book one has kept for just such an occasion. They can also be interminable: long-winded and boring. Harvey's trip home fell into the latter category. A journey that on the timetable promised just under three hours took four and a half: delays, draughty platforms and bad-tempered children made him want to scream. The situation was not helped by the knowledge that there was nothing to look forward to once he arrived.

Zoe Peatman was waiting for him at Oxford station. The usual pleasantries dispensed with, the carer said she would take Harvey straight to the John Radcliffe Hospital. 'Your dad's not in any pain, but he is extremely confused: thinks he's in a hotel, but complains about the bed, the food and the staff!'

'Nothing new then? Every time I phone it's a list of grumbles. He didn't used to be like that and I always feel so sorry that his life has become such a burden. He doesn't seem to find any pleasure in anything.'

'He still enjoys his food and we go out for lunch a couple of times each week. I have to choose from the menu, but he invariably clears his plate.'

Three days later, twice-daily visits to the hospital endured, doctors consulted, and residential Homes visited, it was decided that his father would be better off moving into the Lily Bank Nursing Home, the one recommended by Doctor Barchester as being ideally equipped to cope with his father's needs.

Contacting his brothers, he wondered what their reaction would be, their father having pleaded with them all not to "put him away in one of those god-forsaken institutions". Surprisingly, they both agreed it was for the best, and even thanked him for making all the arrangements.

Needing to clear his head, Harvey went for a walk beside the town's canal. Phoning Serena he asked for any updates. What he heard had him almost dancing along the path, making two ducks who had been sitting on a grassy bank take flight.

'I need to go away more often. I'll be back in a few hours and will let you know when you can expect me.'

Chapter 33

The Incident room was buzzing, animated in a way that had been absent for weeks. A round of applause greeted Harvey as he walked in. He knew he was the one who should be acknowledging his team's progress.

'Good evening, and thanks for staying.'

'No way we were going to miss seeing your face when we tell you what's been happening.' Even Mr Gloomy, alias George Eventide, sounded up-beat.

'Do you want the good or the very good news?' Serena hadn't been able to relax with her boss for weeks, but this evening some levity felt appropriate.

'How about the good, then we can up the ante.'

Serena was enjoying herself. 'SOCO found a glove in the shed after Mr York's body was removed. A most distinctive item and not one that his daughter recognised. She said he never wore gloves, never had, even in the coldest weather. It's woollen, and although it's adult size, it has a picture of a giraffe on it.'

Grinning like an overexcited toddler, Harvey said, 'Now where have we seen one like that before? Wasn't it a certain gentleman wearing a pair of what we all said looked like children's mittens to our soiree?'

'Indeed, he was, sir. I remember commenting on how out of place they looked on an adult, though they were very thick wool, and you said he probably wouldn't be bothered what they looked like as-long-as they kept him warm.'

'Thanks for the fashion update Inspector Peil.'

'Sir, the next bit follows on. It is… to say the least… unexpected. About half an hour after you left the mortuary Alfie Morrison rang and asked to speak to you. When I explained that you had been called away on a family matter he gave me the news…somewhat reluctantly.'

Harvey was aware that the atmosphere in the room had changed and wondered what was coming.

'It wasn't murder. Edwin York died of natural causes: a massive heart attack. The strangling took place post-mortem. He said he only discovered it once you'd gone.'

Unsure how to react to this unexpected development, Harvey gazed around the room. Time to deal with that particular nugget of information later. Turning back to Serena he muttered, 'You said there was more good news.'

'Yes indeed, really great news.' Hands created a dramatic drum roll heralding the information that all, except their boss, already knew. Every eye was on the inspector as she recounted the story. 'You remember that the Barrington trustees installed CCTV cameras at strategic points around Elizabeth Park soon after the third murder. Well, when we were given the updated picture of Harry Whistler, minus beard, shaggy hairdo and tramp's clothes, Clare Jennings had the bright idea of taking a copy to the people who view the park's footage, asking them to look for him. And bingo! Yesterday we received a phone call to say that Harry Whistler was on film entering the park. He was located this morning, sleeping behind the Victorian café.'

Harvey wanted to jump up and down, a personification of the pogo stick he had loved as a child. Instead, he thumped the nearest table, upsetting a half-drunk cup of cold coffee, and yelled, 'We've got him, we've bloody well got him.'

'He was picked up just after dawn, has been cautioned and informed of his rights. As it's a murder inquiry I've managed to extend the period we can keep him in. Plenty of time to conduct the interviews and then charge him.'

'Has he asked for a solicitor?'

'No.' Several muffled sounds made their boss realise he'd asked an amusing question.

Serena managed to keep her laughter under control. 'When I informed him that he was entitled to the services of a lawyer his language became very basic. He's obviously well versed in Anglo Saxon, and I rather think the good people of Fordway heard every word. To precis: he doesn't need a deleted expletive lawyer, so we can all disappear up a certain part of our anatomies!'

'So, no representation.'

'Not quite, DCI Tarquin. No, not quite.'

Eve

How ironic. How ludicrous. Why did it have to be me on duty today? I'd spent the morning with a selection of the town's villains, then had lunch in the canteen sharing a few stories of life as a duty solicitor with Shona Carpenter, our young trainee whom I'm mentoring. As there was no one else was in the cells needing to see me, I was hoping to return to the office and catch up on some paper work.

Serena Peil arrived just as we were getting ready to leave. She said she needed to speak to me alone, and I said I'd catch up with Shona back at the office. To say Serena looked sheepish would do a disservice to any member of the breed. I've seen her at work before and she always looks the part: totally professional. Today's outfit of dark grey suit, red blouse, silver earrings and extremely high heels, the kind I love to look at but can't wear for more than a few minutes, was particularly stylish.

Her demeanor didn't match her looks. Small talk was obviously not on the menu and she launched straight in, a drone finding its target.

'We've just arrested your father on suspicion of murder.' Not waiting for any response, just as well as I had been rendered speechless, she continued. 'He said he doesn't want, or need, representation. However, as I knew you were in the building, I thought you might want to see him.'

The general advice is not to represent a member of one's own family. Nevertheless, there was no way I was leaving until I had talked to him. Serena had, quite rightly, not given me any more information. I knew enough: Dad was in the cells; Dad was suspected of three murders; the police were building a case against him.

We met in the interview room. I was shaking. He looked belligerent. As he walked in he told me to leave, not his exact words, but that was the gist, that I was wasting my precious time and I couldn't expect any payment. 'I haven't done anything wrong, so I don't need you or any other stuck-up lawyer. And I know you're here to gloat. Harry Whistler incarcerated...it's about time I paid for my sins.'

I've spoken to the boys. Will my brothers always retain that youthful designation? They were all adamant that I am the last person who should represent Dad. Rather sad that each one of them assumed that he will need a lawyer. Do they think he is capable of murder? I've got a meeting with the DCI in the morning and will know more then.

Jacob

Dad is in the cells!

Mum is the only one who never contributes to this epic. It would be interesting to have some input from her, to hear her voice occasionally and now is surely the time. For years, she's been like an actor on television, the kind who walk on, thrust a paper at a doctor to be signed, and don't utter a word. I gather they are known as "background cast members" and are not permitted to say more than thirteen words in any scene or they become contracted. Mum's contract ended the moment he walked out. When he lived with us I never remember her disagreeing with Dad, or standing up to his self-serving religiosity. His form of Christianity had more in common with the Old Testament, overflowing with a vengeful Yahweh, always looking to see which of the Ten Commandments had been broken; punishment inevitable. And I seem to remember that the loving, forgiving deity Jesus revealed was conspicuous by His absence.

What is Mum thinking?

Will she say if she thinks Dad is guilty? Probably not: how can one say that of one's husband, though he hasn't been that for many years. She never really resurfaced after Dad went. Had she spent too many years bending to his will, no deviation from the long-distance straight and narrow, the only path leading directly to the next world? Her life now consists of looking after Andrew, who really ought to grow up and move on, with the occasional foray outside the house: coffee with Mary, or the cinema with Joan.

Over the years, we've all tried to help. Counselling sessions were organised. She attended one and declared it a waste of time. Several holidays with Eve were a disaster – Mum coming home early, concerned that Andrew couldn't cope on his own. Offers of day trips were invariably rejected, and the occasional meals out, usually at David's restaurants, were almost always a trial.

Soon after Dad vamoosed, once the shock of his departure was easing, David and I agreed that Mum was better off without him. We were sure that she would emerge from the experience and make a new life, one that she controlled. It never happened. Never. Come on Mum, time to take a stance.

Mum

I *am* going to write. Not about me. You are all good enough at telling me what I should do, say and think. No, it was the local news that's forced me to speak. You've all seen that the body of the old man who disappeared a few weeks ago, has been found…in a shed on the allotments. It was discovered in Jacob's! He arrived yesterday evening to tell me. I knew that Harry stayed there sometimes. Jacob left the key in the same spot, knowing his father would use it to gain access. Jacob thought he only slept there occasionally and didn't seem to mind. The lad is far fonder of his Dad than he admits, and it was a kind thing to do.

I will say this once: Harry was many things, and a difficult man to live with, but he is no murderer.

DCI Harvey Tarquin was enjoying the morning's briefing, a feeling he hadn't experienced for many weeks. He could almost touch the sense of progress that filled the room. He was reminded of the moments when one number, placed correctly in a Sudoku, starts to solve the puzzle. Much as he was addicted to the brainteasers, he hadn't settled to one for several weeks.

The reassembled team looked energised, keen to begin the day's tasks. All other incidents, the overnighters in for a variety of minor misdemeanours, were to be dealt with by the officers in the room on the lower floor, the one with the nickname BOB: bloody obvious and boring, the routine investigations that still needed to be investigated.

'Good morning to you all. I trust you slept well as we are going to be working long days. I do hope you left photos with your nearest and dearest to remind them who you are.' Not having heard the boss attempt humour, most of the team were unsure how to react, the muted laughter failing to fill the room.

'Inspector Peil and I will be interviewing Harry Whistler this morning. Even though he is adamant he doesn't require a lawyer, his daughter has asked to be present. Acting for a family member may not be the best practice, but is perfectly legal. Apparently, providing she serves her father honestly and competently there is nothing to stop her representing him. The fact he doesn't want her is another matter, though once we start to build the evidence against him he might change his mind.'

'The three dead in the park were all known to him, but are we also including Edwin York?' Clare Jennings asked, still obsessed by the old man's death. 'We know the strangling was after he died. Did someone want us to link it to the others? And we don't know...'

Interrupting her, Harvey said, 'Today we'll be concentrating on the part he played in the demise of the homeless.'

The remainder of the briefing was taken up with a variety of tasks being divvied up. Every witness was to be re-interviewed, groans from those assigned to the town's rough sleepers. All family members were to be spoken to in the hope that something new might surface. George Eventide and Roger Symmons were asked to review the autopsy reports and look again at the evidence bags. Photos from the crime scenes would need to be closely scrutinised.

'We need to start from the very beginning. Look at everything as though you're seeing it for the first time. We need sufficient evidence for the CPS. They won't take this to court unless we have a strong, indeed a compelling case.'

'Not trying to be funny, but won't someone have to interview Eve Whistler? If we're talking to all family members we can't leave her out.' Roger Symmons glanced around for support.

For the first time that morning the DCI looked uncomfortable. 'Indeed. Serena and I will do that.' It wasn't something he was looking forward to. The conflict of interest all too obvious.

Eve

I dressed smartly, took ages over my hair and make-up, ate a reasonable breakfast, and told Philip I hoped he'd have a good day. He has been amazing, saying all the right things, even if I found some of them hard to believe. I was in control.

What a fool! As soon as I walked into the station, expecting to spend time with Dad, I was shown into the interview room. To my horror, no X rated film has anything on the next hour, it was me who was being interrogated. That is the appropriate word; no good cop/bad cop routine. Both were on the offensive.

Explaining that they were "talking" to everyone involved with the town's homeless did little to allay my fears. No allowance was made for the fact that I will be my father's lawyer, whether he wants it or not. Reminding them of that did little to stop the barrage of questions. At one point, I felt like a boxer who wonders whether to stay down, or get up and wait for the killer punch. They are obviously of the opinion that over the years, and especially recently, I have had far more contact with Dad than I am admitting...and that I know something. Do they think he confessed to me? Do they think that I believe him to be guilty? In which case I wouldn't be allowed to act as his defence lawyer.

Serena, in full interview mode, sitting straight-backed, no hint of a smile and wearing another "I'm-a-professional" outfit, asked about the comment Dad had made the first time they saw him. It was the one that threw me when she mentioned it at yoga. I was more prepared this time and said that I had no idea what he meant. From the look she gave her boss, I don't think she believed me. Lying to the police isn't a good start, but there was absolutely no way I was going down that particular path, the one with the sign post with neon letters saying, "This way to jail".

After what felt like an eternity I was taken to see Dad. Despite his recent clean up I had never seen him look worse. Haggard is the word that springs to mind. He was an appalling shade of grey, and stumbled into the bleak room set aside for clients to meet their lawyers. He refused to sit, saying that he wasn't staying, that he had merely come to tell me to get lost, the words employed slightly better than the ones he used yesterday. I tried to make him see sense, that he would need legal advice. His only other comment was that as he is an innocent man there will be no need for a trial, and so my services will not be required. However, I *will* be there any time he's interviewed.

Following that totally frustrating meeting I asked DCI Tarquin to keep me informed. For once, the rest of the day dealing with my usual reprobates felt like an unexpected holiday.

Chapter 34

Interviewing Harry Whistler reminded Harvey of a training course he had attended as a young officer. The idea had been to provide the interviewer with a variety of strategies. The course had been entitled "Asking the Right Questions". Sheets of information had been distributed. At the top of the first page there was a statement, written in bold. **"In school, it's all about how well you answer the questions: in the interview room, it's all about the quality of the questions you ask."** The lively tutor, a woman nearing retirement age, who wore the same brown suit to every session, had seen and done it all. She said that one of the most important attributes a policeman could have was patience. Most interviews lasted far longer than expected and, if care wasn't taken, the accused could end up in charge.

It was only when Harvey became the senior officer asking the questions that he appreciated her main piece of advice: 'Never let them see they've riled you. If that happens stop, and reconvene later. Keep a serene expression on your face and reword questions, as many times as you deem necessary.' It had been an excellent course – not true of most he had been forced to attend – and Harvey recalled the role-plays; each new-recruit asked to act the part of a villain or an interrogator. Although it was many years since he had sat in those inspirational sessions, he had learnt very quickly how irritating silence could be. Today, facing the mute Mr Whistler, he had reworded every single question, and had then fantasised about punching, yelling and throwing him through the window. Reactions not advocated on the course! He had no idea whether he had managed to maintain the serene expression suggested by the woman, whose name he could no longer recall. Probably not.

Half an hour of silence had been followed by *no comment*, then a further ninety minutes of *no bloody comment*. It was only when the second victim, Charlotte Carroway, had been mentioned that Harry Whistler had shown any emotion. No words had been forthcoming. Harry had sat and wept.

'Well that was a monumental waste of time. His daughter was no use, though I believe he refused to see her beforehand. She doesn't strike me as the kind to advise her client to go down the non-answering route.'

Serena was as frustrated as her boss. 'At least she is now aware that we have quite a bit of evidence against her father: he didn't deny being in the park on each occasion; he knew all the victims; had fallen out with Terry Wendover; he is a religious man and there were crosses in the victims' mouths. The three homeless were all at some point his friends, and the first two bodies were treated with great respect.'

'But not the third, and the modus operandi is definitely different with number three: Mr Wendover's body was incinerated!'

'As you said sir, they'd had had a falling out. Perhaps that one was more like revenge.'

'What really worries me is that Edwin York was almost certainly killed by the same perpetrator, and I can't see any connection to Mr Whistler.'

'Apart from the giraffe gloves.'

'We'll begin again tomorrow. I asked Miss Whistler to be here for nine.'

David

Eve called after tea, in a bit of a state. She was upset because they seem to have more evidence against Dad than she was expecting. She said the interview was horrendous. Dad refused to speak to her beforehand, so she couldn't advise him, and he spent the entire time staring at the floor and refusing to answer any questions. Apparently, he still gets upset when the girl's name, Caroline? Charlotte? is mentioned.

I have a horrible feeling Eve suspects he may be guilty. When I suggested that she might not be the best person to represent him she burst into tears, and said she wasn't giving up. It's not a case of that. Pragmatism is needed, not something that I think she can manage in the circumstances. She got even more upset when I reiterated my view that he might... I may have said would...be better served with a different lawyer: one who has less emotional involvement.

Jacob

Typical David. The rest of us *say* things; he *reiterates*! But...how truly delightful. Dad is guilty after all.

Eve

If that is the best you can do Jacob, don't bother.

The police station in Fordway had been built in the 1960s, and was a prime example of Prince Charles's description of modern buildings as being *monstrous carbuncles*. At the time, a joke in the local paper said that no one would admit to having designed the ugly building; it had merely been constructed by a builder who had over-ordered a consignment of concrete blocks. Over the years, it had gained the nickname of the *Crime Cuboid Centre*, and familiarity had not endeared it to the locals.

Some effort had been made to improve the interior. A new entrance appeared almost too welcoming, and negative comments had been made about some of the more recent colour schemes. Rooms had been decorated in pastels, an attempt to put the innocents reporting crimes at their ease. Two specially designed rooms, used for sensitive issues, such as domestic violence, rape, harassment or stalking, had won awards and other stations had copied the décor.

The twelve cells, where the accused could be held before questioning, or whilst they waited to be taken to the magistrates' court, were below ground. They were as grim as the day they were installed. No daylight relieved the hours the accused spent, either in solitary splendour, or, for the unlucky few, sharing the drab cells, enjoying the company of another defendant. Each cell boasted a bed, an extra one added when needed, an open-topped toilet and a small wash basin.

Most of those incarcerated felt that sharing was not desirable. Unfortunately, it had proved necessary for last night's guests, following the arrest of a dozen young men involved in a drunken brawl.

'Room service.' Rick Jones rattled the keys as he opened the cell door. 'You were the lucky one last night Mr Whistler, an en suite all to yourself. Everybody else was doubled up.'

'Don't I bloody know it. Didn't get a wink of sleep. Talking, singing, arguing all night. Worse than being on the streets, at least we respect each other's privacy.'

Leaving the breakfast tray, Rick locked the door.

Harvey hadn't slept. Up in the early hours, a cup of tea of little help. Before seven he was driving to Fordway, thinking that now his promotion was permanent he should move closer to work. Houses in the town centre were well within his price range, but he would look for a quieter location, one where he could adopt a couple of cats.

Realising he was too early, he decided to park at the station and walk by the canal. As he strode along, his arms swinging as if to a rousing march tune, he thought about all the people who had once worked on the waterway. It had been built in 1772 as an essential form of transport, for both raw materials and finished goods. Today, only 42 miles was still navigable, and it was pleasure boats, not cargo carriers, that traversed it. A long boat was going in the opposite direction, and Harvey exchanged waves and greetings with the man fortunate to be enjoying a day's leisure.

Lowering skies and intermittent drizzle did little to dampen his spirits. Nevertheless, the euphoria of Harry Whistler's arrest seemed like a distant dream. Returning to the station, he was surprised to find Serena already at work.

'Good morning, sir. Is it still trying to rain? People are funny with their umbrellas. Some put them up at the first sign of moisture, then realise they don't need them when there's no downpour. When I walked here this morning it looked like the dance of the brollies ...up, down, up, down...and so many different styles and colours. Mine is a Christmas present from my mother. It's got bees and butterflies on it!'

Realising that there were far more serious issues to discuss, Serena asked how her boss how he envisaged the day going.

'We need a new approach with our friend. He's too good at staying quiet. Let's start by warning him that these days "no comment", or not responding at all, is not in a defendant's best interests. A judge, and indeed the jury, may view such reticence adversely, and it may prove harmful to his defence.'

'Probably a good idea to say that to his daughter before we start.'

'I'm sure *she's* aware of how it comes across, but I doubt she's having much influence on the old man.'

The old man was brought swearing and cursing into the interview room. Eve walked behind him, looking as though she was the one under investigation. The two had spent some time together, Harry agreeing finally to talk to her. His appearance hadn't improved. In his mid-sixties, she thought he could easily be mistaken for someone two decades older. Despite the lack of beard and shaggy hairstyle he looked unkempt, and she wondered if he had taken advantage of the shower that would have been offered. She remembered that her grandfather had aged almost overnight, and had then suffered a fatal heart attack a week later.

The room chosen for the interview was in the bowels of the building, devoid, like all those underground, of natural light. It was not designed to put anyone at their ease, and even officers had been known to comment that they felt uncomfortable there. A rectangular table stood centre stage, the four chairs placed in twos opposite each other. Writing paper, pens and a large tape recorder filled most of the table's surface. The two-metre long fluorescent light would have awoken Sleeping Beauty: the kiss redundant.

'Interview with Mr Harry Whistler, 9.30 a.m. 30th May. Those present: Mr Whistler, his solicitor, Miss Eve Whistler, DCI Tarquin and DI Peil.'

'You can stop the tape right there. 9.31 a.m. Don't waste your time or your breath. I am not answering any of your bloody stupid questions. I will say just one thing. I did not kill any of my friends in the park. I'd know if I'd done it. I drink, but I've never taken drugs. Terry tried to get me involved, said it was like being on a rocket, leaving the earth's atmosphere. Never appealed. When I drink, I remain in control, and I am a hundred per cent certain that I am not the person you are looking for.'

It was the longest speech Harry had delivered, and was followed by a brief silence.

'Mr Whistler, when you were first arrested you said you were glad. You said you were guilty of murder and needed to be punished.'

'Not by you, DCI Tarquin. Yes, I broke the sixth commandment; I have had my first punishment: living on the streets. Whilst that was the case there was no need for anyone else to be involved. It was between me and God. The Good Lord now wants me to receive a different chastisement, one decreed by a judge and jury. Your accusations lack credence. However, a jury will, almost certainly, find me guilty. The judge must then imprison me. That will be the remainder of my earthly punishment. Life in prison.'

Silence filled the room. No one was sure how to respond.

'Mr Whistler, are you now admitting to the murders of your fellow vagrants?'

'No. Absolutely not. Some other bastard killed them. I am resigned to being punished for something else.'

The next hour was like trying to hold water in one's hand. Every time the detectives thought they might be making progress, Harry slipped through their fingers. He maintained his usual silence, or told them they were being ridiculous, that they had no evidence against him: no eye-witnesses; no fingerprints; little DNA; no real evidence; no motives. They couldn't even place him in the park on the nights in question.

'Mr Whistler, you had a very strong motive for murdering Terry Wendover. The man had accused you – in public – of the first two killings.'

'Yes, he did, and I had a right go at him afterwards. However, I don't go around killing people who've bothered me. And I rather think you haven't got enough to say I do.'

'You knew all three victims rather well, and were almost certainly in the park on each occasion.'

'And that's it. Let me tell you something. The homeless are regarded as the lowest of the low. People look at us like a dog turd they've stepped in; that is the ones who look at all. Most avoid eye contact and walk by on the other side. What no one understands is that we are a close-knit community, with our own rules and mode of conduct. Yes, we fall out, but that's true of every stratum of society. Even the posh nobs fight and brawl. Have you seen Fordway on a Saturday night?' He glowered at the two officers.

'We support each other, look out for each other. If anyone gets in trouble, we try to help. Six of us went to court when Bigman was hauled up before the magistrates.

That was a stupid trumped-up charge. Not moving on when asked to do so. Wanker of a young officer wanting to make an arrest. Waste of court time and public money. Bigman got a warning, a CD for six months. As if they could hand down a fine or give him hours of unpaid work. We all cheered when the chairman delivered his so-called verdict. The toff was smiling when he asked us to respect the Queen's Court. Respect? We were looking out for our mate.'

Serena and Harvey exchanged a glance, acknowledging the truth behind his words. The police had been known to comment on the fact that it was the homeless who drew the largest group of supporters in court, rather like the die-hard regulars at a non-league match.

Harvey thought back to his encounter with Bigman, alias Edward Jonathan Trendell, in the café in Elizabeth Park and silently agreed with the man sitting, looking defiant in front of him. Bigman had been a gentleman, had retained his dignity in the most exacting of circumstances, and he suspected that was true of many of his fellow down-and-outs.

Tears threatening to escape, Harry continued, his voice surprisingly strong. 'Tommy Granger was as near to a friend as I've had for twenty years. He'd fallen on very hard times, but had retained some sense of self-worth. Why in the name of all that's holy would I want to kill him? Terry Wendover and I had our differences, and he could be an awkward git. However, I'll never know why he accused me of the first two murders, and I got no answer from him after your stupid get-together. However, I did not kill him. I. Did. Not. Kill. Him.'

Pausing for a few moments, he continued, the tears now coursing down his face. 'As for Charlie. She brought new energy to the park. She was so young, so fresh, so full of life. We all loved her...and I don't mean in a sexual way...we wanted the best for her. Given time, we'd have helped her to get back on track, to resume the sort of life a girl like her should be living. Never in a million lifetimes could I have hurt her.'

Either the man in front of them was a consummate actor, or he was telling the truth.

Chapter 35

Eve

They've let Dad go! Two long interviews today got them nowhere. The afternoon one was tricky as Edwin York was introduced to the proceedings. He was found in the Jacob's shed (sorry, I think our brother calls it something else) on the allotments. Dad's DNA was all over the place. Dad admitted that he had, on a few very rare occasions, slept there, and that he thought you knew about it Jacob. However, he was adamant that he had nothing to do with the elderly gentleman's death.

The time of death is as woolly as an unshorn sheep, so there is no way of knowing if Dad was even in Fordway at the time. He can't provide a defence as he has no idea when he went to Manchester, or even how long he's been back. Let's be honest we wouldn't know he'd been away unless Andrew had seen him in Platt Fields.

I didn't know about the glove until DCI Tarquin brought it out. Talk about a detonator! Exhibit X! Dad had to agree that he did have a pair like it – he could hardly deny it with me sitting beside him. Needless-to-say he had an excuse ready. Apparently, he only wears gloves when the temperature drops below zero. He has no need of them at other times, so he hasn't taken them out of his rucksack for months.

'Mr Whistler, the gloves are a most distinctive design, not your everyday apparel. It's most strange, not to say suspicious, that a glove you admit to owning turns up at a murder scene, and with your DNA all over it.'

'I've said I went to the shed, but not since the bad weather. That must have been when I dropped the glove. Months have passed since then.'

For some reason, Dad was talking a lot more today. Not sure whether that made him appear guilty. His final statement was interesting.

'I'll say this once more: I am a killer, but almost certainly not the sort you'd be interested in. What I did wouldn't be worth pursuing. The CPS would say it wasn't in the public interest to bring it to trial. God is my judge; no need for a jury. When the Great Day of Judgement comes, when all stand before Him and receive His chastisements, and forgiveness, I will answer for my sins. I am not the murderer you seek. I did NOT kill my fellow vagrants and I did NOT kill Edwin York.'

Oh boys, listening to him reduced me to tears which I fought hard to hide. I think both Serena and the DCI were also affected, as the room felt like a vacuum, all the energy sucked out.

When they saw me afterwards, DCI Tarquin said they were releasing Dad pending further inquiries. We all know that, at least for the moment, there is insufficient evidence. So, he is a free man again.

David

Thanks for the update, Eve. It must have been horrendous for you. On behalf of the family I want to say it's so great you always being there for him. Jacob was with me when we received the news. He had called here after work and it was on the local radio. He was quite upset. I think that's a euphemism. What do you think will happen next? You said, "pending further inquiries". Does that mean he remains a suspect?

Andrew

How naive are you David? Of course, he remains on their radar. Are you the only one who really believes in his innocence? Eve hasn't said they've got anyone else in mind. So, dear brother, you do the math (I know, an awful Americanism).

The stillness in the room spoke more eloquently than any of the officers who were present: all sat at their desks trying to look busy. Everyone knew that Harry Whistler had been released, that the interviews had proved to be a futile waste of time.

'I thought we had him. I really thought this was it.'

'We all did, sir. When someone is arrested, and says they have committed a murder, it's natural to assume that we have our killer.'

'He so called confessed the first time we met him, long before he was a person of interest. We both remember his final comment as he left, the afternoon we talked to him as a member of the town's homeless. You said when you mentioned it to his daughter that she'd looked uncomfortable.'

'Far more than that. I'm sure she knows exactly what her father means when he says he has killed.'

'Sorry to lay this on you, but I think you'd better have another little chat with Miss Whistler.'

Jacob.

I went back to the allotment for the first time this afternoon. No body thank goodness! The SOCO team had left the shed in a right old state: plant pots upended, a rake and my new spade left lying on the floor.

Outside wasn't much better. New plants trampled, and the garden seat left on its side. Hope they found what they were looking for.

When I see Dad, I will inform him that he is no longer welcome there. I don't think he's used it much, and he certainly won't do so in the future. The locksmith arrived soon after I did. Yes, I should be able to do that kind of thing myself, but felt it should be done professionally. I will keep one of the new keys with me. Neither will be accessible to him, no more leaving one under the second plant pot. I gave the spare to Edith, so she can continue to borrow the tools. No need for her to suffer because of him, the murdering bastard.

Serena Peil wasn't sure whether to make an appointment to see Eve, or to turn up at the lawyer's office unannounced. In the end, she went for the latter option, and the following morning was waiting as Eve walked into the reception area.

Not having slept well, Eve looked pale. An attempt had been made to make herself look professional, but no amount of makeup could hide the black smudges under her eyes, or the worry lines creasing her forehead. Seeing the inspector, she flinched, an involuntary movement she was unable to hide.

Pleasantries and coffee dealt with, Serena spoke softly. 'Sorry to bother you, Miss Whistler.'

'It sounds like an official visit. Surname employed DI Peil.'

Trying not to look as uncomfortable as she felt, Serena launched in, a cat determined to catch the mouse. 'DCI Tarquin and I just wondered whether you can clarify something. Any extra information would be most useful. It's about your father's claim that he is a killer. On two occasions, he has told us that he has committed a murder.' Seeing Eve's stricken face, she continued, speaking so gently that anyone listening would have thought she was counselling the woman. 'We think you know what he means, and it would be very helpful if you would tell us. We would be in dereliction of duty if we ignored his comments.'

A long silence ensued. Just when Serena was thinking there would be no response, Eve spoke. 'I cannot possibly comment on anything my father said. As his lawyer, I am unable to give you an answer. As you are only too aware, lawyer/client confidentiality is paramount under English law. However, I will remind you of something that he said: "God will be my judge. No earthly court is needed."'

'Miss Whistler, DCI Tarquin and I are both very concerned that a man has admitted murder, and we really can't wait for divine justice.'

'I must request that any further discussion is undertaken with him present. As I have a full day of cases I must now ask you to leave.'

Andrew

An invitation to the twins' shindig arrived this morning. Mum is keen to say yes.

I thought David and Jacob would wait until next year when they can celebrate their "Life Begins" birthday bash.

Has there been a joint party since they were eighteen, just before a certain member of the family absconded? I used to feel sorry for them having to share their big day. Needless-to-say that was when we passed as a normal family and things like that mattered. Rather selfish of David – what's new? – to organise the evening at his Wild West restaurant. I for one will not be going in fancy dress, and the invitation does say it's optional.

Eve

It's a lovely idea. Just what we all need. I've ordered my cow-girl outfit online; so many to choose from, people must be acting out their fantasies! Philip isn't too sure about the one that is coming for him. It's advertised as "The Most Authentic Western Sheriff this side of the Atlantic!". It's all black, with close-fitting trousers, long-line jacket, waistcoat, dicky-bow tie and badge. We laughed when we read the washing instructions: 'Machine wash on delicate, do not bleach, do not tumble dry, do not iron, do not dry clean.' Philip's comment was that all that advice was redundant as the costume will be worn once, and once-only. The man has no sense of fun.

I told him it will make him a dead ringer for Gary Cooper in '*High Noon*'. I love the old black and white films and have a whole collection on DVD. Unfortunately, it would take a master cosmetic surgeon to make me look anything like Grace Kelly, but I can sing a mean rendition of "Do Not Forsake Me Oh My Darling." That should clear the restaurant.

I was telling him about the twins' tenth birthday party which ended up in a free-for-all. They'd invited every boy in their Year 5 class. Yes, very sexist, but at the time girls were still a foreign species. Sunshine and showers had been forecast, and we all know what that means. Halfway through the afternoon the first shower arrived, though a deluge would have been a more accurate description, and fifteen, I think that was the total though it felt like three times as many, wild boys careered into the house. I'm sure Armageddon will be less dramatic: they knocked over chairs, upset the table weighed down with party food, then started to play-fight. Can't you hear Mr Mellor in the playground informing anyone within earshot that play-fighting was banned. 'It always, and boys I do mean always, leads to fisticuffs and tears.' Fisticuffs doesn't even begin to describe what transpired. Michael Bolton's parents were summoned, Geoffrey Aimsley was taken to Casualty with a sprained ankle, and David and Jacob were sent to their room. Hopefully, this summer's extravaganza will be less eventful, though probably nowhere near as memorable.

The idea of the party has cheered me up and given me something else to think about. Recent events have left me more upset than I realised, and Serena's visit didn't help. She pressed and pressed, and the atmosphere became totally embarrassing. We were both prickly, though she must have known that as Dad's lawyer I couldn't say anything that would betray his trust.

Jacob

Betray his trust. What the hell does that mean? He lost all rights when he walked out. As for your exaggerated memories of our tenth birthday, it wasn't as apocalyptic as you've made it sound. Yes, when he came home, Dad sent us upstairs, but by that time – he was never one to join in with family fun, for ever in absentia until the celebrations were over, some delay at work inevitable –

we had managed to salvage most of the food, and almost all the guests were still there when we blew out the candles. You must remember the cake: shaped as a one and a zero, it had layers of chocolate and was topped with flakes and slices of Mars Bar. It had been ensconced in the larder and was delicious.

David

Do you know, I had forgotten all about that party? I'd hoped the grey matter wasn't ageing quite so rapidly. Eve's given me a great idea, we'll call this year's do *High Noon*, though a bit of gun fighting will be tame in comparison with that afternoon twenty-nine years ago.

Jacob

There you go again David. In charge. No doubt you'll be the sheriff who wins the day, and the rest of us will be the stooges.

Read on dear siblings. One of my favourite moments in the incomparable 'Fawlty Towers' was when Sybil yelled down the phone, 'Pretentious? Moi?' That is my dear brother to a T. He lives in a 'I've-made-it-and-I'm-going to-flaunt-it' house, drives an enormous people-carrier – nothing so plebeian as a car – has a beautiful wife and two girls who are perfection personified. He boasts about them at every conceivable opportunity. I'm just so glad I'm not a recipient of his round-robin inserts at Christmas.

I own a small apartment and an allotment.

Most of the time none of this bothers me. That is until he lauds it over me and makes me look inept: number two, the also-ran. When he suggested that we get together on our birthday, I imagined our usual curry or pizza with a few beers. Next thing I know it's a full-blown spectacular. Fancy dress optional. Has he forgotten we seldom do things *en famille*, and that when we do they seldom go well. Can't wait...for it to be over.

Harvey had taken the day off. He knew any work he might have undertaken would be substandard. Having made up his mind to move he was visiting the three estate agents in Fordway. Nothing so far had yelled at him that it was the one. He had made four appointments to view, and hoped at least one would look better in the flesh.

Popping into The Cup Cake café he sat with a large coffee and two cakes. He thought of them as children's fare, far too sweet for his liking, but it was those or nothing. The place was deserted. Too late for the coffee brigade and too early for the lunchtime customers. Choosing a window seat, he looked at the details of his first viewing. As he re-read the blurb the semi-detached house grew on him: in a quiet cul-de-sac; a fifteen-minute walk from work; newly installed kitchen and bathroom, and with three reasonably sized bedrooms. The price was slightly more than he wanted to pay, but it sounded like an ideal location for the pair of moggies he was tempted to acquire.

The estate agent was waiting as he drove up. The area wasn't one he knew, which was to its advantage: not visited regularly by the police. Unusually, the blurb had not done full justice to the house, which was ready to move into. As he was about to get back in his car, thinking that he might make an offer, and wondering how much below the asking price he dared go, Mozart resonated, disturbing the quiet road.

'Good morning, sir. Sorry to bother you.'

'No doubt it's important,' Harvey replied hoping it wasn't merely an update on her meeting with Eve Whistler.'

'Two things. Talking to Miss Whistler was a waste of time, but we rather suspected that would be the case. She played the lawyer hand to perfection, like an expert poker sharp, holding all the good cards. Needless-to-say, I wouldn't have bothered you with that...it's just that another elderly person has gone missing.'

'I'll be there in ten minutes.' An offer on the house would have to wait.

Serena was waiting and launched straight in. 'Phone call at 11.45. Misper, a Mrs Lillian Henshaw. Aged eighty. Married to Stuart. She set out to visit her daughter, Janine Dakers, this morning and never arrived. It was a regular arrangement. Her daughter lives three roads away, and she always has the coffee ready at ten thirty. Janine works in the local primary school, St Matthew's, and the two get together every Saturday morning and more often during the school holidays. When her mum didn't arrive, she waited for half an hour, thinking something might have delayed her. It was then she contacted her father who said that Lillian had left the house at the usual time, armed with shopping bag and umbrella in case they went into town. Stuart Henshaw had walked to his daughter's, covering his wife's normal route, but there was no sign of her.' Serena's succinct account stalled.

'What else do we know about the family background?'

'As I said the lady is eighty. However, there has been no sign of illness, either mental or physical. I've arranged to talk to the husband and daughter. They are staying at their own addresses in case Lillian turns up. Apparently, there's no history of confusion. However, this could be the first time she's become disorientated and gone the wrong way.'

'I sincerely hope that's the case. We'll take Clare Jennings along and she can act as Family Liaison Officer. She needs to get her confidence back after the Edwin York debacle.' Both hoped this wouldn't be a repeat of the case that everyone wanted to forget.

Stuart Henshaw opened the door as the three police officers walked up the path, a large golden Labrador by his side. They had seen the man standing nervously, mobile phone in hand, looking out of the window. The large house was outside Harvey's price range, but he knew that tragedy had the unwelcome propensity to invade all homes, whatever their value.

Looking every one of his eight decades, Stuart stood shaking, his world, for the moment, reduced to rubble. He was tall, over six feet, but looked shrunken. Smartly dressed in black trousers, black polo shirt and fawn jumper, he informed the officers that he was on the phone cancelling his afternoon golf. Serena and Harvey exchanged glances indicating that, in the circumstances, this was extremely organised. Phone call over, old fashioned manners prevailed, and coffee was offered and accepted. Serena said she would find everything in the kitchen and left Harvey and Clare to gain as much information as possible about the missing wife.

His voice as shaky as his legs, he repeated the story he'd already given. 'Lillian always has the morning with our daughter. They love to gossip and have coffee… always ten thirty…always Saturday, except when school is closed for the holidays and they can meet during the week. Janine works full time at St Matthew's primary school and likes to meet up with her mum at the weekend.' The man seemed unaware that he was repeating himself. 'Lillian walks on her own, it's only ten minutes away. Sometimes they stay at Janine's and have a spot of lunch, other times they go into Fordway. Janine drives, they do some shopping and then go to The Pantry for lunch. I never worry if Lillian's out a long time as I know she's with our daughter. Janine brings her home, usually mid-afternoon.'

As Serena walked in with a tray of drinks she heard Stuart repeat the word "usually", then burst into tears.

'Oh, dear me, I'm so sorry. I never normally blub.'

Assuring the distraught man that it was perfectly understandable, time was allowed for the drinks to be dispensed.

'Has Lillian been her usual self recently? Has she been at all unwell?' Harvey asked the questions as carefully as possible. The man sitting defeated, in the armchair that was obviously his own, reading glasses, tobacco tin and a tome on World War Two on the nearest table, was no fool and would understand the meaning behind the enquiries.

'If you're asking is she starting to lose her marbles, the answer's no.'

'Has she ever varied her Saturday morning routine?'

'No, it's completely out of character. She and Janine meet every Saturday, unless one or other of them is away on holiday. Janine goes abroad some half term breaks with a few of her friends, and in the summer, she likes to try one of those adventure trips. South America is booked this year. Lillian and I prefer to stay in this country now, we both like to avoid the hassle of airports. When we were younger they were acceptable. Age makes one long for an easier life.' Realising he was rambling, he stopped and stared at Harvey. 'Sorry, you don't need to know all that.'

'That's fine Mr Henshaw. Have you got a recent photograph of your wife?'

Rising unsteadily to his feet, the stricken man walked across to the marble fireplace and took one from the overcrowded ledge. 'This is one of all of us at a nephew's wedding. It was taken last year. I think it's the most recent, though Janine might have one on her mobile: she's always clicking away on it.'

As he sat down again he seemed to have aged, the lines on his face increasing as though an artist was adding final brush strokes to a portrait.

'Can you tell us what your wife was wearing this morning?' As Serena asked the question, Stuart Henshaw jumped, a spasm that brought him back to the awful reality of the situation.

'Her fawn mac. She thought it might rain. Probably her brown shoes, she finds them the most comfortable for walking. She had her shopping bag...it's quite distinctive and I always tease her about it...a bright red tartan. When I say anything, she tells me it's a good size, holds a lot.'

Serena said that PC Clare Jennings would stay with him as the Family Liaison Officer. Anything else he thought of could be relayed back. It was as they stood up that she did a double take. The room they were in was a long through lounge, with windows at both ends. The front ones looked out at the road; it was the one at the rear that stopped her mid-sentence.

Draped full length curtains, plus matching pelmet, surrounded an enormous French window. The garden beyond was immaculate: a well-tended lawn was surrounded by various shrubs and borders filled with flowers of every hue. Either Mr or Mrs Henshaw was keen on gardening, or they employed someone.

At the end of the long garden was a high hedge with a wooden door in the middle. Serena was transported back to her first reading of *The Secret Garden*, a perennial favourite for many years. It was the novel that had started her love of literature, and the gate she was looking at was exactly how she had imagined the one in the book, the one through which the children had escaped and had their adventure.

'Mr Henshaw, where does the gate at the end of your garden lead?'

'Oh, that's Elizabeth Park. The gate was there when we moved in. It was left in situ as we like to take the dog in the park, he does love his walks. Our daughter was worried at first that it might not be safe, but no one has ever used it to come into our garden, and we keep it locked. Without that easy access, we would have to walk at least a mile to the nearest official park entrance. Bob would have had his walk by then.'

Almost afraid of the answer, Harvey spoke slowly, 'Can you go through that part of the park to your daughter's?'

'In good weather, it's a short cut: through the gate, across the grass, and on the path to the main gate. Janine lives two minutes from there. We never use it when it's been raining. The grass becomes a quagmire, really muddy.'

The morning had been dry.

'Do you happen to know which way your wife went this morning?'

'Probably the park. I was reading the paper and didn't watch her leave, but that's the route I took when I went to look for her.'

Promising to keep in touch, and assuring the old man that people almost always turned up, the officers repeated that Clare would be there for anything he needed.

Within minutes, police were searching the park, and sniffer dogs had been requested. The Search and Rescue helicopter was scrambled, at a cost of fifteen hundred pounds an hour. CCTV footage covering the paths, theatre, bandstand and café was scrutinized. There was great interest when Mrs Henshaw was seen leaving the park by the main gates.

Then nothing. Once she left the park, Lillian Henshaw vanished.

Chapter 36

Eve

I can't wait for tomorrow!! Hope you aren't expecting exciting presents, the ones I've got are, to say the least, plebeian.

It was good to get back to something like normality today, though most of the people who live in Fordway wouldn't regard Briony Adams as normal. Any time I see her name on my list of clients I groan. I did so aloud today, much to the custody sergeant's amusement. Someone once joked that her initials are the same as the degree she gained in Fine Art from Birmingham University. Not many of our clients can write those letters after their name. The story is that drink and soft drugs fueled her through her final exhibition, then led to her downward spiral.

'Sorry, Miss Whistler, everybody's least favourite nutter is with us again. Do you need a strong coffee before you see her?'

Sergeant Brown is a pleasant man who retains an amazingly positive outlook, despite dealing with criminals, ne're-do-wells, the great unwashed, as well as those who have been wrongly arrested...all on a daily-basis. His passion is golf and he is always keen to update me on his latest handicap on the various courses he visits.

It means very little to me, but my response of appropriate noises seems to satisfy him.

'Two birdies at the weekend, and on a new course. John and I were invited to the one that's opened recently on the far side of Preston. Lovely greens and a good variety of holes. We both did OK.' John is his eldest son, the other one, Paul, is far away in Australia, a source of regret, family deemed important.

The sergeant, he's old-school so no first names, also updates me regularly on how his beloved Bolton Wanderers are doing: he and his son are season ticket holders. 'I was born within shouting distance of the original ground, Burnden Park. Mum reckoned she could hear us when we went to stand on the terrace each home game. We were all there: Dad, my uncle Colin, Paul and John at the last ever Wanderers' game played at that venue. April 1997. It was the final game of the season and we were already Champions of Division One. That afternoon we defeated Charlton Athletic 4-1 after being one down at half time. I think we were all fighting back the tears when the crowd gave a memorable rendition of Auld Lang Syne.' I have also been told that his grandfather was at the ground in 1946 when thirty-three Bolton fans lost their lives in a crush, and more than I need to know about the new, and much despised, ground – nowhere near the centre of Bolton. 'Stupid location, a ground needs to be at the heart of its supporters, and to make matters even worse it's already had two names: Reebok and Macron. All because of sponsorship.'

Following coffee and a chat that went on longer than I wanted, the moment came when I could no longer delay the inevitable: act as duty solicitor to the incorrigible Briony.

She must once have been attractive. Tall and slim, with long dark brown hair, her body has been ravaged by her prolonged addiction to alcohol. Her skin has the pallor of the terminally ill and her clothes haven't seen the inside of washing machine for many weeks, if not months. This morning the alcohol fumes emanating from her made me feel nauseous and I avoided sitting too close.

'Good morning, Briony.' I got no further before the usual mantra began.

'I did it and I'm really sorry. Bill and I had been in town drinking and I lose control when that happens. Am I on one of the cameras? Am I in really big trouble?'

'I'm afraid it was all caught on a camera. You'll be in court this morning; if you plead guilty the case can be dealt with there and then. Better than coming back for a trial, and I must advise you that the verdict would probably be the same, though for a guilty plea at least you'd get a third off your sentence.'

'What did I do? What was it this time? The last thing I remember is Bill getting on the bus and me paying. Next thing I wake up in the cells.'

For more years than any of us want to remember, this has been the norm. Drink, use foul language, become violent, police called, verbally and at times physically abuse them, night in the cells. The sad thing is that she is always repentant, unlike some others I could mention. On the very rare occasions when I have seen her totally sober, I realise that, given different circumstances, like a partner who wasn't also addicted to booze, she could lead a life that wouldn't involve regular appointments in court. I have been told that many moons ago, long before my time and before she got together with Bill, she worked in her local Spar...that is until the day she was caught stealing some vodka.

Whenever any CCTV footage is shown she weeps. The last time she begged the legal adviser to turn it off. She kept telling the magistrates how very sorry she was and that she'd never do it again. As her list of convictions makes *War and Peace* look like a short story that scenario was viewed as most unlikely.

Today's Bench were brilliant. Despite the video showing Briony at her most repulsive, effing and blinding at a passenger on the late-night bus, then punching the bus driver when he tried to intervene, the decision was made to offer help rather than punishment. They persuaded Mr Kitson, the probation officer on duty, to arrange a series of meetings to try to address her drinking. It remains to be seen if she turns up for the appointments, though the chairman, a delightful character called Jeremy Sinclair, warned her of the consequences of not obeying the court order.

'Should you not attend the appointments the probation service has offered you, you may well find yourself back before the magistrates, and last night's appalling incident will be reviewed. Your catalogue of misdemeanors is extensive, and you are very close to receiving a custodial sentence.' When I explained his words afterwards she looked shocked, quickly followed by another bout of weeping. The threat of prison may be the spur she needs. That is until she starts drinking again.

A busy day, hope tomorrow is quieter as I've got hair and nail appointments afterwards. Not exactly wild west style, but a girl has-to-do what a girl has-to-do! Try reading those last words with an American accent, preferably a southern drawl.

David tells me he's invited a lot of friends to the party. Dad will be the elephant in the room, and for Mum's sake we can't mention him. We all need an enjoyable event.

Jacob

So, David has his gang, though I rather think there will be a herd of elephants, a veritable safari, stampeding on the plains of Rusholme.

I am bringing Del. No, we're not an item, or whatever the modern equivalent is. She teaches at the primary school where I started to work recently. I give guitar lessons to several pupils in her class. We got talking one day and she accepted my invitation. She's into drama and loves dressing up. Think she's coming as Annie Oakley. When I was in St Matthew's at the beginning of the week, the school secretary was very upset as her mother has disappeared. No doubt you read about it in the local paper. She vanished on Saturday and there's been no sign of her since.

If only Dad would do that. Vanish. Preferably permanently. Once he's incarcerated – the sooner the better – we can all get on with our lives. Has he any idea of the anguish he has caused? To not know where someone is must be one of the worst things that can happen. We had a decade of such uncertainty, only for him to reappear and be linked to a series of murders.

Once he's enjoying board and lodging at the tax payers' expense, will he write his memoires? That is the most apt word as it starts with me, always his primary focus.

Chapter 37

Wednesday morning and still no sign of the missing woman. She had been caught on the camera by the main entrance to the park, walking quite quickly and turning right out of the gate, the route that should have taken her to her daughter's. No cameras were positioned to view her further.

Harvey was thinking out loud, his fingers moving faster than his words, drumming on the windowsill in the room that only he occupied. 'She disappeared somewhere between Elizabeth Park and her destination. We've walked it and it's about a third of a mile...at the most. Despite her age, she's a fit woman and it should have taken her ten to fifteen minutes. She had her mobile phone but didn't use it. No calls have been made on it since. The last one was to her daughter to say she was on her way, so she obviously intended to see her. The husband, Stuart Henshaw, is adamant that she was in good health and had no worries. He says everything was normal. Normal until an eighty-year old lady goes AWOL. Where the devil is she? And more to the point is she OK?'

Serena entered as he was uttering this last phrase. It wasn't quite seven, but the pair had been arriving earlier and earlier, two birds hoping the old saying about worms might come true.

Greeting her boss, Serena gave him the strong coffee she had purchased en route.

'The reenactment is scheduled for 10.30, sir. It's not Saturday, but we can do it again at the weekend if today doesn't give us any leads. A Mrs Fosdyke is acting the part, and we've got clothes that match the description of those worn by Lillian.'

Harvey had never been a great advocate of reruns, believing them to be a waste of time and money. They were seldom helpful in an inquiry. Looking extremely worried, he muttered, 'I've decided we need to speak to our homeless friends again. They didn't give us anything on Saturday, but someone must have seen her, and they may be our best hope. Have the CCTV cameras been checked again? We asked Roger Symmons to widen the timescale and include Friday evening. We need to know who was in the park.'

'He was working on it yesterday, sir. I'll see him when he comes in.'

Eve

The day of the party! Why, just for once, couldn't work have put me in a celebratory mood? I should have known it wasn't going to be a good day when I was summoned to the police station at the unearthly hour of midnight – actually, a few minutes past the witching hour, so definitely today. Only the vampires are happy to be out and about at that inauspicious time.

Sergeant Brown was once again on duty, though there was no friendly greeting this time. 'Over the many years of doing this job I've been verbally assaulted, punched, kicked, spat at and bitten. But not all at the same time! Sorry, Miss Whistler...she's back. Arrested an hour ago, and this time it's serious.'

My brain hadn't quite woken up, and for a few seconds I didn't know to whom he was referring. 'Sorry, Sergeant, who do you mean?'

'The lady, I use that word extremely loosely, who got off so lightly yesterday. What were the magistrates thinking, letting her off with a few cosy chats with some do-gooder probation officer? As if that was going to work: once an alcoholic, always an alcoholic.'

Never having heard the man in such a negative mood, I was rather shocked by his lack of empathy. He had often spoken of the need for second and even third chances for the people he dealt with.

So, Briony was back, less than twenty-four hours after being given her get-out-of-jail-free-card.

'You'd better tell me what's happened,' I said, in truth, not wanting to know and longing more than ever for my bed.

'When she left us yesterday, she and her waste-of-space partner went on a day-long binge. Started at The Grapes and ended up, several hours and many hostelries later, at The Black Sheep. Almost inevitably with her, there was, what shall we call it, an incident. She and lover boy were outside in the smoking area when someone knocked into her. I'm not sure how the ensuing fracas developed, but the girl who'd bumped the lovely Briony ended up on the ground, with a glass of goodness knows what thrown over her.'

I wanted to laugh, but the look on the sergeant's face prevented any mirth. 'I've never seen her as bad as she was when the young constable brought her in. From the look on his face, neither had he. Her language was the usual appalling misuse of the English language, makes what I hear at the football sound chaste. It was as I was showing her to her abode for the night, B and B, en suite at no extra cost, breakfast in bed, or at least in her boudoir (George was back to his usual self), that she kicked off. Literally! She was like a whirling dervish: arms, legs, head all going for me. It was when she bit my shoulder – got a mouthful of uniform for her trouble – then spat at me, that I almost lost it. Fortunately, Sergeant Masters was assisting me, or I'd have been the one up before the bench for Grievous Bodily Harm, and as a responsible member of the community I would have received a stiff sentence. There would have been no let's-talk-about-this for me.

I waited in the interview room for what felt like hours. As Briony was being escorted from her cell the litany of apologies had already begun.

'Whatever you say I did, I didn't mean to do it. You've got to believe me. I can't be guilty if I don't know what I'm being accused of. It's the drink that's to blame: not me. The booze and Bill. He leads me on, makes me have more than I should. You'll tell the magistrates that I'm really, really, sorry. Really, really…'

The script hadn't changed, and whilst during daylight hours the soliloquy comes across as merely pathetic, in the middle of the night it makes me want to rant and rave, scream obscenities and punch out her lights! None of the above would be deemed appropriate behaviour for a lawyer, so I informed her that I would see her later, when she had sobered up.

Once home, it was incredibly annoying to know that whilst I lay awake, trying not to disturb the still-slumbering Philip, Briony was sleeping soundly. As a defence lawyer I should be au fait with the phrase "there's no justice". I hear my clients say it often enough. As the first light appeared through the crack in the curtains, the words had never felt more apposite.

Before re-acquainting myself with my client, other words spring to mind but are not for public consumption, I went to the office and made my suggestion that we are not summoned to the station until our clients are sober enough to interview. Isaiah Solomon is an excellent lawyer and an extremely understanding boss. Although he has been the senior partner for two decades he remains approachable.

'It's a good point, Eve. However, as you know, once someone in custody requests the presence of a solicitor, we are duty bound to respond. It is, to say the least, one of the more irritating aspects of the job, but it is beyond my remit to change it. I suggest not seeing her again until after lunch. Even she should be more compos mentis by then.'

By this afternoon Briony was reasonably sober, though our interview was a matinee performance of the midnight script. As she stood sobbing before the magistrates, it was obvious that they had lost patience and today's trio sent her to Crown Court. Assaulting yet another officer in the line of duty had finally caught up with her. Lucky Fordway, she's out on bail, due before a judge and jury next week.

So far, a horrible day. Philip and I are about to don our costumes. Do hope the evening goes well.

Chapter 38

The incident room was subdued: no helpful information had been forthcoming following the reenactment. One dog walker said he went to the park every morning. 'I saw someone who looked very like the stand-in leaving the park as I entered, but I couldn't be sure which day. It might have been Saturday. She was an elderly woman, very sprite for her age. Comments were exchanged about the weather. We both wondered if it was going to rain.'

'That's no use. We know she left the park, it's on CCTV. We know she was alone. What we need to ascertain is what happened afterwards.' Roger Symmons was disappointed that the cameras had been of little help. 'Lillian Henshaw is seen walking past the bandstand where she's caught on one camera, and then a couple of minutes later she exits by the main gate. That's recorded on another camera. We can tell she turns right out of the park, which is the route to her daughter's. Unfortunately, the camera only covers the first few metres outside the gate. So, all in all, we have absolutely no idea what happened next.'

'Did the cameras help to ascertain which of the homeless were in the park?' Harvey wasn't sure what he wanted the answer to be.

'Big man, and someone who is new to us, are seen entering via the back gate late on the Friday evening.

They leave at lunch time on the Saturday. No sign of our friend Mr Whistler, either entering or leaving.'

The sense of anti-climax was palpable, the room a burst balloon. Clare Jennings spoke for them all: 'We wait for a body to turn up.'

David

Hope everyone enjoyed the party as much as I did. Some of the outfits were amazing. It's so good when people make a bit of an effort. Did you all enjoy the food? The buffalo burgers are one of the chef's specialties! Thanks for adhering to the order not to buy presents, apart from Eve, though the latest Richard Dawkins book is always welcome. Not quite sure what Dad would have made of it!

It was enough to have you all there. And there were no fallings out, even when Eve, finally, disclosed Dad's deepest, darkest, best-kept secret. I don't think MI6 would be interested, or even the redoubtable DCI Tarquin. Not quite sure why she hasn't told us before.

Jacob

David, are you stupid or just totally devoid of imagination? Do you not understand the way the English judicial system works? Dad broke the law! A law that is embedded in every legal system in the civilised world. I'm sure the police would be very keen to investigate his crime. I use that word advisedly. Dad committed a crime and is still the prime suspect for several recent misdemeanors. Anyone any idea what the body count is up to by now?

Eve

It was a great party. Thanks for doing all the organising, David. I feel bad about disclosing Dad's secret, but it's probably time you all knew, and it does start to explain why he needed to escape, to start his new life. I'm just glad we are the only ones who know. I don't think Andrew would be able to cope with it and Mum must never find out.

On a brighter note Philip has asked me to marry him! He proposed when we got home. In the kitchen, by the cooker: not the most romantic of settings, maybe he plans to turn me into a hausfrau! Was it the *High Noon* connection that encouraged him? We were still dressed appropriately. I have asked him to give me time to think about it. My first foray into marriage wasn't exactly a roaring success. I'll let you know...

Jacob

Go for it! Philip's so different to your first husband. Del and I got on well. It's early days, but we're going out again at the weekend.

Andrew

Mum enjoyed her sons' party. End of.
How come you all know the enigma that is our father. Those last two words are not meant to be religious, just looked more appropriate than Dad. What *did* he do? You will tell me one day, so it might as well be now. Or shall I write an article for the local paper about family secrets, making it obvious it's based on personal experience? That might create a frisson of interest... from the readers or the DCI. Your choice, siblings of mine.

Chapter 39

Unadulterated blue: no clouds gate-crashing the day. This being the north of England, summer clothes were flaunted whilst the temperature allowed. Shorts and the skimpiest of tops had been woken from their long hibernation. People who should have known better were putting unattractive body parts on display.

'Do you think the Queen could sign an order, forbidding girls with legs like that to uncover them in public?' Serena's comment was not appreciated. The traffic was at a standstill, people desperate to escape the humidity of the town for the hills or seaside. 'Blackpool will be busy today. Hope they ordered enough ice cream.'

'I'd rather like to spend the rest of this journey in silence. Unless you have anything of note to impart.' Harvey knew he was growing increasingly curmudgeonly: was it age or the stress or the murders that remained unresolved? A new one added to the list.

The call had come less than fifteen minutes ago. The body of an elderly woman had been discovered in a house near Elizabeth Park. Since receiving the call, Harvey had been set to silent mode, his rebuke of Serena the only words spoken.

'Sorry, sir. Have we any details? Was the house part of our original search?'

Concentrating on the road ahead, Harvey managed a precis of the details he'd been given, his voice like a radio announcer delivering the headlines. 'A body has been found in a detached house about a hundred yards from the park entrance. The house may not have been searched in our original sweep of the vicinity as it has a Sold notice in the garden. Apparently, it's been empty for several weeks, the new owners didn't arrive from Dubai until today: the wife had a long-term contract out there. One imagines they got one hell of a shock when they went into the kitchen. You don't expect to find a body on the floor of your new home.'

42, Windsor Road had a long, sweeping drive, an extended curve making the front of the house invisible from the road. The house had been built about the same time as the park, and the front door was a wonderful piece of Victoriana with ornate stained-glass windows. Waiting, looking rather shaken, a young constable was recording the names of everyone accessing the crime scene.

'DCI Tarquin and Sergeant Peil. And you are?'

'PC Johnny Timpson. Mr and Mrs Dewhurst are in the back garden. They didn't want to stay in the house and are both rather upset.'

Just as the two senior officers were about to walk around the house and speak to the new owners, the cavalry arrived: SOCO, on-call doctor and Alfie Morrison, looking uncomfortable, no longer the ruler of his fiefdom.

Serena was dispatched to talk to the unfortunate couple whose house had been forever tainted. Harvey donned the ubiquitous paper suit of protective clothing. Hood up, mask on, he added gloves and the booties which always made him think of a toddler thrusting his feet into wellies before the glorious business of splashing in puddles. How wonderful if that was the way he was going to occupy the rest of the morning. Walking in he was aware of the irony of a property devoid of everything...except for a body.

Lillian Henshaw had been propped up by the French window, situated at the far end of the large diner-kitchen. Her husband's description of the clothes she had been wearing, now almost two weeks ago, had been accurate. Only the addition of a woolen scarf, wound tightly around her neck, was a most unwelcome addition. She looked strangely perplexed, as though death had crept up and surprised her. The stench in the room was a mixture of decomposition, and the unfortunate proclivity a body has to evacuate both bladder and bowel.

'Oh my, when I volunteered to assist the police, I never dreamt I would be summoned on so many tragic occasions. I assume this is the old lady who went missing, the one who's been on the local news. My husband saw the reconstruction by the park gates. He takes Bess for her walk there most mornings. Unfortunately, he was unable to help with the inquiry; didn't recall seeing the poor woman.' The GP knew she was talking too much, a habit she seemed unable to control when under pressure. Not a good trait in her work and one she was keen to lose. 'Death confirmed. Time of death: 10.39. Actual time hard to say. Not recent, well over a week, maybe nearer two. I'm sure Mr Morrison will be more helpful.'

Thanking Dr. Culkin for attending, Harvey turned to Alfie. 'My usual question: how soon can you perform the PM?'

'PM this p.m.' It was as near as anyone was likely to get to humour. 'I assume you and the lovely Serena will be in attendance. I'll see you then. In the meantime, hope SOCO find something useful. Murder number five is five too many.'

Serena and Alfie passed in the doorway. 'Mr and Mrs Dewhurst are going to stay with her sister. I explained that as this is a crime scene they wouldn't be able to move in today. Not that they wanted to! I've got the address – it's not too far away, in Burton-in-Lonsdale – and promised to let them know when the house is available. Mrs Dewhurst is all for putting it back on the market.'

Harvey surveyed the scene. No sign of a struggle; there had been nothing to disturb in the room which was depressingly bare. Forlorn looking spaces stood awaiting their new inserts: fridge, freezer, table etcetera. All the accoutrements necessary to bring life to the room. For now, there was only death.

Photos taken, the forensics team was busy dusting for fingerprints.

'You'll need to do all the rooms, doors and surfaces. Whoever did this might have gone into any room. Better check the toilets as well.' The look he received reminded him of the saying linking grandma and eggs.

'We'll be some time here, sir. We know you want the results today. You might have to be patient and wait until tomorrow. The house doesn't appear to have an alarm fitted, unusual on this road, and we think the point of access was the kitchen. A pane of glass had been removed from the back door, just above the Yale lock. We'll give that area an extremely thorough examination.'

Leaving the house, Harvey prayed that the people employed on such meticulous, and to him mind-numbing probing, would find something: something to move the inquiry forward. For weeks now, it had been like a car stalled at traffic lights. Annoying to the driver; infuriating for those it was holding up.

Chapter 40

The homeless were enjoying the good weather. Clothes all dry, sleeping quarters the same, and the public more willing to donate money and sandwiches: goodwill more to the fore in the lovely conditions which had lasted longer than usual. Bigman and Harry were in Ash Tree Park, sharing a bottle of cider. Following a long discussion about his time in custody, Harry told his friend that he was thinking of moving on. Permanently this time.

'I've had enough of Fordway. Too many people know me and I'll always be on the police radar if I stay. Two coppers on the beat gave me a filthy look yesterday, and all I was doing was walking along Broad Street. I don't need the hassle, especially as I've not done anything. I keep expecting to be arrested again, so I'm leaving. Might go back to Manchester.'

Looking disappointed, Bigman replied, 'I'll miss you. It's not the same when you're not here, especially since we lost Tommy and Charlie. Not so bothered about Terry, not that he deserved what happened. Still can't get my head around him being incinerated like that. What was that all about?'

'That's another reason to move on. Are any of us safe here? Someone's got it in for us, though what they've got against us is anyone's guess.'

'How long will you go for?'

'As I said, forever. Nothing for me here. Wouldn't be so bad if the family were in absentia. I met Jacob the day I was released, and he asked why they'd let me out; said I should be locked up for life.'

'Your daughter's OK, isn't she? Didn't she act as your lawyer when you were being questioned?'

'Interrogated more like. Yes, she's the best of an iffy bunch, always was. Takes after her mother, unlike the boys who are selfish, self-absorbed idiots. One thinks he's made it as he has a portfolio, his words, arrogant twit, of restaurants; his twin brother teaches the guitar to kids who are probably forced to attend his sessions, whilst the third thinks he's made it because he writes puerile articles for the local rag. They all know what I think. I've seen them all recently and have had the pleasure of telling each of them how disappointed I am with their choice of careers.'

'Trouble is, Harry, if Eve takes after her mother, do the boys take after you?'

'Three failures. No doubt of my making. Enough to make any father want to abscond. I'll let you know when I'm off...in a day or so. I *will* make a point of saying goodbye. You've been a good friend.'

Alfie Morrison was in a somber mood. There had been too many killings. Most of his work, the aspect he enjoyed, was establishing a cause of death, almost always natural. Then, he was the Inspector Clouseau of Fordway, solving a mystery. Lillian Henshaw made him despondent. It was one unwarranted death too many.

'Good afternoon, Mrs Henshaw, or may I call you Lillian? Although you enjoyed an extra decade on the allotted three score and ten, your demise in such circumstances is abhorrent.' Adjusting the microphone, he began. No football references or songs this time.

Two hours later the facts had been established. Death by strangulation. The scarf, left in situ, had been used to choke the life out of Lillian Henshaw. There was severe bruising to the neck, and miniscule red blood spots were still visible on the neck, face and around the eyes. All tell-tale signs of strangulation. A small gold cross had been inserted in her mouth and was the link Harvey needed. It was, without question, the same killer.

Two phone calls, within ten minutes. The first was to tell Harvey that his second, slightly improved offer on The Haven, a name that needed changing, had been accepted. His new start now under way. The second had him leaping around the incident room, like a kangaroo on a performance-enhancing drug.

'Good morning, Chief Inspector. I think I may be about to make your day. We have been examining the scarf that was around Lillian Henshaw's neck.' Pausing for effect he almost yelled, 'And the DNA on it matches Harry Whistler's.' Managing to take the time to thank the technician, Harvey slammed down the phone and yelled, 'We've got him. We've got Mr Harry bloody Whistler.'

'Never knew his middle name,' Serena's droll aside for once appreciated. The loud applause that filled the room made her ask if it was for the forensic result or her outstandingly brilliant wit.

'Both. Most definitely both. Now the hard work begins. We need to make the case water-tight, so drip free that the CPS will have no option: the bastard will have his day...or weeks...in court.' Stopping to look around at the now excited faces he said, 'Have lunch, then everyone back here at 1 p.m. Be ready for some very hard work, and I'm sorry to say extremely long hours. Everything needs to be reviewed. We start this afternoon. We didn't have enough on him last month but by God we will this time.'

Chapter 41

Bad timing. His father's forte. Over the years, since his Mum died, Harvey's father seemed to have been in possession of a sixth sense, an almost uncanny ability to require his son's assistance at the most inopportune of moments.

The phone call came as Harvey was arriving at work. Day One – capital letters most appropriate – of the "Harry Whistler denouement", or as George Eventide had put it, 'Time to progress to joined-up handwriting, not forgetting to do the usual to the i's and the t's, and nail the bastard. This is my last, my final case, and when we hear the key turn on his cell door, it will be one of the most satisfying. It's a grand way to ride off into the sunset.' The final phrase was uttered like a line from a B movie. Few had heard George so upbeat.

Mozart could never have imagined that his music would be employed to herald news, both good and bad, these days mostly the latter. Harvey was half-inclined to change his ring-tone to something discordant: Schoenberg might be appropriate. As he answered the call, Harvey's heart sank.

'Good morning, Mr Whistler. It's the Home here. I'm extremely sorry to have to contact you, but your father has had a slight stroke. It happened a few hours ago, and to start with we thought it was just one of the funny turns he's been having. Unfortunately, when the doctor came he said it was a transient ischaemic attack, or TRA. Laughing (rather inappropriate in the circumstances), the care assistant he didn't recognise, added that Dr Ellerton had simplified the terminology and said it was commonly known as a mini-stroke.'

'How is he now?' Harvey asked, not wanting an answer that would require his presence.

'Comfortable. However, as you may be aware, a TRA must be treated seriously as it is often a warning sign that the patient might be at risk of having a full-blown stroke in the very near future. That's one reason I've called you.'

No, not serious, Harvey thought, then realised he was being selfish. This was his dad they were discussing.

'He's been asking for you, your brothers as well. You're the main contact number we have so it seemed sensible to talk to you first.'

Knowing what the reply would be he asked, 'Are you saying I ought to come?'

Following a speedy discussion with Serena, he returned home for a set of overnight clothes and toiletries. Although he was hoping to return later that day, he wanted to be prepared to stay. It all depended on what he found in Oxford.

Driving seemed the more sensible option. It would be far quicker than the train, and would have the added advantage of allowing him to return without the restrictions of a timetable. Sat Nav informed him that his journey was just over one hundred and eighty miles and should take three hours and twenty minutes.

Fortunately, the M6 was clear, no accidents or road works. The M54 was very different: a squally shower had created a slippery surface making a lorry jack-knife, hit the central reservation and block the two south-bound outside lanes. There was nothing to do but sit patiently as the traffic crawled past the obstruction at an irritatingly slow pace. Harvey thought sloths would have made faster progress. Indeed, David Atttenborough's *Planet Earth* extravaganza had shown that they could certainly do so in the water. By the time he arrived Sat Nav's estimation was out by over two hours.

Meeting him at the door, the recently appointed Manager, a lady of indeterminate age, seemed keen to get the niceties out of the way. 'Good afternoon, Mr Tarquin. I'm Vera Dintner. Very glad you could make it. Your father has been extremely agitated and says he won't settle until he's spoken to you. You haven't seen him for a while – sorry, that wasn't meant as a criticism – and unfortunately I think you will see he's changed to some degree.'

Leading him along the corridor, that he was pleased to note smelt of air freshener rather than lunch, or worse, he wondered how much his father had altered. Her words had made him feel bad. What was more important…work or family? He knew of many people who had arrived at the correct answer too late.

His father's room boasted a curved bay window which overlooked a small garden. It was one of the most expensive rooms in the Home, Harvey and his brothers thinking the extra cost was worthwhile. It wasn't only the outlook that had persuaded them to spend more. The room's layout made it look enormous. Sets of shelves in the two alcoves were jam-packed. First and Second World War books, and his father's collection of tin soldiers, amassed when he was young, filled every surface.

'Who the devil are you? Go away! I'm expecting my sons. They should be here any minute and they won't want to find other people in my room.'

Mrs Dintner's statement had been a gross understatement: any link with the truth as close as a politician's answer to a tricky question. Bill Tarquin appeared to have shrunk, the bedclothes scarcely disturbed by his meagre frame. His face had taken on the skeletal appearance of the seriously ill, and all colour had faded, leaving a pale reminder of his former self. Only his voice had retained its vigour.

'He has been very confused at times, whilst on other occasions he's still very with it. The doctor is calling later and I'm sure he'll be able to give you further information.' Great, thought Harvey, buck-passing time. Surely, they were paying enough to have someone in charge who could furnish him with far greater detail.

'Get out. Leave me alone. I don't like strangers.'

'It's me, Dad. Harvey. I've come to see how you are.'

'Harvey? You're not Harvey. Do you think I don't know my own son? He's coming later, so I will ask you one last time to go. Get out!'

Realising he was upsetting the old man, Harvey left the room. Coffee and biscuits were offered and accepted. He sat stunned in Mrs Dintner's office as she rang the surgery to see when the doctor was hoping to visit.

Chapter 42

Without her boss, Serena was feeling stressed. No sign of the elusive Harry Whistler. Patrols had been dispatched to search both parks and every street, nook and cranny in Fordway. Each officer had a picture of Harry. Members of the public were being asked if they had seen him. So far, no one had.

The inspector had not wanted to contact Harvey, but knew his approval was needed before the media could become involved. The local paper would make the story front page news, and this week's edition of *Crimewatch* had been asked to include a short piece on the missing man. Two photos were to be shown. The before: with beard, shaggy hair and ragged clothes, and the after: the clean-shaven, incarnation.

'He could be used in one of those before and after adverts. Everyone would buy whatever he used!' George Eventide remained upbeat. Returning to professional mode he answered the phone. 'Inspector, we've got a call you might want to take.'

The voice at the other end of the phone sounded nervous, the words delivered hesitantly, a gap between each sentence. 'Good morning. My name is Sylvia Brotherton. I don't know if I can be of any help. My husband said I should speak to you. So, I said I'd call.' Her voice became more confident. 'It's just that a very pleasant young police officer showed me the photo of the missing man, the one you want to question. I was doing my shopping on the High Street, just about to go the butcher's, we like a pork chop and he does good ones, much better than the ones you get in the supermarket.'

From long experience, Serena knew that people often went ten times around the houses before they got to the point. Longing to ask the caller to hurry up, she waited patiently, making the appropriate noises.

'Well, when the young policeman – what a good looking young man, I said to my husband he could be on the television – well anyway, when he showed me the photo I knew I'd seen him. In fact, I've seen him around quite a bit, he's been one of the town's homeless for a long time. He's often walking through the streets, all his worldly possessions in his bags. It's so sad, no life.'

Serena felt impelled to interrupt. 'Mrs Brotherton...'

'Please call me Sylvia. Mrs Brotherton sounds so formal.'

'Thank you, Sylvia. Was there one particular time you want to tell me about?'

'Yes, oh sorry, I've been rambling. I don't want to take up too much of your time. The thing is...it was just before that young girl was found. Was she called Claire? No, I seem to recall it was Charlotte. I remember thinking it was such a pretty name. Well...when I heard on the news that she'd been found I said to Hugo...that's my husband, we've been married over fifty-five years...that I'd seen someone running from the park the previous evening. I take my dog for his final constitutional along the road by Elizabeth Park, we only live a few houses down from the back entrance, and there he was. What made it stick in my mind was that you don't often see a member of the homeless community running. He looked upset and was most-definitely in a tremendous hurry. Looked like he was training for the Olympics. When I looked at the photo this morning I thought…that's him…the running man. I know it was a long time ago, but there was something about him that was memorable that night. I think it was his eyes. We only exchanged a glance, after all my running days are well and truly over, no hope of keeping up with him, but his eyes looked almost manic. Very piercing.'

'This could be most helpful, Sylvia.' Serena knew the lady would have to be certain if she was going to act as a witness in court. Otherwise the CPS would tear her evidence to pieces, finer than any paper at the wrong end of a shredder.

'Are you sure that the man you saw running away from the park is the man we are looking for?'

'Some people would say that all the poor vagrants look the same. Not to me. I worked as a volunteer at the homeless shelter on Chester Avenue before a lack of funding closed it down. Iniquitous. Those poor souls need assistance and the shelter provided some of life's essentials: meals, clothing, a bed for the night. Although I don't recall seeing the man you want at the shelter…it's been closed for years…I look carefully at all the down-and-outs I meet. It's still good to try and help…with sandwiches and coffee…not money, most of that would go on drink…and so I get to know their faces. They are human beings; each has retained his own unique look. That man certainly had eyes I would know anywhere.'

Interrupting the flow, Serena thanked Sylvia Brotherton and said that someone would call to take a formal statement. 'Please tell your husband that your call has been most helpful.' Serena hoped that would prove to be true. How many others were sitting on vital information? Ringing the paper for the second time that morning, she asked them to highlight how important it was for anyone with any information to contact the police. Unfortunately, the local paper wasn't published for three days.

Doctor Ellerton arrived at the Home, as soon as his early afternoon surgery finished. 'I wanted to see your father again, and if possible to catch you before you head off.'

Harvey had been sitting in his dad's room for the past hour, the old man fast asleep. As gently as if he was dealing with a newborn baby, the doctor woke the senior Mr Tarquin and asked how he was feeling.

'I'm OK, apart from all the people who interrupt me. They seem to think they can just waltz in and treat my room as their own.'

Following an examination, the doctor indicated that he and Harvey should talk elsewhere. 'I don't know if I can be of much help. I know you've been told that your father had a mild stroke this morning. It doesn't appear to have done much damage. However, one TRA can be the prelude to others, or more seriously to a full-blown stroke. It's extremely difficult to predict what happens next: your father could live for years and die of something completely different, or suffer a huge stroke tonight and that would be that. Harvey suspected that having used the D word once, he was disinclined to repeat it.

'My brothers are both working abroad. I have spoken to them and they both asked about returning to England. I said I'd contact them again when I had a clearer picture.'

'I'm afraid it's as clear as the proverbial mud. What I would say is that his dementia is progressing rather rapidly.'

Harvey realised that he was near to tears as he repeated his father's misunderstanding when he first arrived. 'Then, the second time I went in to see him he knew me and said how wonderful it was that I was there.'

'That's not at all uncommon. For a long time, the brain affected by Dementia seems to move in and out of the ability to recognise faces, even the familiar faces known for decades. That particular ability gradually departs, and very soon Bill won't know you...or your brothers, so from that point of view they may be as well to come and see him.'

Thanking the doctor for his time, and obvious concern, Harvey decided to ring Sam and Jeremy and arrange a time when they could all visit their father together.

Before leaving the Home, he went to say goodbye to his father. 'Still here, I thought you'd gone back. Nearly tea time. Is your mother coming? It's her favourite: steak and mushroom pie.'

'She's coming later, Dad. Said to give you her love. I don't think she'll be long.' Staccato sentences all he could manage. The doctor's suggestion that the mind slips in and out of lucidity looked accurate. Time travelling was all too obviously another issue.

As he headed back up the motorway he wondered what had been happening in Fordway. The incident room foremost in his thoughts.

Chapter 43

The day in Fordway had proved frustrating. Four phone calls had been received, all claiming to have seen Harry Whistler. Each one had been followed up: each one had been futility personified. Serena had coordinated the many tasks necessary before the CPS would consider taking their suspect to court. As she'd delegated the various tasks she'd felt an almost overwhelming despondency. She was sure Mr Whistler was their man, it was just unfortunate that there seemed to be so many holes in the case it looked like the scarf she had attempted to knit in Year 6.

When Harvey phoned, very late in the afternoon, he assured her he would be back at work in the morning. Serena was more relieved than she was willing to admit. The day without him had been hard. Maybe she hadn't been as ready as she thought for the promotion she had sought. 'I'm just praying that the item on television tonight might bring more evidence. I think we need it, sir.'

Neither of the senior police officers slept well. Both knew what was necessary. A comprehensive file: watertight evidence and wide-ranging statements, all incriminating Harry Whistler. Only then could they show the file to the prosecutor, the one who worked for the Crown Prosecution Service, the one who decided if the evidence they had amalgamated was strong enough to provide a reasonable (sensible, rational, realistic?) chance of conviction in court. *The Evidential Test*: the words bounced inside Harvey's head, like a crazy game of squash. If the evidence wasn't watertight, the case would stand as much chance as the Titanic had done.

He knew the case would pass the *Public Interest Test*: five murders crossed that threshold. Falling asleep, just as dawn was breaking, Harvey was plagued by a series of dreams, each one ending with a jury laughing him out of court.

Despite his horrendous night, Harvey had been the first in, head pounding and stomach heaving. Reading the statement from Sylvia Brotherton helped to kick-start the day.

Clare Jennings arrived, looking as tired as she felt, not good so early in the week that lay ahead. She was seething at the sexist joke Roger Symmons had just told.

'Why was the husband in a hurry to mend the kitchen light bulb?'

'Because his wife had donned her pinny, ready to make his dinner.'

'In what century, could that pathetic excuse for a joke be regarded as amusing? It's stereotypical and demeaning to women, something the modern police force should have eradicated decades ago.'

Walking in at the end of the joke, Serena was surprised by the young PC's reaction. Trying to calm the situation she said, 'And who calls them pinnies these days?'

'My grandma. We buy her a new one each Christmas. This year it was covered in pictures of chickens: ideal for cooking eggs.' The pitying looks he received told the sergeant that it was time to start work.

Serena and Clare stood by their boss's desk. 'Good morning, sir. I see you've read Mrs Brotherton's statement. Clare visited the lady and recorded her words. I'm not sure it helps very much, but at least it places Harry Whistler in the vicinity on the night Charlotte was killed.'

'Yes, and that's about it. Any defence lawyer would drive a two-ton truck through it should we call her as a witness. We need a great deal more.' Seeing the young woman's face, he added, 'Sorry, I don't mean to sound negative and you've done a very good job of writing it up.' The last thing the team needed was any type of criticism; Harvey knew he had to keep them positive. Clare was one of the best, and certainly the most enthusiastic, young officers he had worked with and she needed to know her efforts were appreciated.

The team had been asked to meet at eight. Most were positive, talking in animated voices, though everyone knew that this was one of the trickiest moments of any investigation. It was the time when there was a belief that the right person had been identified, though he still needed to be apprehended again, and weeks of work lay ahead. Sufficient evidence had to be put in place to prove their theory.

George Eventide spoke loudly enough for all those assembled to hear. 'Getting a conviction is like taking a driving test. You start with the written paper which is child's play, provided you've mugged up the answers, but anything can happen when you get behind the wheel. My daughter failed again last week. Her third attempt. Silly muppet forgot to indicate before pulling out. I don't know how many times I've had to remind her about that. The worst of it is I'm the muggins who'll still be taking her out practising. Hard on the nerves.'

'And expensive,' Roger Symmons quipped, before realising Harvey was waiting for Serena to start the briefing.

Most of the team knew where Harvey had been the previous day, and many made the appropriate noises. It was, however, a fact of policing that life outside the station must not intrude on the vital work they had to do. Allowing personal problems to intrude would be like letting a bull loose in a field of cows at the wrong time: the farmer's planning jettisoned.

'Good morning everyone.' Serena had compiled a list of the tasks that needed addressing. As she distributed it, there were comments about its length, and some smirks about the first item written in bold: APPREHEND HARRY WHISTLER! It was most unfortunate that they didn't have their suspect in custody.

Ten officers were assigned to answer the calls, those that were inevitable following the previous evening's television programme. 'As we know they may or may not prove useful. Anything of interest must be relayed to me ASAP.' Serena sat down, knowing her boss wanted to lead the rest of the meeting.

Just as he was about to begin, one of the officers manning the phone rushed in.

'A man has just been in contact with information about Lillian Henshaw. It sounded interesting, so I asked him to come in to give a statement.'

Gerald Smithson walked into the interview room like a conductor about to direct an orchestra. Serena and Clare both said afterwards that they felt like standing up and applauding his entrance. Mr Smithson was well-known locally, an entrepreneur with several businesses to his name. 'Smithson' could be seen in huge red and black letters on lorries and trade entrances throughout the area.

Serena opened the conversation. 'Good morning, Mr Smithson. Thank you for your time. We realise you are a very busy man. You said on the phone that you have some information regarding the last night's appeal.'

Sitting very straight in the chair, a position they assumed he adopted in Board Meetings, he launched in. 'I'll get straight to the point. The Henshaw's were neighbours…and indeed Stuart still is. What happened to Lillian was outrageous, and my wife and I have tried to help Stuart. Anyway, a few days before she was murdered I was in town, and I saw her having a heated conversation with a man I didn't know. At the time, I didn't think anything of it, and certainly didn't think he was one of the homeless scum who mar our streets. It wasn't until last night – when they showed the cleaned-up version of the vagrant you want to apprehend – that I began to think he was the one arguing with Lillian.'

'You say a few days before. Can you be more exact?'

'I can be absolutely exact. It was my wife's birthday and I had gone to town to buy some flowers. June 15th and poor Lillian was killed on the 18th. I'm just sorry I didn't intervene. However, when I came out of the florist's they had both gone.'

'It might have been helpful if you had come forward earlier. We could have organised a line-up. Always easier to identify someone before there is a long time-lapse.' Serena was trying, but not completely succeeding, to reign in her frustration.

Holding up his hands, once again looking as though he was preparing to lead a group of musicians, Gerald Smithson replied, 'I realise that now, though to be honest with you, I didn't give the fracas a moment's thought until last night.'

'Mr Smithson, have you got time to do a picture ID this morning? I'm sure we can organise one quickly.'

An hour later they had their picture. Harry Whistler had been identified as the man arguing with Lillian Henshaw two days before she was murdered.

Feeling very pleased with themselves, Serena and Clare reported back.

'Good work, though once again an efficient defence lawyer would say he was obviously going to pick Harry, as the man's face had been on TV less than twenty-four hours before. The only way such a witness would be of any use is if '*Crimewatch*' isn't mentioned.'

'Sir, we do now have corroboration that Harry and Lillian knew each other. Maybe she wasn't fond of the homeless. Maybe she was rude to him and the argument rankled. Maybe he lured her into the empty house and strangled her. Maybe it was pay-back time.'

'Unfortunately, inspector, that's a lot of maybes!'

Clare Jennings had been assigned the task of producing a summary of all five incidents, based on the universal triumvirate of means, motive and opportunity.

'See what you can produce, Clare. It may be a way to see what is important, without the clutter of details.'

'Don't think I'll do a Venn diagram, might be too complicated. Probably try doing it on a spread sheet.'

Harvey, stuck somewhere in the middle of the twentieth century, didn't know if she was being funny, so decided to say nothing.

Chapter 44

Eve

My life is mimicking that awful play I sat through a few weeks ago: 'Waiting for Godot'. Philip wanted to see it, he'd studied it for A level and raved about its deep meaning. It arrived in Preston last month, part of its country-wide tour, following an eighteen-month run in the West End. I feel like one of the characters, Vladimir or Estragon, who spend all their time postponing real life as they sit anticipating the arrival of Godot. My Godot is Dad. Still no sign of him, though every police force in the universe is looking for him.

Thank goodness for work. I can't deal with Dad's case until he's apprehended – which is bound to happen eventually.

Eric Chorlton certainly managed to distract me today. He's what might be called an habitual criminal, mostly misdemeanors of the less serious variety, leading to fines and community penalties. So far, he's avoided a custodial sentence…surely that's also just a matter of time!

During the pre-court interview with him it all seemed straightforward. He was charged with handling stolen goods, something that was a change from his usual petty thefts. I warned him that this was a far more serious offence, and given his extensive record, the magistrates might hand down a stiff sentence. Unfortunately for him he was in Court Number One, before a trio of magistrates, the chairman well known for delivering the most severe punishments allowed. Their Sentencing Guidelines were formerly a huge tome. Now, still covering every misdemeanor, they are accessed via an app on their iPads.

Mr Chorlton's story was that he had been foolish, and had allowed his brother-in-law to persuade him to transport a range of items stolen from two houses. He claimed to have played no part in the robberies. However, he agreed to take three lap-tops, several items of jewellery and a television, from Fordway to a pick-up point at the Burton-in Kendal services on the M6. Unfortunately for him, he had been caught on CCTV moving the goods to a waiting vehicle.

As I spoke to him it became obvious that he had no understanding of the seriousness of the offence. He told me he was confident he would be given another fine or possibly a curfew, 'Or more bloody hours of unpaid work. I hate that. Everyone sees you wearing the clobber that shouts "criminal".' I had to refrain from saying that is exactly what he is.

Telling him that his offence fell into the Category 4 band, the lowest, due to the value of the goods, cheered him up. That was until I pointed out that the starting point for the magistrates to consider was a high-level community order: almost certainly the dreaded hours of unpaid work. It was when I warned him, that given his antecedents, they could impose up to twenty-six week's custody that he blanched, performing a most impressive chameleon-like change of colour.

As always, I did my utmost to speak positively on my client's behalf. 'Mr Chorlton regrets his actions which he now realises were extremely misguided. The court will have noted that he has not been involved in such activity before. He assures me he has learnt his lesson and that he will have nothing to do with stolen goods in the future. He says he was helping his brother-in-law, whose case comes before you next week, and needed the money as his wife has recently given birth to their first child. Being unemployed, Mr Chorlton was grateful for any extra cash, babies needing a great deal of equipment.' Even to my ears it sounded weak.

Elizabeth Jones, the Chairman, looked most unimpressed and whilst they retired to deliberate I warned Eric that he was about to receive a strong punishment.

Mrs Jones has an aura: she speaks as though addressing a far larger gathering than was present in court today. I could picture her a century ago rallying the Suffragettes. 'Mr Chorlton, you admit to being "foolish",' the last word dripping with so much sarcasm I thought a tap hadn't been turned on. 'You are, however, an adult and must take responsibility for your actions. Your brother-in-law did not force you to transport his ill-gotten gains, and your family would be far better served by having an honest husband and father. Your list of previous felonies is lamentable and has persuaded us to treat this latest wrongdoing very seriously. We could find no mitigating factors which might have persuaded us to lessen your punishment.'

By this juncture, Eric looked twenty years older, the chairman's voice adding months with each word. As he stood beside me I could feel him shaking; shuddering and jolting uncontrollably.

'We have taken your guilty plea into account, though as you were literally caught with the proverbial red hands we feel you had little choice in the matter. The three hundred hours of unpaid work has been reduced to two hundred, and we also impose a four-month curfew from 8 p.m. to 8 a.m.'

Although not happy, Eric looked relieved to have avoided prison. It was Mrs Jones' next words that left me speechless and him anything but.

'As your car was used to convey goods you knew to be stolen, and was driven purely for your own gain, you are to be disqualified from driving for four months, beginning immediately.'

What followed was, in retrospect comical. I think the colloquial phrase would be that Eric went bananas. I will paraphrase what he yelled: you can't do that; it's not allowed; where in your book does it tell you to take away my right to drive? You are all just a pathetic bunch of middle-class hypocrites who think you're better than the rest of us.

Dear brothers, please add a liberal sprinkling of expletives which I have deleted.

His ranting was then accompanied by loud sobs, stamping feet and hands being banged on my desk: a symphony of cacophonous sounds. It was when he progressed, like a car moving up several gears (a simile that, in the circumstances, I find amusing), and began to threaten the trio on the Bench, that security was summoned, and he was taken down to the cells where he spent the rest of the day.

I do wonder who picked him up and drove him home.

The remainder of the day was dull. At least Eric diverted my mind, if only for an hour. Please keep in touch, I need all the moral support available. And I fear it will get worse.

Just an aside...how is the romance going Jacob? She seemed like a pleasant girl when we met her at the party.

Jacob

Yes, she was lovely. Note the past tense. She said the relationship "wasn't going anywhere." Funny that coincided with the press's interest in Dad. I wonder how she'd have put it after that bloody television programme got involved.

Once again, the bastard ruins my life.

Eve

Sorry, Jacob. I'm here if you want to talk.

Jacob

Thanks, but no thanks. The less I see of our family the better.

David

As always, Eve, you seem to be bearing the brunt of the Dad saga which is going on and on... not sure whether ad nauseam or ad infinitum is the more appropriate. Do consider my offer to pay for a barrister to defend him. I know you are more than capable, but it will be stressful. I have no doubt that the CPS will employ a top person to prosecute Dad. We must also be aware that once it starts, every day of the trial will create news headlines: a media circus. All the nationals as well as our local paper will have reporters there who will relish every salacious detail. We can forget about enjoying any privacy.

Keep in touch, and remember you are always welcome to bring Philip to any of the restaurants...no charge!

Andrew

A barrister. Now I've heard everything. David remains the dictatorial, domineering brother we all endured as children. These days he can be even more overbearing. Money doesn't make him our superior.

David, you cannot make decisions that affect us all. I notice there has been no sign of asking what the rest of us think. Well I can tell you one thing...your wealth can't buy this one dear brother. Do you really suppose that even the most capable, and horrendously expensive, lawyer will prevent Dad going where he belongs: jail?

Jacob

I like David's "Dad saga". Do you all realise his self-centered actions have been affecting the entire family for over two decades. Time for it to stop, though will he return, like one of the zombies in the film 'The Night of the Living Dead'? Do you remember when we rented the video from the shop on the corner and scared ourselves witless? That's how I regard Dad these days: part alive and part dead. He even looks like a reanimated body. Without too much emphasis on the animated.

Andrew told me that Mum is back on the tranquilisers. Apparently, she gets up at ridiculous hours of the night and wanders around the house, then can't wake up in the morning.

The sooner the man is apprehended, tried, and locked up for the rest of his miserable life the better. Maybe then we can get on with ours.

Eve

Am I the only one who retains the hope that he is innocent?

Chapter 45

Harry Whistler

Victim	Means	Motive	Opportunity
Thomas (Tommy) Granger. Aged 70. Member of the homeless group in Fordway.	Strangled with his own scarf. Cross inserted in his mouth. PM. Body hidden in the bushes. Laid out with reverence, all his possessions placed around the body.	Argument? Falling out over drink, or sleeping area? Disagreement over the new girl, Charlotte?	In Elizabeth Park, a common meeting place. Once the park shuts at dusk, the homeless are known to sleep there. The park is only opened at dawn, so there was very little chance of being interrupted.
Charlotte Carroway. Aged 18. She had recently joined the homeless in town.	Strangled with her scarf. Cross inserted in her mouth. PM. Body also laid out in the bushes.	Did she reject his advances? Was he jealous that others were also interested in her?	Elizabeth Park. Harry "helped" her settle in Fordway. They are known to have spent a lot of time together.

Victim	Means	Motive	Opportunity
Terry Wendover. Aged 65. Long-term down-and-out. Ex con. Might have known Harry from his time in Glasgow. Terry spent time there and some think Harry also lived there when he left his home in Fordway in 1995.	Strangled, then body burnt. No cross, or it may have been incinerated by the fire. Body not hidden. Was the killer interrupted? Why the escalation in violence?	Terry and Harry had a history of altercations. The day before Terry's body was found he had accused Harry of the first two murders. They were seen arguing outside the police station.	Elizabeth Park. Both lived there much of the time. Once again, an easy venue with little danger of any witnesses.
Edwin York. Aged 64 Pensioner with quite advanced Dementia. The carers reported him missing.	Died of a heart attack then strangled post-mortem with a length of heavy-duty Jute twine. Similar twine found in the shed where he was discovered. Cross inserted in his mouth. PM.	Harry Whistler is known to have slept in the shed. Did Edwin York disturb him? Harry knew his son didn't like him using it.	Edwin York had disappeared from his house two weeks before his body was discovered in Jacob Whistler's shed on the Aldwin Road allotments. The shed is situated at the far end of the allotments and is not overlooked.

Victim	Means	Motive	Opportunity
Lillian Henshaw. Aged 80. Pensioner. Good health, lived with her husband and was going to visit her daughter on the morning she disappeared.	Strangled with a scarf that contained Harry Whistler's DNA. (Unusual deviation, though the weather was warm, and she wasn't wearing one of her own.) Cross inserted. PM.	A witness says he saw Lillian in an altercation with a man, two days before she went missing. When he constructed a picture of the man he had seen having the argument, the result was very like Harry Whistler.	Lillian Henshaw's body was discovered in an empty house a few metres from the entrance to the park. Did he persuade her to go into the house, then kill her? Was it revenge following a disagreement in town?

The spread sheet was given pride of place on the board in the Major Incident Room. It was now a hive of anticipation. A new queen bee had been threatened: a more experienced officer brought in to lead the case. A Detective Chief Superintendent, Janette Masterson, had visited and had been assured that the team, led by Harvey, could cope.

'DCI Tarquin, you and your team appear to be making good progress, though it's taken longer than would, ideally, be acceptable. I can see that you have identified the man responsible for these atrocities and it is therefore my considered opinion that, for the moment at least, the case can safely be left in your capable hands.' Harvey thought she could have said the last sentence in fewer words, but it was hardly surprising knowing the senior officer's propensity for wordage. There was a YouTube video of her giving an interview where one sentence was so long that when the end arrived no one could recall the beginning.

As soon as the senior officer left, everyone returned to their assigned tasks. A feeling of euphoria filled the room. This was the stage in an investigation that the officers enjoyed. Despite the knowledge that there would be no early nights, the men and women involved loved amalgamating all the evidence and slotting the pieces into place like a jigsaw that, when completed, would lead to a conviction. They were certain they had their man. All they needed now was irrefutable proof.

Harry Whistler remained a free man. Three weeks on and no one had recognised him. Any resemblance to either of the photos that had been circulated was, by now, purely incidental.

Following his conversation with Bigman, returning to Manchester had felt like the best option. He had liked the city during his time there. Once there, the police continued to show a quite puzzling level of empathy, making him wonder if they'd all been on awareness courses, encouraged to see the rough sleepers as valuable members of the community. He was seldom moved on, the men and women on the beat more likely to stop and chat, and tell him about the new shelters that had opened in Moss Side and West Didsbury. Neither appealed, both too far to travel. He had spent a few nights in the well-established one, run by St Barnaby's church, situated on one corner of Albert Square.

Within hours of arriving in Manchester he had, yet again, changed his appearance: head shaved, glasses bought at a pound shop, and beard regrown, a goatee which was kept well-trimmed. Clothes, all in garish colours, had been purchased from several charity shops. He knew the police would be looking for him and would not think to look twice at someone so obvious. He knew he "stood-out", the last thing they'd be expecting. Not much of a disguise, but so far enough to stop him being arrested.

Then…a careless choice of night time lodgings. Harry made the mistake of trying a new venue. It was a damp night and the doorway looked deep enough to provide some refuge. Arranging his bedding, he looked up to see a young PC giving him a long, hard stare.

'Excuse me, sir, you can't sleep here.'

'I'm staying, not interfering with anyone.'

'Have we met before, sir? You look familiar.'

'At last, at bloody last. We've got him. Arrested in Manchester last night by an alert bobby. Mr Whistler spent the night in the cells in Bootle Street cells and is, as we speak, being conveyed here, care of the Greater Manchester constabulary. Bless them.'

The cheer that followed Harvey's announcement might well have been heard in Manchester.

'Interview to commence at 1p.m. Hopefully we'll soon be in the position to inform the CPS that we are ready to proceed to trial.'

'Shall I inform Eve Whistler? Even if her father doesn't require her services, she ought to be here.'

'Thanks, Serena believe me…the man will need every bit of help he can find.'

Eve had spent the previous evening at the doctor's surgery. As a child, she had been prone to bouts of eczema. Every GP she had seen had checked for allergies, or newly introduced products that might irritate her skin. Eve had always known that, in her case, stress was the cause of the unsightly and painful cracks and blisters that were once again covering her hands.

Dr Melling was new to the practice, but was aware of Eve's background. As Eve introduced herself and began to explain the reason for her visit, she realised she was weeping. A torrent of tears seemed to escape with no warning. Afterwards, she was to tell Philip that flash floods have taken longer to materialise.

Passing across the ubiquitous box of tissues, the doctor told her to take deep breaths. There was no hurry, Eve was her final patient, so she wouldn't be keeping anyone waiting.

Three quarters of an hour later, she left with a prescription for ointment and the name of a counsellor the doctor had recommended. 'You are under a lot of stress and it might be helpful to talk to someone. Mr Addis is excellent, and I think you'd find him a good listener. In the past, he's helped a number of my patients.'

As she left the surgery, Eve thought her life resembled a "car crash", the words her boss used to describe the chaotic lifestyle endured by some of their clients. Had she, somewhere along the road, missed the signpost that said "Eve, this way"?

Court Number One had a full list. Having been there all morning, Eve was now in the unenviable position of attempting to defend the totally indefensible. Today's chairman had just informed her client that the suspended sentence, announced by a previous bench a mere two weeks ago, was about to be activated.

'Miss Simpson, it was explained to you at the time that a suspended sentence was a serious matter. It meant that, should you offend again, within the six-month period of the suspension, the prison sentence would be activated, and any subsequent punishments would be added to the eighteen weeks that were suspended. You are before us today for not just one, but three further thefts. This Bench has therefore no option but to send you to prison for twenty-one weeks.'

As Joanna Simpson was handcuffed and led down to the cells, one of the ushers arrived and handed Eve a note asking her to contact DCI Tarquin as soon as possible.

It was beginning: how would it end?

Chapter 46

The interview had stalled. The only words Harry Whistler had spoken for the past two and a half hours were, once again, "no comment". A short break, when Eve had begged him to be more helpful, had made no difference.

It had been a meeting that neither would forget. They had almost staggered to the interview room, a pleasant venue this morning with unusually large windows, the sun streaming in. The setting appeared to mock the gravity of the situation. Harry fell onto a chair and scowled.

'Dad, we have been allowed this break so that I can persuade you to answer the questions being asked with more than a "no comment". As your lawyer, I must advise you that you are really, and I do mean really, not helping yourself. We've got thirty minutes to think about your answers.'

Harry stared straight ahead and then started to speak belligerently. 'I am innocent. Unfortunately, you will not be able to prove it. I will swear on the Bible that the charges are untrue. You know what that means, even if they don't. I am aware that people lie on oath, but as I know God is listening I will tell the truth.'

'Dad, there is an avalanche of evidence against you; only you can refute it. Please give me something to work with. I believe you, but I need help to convince the jury. You *are* going to stand trial and as your lawyer I must have the ammunition to repudiate all the charges. DCI Tarquin will tell you that when you come up before the magistrates' tomorrow morning the date will be set for the case to go to Preston Crown Court. This is so serious, Dad. Give me something to work with.'

Mum

My dear children, how must you be feeling? Would that I could take this anguish from you. A mother yearns to protect her offspring: to stop all distress, to make life better, or at least more bearable. Today that proved impossible. Over the years, each of you has suffered. Your father's desertion was a negation of his duty and caused such deep hurt. Every one of you needed him, you were all so young. However, he thought only of himself. He must have had his reasons for such absconding and over the years I have tried to understand and forgive.

Things happen. I know that. Things one doesn't want to happen. Events occur that are beyond one's control. Events for which one cannot prepare. When I promised 'for better or for worse' I never thought that vow would be so sorely tried. It's strange that one can think the worst has happened, only for something even more dire to rear up, like a leviathan from the depths, invading one's life and pulling one under.

This morning, sitting in the Magistrates' Court, watching my daughter defending Harry was almost unbearable: so painfully excruciating I hurt physically. I have no idea why I was reminded of the day, a long time ago, when I was felled in a hockey match, my opponent's stick hitting my leg, not the ball. A visit to casualty showed a broken shin. Oh, dear Lord, were that the extent of today's suffering.

Today: what willpower was needed to remain in my seat. To listen as my husband, the man I married, the man, who despite twenty years of desertion I still regard as my life-long partner, was accused of five murders. Three of his fellow-down-and-outs, and two elderly people.

Today: it was mostly formalities: name, date of birth, address (no fixed abode; dear me, the pain those words continue to engender) and, after what felt like a lifetime, the pleas.

Today: five charges, read separately, an agonising break between each one.

Today: five responses. 'Not guilty'.

It was a day that will be forever locked in my memory. A warning voice tells me that there will be many similar todays.

Harry looked calm and spoke in a clear voice. No hint of nerves. Was he the only one unmoved by this unprecedented and most heinous of occasions? Eve looked nervous and I saw her fiddle with her hair. She used to do that as a child when she couldn't do her homework, or one of the boys was irritating her. Both father and daughter were dressed appropriately. Harry in a dark suit, white shirt and blue striped tie, all bought by David. I have been told there are other outfits for future appearances. For some reason that strikes me as so sad – the man has dressed like a tramp for two decades and is now a 'picture of sartorial elegance', David's somewhat ill-chosen words. Harry had obviously shaved, both his face and his head. When I first knew him one of the things that attracted me to him was his shock of the blackest hair.

I have never watched Eve in court before. She was the consummate professional, a difficult act with such a client.

The case has been sent to Crown Court. We all knew that would be the outcome. Why then did I gasp when the chairman spoke those damming words. 'Mr Whistler, the crimes of which you have been accused are beyond this court's jurisdiction. Your case will therefore be heard at Preston Crown Court, the trial to begin on September 8th. No request for bail has been made and you will be remanded in prison until the trial begins.'

The date set seems so far off. How will we get through those twelve weeks, those eighty-four days?

David brought Andrew and me home. He insisted that we eat: tomato soup and cheese on toast. Hard to swallow, my throat constricted by the tension of the day. Andrew was silent during the meal, then claimed to be exhausted and retired to his room. I doubt I shall see him again this evening. Probably for the best as we wouldn't know what to say, like meeting someone recently bereaved, the appropriate words performing a vanishing act.

I told Eve not to visit or phone. She has done enough today, and for her the next weeks will be like Odysseus facing his Journey of Endurance. David has promised to support her. Sadly, I don't think Andrew and Jacob feel the same way. They don't approve of her acting as Harry's lawyer. Andrew muttered that if she thinks Dad is innocent she must have borrowed Lady Justice's blindfold.

Eve

The process has begun. Thank you for your phone call, David. Glad you took Mum and Andrew home. From the look on his face, I don't think Andrew will go to Crown Court.

Weeks of torment lie ahead. It feels as though Dante has created an additional circle of hell; a personal one with no exit. Jacob has been in absentia recently, perhaps unable to deal with the trauma...or us. Media intrusion certainly doesn't help, encroaching on our lives, nothing left to the public's imagination. The press has already condemned him, no hint of innocent until proven guilty.

My body feels as though it has been scoured, inside and out. No part has been left untouched. It's like the time Mum ordered that specialist cleaning company to "bottom" the house, a wonderful northern word Philip didn't know. When they'd finished, the house didn't feel like ours and that's how I feel about my body.

I ache, groan, give in to bouts of tears and thump the walls. Philip asked if I wanted to start planning the wedding. I said "yes" a few days ago and we are engaged! I was waiting until we met to tell you. 'It will give you something positive to think about. A happy occasion.' He looked crestfallen when I muttered something about it needing greater attention than I could give it until the trial is over.

Everyone has experiences they long to end and, without doubt, this falls into that category. Wars, famines, earthquakes all damage lives, destroy them, often beyond restoration, and I realise that compared to their suffering the weeks ahead are of far less significance: except for those of us directly involved, caught in the firing-line of the media, the lawyers, the judge and an uncooperative, truculent defendant.

There is some relief that the process is under way. It feels like a concerto with three movements: today was a pedantic adagio in front of the magistrates; the next six weeks will be a lento while we wait for the presto in Crown Court. Unfortunately, our soloist is not willing to play his part. His final comment this afternoon made me feel like weeping. 'Don't even think of calling me to give evidence. I'm not bloody well standing in the witness box.' He should realise it's his future that's at stake.

Chapter 47

Bad timing. A few weeks before the trial was due to begin Harvey's brothers were both available to visit Oxford. They had been informed that whilst their father had not suffered any further strokes, and was in reasonable shape physically, his mental capacity was deteriorating rapidly.

'Your father is far more important than this case. You'll regret not meeting up with your brothers and seeing your father together. I know I missed seeing my gran just before she died because I thought I was so essential to a Domestic Violence case. It's haunted me ever since.'

Harvey knew Serena was speaking as a friend, but felt ridiculously irritated by her. He would travel to Oxford, though it would probably prove to be a futile trip. He knew he should look forward to seeing his brothers, but the timing was appalling. In-all-likelihood, his dad wouldn't know any of them, and would almost certainly rant and rave, leaving everyone miserable and frustrated.

The Harry Whistler case wasn't as watertight as he wanted. There were several weaknesses that a good lawyer would exploit. Even Serena, who until this week had been optimistic, had voiced her doubts, worried especially about the dearth of eye-witnesses.

'Please go, Harvey,' the inappropriate use of his name raising his blood pressure even further, 'I'll keep you up to date at this end, though I think we've done everything we can, apart from having final conversations with the eye witnesses; the few there are. I'll make sure they have their evidence in an orderly fashion.'

By the time Harvey arrived, Sam and Jeremy were already at the Home. Bill Tarquin was in the day room, the television informing anyone listening how to make the perfect soufflé.

'Another visitor? This is my lucky day.' Bill appeared to be more compos mentis than on Harvey's last visit, until he was told by his youngest brother that their father had no idea who they were.

'He asked if I was his grandad! I know I've aged, but surely not that much. Now had it been you, Harvey...' Sam smiled, realising his faux pax. Harvey knew he looked haggard, his norm at this stage of any investigation.

Lunch was served in the dining room, painted in a luminous yellow, which Sam suggested was to keep the inmates awake. The Home had an excellent reputation for its cuisine and the menu on the board looked well-balanced. Unfortunately, when it arrived, whilst their meat and potato pie with three veg was well presented, their father's meal was in liquidized form.

'He's been having difficulty swallowing. It sometimes happens as the dementia progresses. People forget how to chew and swallow pieces of food, so it's got to be blended.' The young carer introduced herself then began to feed the old man. As with a young child, a lot escaped and dribbled down on to the cloth around his neck. 'Your Dad had a good appetite until recently, but isn't as bothered about food now. It can take ages for him to eat enough.' Each brother thought that they would feel the same about the mush on the plate.

Two hours were spent in their father's room whilst he slept like an infant enjoying its afternoon nap. 'He really has returned to second childhood. Isn't aware of who we are. Not for a second.' Jeremy then suggested they go to the local pub. Having done his duty, Harvey apologised and said it had been so good to see his brothers, but he had to return to Fordway.

'How's the murder mystery going? Was it Mrs White with the lead pipe in the library or Colonel Mustard using a revolver in the ballroom? Do you remember how we all loved *Cluedo* when we were young; must have known we were going to have a top detective in the family.'

As he stood to say goodbye, the thought struck him that his brothers had summed up his life. He was a DCI. Both Sam and Jeremy had talked about their respective jobs, but had added so many of the other things they did. Sam was keen on his five-a-side football team. 'We're not much cop, it's just a lot of fun.' He had also enthused about his voluntary work in a local hospice. His younger brother had only recently returned from Germany to work in Surrey and had immediately made a new life for himself. Jeremy was travelling the world, away to some new destination at every opportunity. Harvey was aware of the envy he felt. When this case was over, and Mr Whistler was behind bars, he must find things to do outside work. Middle age was looming. Time to reassess his life.

'Sylvia Brotherton doesn't want to give evidence.' Not the greeting Harvey was expecting. The previous evening, arriving in Fordway tired and dispirited, he had gone straight home. There had been no message, so he had assumed that his services had not been required.

'Not give evidence? Why not? When did she come up with that gem?' Realising he was almost shouting, Harvey stopped and took a moment to calm down.

Although Serena was as upset as her boss she knew better than to show it.

'She's the only witness linking Harry Whistler to the second murder. She was adamant she saw him running from the park on the night Charlotte Carroway died.'

'Yes, sir, and she hasn't changed her story. However, she doesn't want to go into the witness box, says she's been having sleepless nights. I've asked witness protection to become involved and Mr Millsaps is seeing her this morning. Jon is good and if anyone can persuade her to go into court, he can.'

'On a more positive note, I had a long meeting with Gerald Smithson. He's so different: can't wait to have his day in the limelight. He's keen to tell the world about Harry arguing with Lillian Henshaw in the middle of Fordway a few days before she was murdered.'

'And what about Jacob Whistler? Will he give evidence about his father using his shed?'

The look on Serena's face told Harvey that the answer was no. 'I can understand that one, sir. It is his dad who's on trial and he would be a witness for the prosecution. A lot to ask.'

'Can we remind him that the man he is protecting might be is father, but that he is, almost certainly, guilty of five murders.'

Looking as despondent as he felt, Harvey groaned. Head in his hands, Serena had to strain to hear his monologue. 'Five murders. It's taken so long to bring the man to justice. I keep going over and over why we didn't move faster. If we had, maybe, just maybe, we could have stopped the later ones, especially the last two. We still haven't established a real motive for any of them. Lots of ideas: the falling out with Terry Wendover, the getting too close to the young girl, the alleged argument with the old lady. But, I do wonder if the jury will think any of them strong enough reasons for murder. I know it's him, I just know it. However, I am not convinced that we've done enough to convince the twelve who matter.'

Not sure how to respond, or even if the words had been meant to be heard, Serena remained silent.

'Thank you for all your hard work Inspector Peil. Should the verdict not be the one we want, the blame will be mine: entirely mine. Try to have a good night's sleep; the next few weeks are going to be hard. I just pray the evidence will prove sufficient to convict Mr Harry Whistler.'

Chapter 48

Fordway Gazette

Tramps in the Park Trial Begins

Preston Crown Court is the setting for one of the most notorious trials of recent years. Harry Whistler, a rough sleeper, who frequented Elizabeth Park in Fordway, is accused of no less than five murders.

The man in the dock did not give the appearance of someone who has been homeless for twenty-two years. He was dressed in a grey suit, pale blue shirt and dark blue tie. He looked confident as he took his place in the dock.

The judge, His Honour Toby Halsey, warned the members of the jury that they should try to 'obliterate from their minds' anything they might have read about the case over the past weeks. They were told not to look at the papers, the internet or watch any television coverage. 'You must, and I repeat must, not be influenced by any outside reporting. When the time comes, your verdict must be based solely on the evidence you hear in this court room. It is a disturbing case and you will be affected by some of the things you see and hear. I must remind you that, as a member of the jury, you cannot discuss anything outside this building.'

The Crown Prosecution Service is represented by top barrister, Ms Helena Morteson-Porteous. In her opening address, she said that the evidence against the accused would lead the jury to only one conclusion: guilty. The names of the five victims were read out: Thomas Granger, Charlotte Carroway, Terry Wendover, Edwin York and Lillian Henshaw.

The case continues.

David

Agony. I sat with Mum who insisted on attending. When Dad was brought up from the cells, handcuffed to two warders, I thought I was going to cry. How Mum sat there so calmly I don't know. At one-point nausea forced me to leave.

Eve has got quite an opponent in the barrister for the prosecution. Ms Helena Morteson-Porteous is one of the country's up-and-coming stars. I looked at her profile on the internet. Her background is a First from Oxford; top in her year on the Bar Professional Course. She is based at one of the elite London Chambers and is obviously highly regarded. On one site, she commented that her initials were perfect for the job: HMP. The desired venue for the people she prosecutes.

Eve looked more confident than I suspect she felt. Only day one. It feels as though we are all on trial.

Eve

Yes. As you put it so succinctly, David, she is 'quite an opponent'. When she began to speak, I felt like a non-league player about to face one of the top Premier outfits in an early round of the F.A. Cup. I don't know much about football, but any giant-killing is so rare it makes the headlines. I have a strong feeling that David and Goliath may well be a myth.

Dad is amazing: no sign of nerves. I am a wreck, but thanks for saying I don't look it. A tutor once told me that a lawyer is like a chameleon, adopting different facades, playing as many parts as necessary to impress the jury. 'Above all, you need to be word perfect; know your part.' My part in the drama will be to appear super-confident, the assured professional who believes the man she is defending will be found innocent. I am as prepared as I can be: all my arguments are ready for tomorrow when the prosecution begins to present its evidence.

Jacob

I was there. Not with the rest of the family. Sitting at the back where I could escape attention. Eve your opening statement was brilliant: you were indeed on the super side of confident, and I felt proud of you. I will attend again, though not every day, and no one will notice me.

The weathermen had forecast one of the hottest days ever recorded in September, beating the previous week's high by several degrees. Children were being kept out of school to enjoy a day at the seaside. Shops reported that they were selling out of ice cream.

A phalanx of journalists sat, like a cackle of hyenas, waiting to scavenge the remains of a carcass. Tablets, iPads and mobile phones at the ready, the resulting reports to be propelled through the ether in preparation for the tomorrow's lurid headlines. Most of those present, had never experienced a trial that engendered such national interest and they were determined to file copies that might advance their careers.

Courtroom Number Five was already hot. Those allowed to witness the spectacle had arrived early. Jackets and jumpers had been discarded in preparation for the day's excitement.

'All we need are some women knitting.' No one was quite sure who had made the comment, but it caused inappropriate amusement.

Harry was led into the dock looking pale and less confident than the day before. All eyes were on the young barrister who stood slowly, taking time to adjust her gown. As she touched her extremely curly wig the more mature were reminded of the disastrous hairstyle prevalent in the nineteen-eighties. Before starting to speak, she gazed around the room, making sure she had everyone's attention. She was determined that not a word would be missed.

'Your Honour, and members of the jury, today I will be calling top people, specialists in their fields to give evidence. At times, what you will hear will be unpleasant. You are asked to listen carefully to their evidence and take it into account when reaching your verdict. I would advise you to take notes. Anything you do not understand can be explained before you retire to ascertain guilt.'

Alfie Morrison was called and strode purposefully into court. Taking his place in the witness box he swore the oath, his Liverpudlian accent particularly strong in the vaulted room. 'I swear by Almighty God that the evidence I shall give, shall be the truth, the whole truth and nothing but the truth.'

'Dr Morrison, Harry Whistler is accused of five murders. I believe you conducted four of the five autopsies.'

'Yes. My colleague performed the first one, on Thomas Granger, when I was on leave. I have his detailed findings here.'

Please will you tell the court the cause of death of each victim.'

'Four were strangled. One, Edwin York, the fourth victim, died of a heart attack and was strangled post-mortem.'

'Thank you. Will you now go into greater detail about Lillian Henshaw's demise?'

If Alfie was surprised that the barrister was beginning with the fifth victim, he didn't show it.

'Mrs Henshaw was strangled. Manual strangulation is sometimes referred to as throttling. The term covers strangling by using the hands, fingers or other articles – as in this case, when a scarf was used. It was still in place around her neck when she was found. In technical terms, the victim's airway was compressed, interfering with the flow of blood in the neck. Mrs Henshaw's larynx was badly damaged leading to her death.'

'How much force would it take to strangle someone in this way?'

'That all depends on the strength of the victim: far harder to strangle a fit young man, but Lillian Henshaw was an elderly lady and of very slight build. I would therefore conclude that it would not have taken much force. Thankfully, it may well have been a quick process and the lady would not have suffered for very long. There was no evidence that she fought back: no skin under her nails or defensive wounds.'

Having begun with the final victim, the barrister worked her way back to Thomas Granger.

Determined that the jury would hear her next point she paused, then summed up Alfie's evidence. 'Dr Morrison, you have told the court that Charlotte Carroway and Terry Wendover were both of medium height. Both were underweight, and malnourished. You reported that Edwin York was elderly and has been described as "frail and vulnerable", though his demise was somewhat different. You said that with his Dementia, he would have experienced great difficulty understanding what was happening, and a heart attack in those circumstances is not unknown, though strangling someone post-mortem is rather unusual.'

Looking at the jury, she spoke slowly. 'Thomas Granger was rather different.' After another dramatic pause, she continued. 'He was a tall, well-built man and presumably much more robust than the other victims. Does that indicate that the murderer must have been strong? It can't be easy to overpower a large man and subdue him long enough to… I think the layman's word you employed was "throttle" him?'

'Yes, in some ways Thomas Granger was certainly a much larger build than the others. There were marks on Mr Granger that might indicate that he tried to fight back, though the bruises could have already have been on his hands and face before the final assault.'

'So, are we to believe that it would have taken some force to strangle him? Could a woman have done it?'

'A large woman, maybe, one with upper body strength. It's impossible to be categorical as to the sex of the assailant. All I can add is that the first victim would have been the hardest to overpower.'

The barrister looked at the jury to see whether this important point had been noted. She allowed herself a small smile as she saw that several people were busy writing. A long silence ensued, broken finally when the next question was asked in a more muted manner.

'All five lost their lives. Did the victims have anything else in common?'

This was one of the moments Eve had been dreading. The crosses inserted in four of the five mouths, the exception being the badly burnt body of Terry Wendover, would, she knew, make the jury believe that there was a religious dimension to the killings. As the pathologist delivered his findings, two of the jurors were heard to gasp. This was something that had not made the newspapers.

As Eve stood to cross-examine the pathologist, she took a moment to control her nerves. The last thing she wanted was for anyone to think she was anything but super-confident.

'Good morning, Dr Morrison. You have told the court that all five were strangled, one post-mortem. Can you say if this is a common method used to kill someone?'

'I can't give a definitive answer; all I can say is that it is not one I have come across before.'

'And how long have you been working for the police as a pathologist?'

'Over twenty years.'

'I would like to quote from a leading academic, Jemma Fielding. She has written several highly-acclaimed studies, where she writes about how killers choose their methods.' Pausing for effect, Eve read from the paper she had taken into court.

'"The general-public believe that strangling is a common method of killing someone. However, strangulation is seldom employed. Those planning a murder are more likely to use a weapon. Where strangulation is used, the murder could be described as a crime of passion: totally unpremeditated. My estimate is that ninety-nine per cent of cases involving strangling have a perpetrator who had not foreseen the act of murder. It is usually the case, where strangling is the modus operandi, that the murderer finds himself surprised by the act. In one infamous trial in Texas, the defendant claimed that he was amazed when he found his hands squeezing the victim's throat."'

Eve stopped, the next extract the most important. '"However, and this is a very important point, where more than one victim has been strangled by the same person, then the acts are planned and often with a high degree of organisation. I repeat they are planned."' Eve paused, then resumed, desperate for the jury to hear her next point. 'The esteemed academic places great emphasis on the fact that where there is more than one strangulation, the murders have been planned. They are not spur of the moment events.'

Judge Halsey looked unimpressed and asked Eve if she had a question for the witness.

'Yes, Your Honour.' Turning to face the witness box, Eve continued. 'You stated that four of the five bodies had crosses inserted in their mouths post-mortem, and the fifth body was so badly burnt that a cross might have melted. The crosses would indicate some degree of planning, of premeditated acts. Can you comment on the likelihood that all five murders were planned?'

'From my examination of the bodies I am certain that they were killed by the same person: same method employed in four of the cases, and the final one made to look the same. Identical religious symbols in their mouths. It is therefore highly likely that all five were planned. One killing, in the heat of the moment, is understandable. Not five.'

'So, in your estimation, these murders were the result of a great deal of planning. Crosses were bought to insert in the victims' mouths. Does that sound like the behaviour of someone who doesn't even know what day it is, never mind the month...or indeed the year? We have in the dock a man who lives a shambolic life, whose idea of planning is where to buy his next bottle of cider.'

'Once again, Miss Whistler, do you have a question? If not, I think you have made your point, so please move on.' Eve knew she had received a warning from the judge.

Lifting her voice, a trick she had learnt to utilise when making a telling point, she continued. 'Mr Whistler has been living as a homeless person for two decades. Do you think it likely that he would have had the wherewithal to be able to afford the crosses you discovered?'

'Whilst they weren't top quality, to purchase five would have required a reasonable outlay. I would therefore think it unlikely that a homeless person would spend their money in such a way. I believe the police have been unable to ascertain where the crosses were purchased, local jewellers not stocking them.'

'Once again, it seems that a high level of planning – and indeed travelling – was undertaken to obtain the crosses. Would you agree Dr Morrison?'

'That would appear to be the case.'

'One final question, Dr Morrison. You have said that four of the five victims were, in different ways, easy targets, without the strength to defend themselves. You have also stated that Thomas Granger was a large man, tall and well-built. In addition, he was in reasonably robust health. Are you of the opinion that a fellow member of the homeless community would have had the power to not only subdue him, but also exert the necessary force to kill him? Such an act must, in his case, have taken tremendous vigour, not something one associates with a rough sleeper, and most definitely not a vagrant of Harry Whistler's age and poor physical condition.'

'Miss Whistler I have been most patient with you. However, as you are very well-aware, an opinion is just that and is not permissible as evidence.' After pausing to glare at Eve, the judge added, 'You have now asked an expert witness to give three opinions: on the ability of a man to purchase crosses, on the likelihood he travelled some distance to purchase them, and on his strength and innate power to strangle someone. Opinions have no place in a court of law.' Turning to the jury box, he continued in a voice that showed a trace of exasperation. 'Ladies and gentlemen of the jury, you are to disregard anything you have heard Dr Morrison say that was merely his opinion. He has dealt admirably with the facts he discovered during the autopsies; only they can be considered when you review his testimony.'

Eve refrained from mentioning that the judge had allowed Helena Moretson-Porteous to ask the witness for his opinion on the sex of the assailant. She knew she must be far quicker to challenge in the future. Even a barrister was fallible.

'I have no further questions for this witness.'

'Members of the Press, I must also ask you to employ caution when you report today's proceedings. The jury has been asked to disregard any opinions they have heard. I would ask you to do the same. Court will rise and resume tomorrow morning at ten.'

Chapter 49

David

Have you been sitting on the naughty-step? That was quite a reprimand!

I spent a lot of the day watching the jury. They are a motley crew: from the man who wears a Sunday-best three-piece suit, to the woman who looks as though she's going to do some gardening, a scruffy top and jeans looking out of place in Crown Court. All ages and most socio-economic groups represented. Better not say classes these days. They appear to be an attentive bunch and listened avidly to your cross-examination of the prosecution's pathologist, particularly the two women who sit side by side on the front seats. The one in blue was making copious notes and nodded on several occasions. She was particularly impressed when you spoke of the cost of the crosses and looked knowingly at Miss Yellow Jacket next to her. Whatever His Honour says, they won't forget the points you elicited from the doctor of death.

Now don't take this the wrong way, just some brotherly advice...I can hear you groaning!

Ms HMP, the redoubtable barrister sporting the scarlet stop-the-traffic lips, showboats at every opportunity. I have a feeling that certain members of the jury are already finding her histrionics wearisome. You are not competing for the Oscar. So, my advice is to relax a little more. Let her be the prima donna; never a popular character!

When you're not annoying the judge, you are mounting an outstanding defence. Dad is lucky to have you.

P.S. have just seen the latest coverage of today's events on the Internet. I don't think the newspapers followed the old boy's advice!

Eve

Thanks, David. I appreciate your support and advice. It didn't feel like me today. I'm not usually so bombastic and never believe in playing to the gallery. I have the arguments ready; a calmer approach appropriate. I just hope I'm not viewed as her understudy. The one who didn't quite make it.

I love your comment on her lipstick: it never seems to rub off and appears to have a life of its own. Unfortunately, I must admit that when I glanced in the mirror at lunch time I looked so awful I did consider rushing off to Boot's!

Still trying to get Dad to take the stand. Still failing.

Fordway Gazette

Gold Crosses Placed in Victims' Mouths: Pathologist Unsure a Rough Sleeper Could Afford Them!

Today, in Preston Crown Court, it was revealed that four of the five victims, in this most horrendous of cases, had gold crosses inserted in their mouths.

The eminent pathologist, Dr Alfie Morrison, gave evidence that the crosses were inserted post-mortem.

When asked about the cost of such items he was adamant that a member of the homeless community would not have been able to afford them.

Questions were also raised about the defendant's ability to commit the murders. The first victim, a fellow rough sleeper was a very large man, and the point was made that he would have been extremely difficult to overpower.

Ms Helena Morteson-Porteous, the glamorous London barrister, will continue the case for the prosecution in the morning.

Another unseasonably hot day. Judge Halsey entered the room looking decidedly warm in his gown and wig. The undercurrent of conversation ceased as all present stood to acknowledge his presence. It reminded Eve of a particularly harsh teacher she had endured in Year 4. At the end of each break all silliness had stopped when her high heels could be heard clacking their way along the corridor. As she walked into the classroom every pupil would be sitting silently at their desk, book open, reading fervently.

Rising to her feet, the barrister announced that she was calling her next witness: Professor Julian Thaxton.

Professor Thaxton was a highly-regarded member of the North West's forensic team. Despite his many years of experience, he looked rather nervous and was asked to repeat his first answer.

'Harry Whistler's DNA was present at all five murder scenes. It was on the clothes and the bedding of each of the three rough sleepers. Traces of the defendant's DNA were on several surfaces, and the door of the shed where the fourth victim's body was discovered.'

As he paused for breath, Ms Morteson-Porteous intervened. 'Professor Thaxton, I would like you to concentrate on the final victim and tell us your findings at that scene.'

'Lillian Henshaw was strangled with a scarf that had Mr Whistler's DNA on it.'

'Can you tell the jury what that means.'

'The scarf had, at some time, definitely been in his possession.'

'Thank you, professor. Could you now tell the court how accurate you consider DNA results to be?'

'DNA is ninety-nine-point nine percent accurate.'

'So...' a long pause followed, 'the chances of the DNA you found at all five crime scenes not being Mr Whistler's is zero point one.'

'That is correct.'

Eve knew that DNA evidence was a favourite with juries, but rather than cross examine Professor Thaxton she had decided to wait to call her own specialist on the subject.

It was late afternoon before Harvey Tarquin was called to the witness box, attempting to look more confident than he felt. He was very aware that every time he was centre stage he became tongue-tied, unable to access the right words, like a foreigner learning the language. His testimony was important: he was representing his team.

'Detective Chief Inspector Tarquin, the man in the dock stands accused of five murders, murders which occurred over a prolonged period...well over six months...' Afterwards, Harvey found it hard to recall what he had said, or indeed the many questions the barrister had put to him, though he knew he had managed to answer them.

Unfortunately, he did recall the exact moment Miss Whistler's cross-examination had discombobulated him.

Had he been a footballer, he knew he would have been credited with an own goal.

The following morning the papers were full of his blunders:

Top Cop Unsure He Has the Right Man
DCI Admits the Police Looked No Further Than the Homeless
Harry Whistler Framed?

Even the broadsheets had headlines that would have made the DCI squirm had he made himself read them:

Senior Officer in the Trial at Preston Crown Court Unsure They Have the Right Man
Doubts Raised Over Five Murders' Investigation

Afterwards, when he realised the extent of his malfunction, he wanted to weep. All the months of team work undone; the man in charge found wanting.

Afterwards, he knew he had allowed Eve Whistler to throw him off course, a dog losing the hare's scent. Afterwards, he realised that all his answers, so carefully rehearsed, had been forgotten; appalling ad-libbing the unfortunate consequence.

Too many afterwards.

It was, perhaps, fortunate that it was the weekend. Harvey doubted he would have been able to attend court so soon after his abysmal agreement with the defence that from day one the police has concentrated exclusively on the town's vagrants when looking for the assailant.

Chapter 50

Jon Millsaps had been busy preparing the eye witnesses. He had taken each person into the courtroom, where they had the opportunity to stand in the witness box. He knew that for most people this was a once in a lifetime experience, the prospect of answering questions under oath a daunting one. People had been known to opt-out at the last moment: not what the CPS wanted. Doubts remained that Sylvia Brotherton would attend court. Jon had agreed to pick her up and drive her there on the morning she was due to give evidence. The rest was down to her.

She was shaking as the usher led her to the witness box. After swearing the oath, the judge told her that she could be seated to give her testimony. Water was provided, some of which spilt as she lifted the glass.

The prosecutor knew this woman's evidence was important, and wanted her witness to be as relaxed as possible, but empathy was not a trait the good fairies had blessed her with, and her voice sounded strident in the high-ceilinged room. After asking Mrs Brotherton for her name and address she asked her first question.

'Mrs Brotherton, do you know the defendant by sight?'

'Yes...yes...I've seen him around the town on many occasions. That is...in the park as well. Yes...I do know him to look at.'

'Thank you.' Stopping, knowing the next answer was vital, she let the silence continue for several seconds. Sylvia Brotherton stared around, longing for her ordeal to be over.

She jumped, as what felt like an interrogation continued. 'Can you tell the court if you saw Mr Whistler on the night Charlotte Carroway was murdered in Elizabeth Park?'

'Well, well, I saw him running away from the park.'

Knowing she would have to exercise patience to extract every iota of detail, the barrister continued. 'Can you tell the court if he looked distressed.'

Eve leapt to her feet. 'Your Honour, that asks for an opinion, not a fact. And therefore, it cannot be admitted as evidence.'

Judge Halsey looked irritated by the interruption. He muttered that the witness could answer, though the jury must be aware that it was going to be the lady's interpretation of the situation.

'He looked upset and was running quite quickly. I remember thinking that you don't often see the homeless moving that fast.'

'You're doing really well, Mrs Brotherton, and thank you for giving your evidence. Can you now tell the court what made you think Harry Whistler looked upset, I think that was the word you employed to describe him?'

A long pause followed the question. HMP rephrased it, inserting 'used' in place of 'employed'.

'Well, he looked bothered. He was frowning and was muttering to himself.'

'Could you hear what he was saying?'

'No, no, it was all over in such a short time. I just got the impression that something had troubled him. He looked wild and his eyes were staring.'

'Can you explain what you mean by staring?'

'I only saw them for a second, but they seemed to bore into me. He looked as though he thought he was being chased.'

'Yes, thank you, Miss Whistler, I will save you the bother of objecting.' Turning to the jury the judge reminded them that opinions were not to be considered as evidence.

'Mrs Brotherton, what made you go to the police?'

'I didn't think anything of it at the time, but when I told my husband he said I must get in touch with the police.'

'Thank you, I have no further questions.

'The court will rise. We will resume at ten-thirty tomorrow morning.

Eve was furious. The jury would have many hours to accept Sylvia Brotherton's unchallenged testimony. It would have been helpful to cross-examine her straight away. There was no guarantee she would even attend court again.

The days were wearying, and the nights had grown steadily worse, odd snatches of nightmare-cursed sleep making Eve long for daylight: only for the agony to continue.

After years of not seeing a doctor, she needed to make a second appointment in just a few weeks. She had been surprised to be offered an evening appointment, her surgery usually working on a fortnight's notice. 'We had a cancellation, at least the patient rang in to free the time up for someone else. A lot of people don't bother. Thirty missed appointments last week!' The receptionist sounded understandably annoyed.

Dr Tanner was a man she hadn't seen before. As she sat in the waiting room, the doctor running over half an hour late, she thought about her friend's comment on the man. 'I'm sure he's a good doctor and he's certainly thorough. The downside is that he must have missed the lectures on bedside manner, though apparently (and this is merely tittle-tattle) he is very well acquainted with an array of beds in the area!' Laughing at her own joke she had continued, 'Remember, if you go with a headache you probably don't need to disrobe.'

An hour later Eve was leaving, clutching a prescription for sleeping pills. 'They're non-addictive, but try not to use them once your life is back on an even keel. I see my colleague suggested some counselling sessions. Do think about them, though your eczema appears to be under control.' Eve knew it would take more than pills or talking sessions to get her life back on an "even keel".

The knowledge that she would soon be called upon to present her father's defence hung over her. She had undertaken such duties on many occasions, but never with so much at stake.

The heat wave had been replaced by rain, the kind that is heavier than it appears. Wet coats and dripping umbrellas gave the court room a musty smell.

Looking even more nervous than the previous day, Sylvia Brotherton was obviously holding back the tears as the judge reminded her she was still under oath.

'My learned friend asked you some questions yesterday, and this morning I will be asking you to clarify some of your answers. Try not to worry. I am not trying to trick you, or make you say anything you don't want to tell us.'

As she began, Eve hoped the witness would retain sufficient self-control to remain in the box. She had seen people unable to continue, the trial suspended whilst they were persuaded to carry on.

'Mrs Brotherton, you said that you know Harry Whistler by sight. Many people think that all the homeless look alike: unkempt, scruffy clothes, unwashed. How certain are you that the man you say you saw running away from the park was indeed the defendant?'

The witness spoke quickly, keen for the court to hear her positive view of the rough sleepers. 'I don't consider the homeless to all be the same. They don't all look alike and certainly dress differently. Harry Whistler is one of the better dressed and always has a warm coat in the winter. Some have dogs with them, but not him.'

'I'm sorry Mrs Brotherton, but you have not answered my question. Can you be a hundred per cent certain that the man you saw was Harry Whistler? This is vitally important.'

The pause spoke louder than a hundred words. 'It was him, or I'm sure it was. It was getting dark and he passed me very quickly. It was his eyes I noticed.'

'So, in other words, you are not completely sure that the man you saw that night, running from the park, was the man you say you recognise as Harry Whistler. The man on trial for five murders.'

'No one can be absolutely sure about anything. All I know is I saw a man looking as though he was escaping from something.' After pausing for a moment, she added, 'And I'm as sure as I can be that that man I saw was the defendant.'

As it was not the response Eve had wanted she decided to move on: 'The man you saw was moving quickly, I think that was your word. Would you agree there could be many, many reasons why a person moves fast? Most people who jog or run are not doing so because they've just killed someone.'

'I never said I thought at the time that he'd murdered anyone, just that he was running away from the park that night and something seemed to be bothering him. The following morning, I heard about the girl being found dead.'

'Mrs Brotherton, you told the court the man you saw, who we now know may or may not have been Harry Whistler, looked upset. The words you used were, "He was frowning and muttering to himself." I don't know about you, but I often do that... and I haven't just strangled a friend.'

'Miss Whistler, do you have a question for this witness?'

'Indeed, Your Honour. Would you agree that someone frowning, and muttering, might just be in a hurry to get somewhere?'

'I suppose so. But he did appear to be agitated...and was glowering, that's the word I'd use...glowering.'

'Once again, I would put it to you that people glower for a great variety of reasons, most of them nothing to do with murder.' Staring at the witness, intimidation not usually a facet of her repertoire that she enjoyed using, Eve asked her final question. 'Why did you leave it so long, before contacting the police? Was it the case that seeing the vagrant was of such little consequence that you wanted to ignore the encounter entirely?'

Another pause, a question Sylvia hadn't been expecting.

'Remember, Mrs Brotherton, you are still on oath.'

'I'm not sure, and right now I'm sorry that I did.'

'You say he was running. Which way did he go once he left the park?'

'Oh, dear me, away from the park, yes away. He ran out of the gates and turned right, towards town. I only saw him for a few seconds, but I think that was it.'

'You used the word think. Can you be more certain?'

'Yes, he definitely turned towards town. It was getting dark and I assumed he was going to shelter in one of the shop doorways. There are always a lot of the homeless who use them. It's true that since BHS closed, its large entrance has been a real home-from-home for about six of them.'

'Mrs Brotherton, am I correct that your evidence is based on a fleeting glimpse? In the dying light, you saw a man running; you assumed he was one of the homeless; you assumed he was upset; the following morning on hearing that a young girl had been murdered in the park you assumed the murderer was the man you had seen – for a few seconds – the evening before, running out of the park. Would you agree that's a lot of assumptions?'

The witness looked unsure whether a reply was required, so said nothing. Weeping quietly, the woman left the witness box.

David

Poor Mrs Brotherton. I felt sorry for her today. Well, almost. The CPS must have known that her evidence was rather shaky, and she wasn't the most confident witness.

At one point, you reminded me of a programme I watched where a seismologist finds fault lines and knows they could easily result in earthquakes! As I'm sure you're aware, she probably did see Dad that night and the prosecution will be livid that such testimony was questioned so fiercely. Dogs and bones springs to mind!

Are you ready for tomorrow? Silly question. Lillian Henshaw's husband needs careful handling. He is a widower and will have the jury's sympathy.

No, I'm not the lawyer; just some brotherly advice. Sleep well.

Chapter 51

As the days moved on, Eve found herself more and more nervous. The nights had been granted a few hours of drug-induced sleep, but the remainder of the time was spent rearranging the bedclothes, stumbling to the kitchen to make cups of tea which remained undrunk, and going over and over the previous day's evidence, like a class reciting the times tables. Although she suspected that the latter might result in madness, she seemed unable to control it. Philip had moved to the spare room after Eve begged him to leave her alone, saying she needed time and space to prepare for the following day.

David's advice about questioning a fragile widower had occupied much of the previous night and she knew she would have to be diplomatic: the last thing she wanted to do was to alienate the jury.

Harvey hadn't had long enough to forget his pathetic performance. Since that fiasco he longed for an invisibility cloak as he walked into court. He knew nobody noticed him. They were all too busy salivating, hoping for another day of entertainment. Not much had changed since crowds flocked to public hangings.

Jed Rutland was a last-minute witness for the prosecution, only coming forward a week before the trial began, reluctant to become involved. He had been the park keeper for thirty years. 'I'm in charge of Elizabeth Park, oversee the gardeners and handy men, organise the work for the villains who've been given their hours of unpaid work; not that you could call what they do work. In the summer, the park is open from 8 a.m. to 10 at night and the rest of the year it's dawn to dusk. I know, only too well, that the dossers like to spend their nights in the park – it's not my job to go all around the place, chasing them out. Wish I could, the mess they make.'

'Mr Rutland, you said in your statement that you saw one of the rough sleepers in an altercation with a young girl, Charlotte Carroway, whose body was then discovered the following morning hidden in the bushes.'

'Yes, that lot are always falling out, fighting over sleeping spaces, especially the park benches and the bandstand. So, as I didn't recognise her, I thought she was a member of the public remonstrating with one of them. She was arguing with a man, one of the tramps. I know a lot of them by sight, but I'd not seen her before and didn't know she was one of them. It was when the body was reported on the morning's news that I had my suspicions. Didn't think much about it until I was talking to Karl, that's my assistant, about a fortnight ago, and he said I should go to the police.'

'Thank you, Mr Rutland. Can you identify the man you saw arguing with Charlotte?'

'Him...the man in the dock. He's always in the park, slightly better dressed than some of the others. Got a temper on him. I've seen him in fights before now. Karl has had run-ins with him and agrees he's a bad-tempered so-and-so.'

Leaping to her feet, Eve said that the witness couldn't be allowed to speak for anyone else.

Judge Halsey agreed, and asked the jury to disregard Mr Rutland's last statement. The judge supporting her: twice! Eve smiled as she stood to begin the cross-examination.

'Mr Rutland, it is over ten months, since Charlotte Carroway's tragic death last December. How sure are you that you saw the argument on the night *before* her body was discovered?'

'Like I said, it was the evening before her body was found.'

'But, this was December, so hardly the evening. I think you said the park closes at dusk during the winter months. Can you therefore be more accurate about the time?'

'Well, I was closing the gates, so in December that would be about three-thirty.'

'So, not what most people would call the evening. I'm just wondering how many other inaccuracies you've given the court. Indeed, how accurate is your recollection, almost a year on, that the man you saw with Charlotte was Harry Whistler? I also wonder why it took you so long to have your little conflab with Karl.'

'It was him. I'm absolutely certain about that.'

The final witness of the day was Stuart Henshaw. He walked into court looking crushed: losing his wife to murder making the simple act of breathing a monumental effort. Swearing the oath, words that as a life-long Christian he took seriously, seemed to rejuvenate him, and he declined the offer to sit whilst giving his testimony.

'On behalf of all present, I would like to extend our sincere condolences on the loss of your wife. The court realises that being here today is extremely difficult for you. Any time you wish to stop please say so and we can have an adjournment.' Helena was determined to get the jury on her side.

'Mr Henshaw, could you tell us a little about your wife.'

After pausing so long that the barrister thought she would have to repeat the question, Stuart Henshaw began to speak. 'Lillian was a wonderful wife and a devoted mother. We were married for almost sixty years; it would have been our Diamond Wedding Anniversary next year. She was a good person, always tried to see the best in everybody. I cannot understand why anyone would want to hurt her. Every Saturday she walked from our house to our daughter's; until the day she didn't arrive.

It's so hard to think it might have been one of the town's homeless who killed her. She never had a bad word to say about any of them and often stopped for a chat or to give them coffee or a sandwich. She never wanted to give them money in case it went on drink or drugs. I'm tortured by her senseless death...and that's what it was: absolutely senseless.'

Eve had decided to decline the opportunity to cross-examine Mr Henshaw knowing she had little to gain. 'Court will rise for the day.'

Chapter 52

Perambulations of the park were doing little to ease the DCI's worries. He knew he had failed. The case had seemed so strong. Harry Whistler was guilty. Unfortunately, Eve Whistler had put severe dents into, not only his testimony, but most of the prosecution case.

Three weeks in: half way through the trial. Usually by this stage Harvey thought he knew the outcome. Not this time. The Crown Prosecution was not being helped by the attention-seeking antics of HMP (he had also looked at her internet profile). The barrister was like a child playing up to relatives who had come to visit, showing-off at every available opportunity. He knew her conduct was irritating some jurors. He remembered cases that were lost due to the shenanigans of the prosecutor. The woman was over-confident, and he knew that the British didn't take to self-aggrandisement and tended to root for the under-dog.

Mozart interrupted his thinking. 'Hi bro, Sam here.'

Annoyed at being disturbed, Harvey knew he sounded tetchy as he muddled through a few pleasantries.

His brother moved on. 'I've been to see Dad and I thought I'd give you an update. He's comfortable, clean and well cared for; in the circumstances, almost certainly as much as we can hope for. He didn't say much, but went on and on about Scarborough and getting so sunburnt he hadn't had any sleep.'

'That was sixty years ago, an unforgettable family holiday. He always said that they all got burnt on the first day and spent the rest of the week avoiding the sun. I suspect he's living in the past most of the time now.'

'Probably better than the present, even with the sunburn.'

A stab of guilt forced Harvey to say that he would get down soon. There were few excuses. He was free each weekend, but the effort required felt overwhelming. Not good enough, not nearly good enough. The old man wouldn't be there for ever.

Late September: officially autumn, but no one had informed the trees which retained their somewhat faded greens. A year since the first murder, Elizabeth Park forever tainted. As he climbed the hill to the café, which he hoped was open, some sustenance required, he wondered if the team had got it wrong. Had they been too sure that the murderer came from the homeless community? He recalled Serena saying, on several occasions, that they needed to broaden their search – to include the townspeople. He hadn't listened. Indeed, they had looked for a single murderer. Was there only one? The five victims could easily be divided into three sets: the first pair of rough sleepers; the burning of Terry Wendover; and the final duo of pensioners. 'No, stop over-thinking,' he said aloud, making an elderly dog walker smile. Stop over-thinking. There is only one murderer.

'Good afternoon, my dear Mr Policeman.' Bigman's voice boomed across the lawn dividing their two paths. 'Wait there, I'm on my way.' In a matter of seconds, the man was beside Harvey, shaking his hand and exclaiming how good it was to see him.

'You look well, Edward.'

'Thank you, Harvey. And for using my real name. Not many people employ it these days and it's good of you to remember it.'

'Edward Jonathan Trendell Esquire. I never forget a name. Unfortunately, Mr Trendell, we shouldn't be talking. I believe you are being called as a witness for the defence.'

'Indeed. Fancy me being asked to stand in the witness box and answer questions. I'd better brush up a bit, visit the hostel for a shower and a shave. Last week, I think it was then, might have been two weeks ago...anyway, I visited the new Oxfam charity shop. Do you know the one I mean? It's on the corner of Brigand Lane and the High Street. I purchased smart trousers and an almost-new jacket – well, the kind lady in the shop gave me that when I said I had a special occasion looming when I needed to look smart. I didn't think it was advisable to mention the trial. She might be one of the town's hang-him-high brigade!'

Harvey couldn't help smiling, thinking that any question the man was asked in court would receive an extremely long and circuitous answer. He could picture the judge, not renowned for his patience, asking him to curtail his replies.

'If we both promise not to talk about Harry, and I quite understand why that topic would be forbidden, I'm sure we could pop in to the café for a cuppa and something to eat. Especially the latter.' His smile must have added to global warming.

Fifteen minutes later the two men were sitting in a far corner of the room, drinks and toasted sandwiches in front of them.

Edward smiled. 'I know we can't talk about the trial. However, I've just been thinking that it must be strange for you to sit and listen to it all in court: to hear the evidence you've gathered presented to an audience. Rather like an author watching actors deliver the lines he wrote.'

'A wonderful analogy and very apt. The trouble is the lawyers are inclined to force witnesses off-script which has me wanting to leap up and reprimand them. Not that I have room to criticise. I couldn't even get *my* lines right! It makes me wonder if we're all reciting words we've not quite mastered; the prompt having gone AWOL.'

'I gather the daughter is putting up a fairly sound defence, and is a bobby-dazzler during the cross-examinations.'

'Sorry, Edward, we really shouldn't discuss this.'

Both took their time enjoying their snacks, followed by large slices of cake, and a long silence ensued. Looking serious, Edward stared at his companion and spoke softly. 'After the trial – depending on the outcome – I'm thinking of moving on. It's lonely without Harry. I'll just say this. He's a good bloke and has been a wonderful friend. Every year when his family gave him new clothes he passed his old ones on to me. I used to joke that I was only twelve months out of fashion.' Harvey laughed, saying that was far more up to date than most of his wardrobe.

'If they don't let him out, then I have no reason to stay. I've thought of going south. The last I heard my daughter was living in Torquay and I'd love to see her again. The grandchildren will have grown up, so I won't cause any embarrassment. It's still just an idea, but the more I ponder it the more it seems like a good one.'

Harvey felt moved by the man's dreams. He knew Edward's family might not want to have anything to do with him, but heard himself say, 'Let me know if that's what you decide, and I'll see if I can help. Do you have an address? I could find out if she's still living there. I'll need her married name; doubt she's Mrs Bigman! When this is over, a trip down to the south coast would do me good.'

The vagrant's voice wobbled, the tears a lot nearer than Torquay. 'Harvey Tarquin, you are a gentleman, and I might take you up on your kind offer. That is the plan. But only in the unlikely event that my friend is not released, no blemish on his character. I am going to do my utmost to see that that is indeed the case. I am certain that my testimony will sway every member of the jury.'

Although desperate to know what Bigman was going to say, Harvey remained silent. He would know soon enough.

Chapter 53

Three weeks in: half way through the trial. Jacob the only member of the family not to attend Crown Court every day. When he didn't go, David provided him with updates which were received with mixed responses.

'You don't need to give me such detail, dear brother, I can read the papers and look at the Internet. They're both full of all the gory details. I can see that Eve is doing her job well, even though we all know the bastard is as guilty as the proverbial hell he threatened us with when we were children.'

A few days later, his reaction was even more vitriolic. 'You say I should be there, that we should be providing a united front. Since when have those words applied to our family? Dad stopped any hope of that decades ago. Have you any idea what it's like for me going in to work? As you know Lillian Henshaw's daughter works at one of my schools. Imagine what fun that is. The staff either smother me with kindness, endless cups of tea, offers of sympathy and the ubiquitous "if you need someone to talk to", or they avoid me as though I was harbouring some deadly disease. As a peripatetic teacher, it's my duty to make sure the kids play the banjo once a week. It's the only time some of them even touch the instrument, daily practise an alien concept. If I didn't go for several weeks they'd forget everything and we'd be starting with lesson one again.'

David had heard the excuse before and was annoyed by what he viewed as Jacob's selfishness. Eve was doing a sterling job of defending their father, and his mother and Andrew were in court every day, either to support Eve, Harry or both.

It was time to confront Jacob. Arriving at the house, late on the Saturday evening, he was allowed in.

No greetings; no niceties. 'Forget your bloody pupils and get yourself to court every day. Your excuses are pathetic. It's time to show some solidarity. I know you hold Dad accountable for everything, but the rest of the family are not to blame. There are times when we need to all be together.'

'My attendance each day would mean nothing. Eve appears to be producing shots that infiltrate what was expected to be the prosecution's bullet-proof evidence, so she doesn't need me, and I'm sure you, Mum and Andrew make a cosy trinity. I seem to recall being told that was the perfect alignment. I'll continue to be there when my schedule allows.'

Days one dreads. Days that matter. Others affected. Eve had received good luck wishes from all the family, even Jacob. She suspected she needed more than that. Would the defence she was about to mount prove sufficient to sway the jury, to introduce some degree of reasonable doubt; enough for them to acquit?

The courtroom felt tense. Eve felt like a diver standing at the edge of the springboard, ready to launch herself into the long space between board and water. As they walked in, several of the jurors looked apprehensive. They'd heard the prosecution's case and now fussed with paper and pens, ready to listen to Harry Whistler's defence.

Eve had done her best to look professional: a dark grey suit, white blouse and pearl earrings. She'd had her hair cut at the weekend and the mid-length bob suited her.

'I call Dr Reginald Howard.'

'Dr Howard, please will you give the court a list of your credentials.'

'I have over thirty years' experience in forensic science. My Doctorate is on the reliability of DNA when used as evidence. I have been employed by the police in England, America and Australia in cases where DNA was the main factor in establishing the outcome of a variety of cases.'

'Thank you, Dr Howard. We have heard that DNA is almost a hundred per cent accurate. Would you agree with that extremely high estimation?'

'In the three decades that DNA has been used as a forensic tool, courts have rarely been skeptical about its power. However, DNA is not the exact science that many people believe it to be. I am *firmly* of the opinion, through many years of research, that DNA is, at best, ninety-five per cent reliable. Let me try to explain some of my reasons. The accuracy of any DNA sample is reliant on an inordinately high level of quality control and quality assurance. There are certain procedures that must be adhered to in the forensic laboratory. Quality control is vital: measures must be in place to ensure that each – and every – DNA analysis result meets an extremely high standard of quality. Quality assurance refers to monitoring, verifying and documenting laboratory performance.'

After stopping to clear his throat, he continued. 'Human error must be factored in, and the likelihood that the sample of DNA is corrupted must be considered.

I use the word *likelihood* advisedly, rather than *possibility*, and I repeat that the chance that there has been some degree of human error must also be included. Sample handling, mislabelling or contamination are all likely to compromise a DNA analysis. Contamination is the most likely of these and can happen during collection, transportation, or when the sample is being analysed. DNA can, of course, be present due to contact with the deceased when the owner is not the murderer.'

This was one of the points Eve wanted the jury to hear. 'So, are you saying that even when a person's DNA is found at the crime scene, it doesn't prove their guilt?'

'There have been many cases where the accused was in close contact, sometimes on-a-daily basis, with the deceased, but was not the person who committed the murder.'

'Can I just make this clear. Harry Whistler's DNA was found on the three victims in the park and on their belongings. Is it possible that this could have stayed on them, due to previous contact, even if he had not been with them at the time of their murders?'

'Entirely possible.'

'And the DNA found in the shed where Edwin York's body was discovered. Could that have remained for days, weeks or months?'

'Yes, DNA remains in situ.'

'Finally, the scarf found on Lillian Henshaw had Mr Whistler's DNA on it. Does what you are saying indicate that he might have once worn it, but not at the scene of the murder?'

'Once again, entirely possible.'

Chapter 54

David

Eve, you were brilliant. That forensic bloke you brought in was excellent and certainly cast doubt on the traces of Dad found at each scene.

The lady who always sits at the end of the front row in the jury box (Ms Yellow Jacket, you must have noticed that she was wearing it again today), was, yet again, in nodding-dog mode. She bobbed in all the right places! Several others were taking notes, and I'm sure you made them think carefully about some of the statements made by the prosecution's DNA expert.

Well done you.

The next morning's headlines were encouraging:

DNA Reliability Questioned: Doubts About Harry Whistler's Guilt.
Top Scientist Claims DNA Can Mislead
Murders in the Park: Prosecution Evidence Questioned by Top Forensic Scientist

It was Bigman's day in court. Eve had been unsure about putting him in the witness box. Though he would undoubtedly provide a strong character reference for her father, some members of the jury might be disinclined to pay attention to the testimony of one of the town's homeless fraternity.

'Mr Trendell (David had advised against using the soubriquet Bigman), will you please tell the court how long you have known Harry Whistler.'

'I've known Harry for over ten years and we've been good friends.'

'I believe you have both been living as members of Fordway's homeless community.'

'That's quite correct. I've been here longer than Harry and took him under my wing, so to speak, when he first arrived. It's not easy being on the streets and newcomers need a lot of help.'

'Thank you, Mr Trendell. Would you now tell us something about Harry Whistler?'

'Harry's a Christian: lives his faith. I'm not a believer and we've had many a discussion about it. He's not the sort to start an argument, though inevitably they do occur. Some people think he's got a temper. However, I've only seen him annoyed when there is a good reason: one of our group stealing or starting a fight. We don't have much in our lives, but when he can he shares: drink, food and clothes. You can rely on Harry, he doesn't let his friends down.'

'Thank you, Mr Trendell. As you know Harry is accused of five murders. Did he ever speak to you about any of the events of the past year?'

Bigman paused, knowing what he was about to say was important. 'Yes, he talked about them, as did we all. He said murder was always wrong. It went against God's laws.' Looking up, he continued, speaking more slowly. 'Harry Whistler is not a murderer. He did not kill any of the five victims. He was devastated when Charlotte was found, and Tommy Granger had been our friend for a long time. He had his differences with Terry, but not enough to want him dead. As for the two pensioners, what possible motive did he have for killing them? No, I repeat, the Harry Whistler I know is as innocent as I am.'

Looking decidedly unimpressed, the judge said the court would rise for lunch.

Andrew

Not sure Dad's friend added much to the proceedings. That infuriating barrister! Does she have to flirt with the judge? He's old enough to be her grandfather. She spent the entire afternoon pointing out that Bigman was bound to claim his friend (oh, the sarcasm in her voice when she used that word) is innocent.

She did veer from the straight and narrow – Dad would be proud of the analogy – when she called him a tramp: not very politically correct. I saw a couple of the jury exchange glances.

Breaking news: David tells me Dad has agreed to go in the witness box. Now that's something I never expected.

Eve

Nor did I. Advising him what to say has been as successful as asking a toddler to part with his ice cream. All that was missing were the tears and a tantrum. He did start shouting, so loudly the whole of Fordway must have heard: 'Stop it Eve. I will tell the truth. If that is not good enough, then so be it.'

Preston was gridlocked: an accident on the one-way system bringing the early morning traffic to a frustrating standstill. Eve sat and watched the traffic lights perform their slow waltz, the green light occasionally allowing one car through the chockfull junction. Tempers were fraying; car horns a discordance of frustration. Police sirens could be heard in the distance, providing some hope that the situation would improve.

Contacting court, she had been assured that few people had arrived, the judge phoning in to suggest that the trial was unlikely to resume until the afternoon.

Two hours later, feeling jaded and in need of strong pain killers, Eve sat with her father.

'You're on this afternoon, Dad. Is there anything you want to discuss?'

The ensuing silence told Eve all she needed to know.

'Good luck. As you know, my questions will be straightforward. Try not to let the prosecutor rile you. Stick to your story and the jury will listen.'

'Story. What a strange and inappropriate word. I will tell the truth. It's up to them to believe what I say.'

It was a confident Harry Whistler who strode into the witness box. Swearing the oath, he stood erect and looked directly at the jury.

'Mr Whistler, you have been accused of five murders and the court has heard already that you have pleaded not guilty to all of them.'

Not waiting for a question, Harry launched in. 'As God is my witness, I am not guilty. NOT guilty. As a believer, I know to keep the Lord's Commandments, the sixth one being "Thou shalt not kill". I have an immortal soul which would suffer eternal punishment had I killed any of them. Why would I risk His wrath by breaking the commandment he handed down to Moses on Mount Sinai: Exodus Chapter 20.'

'We have heard that the first three victims were fellow rough sleepers, each one well known to you. Did you have any reason to wish any of them harm?'

'No, they were my friends. I was distraught when Tommy and Charlotte died, and even though Terry and I had our differences I meant him no harm.'

'Mr Whistler, did you know either of the final victims, Edwin York and Lillian Henshaw?'

'No. The homeless tend to stick together and we have very little to do with anyone else. People in the town tend to avoid us and we keep our distance. Some kind folk give us food or drinks and occasionally money, but that's as far as any interaction goes. I was sorry when I heard two more people had died. However, I didn't know either of them and I was not responsible for their deaths.'

Knowing that the prosecution was bound to ask about her father's DNA being present on all five victims, Eve chose her words carefully.

'Mr Whistler, did you have close contact with each of the homeless who were murdered?'

'Yes. We shared things: food, drink, sleeping spaces, and in bad weather bedding and clothes. My family give me clothing, and so I pass things I don't need on to others. Apart from anything else it all gets too heavy to carry round.'

'Your son has a shed on the allotments at the edge of town. Have you ever used it to sleep in?'

'There was a time I sheltered there, until the day I met him, and he told me he didn't like me visiting it. Informed me in no uncertain terms that it wasn't a doss house!'

'Thank you, Mr Whistler. A scarf with traces of your DNA was found around Lillian Henshaw's neck. Will you please look at it and say when you remember wearing it?'

'I know I've had one like it; I seem to recall it was a long time ago. The one I've had recently is black and that's mostly blue stripes. I'm not saying it's never been mine, but not for ages.'

'As we have been told DNA never entirely disappears, so someone else might have found the scarf and worn it, with your traces still on it.'

'Thank you, Miss Whistler, I think the jury has heard the point you are making.'

Acknowledging the judge's warning, Eve moved to her final question, the one she didn't want to ask. She knew Helena would be aware of Harry's confession and needed to establish what he had meant.

'Mr Whistler, when you were first interviewed by the police, you said you had committed a murder. Would you explain what you meant.'

Harry stood, head down for the first time since entering the witness box. The jury sat motionless, unsure what to expect, the idea that he had confessed to murder an unexpected twist.

His former confidence gone, Harry began to speak, so softly that people were leaning forward to hear. 'It was a long time ago, though the knowledge of what I did has haunted me every day for over two decades.' The ensuing silence was broken only by keyboards being used, the press agog to file the dramatic evidence.

'My mother had been ill for months, the cancer invading her organs, leaving her bedbound and in constant agony. For weeks, the medicine had hardly alleviated her excruciating pain. One day she asked me to end it all, to help her to die. I said no. Like me, she was a believer and I told her that God would take her in His own good time.' Harry's voice had become weaker, and Eve suggested that he had some water and a short break.

'No, I will finish. For over two weeks, she asked me every day, begging me to send her to a better place, to end her misery, until finally the evening came when I agreed to help. All so simple. Extra morphine might have worked, but the doctor would know some was missing. So…so…she thanked me when she realised I was going to hold the pillow over her face. It didn't take long, and her suffering was over. Little did I know that mine was just beginning. No one suspected. No post-mortem needed. The doctor was summoned and offered his condolences. The undertakers came.' Loud sobs filled the room as Harry slumped down.

Eve waited until her father had regained some composure, then asked, 'Do you still regard what you did as murder?'

'I took a life: that is murder. I knew what I was doing. So, I am culpable.'

'Mr Whistler, most people, having heard your testimony, would regard what you did as a mercy killing. You did it to end her unendurable suffering; you did it because you loved your mother and acceded to her request that you assist her – when she was beyond helping herself.'

Pausing, Eve looked at the jury. 'I have to ask you, Mr Whistler, was that the only time you killed someone?'

'Yes. Once was enough. More than enough.'

Chapter 55

Andrew phoned as soon as Eve got home. Exhausted, the last thing she needed was an irate brother.

'So, that was Dad's big secret. Still not sure why I wasn't in the know. What a lot of fuss about not very much. Grandma offed a few days early: big deal! And then two decades of discombobulation for an entire family. Nice one, Dad.

Another way of looking at it might be that the first time usually proves to be the hardest. Practice might not make perfect, but tends to make for success, though maybe not in Dad's case.'

David

I caught a glimpse of Jacob in court today. He looked awful, and is obviously finding the proceedings as hard as any of us. I was hoping to speak to him afterwards, but he must have left before the end of the day. Last week he told me he was worried that you were putting up such a great defence. That Dad might get off. It's almost as he wants the man incarcerated.

Eve, we're here if you need to talk. If I were you I'd avoid tomorrow's papers.

Harry Whistler Confesses to Murder

The trial at Preston Crown Court took an unexpected, and extremely dramatic, turn yesterday. The defendant, vagrant Harry Whistler, accused of the Murders in the Park, confessed to a previous killing...

David had been right: the papers had all sensationalised her father's evidence. Toby Halsey had requested that the press restrain their coverage of the day's events, adding his disappointment at some of the more lurid reporting of the past weeks.

The judge began the day with a reprimand: whilst the trial was undoubtedly of national interest, it was not being conducted for the public's entertainment. Should any journalist continue to write in such a vulgar and outrageous manner, the court was within its rights to charge the person responsible with contempt of court. 'Should that be the case, he or she may well find themselves before me.' Eve hoped that was a sufficient warning. But doubted it.

Cross-examination was normally the barrister's moment to shine, her chance to discredit the defendant and make a mockery of his answers. Helena knew she had the skill to tie even the most assured witness in the type of knot that only tightened as she bombarded them with her subsequent, and consistently well-prepared, questions.

In Harry Whistler, she had met her equal. If Helena was used to sparkling, Harry had a higher wattage and out-shone her for ninety minutes. He had a response to every question.

'Yes, he had been friends with the three homeless victims.'
'No, he didn't know the pensioners.'

'No, he hadn't bought the crosses.'

'Yes, it was his DNA, though its presence on all five victims could be explained.'

Finally: 'He wasn't the killer.'

'Mr Whistler, you told the court you are a murderer. Why then should we believe you when you say you are not responsible for the five of which you stand accused?'

For the first time, Harry seemed perturbed. His voice had a harshness that had not been there before. 'Were you not listening when this was discussed yesterday? For a supposedly intelligent person you seem to have retained little of what transpired…let's see… oh yes, less than twenty-four hours ago.'

Helena looked pleased to have riled him. 'Mr Whistler, you can't ask the jury to believe that when you admitted to committing a murder you meant the mercy killing of your mother, a woman who had begged you to release her from her suffering. Most people in this room would regard that as an act of love, of kindness, not the breaking of a Commandment. Was that really what you meant when you told DCI Tarquin that, and I quote, "I am a murderer"?'

Not allowing the man in front of her time to respond, HMP informed the court that she had no more questions.

As he was taken back to the dock, Eve felt proud of her father. He had performed far better than she had expected. Far better. Only towards the end had he shown any sign of emotion. She had decided against any re-examination.

The weekend loomed, an unwanted interruption. All evidence presented. Only the judge's summation to be delivered: then the jury would decide.

'Ladies and gentlemen of the jury, you have sat through many weeks of a difficult and, at times, harrowing trial. Five people were murdered: three from the town's homeless community, and two pensioners. All were strangled, though one was post-mortem. Strangling is a method not usually employed by a person killing on such a scale. It is claimed by the CPS that one person committed all five murders, the modus operandi in each case being so similar. Harry Whistler stands before you, accused of all five murders.

You have listened to a great deal of evidence, some of it rather contradictory, which can cause confusion. It is now your duty to decide whether that evidence – and you must only take into consideration the facts that have been put before you in this courtroom – is strong enough to convict him. You are about to make one of the most important decisions of your lives. Harry Whistler: guilty or innocent. None of the witnesses' opinions can be considered: they are not evidence. You must also ignore anything you may have read in the media.

Choose a spokesperson who will guide you through your deliberations. You must take your time and every piece of evidence must be discussed. Should you require clarification of any aspect of the case, I am happy to receive a written request for my assistance. Your decision, when you reach it, must be unanimous and beyond reasonable doubt.'

Chapter 56

Eve

It's over.

Before has become after.

Before: hope.

After: despair.

The jury returned after eight hours: surely insufficient time to have reviewed all the evidence thoroughly. I feel like a tyre that's been suffering from a slow puncture and has finally lost all its air.

I keep asking myself whether I was wrong.

That Dad was guilty.

As his lawyer, I had to believe in his innocence.

As his daughter, I was certain he was incapable of such acts.

The fact remains he's been convicted, so the jury obviously thought he was a man capable of murdering five people.

I remain unconvinced.

The more the trial went on, the prosecution evidence rather unconvincingly attempting to prove his guilt, the more I believed in him.

No unassailable reasons emerged for any of the killings. No eye witnesses, no proof he was even in the park each time one of the homeless was killed.

As for the two pensioners...the question remains why? Why would he want to end the lives of two people with whom he'd had either no, or very little, previous contact?

I was ignored when I said that the alleged altercation with Lillian Henshaw was hardly a motive for murder. Even the DNA link was weak.

It was his glove in the shed; it was his scarf on Mrs Henshaw's body.

But, as I said in my summing-up, he is not a stupid man. He would not have left behind such incriminating evidence.

He has been imprisoned for life; the next stage of his torment.

What he is feeling I can't begin to imagine. I suspect that, like me, he lay awake last night, his mind a maelstrom.

Did I do my best for him? I tried, oh how I tried!

The suspicion lurks that he might have been better served by a more experienced lawyer, or the barrister that David offered to fund. It was my first murder trial, and I failed.

Was I too close to him?

Should I have followed the advice that one does not act on behalf of a relative?

There are no answers.

I must live with the outcome.

When I saw him, after the verdict had been delivered, he thanked me. I was the only one in tears. Enough for both of us.

'I did not do the things of which I was accused and found guilty. I will always be grateful for your loyalty. You alone have believed in me, and I do not deserve such a daughter. You alone were privy to my crime; the life I ended long ago. Prison will be a just punishment.'

Standing, weeping, I tried to embrace him.

'No, Eve. Now is the time for it all to end. I do not want you to visit me again. You must put this behind you and get on with your life. Marry your young man, have a family and be happy.'

With that he asked the officer to take him to his cell.

Chapter 57

The incident room looked as despondent as Harvey felt. It gave the appearance of having been abandoned, mid-activity: half-empty cups and sandwich wrappers littered every surface. Walking in, Harvey wondered why the cleaners hadn't been in to tackle it.

Serena entered the room quietly. 'Morning Harvey.' The use of his Christian name always irritated him. It seemed inappropriate, like a pupil on first name terms with a teacher. 'How are you?'

Having no idea what answer to give, Harvey sat silently, staring at his Van Gogh print.

'A good result. The jury didn't take too long to return.'

It took a monumental effort for Harvey to speak. 'Is it good? Is it the correct verdict? The longer the trial went on, the less certain I became.'

'We collected the evidence; the CPS thought it was enough to bring the case to trial, and twelve members of the community found Harry Whistler guilty. That's more than enough for me.'

'I am so afraid we missed something – that there was a gorilla disco-dancing in front of us. Too obvious for us to see.'

Pausing to think how to make her boss feel better, Serena said, 'When I was a child, at the end of many programmes on the tele, a sign came up saying "The End". For some reason, I loved those words and would always say them out loud. They became a family joke. Well, now is the time to say *The End* to this case.'

Although not sure Harvey was listening, she continued. 'When you get back from your leave, there will be new challenges, more miscreants to deal with.'

Twenty-four hours later, Harvey was keeping his promise and driving down to Torquay, his loquacious passenger filling every second with a miscellany of diatribes against a judicial system that could convict an innocent man.

'It's not safe to live as a rough sleeper, so I'd better be Edward now, not Bigman. Poor Harry never got the chance to return to his family. Eve would have had him back. She's a good one. Instead, he got life in prison, the judge saying that in his case life meant life. No hope of parole. I still know he didn't commit any of the murders. The man has not got it in him.'

Having contacted Edward's daughter, Harvey wasn't sure she was a "good one". Her reaction on hearing that her father wanted to see her had been less than positive. Father and daughter were meeting on the promenade by the seafront gardens. She had obviously wanted the meeting to be on neutral ground, and Harvey hoped that Edward's expectations were not pitched too high.

'Good luck, Edward. It's been a pleasure knowing you. Let me know how you get on.' He somehow doubted he would hear from Bigman again.

As he drove home, he recalled the man's impassioned testimony. There was often some part of a trial that stayed in his mind, long after the rest had been deleted, and it was Bigman's voice that he heard. Eve Whistler had done her best to use her father's friend as a character witness. As always, Edward had spoken at length, this time about the man he had known for years and who had been a close companion in the direst of circumstances.

'People don't appreciate the bond that forms amongst society's rejects. We know how the rest of the world views us: as vagrants, useless, a blot on the town. Because of our lifestyle, we, the homeless, are forced together. We may live rough, but we remain individuals, with our own unique personalities. Not everyone wants a mate, but Harry and I became true friends. Buddies, amigos. We shared everything in a way that the more fortunate cannot even imagine. Food, drink, sleeping spaces and blankets were divvied out. However, more importantly – far more importantly – we knew each other: our histories, and what had brought each of us to such a low ebb.'

After stopping for a moment, Edward had continued. 'Harry Whistler is not a murderer. Yes, he is a rough sleeper; yes, he is down on his luck; yes, he left his family years ago; yes, most of the time he is dirty and smells. None of these things make him a killer. He is a good man, a caring man, a man whose life took a wrong turn. A man who sought chastisement via homelessness. But, I repeat, he is not capable of murder, and if you knew him, really knew him as I do, you would know that I am telling the truth.'

Three weeks after the verdict Harvey was moving into his new house. Since leaving university, where he had endured years of enforced company – house-sharing a most unpleasant experience – he had opted to live alone. He had grown up in a noisy house, both he and his brothers filling the place with friends at all hours of the day...and night. Had the time now arrived to share his space?

A dog wouldn't be a good idea: the poor animal would be left alone for long periods. In any case, no dog could match the one-and-only, the ultimate dog-of-dogs he had loved as a child. Prince was an Afghan Hound, an enormous creature with a coat made of silk, an exotic face, and the body of a fashion-model. His aristocratic looks had belied a clown-like behaviour. He could multi-task: be aloof and comical at the same time. On the street, people would stop the family to talk about the hound – who greeted all-comers as his new best friend – and admire his film-star looks. The aptly named Prince seldom barked; it appeared to be too much trouble, and when the sound did emerge it was a most polite and humorous "wharf", rather than a more-doggy "woof".

Harvey thought it was highly likely that anyone's first pet remained forever special: elevated to a pet pedestal by youth's innocence and aptitude for all-encompassing love.

Prince exceeded the breed's estimated life-span by living for fourteen years. His final year was plagued by a series of ailments, but to the end he remained the same adorable character. The day the announcement was made that he was going to the vet's where he might have to be "put to sleep" (his mother was far too considerate to say the words "put down") was one that none of the brothers, all in their teens, would forget. For days weeping became the norm. Indeed, for many weeks even seeing a dog out enjoying a walk would result in the brothers fighting a losing battle with unmanly tears. That was the down-side of having a pet: one tended to outlive them. Nevertheless, the time had come to make changes in his life, the move being a start...pets to follow.

Packing had been left to the removal firm, the highly recommended Robertsons' Removals, a family firm comprising a father and two sons. They had lived up to their reputation: arriving at the arranged time and putting his life in boxes in less than four hours.

Arriving at his new home, *The Haven* removed, a new name deemed unnecessary, Harvey tried to feel positive. The cul-de-sac was looking lovely, the many trees an Impressionist painting suffused with autumn colours.

As he unlocked his new front door the word "Guilty" resonated in his mind. When the jury had returned to court, after so short a time, he had assumed they wanted clarification: either on a point of law, or a piece of evidence. He hadn't been alone in feeling surprised when their spokesperson, not the man Harvey had thought they would choose, announced that they had the verdict. Each time he thought about the trial, it was like a broken nail catching on a piece of material: part pain, part ridiculously unsettling. Now it was all over he wasn't sure they'd convicted the right man. When Edward had asked for his opinion, he had been unable to form the words, pretending a sudden interest in the Sat Nav.

'So, Mr Policeman, I'm not alone in knowing that Harry was innocent.'

Harvey had decided on his new companions: two kittens, just seven weeks old, but had arranged that he would delay their arrival. They were the most endearing pair. He had selected them from two litters that had arrived recently at the local Animal Rescue Centre. Choosing them had been the most difficult thing he had done since the end of the trial. Both litters had comprised the most adorable bundles of fur, all falling over each other, each kitten doing his or her best to be chosen. He had been to see them again a few days ago, but wanted the house to be settled before he brought them home. A cordless metal Jigsaw had been bought to fit a cat-flap on the back door. He hoped the procedure would be straightforward; the device had cost enough.

He had almost decided on names: the black and white one would be Chopin, his reasoning being that the composer was one of the greatest exponents of the black and white notes on the piano. The ginger one was more difficult. He wanted another composer and had considered Debussy (too close to Depussy!), Ludwig, Amadeus and Grieg. It would probably be the latter: both colour and composer starting with the same letter. Realising that others might think he needed certifying spending so long on such a conundrum, he had kept his thoughts to himself.

A holiday was organised before his housemates took up residence. He was leaving at the weekend for two weeks of walking in the high Alps. Having given much consideration to becoming more gregarious, he had reverted to type and opted instead for a self-guided, non-group fortnight of trekking in the Bernese Oberland. All hotels, hostels and mountain huts were booked, and the prosaically named *Hike the Highways* organised for luggage to be transported each day. He had collected his tickets and detailed schedule, and was looking forward to his "carefree walking in glorious scenery". He was delighted that his itinerary included sleeping overnight in mountain huts which promised few mod-cons.

The aim was to remain as high as possible and not descend to the valleys. He had spent a long time deciding on the huts. Two in the mountains near Grindelwald had appealed. The Schreckhornhutte was 2350 metres above sea level and slept sixty-five. The one he had opted for was the Berglihutte at 3299 metres. It had the great advantage of only accommodating twenty. He had absolutely no desire to be surrounded by hordes of enthusiastic people.

The last time he had hiked in the glorious scenery, which he was both surprised and appalled to realise was at least four years ago, he had been fortunate with the weather. He recalled ten days of sunshine. The well-behaved rain, accompanied most days by a display of thunder and lightning, had waited to make its appearance until dinner time. He hoped for the same this year. Hope seemed to be the word of the moment, one he had not employed for far too long.

Planning was complete. Why then did his mother's oft-used phrase reverberate, like a base drum, making his brain ache: "Man plans, and the gods laugh." If he was responsible for a man being locked up for life, did he deserve such a holiday? Or would the deities have their revenge?

Serena had told him to forget everything. 'Go to your mountains, hike yourself silly, breath in all that pure air, eat fondue and apple strudel, and come back refreshed... and podgy. Harry Whistler is history. Go, enjoy yourself... and send me a postcard! I'm off to Spain: better weather, wonderful beaches and no hills to stumble up. See you in three weeks.'

As he was packing, he determined that once home he would make more of an effort to be more sociable. That was a must. He had mentioned a house-warming party, and would invite Alfie Morrison and his partner, the one the pathologist referred to as she-who-remains-at-home-with-the-dog. The fact that the pathologist spoke more about the dog, named Frankenstein, a moniker that he hoped was usually shortened, said a lot about the couple's relationship which seemed problematic.

Thinking about the man he hoped to know better, he recalled his reply during cross-examination. Eve Whistler had asked what, apart from the undisputed fact that they had all been strangled, the five victims had in common. She was attempting to highlight the fact that whilst three were rough sleepers, and known to her father, the final pair had no connection to him. Alfie, always eloquent, had taken a few moments to think, and had then spoken so slowly and clearly that the journalists would have had enough time to record every word longhand.

'All the victims were human beings. Human beings. Each with a unique past. They all had hopes, fears, successes and failings. Each future was cut short. So cruelly: a few minutes deprived of air, bringing each life to an untimely close. Each denied their hold on life. Killers do not always know their victims. There can be a certain randomness. It is undisputed that three of those we are thinking about today lived outside society's norm, whilst the final pair were pursuing what is generally regarded as a more acceptable way of life, enjoying their retirements. Who are we to judge how others choose to live? I will merely reiterate that all five were members of our shared race: men and women murdered most brutally.'

Most unusually, his soliloquy was greeted with a resounding round of applause from the packed gallery, led by members of the town's homeless fraternity who had been present every day of the trial.

The pathologist would make a good friend. The trial was over: the desired verdict delivered. Harvey knew he should be feeling that life was "on the up".

Time to start packing: walking boots essential.

Less than fifteen miles away Harry Whistler was informed that he had a visitor. Seldom leaving his cell, he spent his days lying so still one warder suggested he was as good as the mime artists who made their living by standing immobile, dressed up in strange outfits, pretending to be statues. 'They're in Preston every Saturday and from what I can see they make a bob or two.'

Harry did not like being disturbed. 'No way. No visitor. I don't want to see anyone. They can turn around and go back home. I assume they've got one to go to.'

'It's your son, Jacob. He seems keen to see you.'

'As we've hardly spoken for twenty years, I can't imagine why he wants to see me now.'

'Shall I tell him you won't see him?'

Harry couldn't help being intrigued. Eve had agreed not to visit him again, and he had assumed that no other member of the family would want to see him – prison as far outside their comfort zone as a polar bear finding itself in the desert.

They'd all written. A strange selection of missives: from the sad (Elizabeth, still concerned for him) to the offensive (Andrew, blaming him for everything and glad that he was now incarcerated for life: 'You'll die in there and good riddance. The shame of having a father who is responsible for five murders'). There had been a lot more in the same vein.

David had offered to stay in contact and promised to write on a regular basis. Jacob's letter had been interesting, a juxtaposition of anger and self-pity. There had been no hint that he would want to see his father, making today's visit unexpected.

'How long do I have to endure him? He won't be here to congratulate me or to sympathise. Gloating more like.'

'Visiting's just started, so you've got an hour.'

'Suppose I can walk out whenever he's said his piece.'

The room was packed. Tables were set out in such a way as to afford each conversation some privacy. Prison officers stood by all four walls, looking extremely bored. Extra men positioned by the two doors looked far more alert, ready to deal with fleeing inmates or distraught relatives. Strident sounds greeted Harry as he entered. Everything had to be said in sixty minutes, and excited children squealed, trying to gain their dad's attention. Arguments flared and were quelled, the time deemed too precious for altercations.

Jacob was sitting stock-still at a table on the far side of the room. Where others wore casual trousers, and sweat shirts, he had dressed for a formal occasion. He was making a statement in his newly acquired dark grey suit, light grey shirt, both teamed with a red tie: a bold contrast. A piece of A 4 paper lay on the table in front of him, bullet points filling the page.

As Harry sat down, neither spoke. The silence stretched, Harry wondering why his son had come if it wasn't to deliver his personal verdict. He felt sure that Jacob wasn't going to let the jury have the last word.

Jacob looked up from the paper that was obviously intriguing him. 'So, guilty as charged, or are you still proclaiming your innocence?'

'I have one murder to my name, but God knows I was not responsible for any of the others.'

'Strange then that a jury of twelve people said you were.'

'They were wrong. The Good Lord knows that, and at the Day of Reckoning I will not have to answer for any of them. God is my witness; the police didn't find many others.'

Jacob had spent his formative years listening to his father bring his deity into every conversation and couldn't stop himself retorting that it was a shame that God hadn't been available for the defence. 'Indeed, Eve could have called God and one other.'

Harry looked up. The words, when they came, causing him a great deal of effort. 'Yes, God and one other. The bastard who murdered them. May he rot in hell. Don't you think I spend every moment of every day wondering who did it? And why I'm in here for his crimes. The police took the easy option and looked no further than me. The reject, the one no one would give a damn about: guilty or not.'

'Isn't being in here, a warm cell, three meals a day, better than being on the streets?'

Harry scowled, 'I'd rather be outside and free. Left to my own devices.' Jacob smiled, glad of those words.

Looking down at the paper he began to speak, so softly only his father could possibly have heard. The words for his ears only.

'Thomas Granger…'

'Tommy, he was known as Tommy.'

Undeterred by the interruption, Jacob continued. 'Thomas Granger: so, so easy. An old man with no fight left in him. The police took their time discovering his body: in the end, I got fed up waiting and rang them. Mr Granger was a close companion of yours, a fellow vagrant; you even claimed he was your best friend, and yet to start with you weren't much of a suspect in his demise. That was a shame. I was sure they would think you had the means, opportunity and motive; a falling-out that led to violence.'

Moving his finger down to the next bullet point, Jacob paused then began again. 'Charlotte Carroway. Only eighteen, rather a shame, she might have reformed and become a worthwhile member of society. You and she were far too close. Goodness knows where that might have led.'

'I loved that girl, but not in the way you're implying.'

'Once again, the police believed you and you weren't investigated, apart from a short conflab. I recall Eve telling me that they believed your account. That you were acting as a "father figure" to her. How ironic. I don't recall you being much of a father to your real offspring. And, let's be honest, if you were as good as she was going to get, maybe she was better off dead.'

If Jacob was looking for a reaction, he was disappointed. Harry sat like a defeated boxer, one who had discarded the towel a long time ago.

'Now the interesting one. Terry Wendover. This time you registered on the police radar. This time they were looking for a serial killer: three the magic number. Your movements were scrutinised. You were questioned. They knew about your argument with the deceased the night before his body was found. To start with they couldn't understand why the violence has escalated, the body incinerated. They should have arrested you for that one. I would have done. Terry had accused you in front of those assembled at that pathetic get-together, then immediately afterwards you are seen arguing, and allegedly indulging in some fisticuffs. Within twelve hours he's dead. I assumed they would charge you. That you had burnt his body as revenge. I was wrong. A great shame. If that had been the end, if the police had looked at the evidence, left so carefully, the final two wouldn't have been necessary. Not needed. Still alive and enjoying retirement.'

Harry sat, head down.

'A great shame the cross I thrust into *his* mouth was never found. I purchased the crosses (a couple still in hand) when I went to Birmingham for a weekend. They were in the window of a small shop, hidden down an alley, not somewhere the police would look. Though I say so myself, that was one of my more inspired ideas, you known to be so religious.'

'Ten minutes.' The prison officer's voice warned that time was short: no extra time for last minute exchanges.

'Have you finished? Fascinating as this is, I'm more than ready to go back to my cell. It's preferable to listening to you cataloguing recent events.'

'Almost there. Two to go. After the three, who let's face it no one was going to miss, DCI Tarquin thought there wasn't enough evidence. Eve told me that the CPS wouldn't prosecute you, that a jury would never convict, unless you could be placed at any of the scenes. Apart from the fact you knew them all, and spent a lot of your time with them in Elizabeth Park, there was nothing to say you'd been involved in any of their deaths. Any DNA linking you could be put down to your close-proximity to them as one of the other waste-of-space vagrants. The crosses were a clever touch and made them consider you – you so "religious", but even they weren't strong enough evidence and were discounted.'

Five minutes were called, and Jacob was keen to finish what he'd come to say. Pointing at the penultimate point he looked up at his father, the man he had hated for most of his life.

'Edwin York: surely this time guilty as charged. Giraffe embossed glove inundated with the all-essential Deoxyribonucleic Acid – sounds so much better than its initials – left at the crime scene. Such an easy victim, frail and lost on the allotment, following me, like a child from Hamelin, not into the mountain, but straight into my shed. When he saw what I was going to do, his old ticker gave up. Saved me the bother. Still thought I'd better made it look like a strangling. I love the phrase post-mortem.

Finally, Lillian Henshaw. Such a gullible old lady, believing I'd been asked to accompany her to her daughter's new house. What a delightful woman, chatting away about the weather, her daughter and her up-coming holiday. I told her, quite truthfully, that I knew Janine as I worked at the same school. The old dame believed me when I said her daughter had purchased the house with the Sold sign in the garden and was going to meet her there to show her around. How pleasing it was to read in the paper that the prosecution had made a lot of the fact that the homeless often doss down in houses left empty.

Your scarf finally did it: gave the police the piece of evidence they needed. Fancy Mum keeping your clothes all those years. Did she really think you were coming home? Could she possibly have wanted to live with you again? I did as she asked and helped David sort the wardrobe filled with decades-old garments: some to go to charity shops, a lot to throw out, and one item to keep. Added to the glove you left, so helpfully, the last time you slept in my shed, I had all the DNA I needed... as did the CPS.'

Jacob was smiling as he reached his final bullet point.

'All me. All so easy. To quote from your favourite book: "The sins of the father..." I don't think I need to continue. Bet you never thought I had it in me. You've always regarded me as a failure: messing about on an allotment and playing "namby-pamby" instruments, your words in 1993. Well, I think you must admit I've succeeded finally. You'll die in here, everyone thinking you've committed five murders. What a result. Yes, without doubt, a resounding success. Goodbye, father. I doubt we shall meet again.'

'Time please. Will all visitors now make their way to the visitors' exit.'

Was it right to do the things I did? No.

Would I do it all again? Yes. Most definitely, yes.